THE KINGDOM

BERKELEY BLACKFRIARS • BOOK ONE

J. R. MABRY

Apocryphile Press

1700 Shattuck Ave #81

Berkeley, CA 94709

www.apocryphilepress.com

Printed in the United States of America

ISBN 978-1-944769-99-4

Cover graphics by Milo at www.derangeddoctordesign.com

CLAIM YOUR FREE BOOK

To find out more about the Berkeley Blackfriar's universe, download your free copy of *The Berkeley Blackfriar's Companion*. Includes short stories set in the Blackfriars' universe, photos of main characters, a complete glossary, a walking tour of the Blackfriars' Berkeley, recipes from Brian's kitchen, a short history of Old Catholicism, a Q & A session with author J.R. Mabry, links to music and videos associated with the books and more!

Click on BookHip.com/DXDCAS
to get your free copy!

REVIEWS

If you enjoy the Blackfriars books, please help other people find them by leaving an honest review on amazon or kobo or wherever you buy books. Thank you!

OTHER BOOKS BY J.R. MABRY

The Berkeley Blackfriars Series:
The Kingdom
The Power
The Glory

The Christmas at Bremmer's Series:
What Child is This?

The Temple of All Worlds Series:
The Worship of Mystery

DEDICATION

This book is offered with gratitude
to the memory of
FRATER QUI SITIT VENIAT
"Under the Mercy"

ACKNOWLEDGEMENTS & CAVEATS

Grateful thanks to all of my friends who encouraged me in the writing of this novel. Special thanks are due to those who read the first draft carefully and made invaluable suggestions, especially B.J. West, Lola McCrary, Dan and Kathie McClellan, Ric Reed, Liza Lee Miller, Bill Armstrong, Kittredge Cherry, Audrey Lockwood, Lizzy Hull Barnes, Liz Stout, and others who prefer to remain anonymous. Thanks also to my editor Jason Whited for making the second edition sparkle. I wish to acknowledge my debt to *Buffy the Vampire Slayer* (the best show in the history of TV), the novels of Charles Williams (oh, when will people discover him?), Garth Ennis and Steve Dillon's *Preacher*, and James Blish's *The Devil's Day* (the demonic processions it depicts inspired the one in Chapter 65). Liturgical rites were adapted from the Roman Catholic Ritual for Exorcism, the Liturgy of the Liberal Catholic Church, and the *UCC Book of Worship*. To shield myself from possible litigation, I have changed the names of some institutions, especially in the Gourmet Ghetto neighborhood of Berkeley in which the friars live and work. Those familiar with the area will no doubt sort out what is what fairly easily.

For your face turns toward all faces
that gaze upon it.
Therefore, those who look upon you
with a loving face will find your face
looking on them with love...
Those who look upon you in hate
will similarly find your face hateful.
Those who gaze at you in joy
will find your face joyfully reflected back at them.

—*Nicholas of Cusa*

THURSDAY

PROLOGUE

WHEN THE DEMON APPEARED, Randall Webber nearly jumped out of his skin. He was an experienced magickian, but the appearance of an infernal dignitary is never a commonplace event, and it shook him every time. He knew that if he stepped even momentarily outside the circle he had painstakingly burned onto his hardwood floor the demon would be at his throat, and in an instant would separate his soul from his body and devour it—or worse.

Webber mustered his courage and put on his best poker face. He was in control here, he told himself. He was the magickian. He called the shots. He commanded the hosts of Hell. He wiped the sweat from his forehead and upper lip and then put his hand in his back pocket to stop it from shaking.

The demon did not speak but appeared in the form of a dragon. It hovered as an image cast upon a small paper triangle about the size of Webber's fist, set safely outside the circle on an end table. The dragon uncoiled its tail in slow motion, gold-flecked pupils staring straight into Webber's own. Webber gulped and willed his voice not to waver as he spoke.

"Greetings, noble Articiphus, commander of many mighty hosts, Duke of Hell. I acknowledge thee and bid thee welcome. I command thee by the holy Tetragrammaton to assume thy human form and speak with me!"

So far, so good, Webber thought. He was still in one piece; the demon was still constrained within the folded paper triangle, and he thought he had just given a flawless performance of a man in command of himself. He fought the urge to run through his mental checklist to make sure he had not forgotten anything. One missing link and the whole house of cards would come tumbling down and he would be demon chow. He fought the urge. He had been careful, and if he had missed anything it was too late now to do anything about it. Right now, he needed to focus.

The triangle shimmered, and a regal-looking gentleman hovered in it dressed in ermine and satin. One half of his face was serene, the other horribly scarred. A diadem sat upon his head, and his face bore a resentful scowl. *Nobody likes to be told what to do*, Randall thought, *least of all a man of power—or a being of power.* "Hail, Articiphus, Duke of—"

The demon interrupted him impatiently. "Cut the shit, Magickian. What do you want?"

Randall's eyes widened. He pushed a lock of long brown hair out of his eyes and consciously straightened his perpetually stooped shoulders. He was expecting the typical exchange of ritual pleasantries, a ping-pong volley of testy manners conducted in Elizabethan English, but he had never summoned this particular spirit before. This one, apparently, had no time—or patience—for small talk. *Very well*, Randall thought, *let's just cut to the chase.* "Is it true, noble Duke, that you have the power to remove souls and put them in other bodies?"

Whether the demon's voice was audible or whether it merely resonated in his mind, Randall couldn't tell. It had an odd quality about it as if Randall were wearing headphones. There was no resonance in the room, so it was hard to tell. He dismissed the thought as irrelevant and willed himself once more to focus. The words were clear, regardless of their source. The big question had just been asked. And for a demon in a hurry to be rid of this pest of a human, Articiphus was certainly taking his time replying.

The demon's eyes narrowed, and he looked like he was trying to stare *past* the magickian. Randall stole a glance behind him, but there was nothing. Out the window he could see drizzle swirling around a streetlamp, forming wispy ghosts that, he prayed, were neither conscious nor malevolent. In this business, however, one could never be sure.

Randall shifted nervously, noting that the meat of his thigh seemed to have gone numb. He slapped it with the flat of his hand. "What say you, noble Duke?" he called, with a note of impatience.

"I. Can." The demon let the two words drop like ice. He squinted at the magickian. "You want to share a body with another soul." He spoke it as a statement, but a raised eyebrow indicated that it was more of a question of clarification.

"No. I want to trade bodies."

Randall saw the demon nodding, understanding. "Man or woman?" he asked.

"Neither one," Randall said. He forced all the air he could into his lungs, expanding them as far as they would go given the acrid sting of the incense that hung as thick in the air of the apartment as the fog outside. "The being I want to swap bodies with is...not human."

The demon opened his mouth to speak but then closed it again, furrowing his brows instead.

"Oh yeah," Randall added. "When I go, I need to take this with me." And he held forth a purplish-green fruit.

"What are you going to do with an avocado?" asked the demon, now truly curious.

Suddenly, Webber was not nervous at all. He knew what he had to do, and he knew he had the means at hand to do it. He didn't answer the demon but only smiled.

FRIDAY

1

Fr. Richard Kinney didn't mind the rain. It was turning out to be Berkeley's wettest winter in decades, but he smiled as he turned his nose to the sky, quietly relishing the tiny splashes on his nose and cheeks.

It was a cold midmorning, though, and he thrust his hands deep into the pockets of his jeans as he walked. He cut through to Spruce Street and turned right at All Saints' Episcopal.

He was a middle-aged friar habited in a black Anglican cassock, yet no one seemed to think his attire out of place—there were plenty of people in the vicinity of the Graduate Theological Union in religious dress. His hair was tonsured—a round bowl of skin poked through his already thinning hair on the very top of his head—and though his frame carried a few extra pounds, he carried them well.

The wind seemed to pick up when he reached busy Shattuck Avenue. So did the rain, and he suddenly wished he'd brought his hat. He didn't dwell on it, though. The Old Catholic Order of Saint Raphael, of which he was the prior, had just finished a very successful series of exorcisms for the Roman Catholic Diocese of Oakland. Not only had they succeeded in banishing a whole host of demons from a Lafayette orphanage, but they had been well paid for their efforts. Good pay—or even adequate recognition—was a rarity in the exorcism business, and Richard gave himself permission to enjoy the success—for a little while at least. *Beware undue pride*, he reminded himself, but he smiled as he did it.

He felt relieved as he darted in the door of the Gallic Hotel's café. The smell of coffee wafted over him like a pleasurable veil, and he paused to savor it, filling his lungs.

The line was unusually short, no doubt due to the weather, and he ordered a cappuccino. Passing his hands through the slits in his cassock, he unzipped his fanny pack and felt around for some change. He paid, and, picking up a discarded newspaper, he found a table and waited for Philip to arrive.

He liked Philip. They had met online about a year ago and had had an on-again-off-again relationship that was both promising and maddening in equal measure.

They seemed, at least to Richard, to be well matched. Philip was a seminary student, embarking on a second career as an Episcopal priest. They had a lot in common, and where Richard was an extroverted, charge-ahead kind of guy, Philip was quiet, reserved, and cautious. A little too cautious, Richard sometimes thought, but he also realized that Philip's reserve provided a useful balance.

They were different in other ways, too. Richard was tall, standing a good six feet, with broad, though somewhat stooped shoulders, while Philip was a smaller man, five foot five, with delicate features that often looked pained when he was concentrating on something.

Philip appeared in the doorway, and Richard waved at him. Philip flashed a grimacing smile and sat down without ordering. "I can't stay," he said, brushing rain from his coat.

Richard had been expecting a kiss, and Philip's brusque demeanor caught him off guard. "Hey, Baby. You look worried. What's up?" He reached out and took Philip's hand. Philip withdrew his hand from the table and sighed. "Dicky, we need to talk."

As if mirroring the weather, dark clouds gathered on Richard's interior horizon, and he didn't like it at all. "That's never a good thing to hear," he said, almost as an aside. "What's wrong?"

"How can I put this?" Philip softened a bit. He leaned forward and squeezed Richard's hand. "You're driving me crazy."

"Innnn...a good way?" Richard asked hopefully. "Like crazy with lust, or an obsessive fascination with my winning personality?"

The levity didn't help. Philip blew air through his cheeks and lowered his head. Richard took that moment to admire the full head of hair his lover sported. *Some guys have all the luck*, he thought. His thoughts returned to what seemed to be inevitably coming. *Some guys that are not me.*

"Dicky, for the past month you've been playing Batman and Robin, scurrying all over the Bay Area chasing bad guys and...doing your thing."

"Yeah," Richard said, realizing his parade, his success, was about to get rained on as well. "My thing. It's what I *do*."

"I know that. I've always known that. But in the past month, I've seen you exactly twice, and one of those times, I spent the whole evening trying to comfort you while you were having one of your inferiority attacks or whatever they are—insecurity, existential anxiety—whatever it was, it was all about *you*."

"I–I've been busy," Richard stammered. "We had a gig, a *paying* gig. And I had a rough spot. You were wonderful, you helped me through it. You gave me exactly what I needed—"

"Yeah, but at no time during this whole month did I get what I needed—and that's the thing." Philip raised his voice but then lowered it when he realized he was attracting the attention of other patrons. "I need this to work for me, too. And it isn't. I have crises too. I have times I need to be carried, and held, and...loved. And you're never there when I need *you*. So, I'm done. We've had some lovely times, Dicky, but it's over. I'm sorry. I really am, but I can't continue like this." He rose from the table and kissed Richard on the cheek. "I'll miss you," he said, and he was gone.

Richard sat frozen—activity went on in the coffee shop around him, but he did not notice. "Sweet Jesus," he finally said out loud and then lowered his head to the table, a bit more quickly than he'd anticipated. His forehead smacked with unexpected force on the wood, and, in his present state, the sensation seemed appropriate, even pleasurable.

He smacked his forehead on the table again, a little harder this time. Then he did it again. And again. "God hates me," he said out loud, between head bangs. "The motherfucker really, really hates me."

"I not fond of you, either," a harsh voice said from just behind him. "And if you break that table, God will not be only motherfucker on your ass." Richard raised his head to see Mr. Kim, the Korean owner of the Gallic Hotel—a small man with a thin mustache coloring his lip, and a grimy towel hanging from his belt. His arms were crossed, and his jaw was set with a *don't fuck with me* rigidity. Richard didn't.

"Sorry, Mr. Kim," he said and laid his head down on the cool of the table, waiting for the stars to stop spinning in front of his eyes.

"And I don't want to hear about you fag-monks' sex lives," Mr. Kim added, in English that wasn't quite broken but was undeniably cracked.

"We're friars, not monks. And this is Berkeley," Richard said. "Our sex lives are tame by comparison to most of the people in here."

Mr. Kim looked around, and Richard followed his gaze as well as he could without moving his head. There were exactly three other patrons in the joint, all of them elderly.

"Uh-huh, whatever you say, *Father*," Mr. Kim said. "And stop spit. It disgusting."

Just then Richard's cell phone rang, a cheesy Casio version of the triumphant "Rise Up, O Men of God," which Richard had picked for the double entendre. Richard raised his head from the table, trailing a string of drool, and flipped open the phone.

Fr. Terry Milne's reedy voice cut in and out, but it was still comprehensible. "Dicky, drop whatever you're doing."

"God hates me," Richard told him.

"What? You're breaking up. Listen, get your ass in gear, and meet us over in the city. Pacific Heights, corner of Baker and Clay. We've got a gig."

"God hates me," Richard repeated.

"Dicky, I can't. I'm sure it's lovely, whatever you just said. I've left messages for Dylan and Mikael as well—we've got demon ass to kick, and we're going to need backup. Ciao for now, sweetie."

2

LANTERN IN HAND, Alan Dane descended the steps of the catacombs beneath his family home. Unforgiving rock, dank and dark, loomed above his head, and he breathed in the familiar cold and musty air. Reaching the bottom, he held his lantern up and surveyed the tomb in which a hundred years of relatives were buried. The Danes were the closest thing to old money that San Francisco had. At one time, they had been rivals of the Sutro clan—and, paradoxically, high-society friends as well.

He was a tall, lean man in his middle thirties, well groomed, and fashionably attired. His hands were large, prone to grand gestures, and sported many rings, among them a large, red jewel on his right hand.

Passing row upon row of shelves cut deep into the rock, he glanced at the mummified remains of his ancestors. He bowed dramatically to the first one and uttered a very formal, "I trust you are enjoying your stay in Hell, Grandmother Dane." He shuffled left and bowed again. "And, Uncle John, I hear the worms feasted well on you, and it makes me glad." He continued to greet his ancestors in this manner all the way down the hall, each time bowing low with a grand sweep of his bejeweled hands, until he had reached the end of the inhabited shelves, at which point he turned to face the hallway and addressed them collectively. "For raising my father in the way that you did, I say to you all, *fuck you*. You have made him the monster he is." *Or was*, he thought to himself, swelling with pride for, at last, having the upper hand.

This was no time to gloat. While it was true that his father would be tormenting no children in the immediate future, it was clear to Alan Dane that his job was far from finished. There were still children suffering, even if not at his father's hands. There were other fathers, other monsters, other sources of suffering. There were so many children to save.

With a sense of mission, he unlatched the large wooden door at the end of the hallway. As it swung open, the lantern light shone upon a richly appointed room, revealing the form of a small boy, sniffling and mewling for his mother.

"Shhhh, it's okay," Dane said, closing the door behind him with a boom that reverberated through the rock. He smiled at the child, revealing true compassion as he withdrew a scalpel case from his breast pocket. "No one will ever, ever hurt you again. I promise." He said it mechanically, as if he were reciting lines, for it was a ritual he had enacted many times. "I am your savior, and I have come to deliver you. Everything is going to be *all right*. Your suffering is finally at an end…"

3

As RICHARD SQUEALED to a stop in front of a Pacific Heights mansion, he saw Terry and Mikael waiting for him on the sidewalk, their arms crossed impatiently.

"Took you long enough," Terry called.

Richard said nothing. The traffic had been terrible coming over the Bay Bridge, but he was in no mood to make excuses, or to be concerned about Terry's legendary nitpicking. He grabbed his kit bag from the trunk and strode over to where his friends were standing.

Terry and Mikael were a study in contrasts. Terry was short, the ring of his tonsure cut so close as to be almost undetectable. The product of a Japanese mother and an Irish father, his black hair and oddly shaped eyes lent him an elfin appearance. He was a nervous, agitated, and extroverted man just nearing forty, his face red with exasperation.

Mikael, on the other hand, was tall—over six feet—with a shock of wild jet-black hair that radiated from his scalp like the rays of a negative sun. He was a calm, quiet man, just barely thirty, the friars' most recent oblate. His tonsure had been symbolic—a lock of hair was cut at his admission but allowed to grow back, as befit a struggling power-punk musician.

As Richard approached, Terry's anger transfigured into concern. "Dicky, what's the matter?"

Richard stopped within arm's reach of his friends and struggled to master himself. "God hates me," he said.

"God can be a right bloody bastard," Terry agreed. "What did the jerk do this time?"

"Philip..." Richard was proud of himself for having held it together this long—all the way over the bridge, in fact. But the shock was wearing off, and the reality was sinking in. He lost it, and buried his face in Terry's black cassock.

"Shh...Honey, there, there," Terry said, stroking his neck and looking up at Mikael with a concerned grimace. Mikael laid his hand on Richard's shoulder and gave it a squeeze that passed for an acceptable, manly, and decidedly straight display of sympathy. "Did he dump you?"

Richard nodded into Terry's shoulder, and the smaller man cursed in response. "That damned nelly wannabe. I knew he would be trouble. You deserve better, Honey." He rocked Richard for a few seconds.

Richard picked his head up and looked, sniffing, at the gray, brooding sky. "No. He deserved better than me. He was totally right. I just haven't been...available."

Terry took Richard's hands in both of his and gave them a good shake. "Dicky, listen to me. We've got a demon in there. We've got an exorcism to do. Are you up for this? Because if you're not, I want you to go straight home. I'll handle it myself—Mikael can help. It'll be a good learning experience for him either way. I would really like to have your help in there, but not if you can't handle it. I don't need to remind you about the dangers. And if you're in an emotionally vulnerable place..." He did not finish the sentence. He didn't have to.

Richard considered. If Terry could see that he was so upset at one glance, then he wasn't going to fool any demon. And demons were nothing if not brilliant exploiters of weakness. On the other hand, it might prove even more dangerous for Terry to try it alone. Terry was a good exorcist—certainly he was brave—but his area of occult expertise was Enochian magick, not demon magick. Goetia—the kind of magick in which one summons and manipulates demonic entities—was Richard's own area of specialized study, and more than once he had saved the Order's collective ass due to his knowledge of the field's most excruciating minutiae.

As for Mikael, he was the magickal equivalent of a driver's ed student. It's not that he was useless, but he had only seen one exorcism previously, and it was a mild one. He was there to learn, not to help—for his own safety and everyone else's.

"Where's Dylan?" Richard asked.

"Under deadline with a big web job, the one he and Susan have been working on all week. It goes live tonight."

"Shit," Richard muttered. He considered going home, but the truth was he simply did not know what he would do with himself when he got there. He didn't really feel like relating the whole story to the others back at the Friary, and given a choice between being here and beating up on demons or sitting alone in his room and beating up on himself, it was not a hard decision. Besides, even if he was in a delicate place, the work would be safer if there were two experienced priests on hand. "Let's kick some demon ass," he finally said, trying to sound resolute.

"You sure?" Terry looked up at him uncertainly.

"No. So let's do it while I'm still in shock." He slung his kit bag over his shoulder, and together they passed through the wrought iron gates. As they approached the doors of the mansion, it occurred to Richard that surely the likes of them would not be admitted to such an opulent place. They were, after all, on the brink of poverty, and that due to circumstance, not pious adherence to their vows.

"Wait," Terry said, turning to Mikael. "Do I look buff? 'Cause I don't wanna face any demons if I don't look buff." He struck a Charles Atlas pose.

Richard answered instead, grateful for an opportunity to lighten his mood. "Ter, you're not just buff, you're butch."

"Fuck butch. Dykes are butch. Fags gotta be buff."

"Well, actually," Mikael said, "Your rouge is a little uneven."

"Oh thank you," Terry said. "Heavy on the right or left?"

"Left. *Your* left."

Terry rubbed at his left cheek while Richard contemplated ringing the bell.

"We don't belong here," Richard said, hesitating.

"I feel it," Terry agreed, "but we do this job, Honey, and we may actually get a paycheck."

"I'll believe it when I see it," Richard said and reached for the button.

"Stop!" a voice forcefully whispered, loud enough for them all to hear. The friars turned, searching out the source of the command. In the shadow of a stand of bushes about a foot away from the house, a slight female figure crouched. Once they had seen her, she put her index finger to her lips, signaling silence. Then she waved at them to follow, and turned, disappearing into the shrubbery.

Terry looked at Richard for a decision. Richard shrugged and set out after her. A couple of steps brought them to the shrubbery, and soon they were winding their way along a little path directly beside the mansion.

After about thirty yards, they cleared the bushes and found themselves beside a wooden gate that loomed over them. Fumbling with a ring of keys, an attractive young woman in blue scrubs visibly battled her anxiety. Eventually, she found the right key, and, pushing her long red hair back with one hand, she peered intently at the lock. She inserted the key and turned it. The lock responded with a satisfying click, and the gate swung inward. Looking around nervously, she motioned them to enter, and following them, shut the gate behind them.

They were in a small, neatly kept garden with high walls and tasteful Greek statuary. The young woman paused, closed her eyes, and caught her breath. Richard noticed that her hands were shaking.

She, apparently, noticed it, too, and pressed them together. Then, seeming to suddenly remember her manners, she extended her hand to the friar nearest her, which happened to be Terry. "Sorry for the intrigue. I'm Jessica Stahl, Mr. Dane's resident nurse."

Terry shook her hand. "Very pleased to meet you in person. I believe you and I spoke on the phone—was that you?" She nodded. "I'm Fr. Terry Milne, and these are my colleagues, Fr. Richard Kinney and Brother Mikael Bloomink of the Old Catholic Order of Saint Raphael."

She shook hands with Richard and Mikael, and seemed to have caught her breath. "I'm sorry about the sneaking around," she said. "But Mr. Dane—the young Mr. Dane—doesn't know I called you."

Terry raised his eyebrows and shot an uncertain look at Richard. Richard cleared his throat. "What, exactly, are we dealing with, here?"

"The elder Mr. Dane is dying—he was diagnosed with pancreatic cancer well over a year ago, now," Nurse Stahl obliged. "He's in terrible pain. The truth is, I've never seen anyone hold on like this. He should have..." She swallowed. "He should be dead. And I don't understand why he's not."

"So why call us?" Richard asked.

She looked around, apparently concerned that she might be observed. "I think—I know it sounds crazy—but I think his holding on—it's *supernatural*. And I know this isn't scientific, but it doesn't *feel* good." Her eyes were large, and she looked at them fiercely as if daring them not to laugh at her.

Terry pulled a notebook from beneath his cassock and began scribbling in it. "Can you describe the behaviors you've observed?"

She nodded. "Sometimes, I think I see his eyes glow—they're kind of red. At first, I thought it was my imagination, but then I was walking through his room in the dark, and...well, I could almost see my way because of it." She felt at her arms and rubbed them. "Gives me chills just to think about it."

"What else?"

"Well, sometimes, if I don't do what he asks fast enough—and that's another thing, he shouldn't be talking at all at this stage, let alone asking for things—but, if I don't, he gets...there's this *other* voice...it's deeper, rougher...scarier. It seems to be coming from every-where. It's...not Mr. Dane. It's someone...some*thing* else."

Terry nodded, glancing at both Mikael and Richard. They all seemed to be on the same page. "Anything else?"

She sniffed and pulled at her hair with a shaky hand. "Yes, once I was attaching a new catheter, and he grabbed my arm so hard I had bruises for a week. Like I said, he shouldn't be able to do that. And so hard...it's not *natural.*"

"How did you hear about *us,* Ms. Stahl?" Richard asked.

"On my day off, I went to the office of the Roman Catholic Arch-diocese. I met with several people—they kept passing me from one office to another. Finally, the bishop's assistant made sure we were alone, and he said to me—really loud, as if he thought someone was listening—that most demonic possessions weren't real and that they didn't have anyone on staff that could help me. Then he handed me your card. And—it was weird—he *winked* at me."

"Unfortunately, that's the way it has to be," Terry nodded. "We handle most of the Archdiocese's exorcism work—and every other diocese, Catholic and Episcopal, in Northern California. But *unoffi-cially,* of course. Very few clergy specialize in this sort of thing anymore. We've actually been busier than you might think."

"Father, if anyone believes, I believe." Her eyes were huge.

"Can we see him—Mr. Dane?" Terry asked.

She led them to the sliding glass door and opened it, revealing a dimly lit room. About three times the size of a normal hospital room, it had all of the same accoutrements, yet it was so spaciously arranged it did not detract from the atmosphere of calm elegance.

For all of its beauty, however, the room was heavy with the stench of bile and disinfectant. Worse than that was a malevolent energy that hit the friars full in the face the moment they entered. Richard cringed at the feel of it, and he glanced at Terry, the most spiritually sensitive of all of them. He could see Terry's face tighten. If forced to describe the feeling, Richard would have simply said it was *wrong.* Very, very wrong. The friars looked at one another briefly and wordlessly registered the feeling between them. It was clear that they all felt it. They were in the presence of sentient evil.

At the epicenter of the wrongness, a withered skeleton of a man lay in a hospital bed flanked by heart monitors and IV bags.

"It's been a tough day," Nurse Stahl said as they gathered around the hospital bed. "The morphine isn't quite cutting it, today. And it..."—she was, Richard gathered, referring to the demon—"If I could sue it for sexual harassment, I would."

Richard nodded, and his eyes softened momentarily. "I'm sorry about that. Tell us about his son."

"The young Mr. Dane is running the family businesses now. He comes up often to check on his father, but there doesn't seem to be much love between them. In fact, one night I overheard him talking to his father—or that thing inside him, I couldn't really tell. It didn't make a lot of sense to me, but that man's got a lot of anger in him, that's for sure."

"Why didn't you tell him about contacting us?"

"I mentioned the possibility of calling *someone* in to help him, and he laughed at me. Not a nice laugh, either. So, I...Look, I don't know anything about the old man. I just know that no matter who he is, or what he's done, everyone deserves to die with dignity, in peace. So, I called you. I thought if there was any way to get that thing inside him *out*—maybe nature could run its course and Mr. Dane could find some rest."

"You did the right thing," Mikael assured her. Both Terry and Richard looked at him. Blood rose up Mikael's neck as he realized he was being stared at.

"Well, *technically*, we can't do anything without the family's approval," Terry said, still looking at Mikael. "But it sounds like we're not going to get that." He looked back at the nurse. "Are we?"

She shook her head.

Terry looked at Richard. "And we have an old man needlessly suffering..."

Richard sighed. "What the hell, all he can do is sue us."

Terry smiled, "And no one has ever won a case on the grounds of unauthorized exorcism."

Richard met the woman's eyes. "We'll do it."

She was visibly relieved. "I'm afraid he's got so much morphine in him he won't be able to speak to you," she said.

"That's all right," said Richard. "We don't need to speak to him, just the thing inside him. And unless I'm mistaken, the morphine isn't going to slow *it* down any."

"No," she said with a frightened and faraway look that was not hard to decipher. "It never does." She looked at the old man with a mixture of compassion and fear. In a moment, she gathered up her courage and addressed them again. "My rooms are just through there." She pointed to a door opposite the one they had come through. "I always have the monitor on, so just call if you need me."

Richard smiled grimly at her. "Thank you. But we want you to turn the monitor off. It's not a request; it's a requirement. And no matter what you hear coming from this room this afternoon, I need you to promise me you'll stay put. I don't care if you hear what sounds like Armageddon coming from this room, for your own safety, and ours, you need to stay put."

"Do you want me to leave?" she asked, looking skeptical.

"Mr. Dane might need medical assistance if things go wrong. But we'll come and get you if we need you. Are you okay with that?"

She looked momentarily relieved, and then frightened—but she had obviously seen enough weirdness in tending to the old man that she was prepared to be brave. "I'm okay...with that."

"Good. Then we're going to get started." This was, apparently, her cue to get lost, and after a moment of hesitation she picked up on it. After a quick check to make sure all was as well with Mr. Dane as she could make it, she retired to her apartment.

Without another word, Terry and Richard began carrying all the superfluous furniture out of the room and into the garden. Mikael followed their example. "Hey, if we want a smoke later, we can kick back out here," Mikael said. He looked a little confused by all the moving.

Terry noticed. "We don't want you to be hit in the back of the head by a flying samovar, let alone a sofa, do we?"

"Oh," he mouthed silently, nodding. He went back inside for a lamp. Once everything that wasn't nailed down or necessary for medical care was safely in the garden, they opened their kit bags and unpacked their vestments. All three donned surplices and pectoral crucifixes, and Terry and Richard put on stoles. Then the priests took their places on either side of the possessed man. Richard lit a charcoal brick for the incense and laid it in a brass thurible.

"Where do you want me?" asked Mikael.

"As far away as possible," Richard said. "You're here to observe. I'll let you know if I need your help. Otherwise, just keep your eyes peeled and learn."

Mikael swallowed hard and wiped a clump of wild black hair out of his eyes. Terry smiled at his nervousness, and in a quiet compassionate voice asked him, "Where is the one place on earth you feel most safe, Mikael?"

Mikael's face screwed up into an almost comical mask of concentration. Then he brightened. "924 Gilman."

"The punk club? Seriously?"

"Seriously."

"Okay, imagine that you're there, waiting for a show."

Mikael closed his eyes and put on the concentrating face again. After a few minutes, he opened his eyes again and shook his head. "It's not working. I'm too nervous."

"Okay," Terry said, "let's try something else. Martin's first stage of exorcism—what is it?"

"Presence."

"You feel it?"

"The moment I walked in the room."

"Good. What's the second stage?"

"Pretense."

"Bingo. What does this look like to you?" He waved toward Mr. Dane.

"It looks like a really sick man knocked out on morphine."

"It does, doesn't it? Don't let it fool you, though. Inside this body is a very conscious, very dangerous being. It may try to hide for a while —to pretend it's just a very sick man knocked out on morphine. But this actually helps us. The demon can't pretend it's anything else but an unconscious old guy. If we get any response at all, we'll know it's the demon talking, not Mr. Dane here."

Richard spooned incense onto the smoking charcoal. Terry quickly set wards for protection and then erected a crucifix in a stand on the tray table in front of the possessed, where it would be clearly visible should he open his eyes.

Richard said a silent prayer for protection. As the smoke of incense wafted through the room, Richard took out a portable aspergill and began to sprinkle holy water over himself and Terry. He threw a few sprinkles in Mikael's direction and then sprinkled the old man.

A violent stirring began. It started with a shudder that ran the length of the body, beginning at the feet and ending with a brief convulsion of the shoulders and head. Then the old man began to shake all over, with shivers that did not subside.

Richard rubbed his thumb across the cotton in his oil stock, wetting it with holy chrism. The moment he touched the old man's forehead with this thumb, and before he could make the sign of the cross, the eyes snapped open, and the sagging face bunched itself up into a taut mask of rage.

"That was quick," Terry noted.

"*Well, what have we here?*" it began, slithering its words like a serpent. "*Two magickians*"—he cast his eyes to the far side of the room and sized up Mikael quickly—"*and a witch? Masquerading as priests. We're on the same team, you know, you and I. Just what do you expect to do here?*"

"We expect to send your sorry ass back to Hell, bozo," Terry said as Richard continued the chrismation. Once the cross of oil was complete, the withered body writhed in pain, and the acrid smell of burning flesh cut through the incense.

Richard ignored the demon and opened his *Ritual*. He began with the standard litany and prayer of divine invocation. Then he turned and addressed the possessed. "Unclean spirit!" he shouted. "Whoever you are who possess this servant of God, by the mysteries of the incarnation, the sufferings and death, the resurrection, and the ascension of our Lord Jesus Christ; by the sending of the Holy Spirit; and by the coming of our Lord into last judgment, I command you to tell me, with some sign, your name, and the day and the hour of your damnation. Obey me in everything, although I am an unworthy servant of God. Do no damage to this possessed creature, or to my assistants, or to any of their goods."

"Fake priest—fuck off!"

"Demon, I command you in the name of Yod-He-Vau-He, in the name of Y'Shua the Nazarene, tell me your name!"

"I am Your-Mother-Drinks-Elephant-Cum, you phony bastard!"

"Really? Elephant cum? Is that the best you can do? In the name of the Lord of Hosts—" Before Richard could continue, a wind of hurricane force upturned the tray table and upset the machinery surrounding the bed. Richard and Terry were both thrown against the sliding glass door, and Mikael hugged the wall.

The wind continued to whip at their clothes, pinning them for several minutes. Then, as suddenly as it had erupted, it stopped. Richard fell forward, and caught himself, but Terry was not so lucky, and lay sprawled on the floor. Richard looked at the door where they had hit it, and saw an enormous web of cracks radiating from his point of contact.

Richard helped Terry up and glanced at Mikael to make sure he was all right. Mikael's eyes were wide, but he nodded—he was okay. "Mikael, call Brian, and see if he can get a handle on who we're dealing with," Richard barked. "Put him on speakerphone."

Brian, Terry's husband, was a Jewish Kabbalah expert—he was also a crack professional researcher at the Graduate Theological Union Library. Mikael speed dialed Brian and hit the speakerphone button. "Hi, Mikael, what's up?" Brian's voice was tinny as it emitted from the cell phone, but cheerful.

"Hi, Sweetie," called Terry across the room.

The demon looked around uncertainly, clearly not used to such openness and lack of shame in queer folk. Shame was, after all, the hook demons most often used to snag people. Yet Terry was so open-hearted, so devoid of guilt, that it gave the demon nothing to clutch at or use against him. When the demon turned to look at Richard, however, he broke into a small, evil grin that seemed to be saying, *"Here, now, is something to work with."*

"Listen, Brian, we've got a beastie here who won't give up his name!" Richard called.

"Big surprise!"

"No kidding. What do you have for us?"

"Ever since Terry left the Friary, I've been doing web research on Mr. Dane's success in business over the last twenty years. I think you've got your work cut out for you, guys. I don't think this is an unwilling possession. I think it's a partnership."

Richard was not surprised. The drive for material success was one of the chief reasons people got involved with demons—that and power. This demon no doubt granted Mr. Dane all the riches he lusted after, and in return got a welcome relief from discarnate existence. Demons love carnal pleasure, and desire it as much as humans do, but their bodies are too subtle to enjoy food, drink, or sex. Without the solid bodies of humans, they can only look but cannot touch, taste, or feel. This inability to enjoy what they so desperately crave is itself a form of damnation, and so such partnerships were not uncommon.

"Do you know who we're dealing with?"

"Well, as you know, there are whole hosts of avarice-demons. But this guy's MO is pretty distinctive. He doesn't just defeat his competition; he likes to kill them—in pretty gross ways, actually—and we've only got a handful of beasties who operate that way. The best match is Griandre, but he's in Moloch's host, and Moloch is in the doghouse right now according to the demonwatch.com folks. So, my best guess is you're dealing with either Orak of Alexandria or Duunel of Maaluchre's host."

Richard was watching the possessed like a hawk and saw his eyes widen at the information. *So much for the famed demonic poker face,* Richard thought. He didn't know which of Brian's suggestions were on the money, but he knew one of them was.

"I've got a suggestion," Brian's thin voice offered through the speakerphone.

"I'm listening," Richard said, still drilling the demon with his eyes.

"If it's Duunel, he's got to have a physical link to Maaluchre attached to every instrument of evil. Since so much of Dane's work is legal, I'd say take a look at his letterhead. The corporate logo might yield something interesting."

Richard nodded and turned to Mikael. "Go ask the nurse if she's got any written correspondence, a contract with a cover letter, anything on Dane's letterhead."

Mikael rushed to the door on the far side of the room and entered without knocking.

"What if it's Orak? And why is he in San Francisco and not Alexandria?"

"He just made his name in Alexandria. There's a good chance he was in Chicago for the better part of the twentieth century. Railroad tycoons and such. If it's Orak, this is going to be a far sight tougher. He's rogue."

Richard nodded. Most demons were arranged into hosts, like military companies, and followed a fairly strict discipline. Rogue demons, though, answered to no one and were extremely unpredictable.

In a moment, Mikael returned with a piece of paper in hand. Richard stepped away from the possessed and snatched it from him. He held it out so that all three of them could see it. The vague nature of Mr. Dane's industries was not illuminated by anything on his stationery. The corporate logo, as was typical, adorned the upper left corner; a simple geometrical design built around the letter D—for Dane, no doubt.

"I think we struck out, here," Terry said. "I can't see anything in that design that looks even remotely sigilic."

Brian's voice crackled a bit but was still decipherable. "I have an idea. Is there a watermark?"

Richard turned around to hold the paper between himself and the brightest light in the room, and promptly swore. "Fuck me..."

Both Terry and Mikael jostled around to get a glimpse of what Richard was looking at. There, plain as day, was the ghostly image of what was unmistakably a sigil.

The demon, more agitated than ever, began to shake.

"Brian, we've got a five-pointed trident, here. The outside tines are intersected by circles—"

"That's Maaluchre's sigil, no doubt about it!" Brian's voice exclaimed tinnily. "You're dealing with Duunel, or I'll eat my kippa."

Richard lowered the paper and gave the demon his best shit-eating grin. "Got you, motherfucker. Anything else we need to know, Brian?"

"Not really...standard sixth-station demon. Nasty, but not particularly powerful politically. But he's no dummy, and he's no slouch, either. He's well connected and keeps up a wide intelligence circle. According to the demonwatch folks, he's originally a desert dweller, putting in a couple of centuries on the Sinai Peninsula, and some time in Saudi Arabia. So, invocations against jinn would probably be effective if you were Muslim. But no need to deviate from the standard Catholic formulas, guys, since you know them better. Oh yeah, one more thing about the desert stuff—he hates water."

"Yeah, we figured that one out," Richard said. "Good work, Bri. Two cookies for you at dessert tonight, laddie."

"Gee, thanks, Dad."

"Keep a plate hot for me, babe," called Terry.

"That's not all I'm keeping hot for you, Honey Pie. It's *shabbas*!"

"Okay, okay, down, boys," Richard said. "It's almost sundown, Brian. Time for you to knock off and light some candles."

"I'm *boruch*-an, I'm *ato*-an, I'm *Adonai*-an. Good luck, guys." There was a click, and he was gone.

Richard opened his *Roman Ritual* to the beginning and approached the possessed again. The old man's body was racked with convulsions as the demon fought against the limitations of its wizened form.

"Hello, Duunel. We can do this the easy way or the hard way. You either come out now, quietly, and without hurting anybody, or we kick your sorry Satanic ass. Now what's it gonna be?"

4

WHEN KAT WEBBER arrived at her brother's apartment, she was surprised to find the door locked. She knocked and waited, growing more concerned as the minutes passed and still he did not appear. She looked around—his car was there, and it *was* the middle of the afternoon. And this was, after all, Alameda, the island-where-time-stands-still, the only crime-free zone in the Bay Area. The screen door should be open to the world. She peered in the front window but was frustrated by drawn curtains, which also disturbed her. She thought perhaps he had nicked down to the Lands' End market for half-and-half or a midday cookie. So, she sat on the curb of the lazy, tree-lined street and smiled at the people strolling with their dogs and baby carriages. But as time passed and he did not appear, her smile faded, and she became openly worried.

Eventually, she passed the point where propriety had any hold on her, and she fished in the bushes for the fake rock with the key in it. The lock yielded easily, and she pushed the door in tentatively. "Randy?"

She entered the foyer and frowned at the stack of gaming magazines that were her brother's equivalent of professional journals. Most days, he was holed up here with a mug of coffee the size of his head, pecking away at his keyboard, programming video games for the Cycore Media Group.

Everything was as it should be. Still, her antennae were up for some reason. Then, when she stepped into the living room, she saw it. Him. Her brother's body lying on the floor—surrounded by a roomful of odd accoutrements. She couldn't process everything she was seeing, and so she zeroed in on the most important thing—him. She rushed to where he lay, hysterically calling his name.

She almost cried out with relief to discover he was warm. She put her ear to his mouth. He was breathing. She felt his neck; he had a pulse. He was unconscious, though, lying in a pool of water that she realized a moment later was saliva.

Tears streamed from her eyes, and she choked back scared, relieved sobs. She fumbled at her cell phone and called 911. She struggled to stay calm enough to give the operator the proper information, and then ended the call to wait with her brother until the ambulance arrived.

As she held his head in her lap, the rest of the scene came into focus. They were sitting in the middle of a circle intersected by a larger star stained—or perhaps burned—into the hardwood floor. The oriental rug that normally covered the floor was rolled up against one wall. Candles had burned down—and out—all over the room. One, a large pillar candle, was still burning as if it had hung around to bear damning testimony to what had occurred there.

Just outside the circle, a triangle was likewise burned into the floor, and on a table within it, a small triangle of white paper. Kat picked it up and noted the strange symbol written upon it in a black-ish-red substance. With horror, she recognized that it was probably written in blood. Perhaps Randy's.

Kat was a Wiccan—a witch, a worshipper of the Goddess—so she was not unfamiliar with the paraphernalia of the occult. The magick she practiced was white magick, nature magick, concerned with the perpetuation of natural rhythms and the mystical attunement of oneself with the cosmos. She was magickally literate enough to know the difference between the kind of religion she practiced and the black magick of Goetic magickians. And there was no doubt what sort of magick her brother had been doing. She stuffed the paper into the pocket of her jeans and knelt beside him, pulling him into her lap. "Holy cow, Randy, what the hell have you been up to?" she whispered, kissing the top of his head.

She realized she was cradling his body like an unholy pieta, surrounded by the instruments of demons, feeling like the bull's eye of a target that the demonic host could not miss. She brushed her brother's stringy hair out of his long, equine face. Indeed, they had not missed. She said a brief prayer to the Goddess and rocked him until she heard the sirens approach and the thundering boots of paramedics on the steps.

5

THE DEMON HAD CHOSEN the hard way. Richard knew he would. They always did. The possessed man's throat opened, and the demon emitted a scream that made all of them wince. "You!" It pointed the man's bony finger at Richard. "You have no authority..."

"I exorcise you, Most Unclean Spirit! Invading Enemy! In the name of Our Lord Jesus Christ: Be uprooted and expelled from this Creature of God..."

"You separate yourselves from the True Church because you are willful, and sinful; your appetite for sin overcomes you and will be your undoing, false priests..." The demon had become unexpectedly articulate, which meant he was scared. Richard knew they were on the right track.

"What's the next stage, Mikael?" Terry asked.

"Breakpoint? The battle of wills..."

"Yup. We're there."

Richard shook the aspergill at the possessed, raining him with holy water as he intoned, "He who commands you is he who ordered you to be thrown down from Heaven into the depths of Hell. He who commands you is he who dominated the sea, the wind, and the storms..."

The demon writhed at the touch of the water, which stung his skin like acid and filled the air with the sick stench of burning flesh. "You suck the cocks of anonymous men in bathhouses!" The demon howled, and a new voice emerged, one that sounded like the massed buzzing of a billion flies. "Who are you to command me?!"

Richard faltered, and shame rushed in. The demon saw his opening and pounced. "You lust after countless women each day. Your lust is a stain upon your soul that no sacrament can absolve! It is a sickness that ravages you, body and spirit. You'd fuck old men and bunnies if you could! You'd fuck anything that moves!"

Terry clapped his hands to get Richard's attention, "Dicky! Don't argue! Don't listen! Half-truths are the doorways to the Lie! Richard! Focus!"

"The Voice. It's the Voice..." Mikael breathed as all color drained from his face.

Richard's eyes narrowed, and he did not refute the demon. He could bear all that was true, he knew, and he could let go of the rest. He did, in fact, find bunnies oddly, even erotically, alluring. His voice, once he had cleared the phlegm born of sudden emotion, was commanding. "Hear, therefore, and tremble, Duunel, servant of the enemy of the Earth! Enemy of the Faith! Enemy of the human race! Source of death! Robber of life! Twister of justice! Root of evil!"

Instantly, every glass item in the room shattered. The windows descended in sheets of minute, sharp shards, and the plastic IV bags exploded, showering the room in saline solution. Mikael covered his face and dove to avoid the hail of glass. The demon was just reacting, not thinking, Richard thought, as the falling salt water caused it even further distress. He set his face with grim satisfaction and raised his voice above the din.

"In the name of He who has power to send you back to Hell! I command thee, Duunel, depart from this man! Surrender, not to me, but to Christ of whom I am a member. His power forces you. He defeated you by His Cross. Fear the strength of He who led the souls of the dead to the light of salvation from the darkness of waiting." Richard smeared the sign of the cross on the old man's chest. "May the body of this man be a source of fear for you." He crossed the man's forehead. "Duunel, demon of the sixth station, servant of the great Duke Maaluchre, I command you to depart! God the Father commands you! God the Son commands you! God the Holy Spirit commands you!"

Richard jumped back as the bed began to float into the air and the old man's body was racked by convulsions that would have killed even a hale man. Then the air was pierced by the sound of a heart-monitor alarm—the old man was having a heart attack.

6

WHEN THE PHONE RANG, Fr. Dylan Melanchthon looked up from the screen he had been staring at for the past three hours straight and blinked. Everything was out of focus.

"Reality rush!" he and his wife, Susan, said together. Their workstations faced each other, so a slight tilt of the eyes or the head would give them a good view of their beloved. "Reality rush" was a common phenomenon for those who make their living staring into the unblinking eye of the computer, and naming it when it happened was a bit of a ritual for them.

He picked up the phone. "Holy Apocrypha Friary," Dylan said distractedly in his Tennessee drawl, hitting save before completely turning his attention. He looked at his wife, her plump, curvaceous form hunched over her keyboard, her pretty face framed by short blonde hair. He smiled. It was good to work at home, to work together. The websites they built contributed heavily to the support of the Friary, and they had a sizable nest egg set aside for retirement already, as well. It was, he knew, a very good life indeed.

A man's voice on the other side was tentative, uncertain. "Can I speak to...is there a priest there?"

"Ah'm Father Dylan. How can Ah help you?" Dylan's back

creaked, and he rose to stretch it, cradling the phone on his shoulder and pressing his spine with both hands. Neither he nor Susan was small, due as much to their sedentary occupations as to their genetic predispositions. Brian and Terry called him a "baby bear," meaning a shortish, burly man with a tendency to be both rotund and hirsute. It was a label Dylan wore with a bit of pride. Even if he wasn't gay, it was oddly satisfying to know that there were plenty of guys out there who would find him attractive. "Um...we need to have our baby baptized. Can you do it?"

"Sure, we can do that," he said. "Why don't we get together and discuss what you're looking for?"

"Well, my family is Catholic, and it's mostly for them."

Dylan had not sought this information, but apparently the gentleman on the other end thought full disclosure important.

"Um...okay. We can talk about that. Can you come to the friary later tonight? Say, 7:30 or so?"

The man could, and would bring his wife and child.

"Brian's making cookies," Susan offered.

"There are cookies in the house tonight!" Dylan told the man, "and we'll have the kettle on." Dylan gave him the address and then hung up and stared at the phone for a second before sitting down again.

"What was that about?"

"Baptism of a child," he said, but as he did so a chill ran through him.

Susan cocked her head and took her glasses off, trying to focus on her husband. "So why do you look like you just picked a pubic hair out of your teeth?"

Dylan looked up at her and gazed for a long moment before responding. "Ah'm...not sure."

7

BISHOP TOM MÜELLER shifted in his chair. His left calf had gone to sleep, and he resisted the temptation to punch it. He was sitting in one of the large meeting rooms in the Mercy Center just outside Tucson, Arizona, in the company of his fellow bishops. The annual meeting of the bishops of the Old Catholic Synod of the Americas was in full, sleepy swing, and he fought to remain erect and alert. When he tuned back in, Bishop Walenski of Wisconsin was practically yelling.

"Christ cannot be represented at the altar by a gay man! Why are we even talking about this? We cannot have gay men—"

"Or women?" interjected Bishop Van Patton, one of the two women bishops present.

"Or women"—he nodded in her direction impatiently—"as representatives of Christ. It doesn't work!"

"Um, if I may ask a question..." Bishop Tom stood. The presiding bishop nodded to him. Tom had only been consecrated a year ago and was one of the youngest and least experienced bishops in the synod. He had so far managed to avoid the ire of the more forceful personalities in the episcopate by lying low and keeping quiet. "Why can't a gay man represent Christ at the altar, Bishop Walenski?"

Bishop Walenski, a plumber in secular life, glared at him as if he were an idiot. "Because Christ wasn't gay!"

Tom sat down again with a grateful nod to the presiding bishop. Tom wasn't sure how to answer Walenski's logic. He knew it was wrong, somehow, but he was not keen on making any enemies in the synod's leadership.

"If Ah may speak?" Bishop Cornwall of Georgia leaned on his walker and got to his feet. Bishop Cornwall had been a lawyer before retirement, and Tom admired how the man's still-nimble mind worked.

The presiding bishop pointed to the elderly prelate, and the old man continued. "Ah'm no fan of faggots in the pulpit, gentlemen. But if you ah goin' to keep them out, you best do it by logical means. Walenski, you sorry sow, Christ wasn't no Polack, either, yet you seem to have no great qualms about seizing upon your own right to represent him—"

Presiding Bishop Mellert sighed and smiled in spite of himself. When he was not wearing vestments, Bishop Mellert was a referee for the NBA—a job that ideally suited him to herd the cats of the OCSA. "Let's keep the discourse civil, Brothers," he admonished.

"And sisters!" Bishop Van Patton interjected angrily. Bishop Van Patton taught feminist theory at Midwestern Theological Seminary in Chicago, and seemed to be the self-appointed watchdog of gender balance among the denomination's leadership.

Mellert nodded and waved for Cornwall to continue. "This is the same threadbare argument used to keep women out of holy orders. 'Christ wasn't no woman, so women can't represent him,' was how the argument went. Remember? Ah do. It weren't that long ago, gentlemen."

Bishop Van Patton glared at the old man but held her tongue.

"If you ah goin' to use that argument, then logic says that only unmarried Jewish men in their thirties—and carpenters, to boot—can represent Christ at the altar. No, Ah say if you're goin' to keep them out—and I hope you do—Ah say do it on moral grounds. The idea of our clergy buggerin' each other while they're singin' 'Here I

Raise My Ebenezer' jus' gives me the willies." He sat down again with all the dignity of a sack of turnips being dropped to the floor.

"If I may?" Bishop Jeffers of New York raised one finger and waited for the presiding bishop's nod. He got it and stood. Jeffers, a onetime actor on Broadway, now served as the maître d' at Vesuvio in Manhattan. Everyone knew that Bishop Jeffers was gay, and one could have heard a pin drop in expectation of what he had to say. "May I interject a note of reason here, gentlemen...and ladies?"

Bishop Van Patton smiled her approval.

"May I recall our 2004 synod when this question completely stopped the meeting in its tracks? We have so much other business to attend to. Might I suggest that the presiding bishop appoint a committee—a fairly balanced committee, mind you, with bishops on both sides of the issue—to study the issue and make a recommendation to the next synod meeting?"

Bishop Van Patton raised her hand. "I second that motion and call for a vote."

Bishop Walenski shook his head and glowered at Jeffers and Van Patton in turn, longing for the days of the old boys' club, where the women stayed in the kitchen and the faggots kept quiet about it.

The vote was cast, and Jeffers's recommendation carried. The presiding bishop wrote "Appoint gay committee" on his growing to-do list. Then he noted with relief that they had worked through the last item on the morning's agenda. He looked at his watch. It was still an hour before dinner. They were doing well. "New business," he called.

Bishop Hammet of Texas raised his hand. The presiding bishop nodded but not before rolling his eyes. Bishop Hammet headed the synod's only Tridentine-rite diocese. He would not ordain women, nor would he allow the mass to be said in English. He ruled his diocese with an iron fist, and so great were his skills at alienating people that three years ago the synod had been forced to create a non-geographical diocese to tend to the ministries of disaffected clergy, including women and gays in Texas, as well as those who do not speak Latin, and everyone else Hammet had managed to piss off.

The bishop they had consecrated for this floating diocese, Bishop Tom, felt his flesh crawl and sweat begin to bead up on his forehead as he saw his chief antagonist rise forcefully to his feet. The two men could not have been more different. Hammet was tall, lean, and came across very much like the Marine sergeant he had been before retirement. Tom, by comparison, was soft-spoken and deferential, with a body type that could only be described as doughy. Hammet was deeply resentful of the floating diocese, which he saw as an attempt to undermine his authority in Texas, and he had very nearly split from the synod over the issue. He still entertained the notion regularly, and publicly, especially after a few shots of bourbon.

Thus far, Tom's work had been largely composed of picking up the pieces of people's lives and ministries left shattered by Hammet. The image of a bull wearing a mitre rampaging through a Catholic bookstore and icon boutique flashed through Tom's mind. He shook his head to clear it.

"Gentlemen..." He nodded in Van Patton's direction but could not bring himself to say "ladies." Van Patton once again donned her trademark glower.

"It has come to my attention that there is a religious order attached to our synod that is the very antithesis of Christian virtue and values. I speak of the so-called Berkeley Blackfriars, the Old Catholic Order of Saint Raphael in California..." He spoke the syllables for California as if they were separate, equally detestable words.

Tom grabbed the arms of his chair to quell the vertigo that rushed through him. There was not a drop of afternoon sleepiness in him now. Only pure, panicked adrenaline. He had been given oversight of the Order of Saint Raphael when he had first been consecrated— mostly because none of the other bishops knew what to do with them. They were an ecclesiastical anomaly, an order of exorcists— friars whose entire ministry stood in direct contradiction to everything the modern church holds dear: rationality, psychology, and order.

Certainly, Tom agreed that there was nothing orderly about the Order of Saint Raphael, but from the moment he met them during his first episcopal visit, he discovered in them kindred spirits. He let them in on his secret fascination with Theosophy, and they had passed him a joint. Thus far, his relationship with the friars had been a marriage made in heaven. They were not just his charges; they were his friends.

"I have it on good authority," Hammet announced, "that the men in this order have no respect for the Catholic tradition. They are hedonists and perverts, and what's more, they are Satanists."

A collective gasp rose up from the assembled bishops, and Tom slunk down in his seat in an unconscious attempt to disappear. It was true they were hedonists, Tom agreed silently. No doubt about that. He had never seen anyone put away as much liquor and weed in one weekend as the Blackfriars had done. Yes, they were addicts and alcoholics, some more than others. And yes, some of them were perverts, if that's how you regarded gay men and bisexuals. But Tom didn't consider them perverted. Terry's marriage to Brian seemed to him to be one of the healthiest he had ever witnessed, gay or straight. Certainly, it was more functional than his own marriage. But Satanists? No, they were not Satanists. Occultists, maybe, perhaps even Theoretical magickians. But Satanists? No. He struggled with what to say, and how to say it.

Bishop Stolte of Oregon asked to be recognized and stood. "My brother and sister bishops, as many of you know, my son Charlie has suffered from mental illness his entire life. At least we thought it was mental illness. When paranormal phenomena began to accompany his seizures, Bishop Tom Müeller suggested I call on the Order of Saint Raphael. They drove up the very same day I called them. They were friendly, respectful, and knowledgeable regarding demonic possession. They quickly ascertained that my son was not epileptic but possessed. Against their advice, I assisted at the exorcism. I can tell you they are the real thing. They wrestled with that demon for nearly twenty hours, but eventually they beat that beast and restored my son to me. They could not have done it if they were not faithful ministers of the Gospel of Jesus Christ. As our Lord said, 'A house divided against itself cannot stand.' They did not cast that demon out by the power of Satan but by the power of the Holy Ghost."

He sat down again, and Bishop Tom was heartened as two more bishops rose and offered testimonies on behalf of the order's ministries in their own situations. Each of them spoke glowingly. He was beginning to feel downright confident when Bishop Hammet asked for the floor again. "Yes, yes," he agreed, "they are very effective at seeming to be on the side of the angels. But the means do not justify the end, gentlemen! Even Satan disguises himself as an angel of light! We have wolves in sheep's clothing right here in our own synod, and they must be rooted out!"

The presiding bishop looked at his watch and sighed. "All right, stand down, Bishop Hammet. We will break here for the night. Tomorrow we will consider Bishop Hammet's evidence against the friars *after* we have concluded the business already on the agenda. Let us pray..."

The bishops stood and bowed their heads, but Bishop Tom remained seated, too stunned to move. Should he call Richard and the others? Of course he should. There wasn't anything any of them could do, but they deserved to know what was being said about them. Realizing he was the only seated person in the room, he stood up quickly, sending his chair flying. Every eye in the room shot open, and in his direction, as the clatter of metal on linoleum echoed through the cavernous hall.

8

NURSE STAHL HAD, apparently, been listening at her door, since as the heart-monitor alarm sounded, she raced into the room and began shouting, "Back off! You're killing him!" The friars stood frozen, uncertain how to respond to this intrusion at the very point of expelling the beast.

"It's just a ruse!" Terry tried to intercept her, but she evaded him like a veteran running back and grabbing the hospital bed now inexplicably hovering a foot or more off the ground. She yanked it down to the floor with a crash of steel. She snatched a syringe from a nearby tray and, quickly filling it, injected the man in the neck. Summoning every ounce of strength, she pounded on the old man's sternum once, twice, and then pushed upon it rhythmically, without ever taking her eyes off the green-glowing monitor.

As she worked, the old man stabilized, and his breathing returned to normal. Wiping sweat from her forehead, she turned and faced the friars. "I was afraid this would happen. I don't care how nasty this demon is, if you try this again, you murder him."

The friars swallowed and looked at each other, angered by the abrupt *exorcises interruptus*, but Richard knew in his heart she was right. They would have expelled the demon, all right, but at the expense of the old man's life. It would have been a shallow victory indeed.

Just then the door at the far side of the room smashed open. A tall, handsome man of about Terry's age burst through, his mouth open in disbelief. "What the *fuck* is going on here? And who the hell are *you*?" He was dressed in a dark blue suit, sans jacket. His sleeves were linkless and flapped around, his forearms wet as if he had just been washing. Rings adorned his hands ostentatiously; a large red stone in particular flashed on his right hand.

Nurse Stahl looked around at the disaster area the room had so quickly become, and her horror showed on her face, plain for anyone to read. "Oh, Mr. Dane, I'm so sorry. I had no idea this would happen—"

His rage was evident, but instead of mounting a defense, Richard froze. There was something about the angry young man's face—something disconcertingly *familiar*. Then his blood ran cold. He knew him—had known him, he realized with a shock, in the biblical sense. It had been at the Jizz Factory, the gay bathhouse in west Berkeley, only last month. He hadn't known Dane's name then, or that he was one of the richest men in the Bay Area, but he remembered every detail of the man's ass.

"Mr. Dane, these are priests," Nurse Stahl said quickly, before Dane did anything to hurt the friars. "They're here to help your father."

Silence hung in the air as Richard was momentarily paralyzed.

"We're from the Old Catholic Order of Saint Raphael," Terry jumped in, extending his hand in greeting. "I'm Fr. Terry Milne. These are my colleagues, Fr. Richard Kinney and Brother Mikael Bloomink, one of our novices."

Mr. Dane's eyes locked on him, and Richard knew he was experiencing his own little shock of surprise. "Mr. Dane and I have met before," Richard admitted, "in a rather...anonymous environment."

Terry rolled his eyes. "Oh Jesus Christ. Well, I guess formal introductions are not necessary, then, since you two already know each other *intimately*."

Mikael was utterly lost but did not ask for clarification. Dane's anger appeared to drain from him, but he seemed uncertain what to say or do. He ran his hands through his hair and breathed deeply, trying to catch his breath. It was obvious he was working hard to master himself.

"So, you're a *priest*?" he said as if Richard were the only other person in the room.

"Yes. I take it you're a tycoon or something," Richard answered.

"And we're both liars," Dane said, a slight smile beginning to curl his lip.

"When we need to be, I guess that's true," Richard conceded.

"Well, it's nice to see you again, *Richard*." He looked around the room at the rest of them now. Then, staring straight at Nurse Stahl, added, "Although I would have preferred other circumstances."

"Mr. Dane, Ms. Stahl called us because she was concerned about your father, that he might be possessed by a demon," Richard interceded. "She did the right thing. He *is* possessed. *We* didn't do *any* of this," he said, waving his hand around the wreckage of the room. "The evil being resident in your father did it."

"And yet," Dane said, "before you got here, nothing had been smashed in this room for, oh, a hundred years?!" His eyes narrowed, and the anger returned to his face. "Who the hell gave you permission to come in here and do an exorcism?"

None of them spoke. Finally, Richard cleared his throat. "Mr. Dane, surely you wouldn't want your father to suffer having a dem—"

"I did," Nurse Stahl stepped forward. "I called them, I told them what I saw, and I asked them to help your father. If you want to fire me, go ahead, but these priests have done nothing wrong. They were just doing...their jobs. And honestly, so was I." She looked down. "I know I should have asked you about it first. But I was afraid...I was afraid..." She didn't finish.

Richard had a good idea of what she wanted to say but couldn't. She was afraid Dane *wanted* his father to be possessed, for some unknown, twisted reason of his own that Richard could not begin to guess.

Dane once again mastered his anger. He placed a compassionate hand on the nurse's shoulder. "I understand. You were just trying to help." He turned back to Richard. "Did you succeed?"

Richard shook his head. "We met with...a bit of an impasse. We were on the brink of expelling the demon, but in your father's condition...we almost lost him."

A satisfied smile passed over Dane's face, but he quickly covered it up with a look of concern. "I'm sorry you troubled yourself for nothing, then. I will...consult with some experts of my own, and decide what to do. I'm grateful that you brought this issue so forcefully to my attention." He shook Richard's hand and gave him a disingenuous nod of thanks. "However, if, in the future, you plan to conduct any rituals that might include members of my family, I will thank you to consult me first." With that he walked toward the door and called over his shoulder. "I trust, Nurse Stahl, you can show these monks to the door."

"Friars," Terry corrected him and then jumped at the sound of the slammed door.

9

KAT WANDERED A FOGGY STREET, the cement covered with occult symbols painted in white and yellow like lane division lines gone horribly awry. She skipped through them as if she were playing hopscotch, daring not to touch any of the lines. But it was getting harder because she was aware that she was being pursued—by what she did not know, but she could feel a chill breath on the back of her neck.

Then, suddenly, the lines stopped. A huge circle appeared, empty of the yellow and white symbols, a large white house at the center of it, across the street from where she stood. Floating out to meet her was a scarecrow of a man with wild black hair, his legs gyrating as if pedaling a unicycle but his feet never touching the ground. He floated straight up to her and kissed her on the lips—

She awoke, to the embarrassing realization that she was drooling on the seat next to her. She looked around and recognized the place. She was in the waiting area of the emergency room of Alameda Hospital.

Comprehension swarmed in. Randall, comatose, and she had been waiting...how long? She rubbed her eyes and squinted at the clock on the wall. Three hours. Three hours, and the doctors had yet to say one word to her.

She moved her head around to work out the kink that had developed in her neck. She had been dreaming, but had it been just a dream, or was it a *Dream*? She could never tell—she just knew that sometimes her dreams were portentous. More than that, they were often *true*—sometimes symbolically, often literally.

She pulled out her phone and checked her email. She rolled her eyes at the seven messages devoted solely to her coven's drama *du jour*. She loved her sisters, but it seemed to her that the Berkeley brand of feminist-eco-pagans was addicted to interpersonal conflict and perpetual emotional processing in a way she had rarely encountered before moving to the area. By comparison, Seattle Wiccans seemed almost sane.

She exhausted her email and began surfing the web. Ignoring the sign prohibiting cell phones, she tried to distract herself. Moving her thumbs like lightning across the buttons, she went to Google and typed in *Satanic Ritual*. Then, in a flash of inspiration, she typed *investigation*.

The first website on the list belonged to a Christian group. Her eyebrows lifted in surprise. *The Order of Saint Raphael*, she read, *was dedicated to the expulsion of demons and the investigation of occult phenomena...*As she continued reading she discovered that they specialized in Satanic ritual and spiritual emergencies of all kinds.

As she read, she battled against an internal aversion to anything even remotely connected to Christianity. She felt anger rise hot in her throat as she thought of the nine million women accused of witchcraft in the past one thousand years that the church had condemned to horrible, grisly deaths. Those women's stories were her legacy, whether any of them had been witches or not. Kat *was* a witch, and proud of it, and an angry defiance welled up within her whenever she encountered Christians.

All Christians were hicks—at least every one she had ever encountered—backward, anti-intellectual bigots who would stop at nothing, no matter how unethical, to coerce the rest of the nation into sharing their own prejudiced opinions. That was why, as she read the order's website, much of what she read simply did not compute. *The friars of Saint Raphael were of a liberal theological orientation and were committed to the well-being of peoples of all faith traditions.*

She could hardly believe what she was reading. She was sure she didn't understand it; perhaps she didn't want to. She certainly did not want to call them, but where else to turn? It seemed that something like fate was involved when she got to the bottom of the website and discovered that their friary was less than five miles away.

The Holy Apocrypha Friary was in north Berkeley, just a couple of blocks from the original Peet's Coffee. She knew the neighborhood well, as a former boyfriend had lived just across Shattuck, near Big Apples. The area was informally known as the "Gourmet Ghetto," as it was home to Chez Panisse and many other fine restaurants. She didn't know exactly where the Holy Apocrypha Friary was, but she was sure she could find it without too much trouble. She scribbled the address on a piece of paper and chewed on her lip, staring at the TV but not seeing it. As soon as she had news about her brother, she decided, she would pay the friars a visit.

10

WHEN THE DOORBELL RANG, Dylan had been in the backyard wrestling with the great golden lab, Tobias. At the sound of it the dog had barked and rushed off to investigate, while Dylan stumbled into the kitchen. Brian was laying a huge handful of kale into a frying pan, and a cloud of steam arose, filling the house with the glorious smell of garlic.

Although Brian was about Dylan's own height, he seemed larger, mostly because he was a hunchback—the large dromedarian hump swelled from just behind his right shoulder, stretching tight the fabric of his flannel shirt. It also forced Brian's head to cock to the left, creating an illusion of perpetual inquiry. "Smells good, amigo," Dylan said, swallowing against the rush of saliva.

"You got a meeting?" Brian asked. "Now?"

"Yeah. Baptism."

"You got grass in your hair."

"Thanks, dude." Dylan picked at what was left of his unruly red mane.

"And you reek of marijuana. Altoids are on the fridge."

"You are mah salvation," Dylan responded almost liturgically, shoving four of the mints into his mouth and crunching them.

Brian looked up at the clock and shot him a look. "Dinner's at eight." However unsettling his disfigurement might seem to strangers, among the friars Brian was the benevolent dictator of the household, a true Jewish mother in all but genitalia.

"Ah'll make it quick. Start without me if you need to."

Brian didn't say anything—a wordless reproach, which, Dylan realized, was justified. An artist deserves to have his friends show up on time to appreciate his art, after all, and Brian's cooking was high art indeed.

The foyer was at the foot of the chapel, and Tobias was sniffing at the door and making rumbling sounds in his throat. "It's okay, big boy, they're nice people." Dylan realized he had no evidence of this as he opened the door and then conceded to himself that, indeed, some things needed to be taken on faith. He grinned, swung out the screen door and offered his hand. "You must be the Swansons! Welcome to the friary, I'm Father Dylan."

A couple in their early thirties stood there, looking like they might cut and run at any moment. Holding on to the end of her father's arm, a little girl of about four bunched a wad of her blonde, curly hair in her fist as she twisted to and fro.

"Hello, little one!" he said to her cheerfully. But seeing the surprise registered on the couple's faces, Dylan realized what a sight he must be after his wrestling match with Tobias. "Sorry about mah appearance. Ah've been...working in the yard. Why don't y'all come with me?"

The couple shook his hand and followed him inside the enormous farmhouse that had once been the only structure in North Berkeley for miles around. The two seemed a little spooked by the gaudy excess of the chapel, and gladly followed Dylan to an adjoining room used by the friars for spiritual counseling.

Dylan's heart melted as he saw that someone—probably Susan—had placed a plate of Brian's famed snickerdoodles on the little table. "Please have a seat—and a cookie." The little girl ran up to the plate and snatched one off. She already had it in her mouth when she looked at her mother for permission. Her mother nodded, and the little girl began chewing with gusto.

Dylan ran his hand through his hair in one more pointless attempt to look presentable. "So, we're doing a baptism for this beauty, eh?" He leaned in and made a funny face at the little girl, who immediately shrank back in horror.

"Well, yes, I suppose so." The man looked at his wife hesitantly. For a moment indecision played over his face. With a grim look of resolve, he started in. "Look, we're not sure we should even be here. And I'm afraid that if I just tell you the truth, you're going to kick us out on our asses."

"Dude," Dylan laughed, "you are so speaking mah language. Why don't you just spill the beans and see how it goes? Ah guarantee you ain't gonna ask me anything Ah haven't heard before."

"Okay," said the man warily, choosing to take Dylan at his word. "Look, my wife and I are not Catholics—in fact, we're not Christians. Hell, we're not even religious. But Connie's family, they're rabid. They've been calling us every day asking us when we're going to get Jamie, here, baptized, sending us these horrible articles from these fucking fundamentalist Catholic websites about how our baby is going to spend eternity in Limbo if she dies. We both think this is complete and utter bullshit, but we don't know how to get her folks off our back! So, we're giving in..." he trailed off with a look of defeat.

Connie picked up the thread. "You—well, not you but one of the monks here—did a wedding for my friend Pam, and she said you were...pretty cool, which I thought was a pretty strange thing to say about monks." Her voice was unusually rough as if she had been smoking three packs a day since infancy. "So, we thought we would just come and talk to you about it, without making any plans or promises or anything, because we're just not sure, well, even what we're doing here, or if we *should* be here—"

Dylan held his hand up to stop the sentence that didn't seem to have an end in sight. "First off, we're friars, not monks—we friars live and work out in the world with regular folk. Second, Ah think Pam is right. Ah think we can probably help. What if we gave your family everything they want—a baptismal liturgy with all the right ritual actions, performed by a qualified Catholic priest—and, at the same time, we craft the words of the liturgy to reflect your spirituality and your real hopes and desires for little…"

"Jamie," said Connie.

"Little Jamie, here. What do yuh think?"

They looked at each other, a little surprised. "Sounds…okay," the man said.

Dylan glanced at the plate of snickerdoodles—they were calling to him. "Why don't we start with you two telling me your own understanding of baptism?" He grabbed a snickerdoodle and ate half of it in one bite.

"Well, I—"

"Ah'm sorry, what was your name?" Dylan asked, his mouth full of cookie.

"John." The man swallowed and started again. "Well…I…I wasn't raised religious, so I guess I don't really know…"

"I hate that original sin stuff," Connie piped up with the ladylike timbre of gravel in a blender. "If baptism is all about wiping away original sin, then we are so out of here."

Dylan laughed. "Thank you, Saint Augustine," he said, shaking his head. "Well, it's true that Western Catholicism has tended to focus on the original sin side of things, but that's not the whole story. The Eastern Orthodox maintain an earlier tradition that says that all babies are born good. Well, morally neutral, actually. They're good just as every other part of God's creation is good, but they don't have any stains on their souls or any nonsense like that."

Connie relaxed a little. As he talked, Dylan noticed that her features softened a little. *Maybe,* he allowed himself to hope, *they're starting to like me a little.* "For the Orthodox," he continued, "baptism welcomes the child into the Community of God."

"But…what does that mean?" asked John.

"Well, that's the million-dollar question!" Dylan laughed. "Some people draw the circle very small—you know, who's in the circle of grace and who's out. Like Christian fundamentalists draw the circle very small, only those who believe exactly like they do are 'in.' Some of them even exclude other fundamentalists who don't belong to their particular sect. The Orthodox are interesting because they mean, on one level, the Church, but they also believe that the entire universe is in the process of being transformed into God's Community. So, in the Church they celebrate in miniature the community of grace that is transforming the cosmos into Divinity itself."

"Wow," said John. "I'm not sure I follow, but it sounds pretty trippy."

"So…Father Dylan, where do you draw the circle?"

Dylan smiled, and it lit up his whole flat Melungeon face. "I think that everything that is, is in the circle."

"So, what is baptism about?"

"I like to think of it as a Welcome to Earth celebration because the whole world is God's Community for those who have their eyes open to it. And my hope is that you'll be able to bring her up so that she can see that." He patted Jamie on the head and handed her another snickerdoodle.

In spite of her obvious efforts not to, Connie began to cry.

"Oh my God," Dylan said, instantly chagrined, "did I say something wrong?" He looked to John for help.

Connie picked up Jamie and held her in her lap. "No, it's okay. I'm just…relieved."

"Awww…bless your heart," Dylan relaxed. He picked up the plate and held it out to her. "Have a cookie," he offered.

11

No sooner had the door shut behind the friars than Alan Dane walked up behind Nurse Stahl. Thinking he had left the room, she gave a little start then opened her mouth to say something. He held up his hand, and a paternal smile spread across his face like a plague as he spoke. "Not a word, my dear. Not a single fucking word. You will now return to your room where you will pack all that you have. Without saying goodbye to myself or my father, you will leave this house in fifteen minutes—less, if you can. Any remaining pay will be forwarded to your permanent address. Go." He waved her away like a mosquito and sat on the bed next to his father.

He picked up one age-spotted hand in his own and held it as he talked. "Well, we *have* had an adventure today, haven't we? I take it those priests gave you quite a workout." The red and glowing eyes of the old man pierced him with fierce and impotent rage, but the demon said nothing.

The younger Dane leaned in to whisper conspiratorially. "You didn't think you'd get out of it as easily as that, did you? Really?" He fixed his father with a malevolent grin. "No, dear Father, you will not have your release. Not yet. Not while I live and breathe. Need I remind you what you did to me when I was young and helpless?

When I could not escape? Did you have pity on me then? Do you really expect any from me now? I know this demon is hard to live with, Father dear, but it keeps your heart beating so that you can enjoy an interminable string of boring, excruciatingly painful days, world without end."

He sat upright again and smoothed out the bedclothes, arranging them neatly. "Don't look at me like that," he said, although in truth, his father's expression had not changed since he sat down. It was frozen in a permanent mask of unmitigated hatred.

"It's not like *I'm* the evil one. *You* were the one who ruined countless lives to build your fortune. *You* were the one who drove Mother to end her own life. You were the one who...did what you did to *me*. I'm not persecuting you, Father dear. I'm simply giving you an opportunity to atone for your own sins. I know, the burden of the flesh is hard, and it would feel ever so good to let go, to shake off this mortal flesh and let your spirit breathe free, but would that be justice? Oh, it would be kind, no doubt, but would it be *right*?"

He grinned at the old man. "And I'm not terribly interested in kindness, not now—no, in that you taught me well. But it wouldn't be fair to let you...expire...without having settled the karmic debt, if only just a little bit, would it?"

The young man shot him a satisfied look. "Oh, no need to thank me. It's what I do, you know. You savaged people. I save them. Oh, you made me what I am, no question, but I seek to undo all the evil you worked at so tirelessly."

The younger Dane wiped at his own brow melodramatically. "I don't expect you to be proud of me, heaven knows. I certainly don't expect you to love me. I don't even need you to like me."

He held aloft the glowing red ring on his right hand and menacingly brought it far too close to the old man for the demon's comfort. His father jerked and wrestled against the bedclothes, trying to back away from the ring, but the young man held him fast. "I only require that you fear me. And suffer. And despair. Is that too much to ask?"

12

SUSAN WAS BURIED in a web page she was proofreading when the phone rang. She picked it up absentmindedly. "Holy Apocrypha Friary," she said almost robotically.

"Susan? Bishop Tom here."

Susan forced herself to break away from the screen. "Tommy! Hey, how's the day trading going?" Then she remembered. "Omigod, the synod is on now, isn't it? Shit, how is the synod going?" The friars had been checking their email every night after dinner for updates. So far, there had been nothing terribly exciting.

"Not well, I'm afraid. Is Richard there?"

"No, he's out getting his pound of demon flesh with Terry and Mikael."

"Dylan?"

"Baptismal consultation. Sorry, you'll just have to speak to a Lutheran," she said, referring to herself, "or a Jew," she added, referring to Brian, "or there's always Tobias. I must warn you, however, that he doesn't pass on information reliably. And he sheds prodigiously. Possibly even over the phone."

"Can you have Richard or Dylan call my cell phone when you can? We're neck deep in shit here."

"What's going on?" she asked, suddenly serious.

"An objection was raised against the order during our session today."

"What kind of objection?"

"Look, Susan, I don't want to alarm anyone unnecessarily, but we're actually on the agenda tomorrow."

"Oh my God! Tom, what are they saying? And who's accusing them?"

"It's the conservatives, of course. They've been out to get the boys for quite some time, and after the Bishop Kaarlson fiasco, they're seizing their chance." He breathed a deep sigh. "They've been accused of Satanism."

"That's crazy! Surely, no one is going to take them seriously."

"Sadly, they are," Bishop Tom sighed heavily, and the weight of it carried over the phone without any loss of effect or meaning. "Susan, they're talking about excommunication."

13

DYLAN KNEW that he was indeed late for dinner as he saw John, Connie, and little Jamie out. "Ah'll email a liturgy for you to look over, especially adapted to your situation," he said. They nodded and thanked him. "Goodbye, Honey," he waved at Jamie. "You be good!" She pumped her head forward exactly once and turned to walk down the steps. Dylan closed the door behind them.

He sighed deeply, taking in the enticing aroma of Brian's cooking, and looked at his watch—ten past. "Ah'm not too late," he announced at the kitchen's threshold, hoping Brian would agree. A huge, rough-hewn wooden table took up half of the room, and Brian and Susan, seated on its long benches, ate sullenly, silently.

"What's wrong?" he asked.

Before she could answer, the front door banged open, and Richard, Terry, and Mikael stumbled in, tired and not a little bit hungry. They dropped their kit bags at the chapel door and joined the rest of the friary family at the table.

As usual, Brian's cooking was exquisite. The evening's menu was mostly Middle Eastern, with lamb, falafel, salads, pita bread, steamed greens, and generous helpings of tahini and hummus on top of it all.

But before anyone dug into any of it, Susan announced, "Guys, you need to call Bishop Tom right away." She filled them in on what Tom had told her, noting painfully the look of shock and anger on her husband's face. Richard, Terry, and Mikael looked likewise stunned.

"Holy shit," Richard said, breaking the shocked silence. "Do you know what that means?"

"Hell, yes," Dylan said. "Ah know what excommunication means. It means we won't be affiliated with the Old Catholic Synod of the Americas. Big deal."

"It *is* a big deal. If we aren't affiliated, we don't have a bishop. And if we don't have a bishop..."

"We're not Catholics," Terry finished his sentence, horrified by the implication.

"That's right," Richard said.

"So?" asked Susan. "You could be Lutheran friars."

They all shot her twisted, pained looks. "What?" she protested. "It's not oxymoronic! They have Lutheran nuns in Germany!"

"If we're not plugged into the apostolic succession," Richard said, "we lose our priestly mojo—worst of all, we lose any power we might have over demons. We have to have a bishop to be connected to the Succession."

"Oh," Susan said. "Is that really true?"

"It is for us," Richard said.

"That would be the end of the line for us, Gents," Dylan said. "So, what can we do?"

"Well, let's not panic," Richard said. "After dinner, we'll call Bishop Tom and get the details."

"He sounded pretty rattled." Susan gingerly stuffed a pita.

Richard let out a tired sigh. "Let's hope these things just happen in threes because, honestly, I don't think I can take another major disappointment today."

"Why?" asked Brian. "What else happened?"

Terry beat Richard to the punch. "Philip dumped him."

Susan's mouth dropped open, and she banged the table with a

plump fist. Richard scowled at Terry. "No," Susan said. "I don't believe it. I *like* Philip! Did he give a reason?"

Richard was suddenly awash in depression. "He said I didn't have time for him—or didn't *make* time for him."

"Oh." Susan picked at her falafel sandwich. "Well, *that's* true. I struggle with that one myself." She glanced sideways at her husband. Dylan shrank noticeably in his seat.

"Thanks a lot," Richard said, the hurt evident in his voice.

"Well, it *is* true." No one at the table disagreed. "I'm really sorry, Dicky," Susan said after chewing a bite. "You deserve a good person like him."

Brian reached for the salad and placed a goodly portion on his plate. "What was the second disappointment?"

Terry piped up, "We had what you might call an unsuccessful exit job this afternoon."

"Well, you've had those before," Brian said philosophically. "What went wrong?"

"I've been asking myself the same question," Richard said, a faraway look in his eyes. "And I honestly don't know. The demon was responding well, and then at the point of expulsion...well, we stopped it."

"Why?" asked Susan.

"We were afraid we were going to kill the host," Terry admitted. "But Dicky's right. It shouldn't have been that hard."

"And then there was the whole Jizz Factory surprise," Terry continued, kicking Richard under the table. "Okay, I know you're always down on me for buying into these conspiracy theories, but I wonder if maybe your...encounter with Dane wasn't an accident?"

All eyes turned to Richard. "Okay, we didn't hear this bit," said Brian, grinning salaciously. Susan looked at Richard with a complex mixture of compassion and disappointment.

"You *did* seem more surprised by it than he did," Mikael noted.

Richard looked down at his plate, hating the feelings suddenly coursing through him.

"Maybe Richard was just more ashamed," said Terry, and the truth of it was evident.

"Maybe he worked some kind of spell on you," Dylan said. "Or maybe he planted something on you! Dude, were you top or bottom? 'Cause if you were bottom—"

Richard slammed the table with the flat of his hand. "I am *not* having this conversation!"

"Oh, but Honey," said Susan soothingly, "you *are*. You have to. We're all in this together, and whatever you did in that bathhouse affects us, too. We're not blaming you for anything; we're just talking—"

But Richard had pushed away from the table and was already pounding up the back stairs.

"And he's gone," said Dylan, staring at the space where Richard had been. "That Dane guy coulda planted a bug or something up Dicky's bunghole; that's all I was sayin'."

"Internalized homophobia," pronounced Brian, gathering dishes. "That's always been Dicky's problem."

"But what do we *do*?" asked Mikael.

"For now, we do dishes," said Brian. He waved at Dylan and Mikael, "And it's youze guyses turn."

14

DYLAN WASHED and placed the dishes in the right-hand sink for Mikael to rinse and dry.

"Do you really think we'll get excommunicated?" Mikael asked sullenly.

"'Sa good question, amigo," Dylan said. "I just wanna know where the charges are comin' from. We never had any trouble before. In fact, we've been commended by the synod more'n once."

"We should have sent a delegate," Mikael said. "Nobody is there to represent us."

"Bishop Tom is there," Dylan said. "But I take your point. Bishop Tom is about as aggressive as a baby chick." He shook his head. "His heart's in the right place, but he ain't gonna stand up to the bastards. He has a thing against rockin' the boat."

"Fucking Bible-Belt pricks," Mikael muttered. "I'll bet my ass it's those Tridentine Mass nutcases in Texas. They hate us."

"Eh, the feeling is kind of mutual," Dylan admitted. "Their bishop don't ordain women, and thinks that all sexual minorities are headed straight to Hell, except for the celibates, o' course."

"Yeah, but we've never tried to excommunicate their fundamentalist asses!" Mikael said hotly.

Dylan chuckled. "They're still brothers, even if they do...have it all wrong."

Just then, out the window above the sink, a young woman strode into view across the street. She was slight, dressed in a short poodle skirt and a black leather biker jacket, her long black hair waving in the wind. She appeared to be pacing, and, it seemed, staring right at their house. "I sure like her style," Mikael whistled. "Do you see her?"

"Huh? Who, 'her'?"

"Her," Mikael pointed out the window, but the woman had walked out of sight again. In a moment, though, she was back. "There," he nudged Dylan.

The portly priest squinted. "Oh yeah. Cool jacket. Is she looking at us?"

"That's what I was thinking. She looks kind of upset."

Dylan nodded. She did. "If she was spying on us," he reasoned, "she'd be more careful 'bout it. Maybe she's still makin' up her mind whether to come across..." Then it hit him. "Wait! She's *tryin'* to approach the house and can't. *Terry!*" he yelled.

Terry came running from the living room. "What? What's wrong?"

"That girl out there—the one looking at us but definitely *not* crossin' the street. Do you see anything we don't see?"

"What?" asked Mikael. "Do you think she might be possessed—and can't approach the house because of the warding?"

"Possessed or *oppressed*," Dylan answered.

"Her aura is distressed, that's for sure," Terry said, squinting. "I can tell that even by the light of the streetlamp. "Wait...yeah, she's got something else hanging around her. Not possession. Not even oppression, really. But Presence. As if something is watching her. Maybe even lying in wait."

"I could go talk to her," offered Mikael.

There was something in his tone. Dylan looked at Terry, and they both grinned. "She's your *type*," said Terry.

"Yup, gothy-punk style, complexion like a corpse. She's his type, all right." Dylan shook his head. "Okay, Lover Boy, go see what she's up to. Take some gall in case she's really on her way in here and we need to send that demon packin'."

Mikael dried his hands hurriedly, rummaged in the sacristy cabinet for a moment, and rushed out the front door. He slowed his pace as soon as he reached the street, and tried to look nonchalant.

Kat saw a tall, lanky goth guy emerge from the house at a sprint and wisely slow down at the street. He seemed to grow even taller as he approached, and she noted how fine his features were, how angular and severe. He was painfully skinny, and his black clothes hung on him like a scarecrow. He reminded her of Morpheus, the Sandman, from the comic book series. So dark, so brooding, so...smiling.

"Hi," he said. "We couldn't help noticing you out here. Can I help you? I'm Mikael." He offered his hand.

"Kat," she said, a little flustered by the fact that this vision was speaking to her. "Webber. Kat Webber. That's. My name. Hi." She grinned back and felt like an idiot.

He didn't seem to notice. "Whatcha doing out here? I mean, other than looking at our house?" He realized how that might sound, and added. "Not that we mind—it's a cool old house. One of the oldest in Berkeley. Maybe *the* oldest. But, I guess, I mean, is there a *reason* you're looking at our house?"

"I was looking for the Holy Apocrypha Friary."

"You found it."

"You don't *look* like a friar," she said, noticing with not a little awe the prodigious inkwork covering his arms. "Not that I'm all that clear on what, exactly, a friar is in the first place."

"I'm a novice, here, actually," he said. "I'll be a friar next month, Frith willing."

"Frith?"

"Never read *Watership Down*?"

She *had*, actually, a long time ago. *What an odd guy*, she thought. "I need to talk to you guys," she said but then looked a little scared. "But for some reason, I can't seem to cross the street."

"We figured. The house is warded." Oddly, the young man sat

down cross-legged on the sidewalk and pulled a large abalone shell and what looked like a midget-size hockey puck out of a shoulder bag.

"Warded? Like, as in magick? Warded against what?"

"Demons, of course."

He said it so matter-of-factly, she was a little taken aback. But she knew he was right. "It's my brother. I think he was doing demon magick. I found this." She pulled out the little paper triangle with the strange symbol on it.

Mikael studied it closely for a few long seconds. "That's a sigil, all right," he said. "Put it away, now. And don't pull it out again. If your brother was doing what I think he was doing with that thing, we're both in danger, now."

"What? I'm not doing magick. Not demon magick, anyway."

"No, but there's magick associated with that thing, and it could put us all in danger." He struck a lighter and held the flame to the side of the hockey puck. Then Kat recognized the object—a brick of self-lighting charcoal, the kind some of the women in her coven used for incense.

"What are you doing?" she asked.

"We're going to separate you from that beastie so that you can cross the street."

"Your warding works pretty damn well."

"It's not us; it's angelic warding, actually. And it *does* work pretty well." He pulled out a plastic bag that looked like it was filled with the bloody entrails of an animal. Mikael blew on the charcoal to speed it along. "But we *are* pretty good at what we do, if I do say so myself. Everyone here has a specialty. Terry's thing is the angel magick, you know, Enochian stuff. You'd be surprised how many thieves and homeless people are possessed or oppressed. The warding keeps the house pretty safe from petty thieves and oppor-tunists. Kind of a positive side effect."

He was too chatty, she thought. Perhaps he's nervous. *Perhaps*, she dared to allow herself to think it, *he's as smitten with me as I am with him*. She told herself she was being silly and tried to suppress the thought.

Then, with gross fascination, she watched as he pulled some nameless, bloody organ from the plastic bag and placed it on the charcoal. It fizzled and spat, and a noxious cloud of smoke erupted into the air. Mikael jumped to his feet and began waving the abalone shell around in front of her.

She had been smudged many times, especially before coven rituals. But she had always found sage a pleasant, cleansing odor. This was ghastly. She screwed up her face and went into automatic, holding her arms up and cooperating with the smudging in due form despite the acrid and obnoxious stench.

"You've done this before!" Mikael said, delighted. She turned, and he began smudging her back.

"Yes, but it was never so unpleasant."

"Unpleasant beasties require unpleasant means, I'm afraid."

He shot a glance toward the window, caught Terry's eye, and gave an exaggerated shrug, a question: *Is it safe?*

Terry nodded vigorously and waved his hand for Mikael to hurry.

"Let's go," he said and waved her in front of him. He held the smoking abalone shell at her back all the way to the front door. He placed the shell on the porch and held the door shut as he yelled through it. "Dudes, sigil alert! I need a warded envelope, pronto!"

He heard scrambling from within, and in a few seconds a dark brown envelope was fed through the mail slot. He turned to Kat and held open the envelope. "Okay, put the sigil in here."

"The paper-triangle-thingy?"

"Yeah, quick! Before the gall burns up."

She nodded and dug in her jeans pocket for the paper. She dropped it into the envelope, and Mikael sealed it fast. He then dropped it in the mailbox. "You can pick it up on your way out," he said, "but I don't recommend opening it again." He pushed open the door, then, and waved her inside.

Tobias greeted her first, his tail moving in quick, happy circles. And then suddenly she was surrounded by a gaggle of men, most of whom looked like they would have felt right at home at a science fiction convention or a Pink Floyd reunion concert. Kat noted that most of the men were in their late thirties or early forties and balding—except for Mikael, who was younger with a head of insanely wild hair.

"Tobias is our guest master," Mikael said, in what seemed a kind of apology for the dog's exuberance. "His hospitality is unparalleled."

Richard emerged from the front staircase, and Mikael proceeded to make further introductions. He then led Kat to the big table in the kitchen where the friars sat while Dylan put the kettle on and grabbed mugs for them all.

"How can we help?" asked Terry.

This wasn't at all what Kat had been expecting. Except for the black robes, there was nothing even remotely monkish about the men seated around the table. Nor was there an air of saintliness hanging over the place. Indeed, it seemed like at any time they might grab a big bowl of potato chips and gather around the TV for a football game.

Hesitantly at first, and then in great gushes of emotion, she described the condition in which she had found her brother. They hung on every word, and one of them, the small, effeminate guy, took notes on a laptop. She was grateful for their attention and felt better just talking about it to someone—someone who wouldn't think she was crazy, that is.

"Where is your brother now?" asked Dylan, pouring hot water into the mugs.

"In the hospital. They say that there's nothing physically wrong with him, but they're going to hold him overnight for observation." Despite her best efforts, she started to cry. "What happened to him? Is he going to be okay?"

The friars looked at each other, and back at her with concern.

Richard spoke first. "I don't know. But we're going to find out. If there is anything we can do to return your brother to you, we will. We promise." He offered her a grim smile that betrayed more determination than certainty. "The first thing we need to do is inspect the ritual site. Do you still have the key to your brother's house?"

She nodded.

"Dylan, Terry, let's go."

A throat cleared behind him. In the doorway to the kitchen stood Susan and Brian, arms crossed over their chests.

"Oh," Richard said thinly, like the sound of air being emitted from a tire. He looked at his watch. "It's almost 9:30, and we've all had a long day. Why don't we investigate at your brother's house first thing in the morning? We'll all be fresh."

Everyone smiled knowingly and nodded, pushing their chairs back.

"Except..." she began, and they all rested their elbows once more on the table. "Well, I'm a little freaked out. I don't really want to go home. Not alone."

"We have a guest room. You're welcome to stay there," Mikael offered. "In fact, it's a really good idea, what with the sigil thingy and all. You'll be safe here. The house is wa—"

"I know, the house is warded," she smiled at him. "I know how well that works. Are you sure it won't be any trouble?"

"Sure, it's trouble," Richard said, getting up and carrying his tea with him. "Guests are always trouble. People are always trouble." But before she could suspect a spirit of misanthropy, he winked at her. "But they're almost always worth it."

"Come on," Mikael said, "I'll show you to your room."

She was secretly delighted to be staying in this enormous and unusual house, and longed to see more of it. She followed Mikael out the back door of the kitchen to a narrow set of stairs. At the top, they walked past several bedrooms that must have belonged to the friars. At the end of the hall, they turned left and entered a small room with a large picture window. A single bed was there, made up and inviting. "That's just the bedspread," said Mikael. "I'll get some fresh linens."

While he was out, she took in the rest of the room. A small desk was set against the far wall, and a single low bookcase was set near the door. Above it hung a large mirror in a rough wooden frame. There were several hooks in the wall but no closet.

In a moment, he was back, and together they set to making the bed. "Can I ask you a question?" Her voice was soft, tentative.

"Sure."

"What was that all about? About starting tomorrow? Because if it was really about getting a good night's rest, I'll eat my pointed witch's cap."

Mikael laughed a hearty, throaty laugh. "You don't miss a thing, do you?"

He straddled the desk's chair backward and leaned his arms on its back while she settled in on the freshly made bed.

"Well, it's *shabbat*."

"Isn't that a Jewish thing?"

"Yes, and since Terry's partner is Jewish, we have adopted some of his tradition. Partly to accommodate him, and partly because it just makes good sense."

"So, what's the significance of *Shabbat*? Not working? I thought we were going to go over there tomorrow. Doesn't the Sabbath extend to sundown the next day?"

"Yeah, but we're not that strict. We try to take Saturdays off, but when something major is up, we do what we need to do. After all, Jesus said, 'When your ass falls into a hole on the sabbath, don't you pull it out?'"

"Great, so I'm an ass you're pulling out of a hole." She mock-pouted.

"We're all asses, and we all have holes," he grinned.

"So, what's it really about? The sabbath thing?"

"Well, see, Old Catholics like ourselves are not required to be celibate, and some of us are partnered. Like Dylan and Terry..."

"Oh." She smiled, and her eyes grew large with comprehension. "Friday night is *nooky night*."

"Bingo."

SATURDAY

15

KAT AWOKE to the inviting smell of frying bacon. She slipped on her jeans and headed to the bathroom. There was someone in it, of course. *What did I expect*, she thought, *in a house with so many people?* She padded down the back stairs in search of another, which she found just off the kitchen.

When she finished, Brian greeted her with a warm mug of coffee. "Hi, Sweetie," he said without even a hint of impropriety to his familiar address. "Catch Susan in the shower up there?"

She nodded, and he rolled his eyes. "We tease her that she should just move a bed into the bathroom. How do you like your eggs?"

"Um...just fried, I guess."

He nodded. "Yolks hard or runny?"

She smiled. "Runny, please."

"Coming right up."

She watched him as he worked. He was assembled with fine, bony parts that didn't quite fit together right. He had a slight hunch in his back, and he moved with more pain than she had noticed last night. She wanted to ask him about it but didn't know how to do it without being rude. She mentally put it on her list of things to ask Mikael about the next time they were alone.

"I need to check in on my brother..." she began.

He waved toward the phone on the wall with his spatula, but she had already pulled her cell phone out of her pocket. Her fingers shook slightly as she dialed, and she sipped at the coffee as a conscious gesture of normalcy. She was connected to the nurses' station quickly, and asked for an update on Randall Webber's condition.

"No change," a nurse told her, matter-of-factly. "He's stable, but he's not conscious."

She thanked the nurse and fought back twin waves of panic and depression. "Where is everyone?" she asked Brian.

"Chapel—morning prayer. Why don't you go in and see? They'll be done soon, and I'll serve you all together."

"Can I take my coffee?"

He smiled big at her. "Why not? I hear Jesus loves coffee."

She furrowed her brow at this silliness and tentatively walked out of the kitchen. A plaque beside the door announced that she was entering the Montague Summers Memorial Chapel. She gasped. Last night, it had been dark, and she had not noticed it at all. But with the sun streaming through the window above the altar, she was almost paralyzed by its gaudy glory. Just below the window was what appeared to be a community altar, with more candles and sacred objects than she could count: crucifixes, scrolls, icons of saints as varied as Saint John of the Cross and Harvey Milk, a framed *Rolling Stone* cover of Jimi Hendrix, statues of Shiva and Ganesha, and even a posable figurine of Homer Simpson were positioned lovingly on the deep-blue altar cloth.

Just in front of this was a freestanding altar, dressed but unclut-tered except for two candles on its right and left sides. The friars were seated in chairs lining the walls to her right and left, facing each other, fully vested in albs, with some in stoles as well.

She slipped into one of the empty chairs on her left and raised her head at Mikael's nod of greeting. The friars were singing a chant in what seemed to be Latin. She found the music relaxing and was surprised to find she felt warm and at home.

On the wall that faced her she noticed an enormous collage that almost dominated the room. It was the face of Jesus, looking odd and almost deformed. As she looked closer, she saw that his face was an impressionistic collage of many photos, most of them, it seemed, cut from magazines. His left eye was definitely the dark and almond shape of someone from the East; his nose, exaggeratedly Semitic, was made up of a sandy beach scene; his mouth was framed by a dark and curly beard made out of a picture of a large black poodle. His right ear was lily-white and delicate, like a child's or that of a petite woman. A hundred scenes, creatures, and faces seemed to have been pilfered to form this one face.

Kat couldn't decide if the Frankensteinian icon was horrible or beautiful, but then she noted with a start the words that hung above it. Cut from large capital letters of many different fonts, the banner read, "THIS MAN EATS WITH FUCKUPS AND SINNERS."

In spite of herself, a sob arose from deep within her and threatened to spill out into the quiet air. She choked it back and wiped at her eyes with the back of her hand. *What was that all about?* she thought, embarrassed, hoping none of the friars had noticed her rush of emotion. If they had, they didn't show it. They kept up their chant until it trailed to a natural end.

Then Mikael rose, reverenced the altar with a brief bow, and removing a snuffer from its hook at the side of the altar, extinguished the candles.

"God is great, God is neat. Good God! Let's eat!" announced Dylan, heading for the kitchen.

"Dylan, that doesn't even work as a poem," said Terry, shaking his head.

"In magick, as in religion, it's the intention that counts, not the execution."

"Do not listen to this man," Richard protested, catching Mikael's eye. "That kind of talk will make you demon fodder, and he knows it."

"Ah know Ah'm hungry, that's what Ah know."

"Maybe it's true in shamanism," Terry offered, ever the conciliator.

"Good morning, Kat," said Mikael, sitting down next to her. "Did you sleep well?"

"I did." The words caught in her throat, and she felt another rush of unwelcome emotion. "That was really beautiful," she finally managed. "Your singing."

"That's how we pray here. 'He who sings, prays twice,' said Augustine. He's not my favorite saint by a long shot, but he did have a few good one-liners." He noticed the blush in her cheeks and the wetness in the corners of her eyes. "You okay?"

"Yes...well, I think so. I'm...moved. I just need a moment."

"Okay, well, I'm going to disrobe, and I'll see you in the kitchen. Let me know if you need to talk, okay?"

"Yeah, sure." He left the room, and she fished in her pocket for a tissue. As she blew her nose, her gaze returned to the face of the patchwork Christ. His black mouth was open as if he were about to speak.

She stood and shoved the tissue into her back pocket. Then she went and stood directly in front of the collage. In spite of herself, she spoke to it aloud. "You're weird, but I'm listening," she said and then went in for breakfast.

Brian had managed to keep everyone's eggs warm without ruining them, and even Susan had emerged from the bathroom in time to get hers while still hot. Everyone tucked in but Richard, who leaned on his elbows and felt at his beard nervously.

"Dude, you doin' okay?" Dylan leaned into Richard affectionately.

Mikael whispered to Kat, a little too loudly, "His boyfriend dumped him yesterday."

Richard drilled Mikael with an evil eye and ignored the subject altogether. "Okay, this isn't going to be a popular suggestion," he said, "but we need to deal with the whole sigil situation."

Mikael's shoulders sagged. He had been afraid of this.

"What?" asked Kat, "Do you mean that paper-thingy with the symbol on it?"

"Yes," Richard said. "It's a sigil that has been demonically empowered. Whatever the demon was called up to do is mystically connected with that piece of paper. And whoever has seen it, besides the operating magickian—that's your brother, Kat—is susceptible to attack. That's why you couldn't approach the house last night."

"Because there was a demon..."

"Riding your ass. Yes."

"Well, what can we do about it? Isn't there some spell—"

"We're exorcists, not magickians," Richard explained. "We study magick, but we don't *do* magick. I can explain at another time, but for now, no, there's nothing we can do as long as the working is in effect."

"What do you mean, in effect?"

"I mean that whatever your brother employed the demon to do, it's probably still doing it. Your brother is in no position right now to release the demon from his command."

"But what does that mean? What is going to happen to me...or to you?" She pointed at Mikael, since she had shown him the sigil.

"It means that whatever happened to your brother is likely to happen to you if...well, if you leave the safety of a warded place. Like...this place."

"You're saying I have to stay here? I have a job! I have a life!"

"Well, you won't have much of a life if you end up catatonic like your brother," Richard said, a little harshly. "And you won't be able to work, either."

"So, I'm trapped?"

"Of course not," Dylan said with real compassion. "You're free to go anytime you want. We're just saying...it isn't really safe to do so. We're suggesting you hole up here for a while until we can investigate and see what we're up against."

"It's not so bad," Susan said. "Just call in sick. Consider it being down with the flu for a few days. You have your own room, you've got internet access, and Brian's a hell of a cook. And the company's not so bad, is it?"

Kat looked at Mikael and tried not to blush. "Looks like I'm camping out."

"Could be worse," Mikael smiled a weak smile.

"It could be, yeah."

"What about me? I saw the sigil, too," Mikael said.

"That's complicated," said Richard. "We've got to figure out what Kat's brother was up to. I think Dylan and I should go check out the scene of the ritual at Kat's brother's house. I don't want to go in there alone in case there's still demonic activity. Terry, can you go and visit...what's your brother's name again?"

"Randy...Randall."

"Terry, you visit Randy, and see what kind of reading you can get off him. See if he's in there, the condition of his soul—whatever you can glean."

"Will do."

"What about me?" whined Mikael.

"You and Kat can give Brian a detailed description—verbally, mind you—of that sigil. Then you and Brian hit the books. If we're lucky, we can find out which demon we're dealing with here. Then, I want you to run down whatever addresses we uncover at the scene. I want to find out who Randall Webber was working with and where to find them."

"But wait, he can't leave the house. He's in as much danger as Kat."

"Terry, how hard would it be to ward Mikael's car?"

"Not very. I could do it in about ten minutes."

"Fine. Mikael, burn gall to get out to your car, and keep that shit handy just in case. You cannot leave that car, you hear me? If you have to stop for gas, burn the gall. If you have to pee, use a Snapple bottle—make sure to take one with you. If you have to shit, burn the gall all the way in to the gas station loo and all the way out, devil may care who sees or what they think of it. You got it?"

"Got it, chief."

"All right. Mikael, you could be gone all day, so make sure to phone Susan every hour on the hour to check in. The rest of us, shall we meet back for lunch?"

Nods all around. "Then let's get cracking."

16

DYLAN TURNED the key in the lock and entered the room tentatively. "Should we do a banishing?" he asked.

"Good question," said Richard as they hovered on the threshold. "If we do, we clear out the space of any negative energy and protect ourselves, and that's good..."

"But we also dispel any readable energy as well," Dylan finished his sentence. "What do you want to do?"

"I say we preserve the scene and risk it," Richard decided.

"*Imitatio Christi*, dude. Let's sacrifice ourselves!"

"You know, for a straight man, you're absolutely the biggest damned drama queen in the order."

"Ah weel take that as a cahhmpliment," Dylan drawled exaggeratedly, his best Scarlett O'Hara impersonation.

They entered and waited a moment for their eyes to adjust. At first, it seemed to be a typical single man's home, except for the clammy feeling of cosmic dread that hung heavy in the place.

"You feel that?" Richard asked.

"Oh yeah. Heavy nasties goin' on in here, that's fer damn sure."

Dylan went off to the right to investigate the bedrooms. Richard glanced at the piles of gaming magazines, the less-than-tidy kitchen.

Then he rounded the corner into the living room. "Fuck..." he breathed.

Dylan caught up to him in a moment. "Hey, dude, bedrooms are a disaster, but nothing paranormal—whoa..."

Together they stared in awe. It was, in their eyes, a thing of beauty. The Circles of Evocation had been literally burned into the hardwood floors, creating a permanent working space that was both functional and elegant.

"God, how many hours must this have taken?" Richard wondered aloud, squatting to get a closer look. "It looks like it was done with a pen wood burner."

"Some project, that's for sure."

The outer circle was about nine feet in diameter, a second circle set within it about a foot all around. Within the second, smaller circle, four Stars of David were set in each of the cardinal directions. The bottom tips of each of the stars formed the corner of a square in the center of the circle, each side of which was inscribed with one of the four letters of the Tetragrammaton. Just to the east of the circle was a triangle, each side about three feet long, with one side facing the circle. Within it was a little table containing a small white triangle of paper propped up behind a censer.

"Ain't no question what this guy was doing here," Dylan said, walking around the circle, still in awe.

"No, and he wasn't taking the easy way, either."

"What do you mean?"

"Well, most magickians who know what they're doing use the *Heptameron* grimoire—it's the simplest and most foolproof method. But this isn't the circle described in the *Heptameron*. This is the one from the *Clavicula Salomonis*, which is outrageously complex. Most people who use it are dabblers, and of course it always backfires on them because they're just after kicks. They don't want to do five years of preparation for a simple ritual, and so they cut corners and end up frying their livers when their evocation only results in a partial manifestation of the demon."

Using a handkerchief, Richard picked up a wand from the floor and studied it. "This is almond wood. This guy did the prep, all right. He knew *exactly* what he was doing. And he was definitely raising demons, but to what end? What was he *up to*?"

Dylan wandered to the bookcase and whistled. "Quite a library, here, dude." There were new, critical editions of all the major grimoires, and some ancient-looking leatherbound volumes he did not recognize.

Richard continued to study the circle, noting that just inside the circle was a table, and beside it on the floor, a crumpled tablecloth. In his mind's eye Richard reconstructed the scene—the evocation, the magickian passing out, catching the tablecloth on his way down, pulling it all to the floor. Gently, he parted the folds in the tablecloth. A boat containing the Perfume of Art—otherwise known as incense, and a metal censor. "He's lucky the house didn't catch fire when this shit fell," Richard said aloud.

Dylan was still studying the library. "Dude, Ah shouldn't be looking at the books on the shelves—but the ones off the shelves!" He picked one of them up. "Milton," he said, "Opened to the scene of Satan's initial oration in Pandæmonium."

Richard nodded and continued to study the triangle. "Here's another one, dude," Dylan said, moving to the sofa. "This one is describing...holy cow...it's in Latin, but Ah think it says, 'The Displacement of Souls.'"

He had Richard's full attention now. He vaulted over the wreckage of the room to where Dylan was standing, hunched over a volume on the couch. The text was in Latin but was pretty standard stuff, and Richard was able to scan it pretty easily. It wasn't a spell or a collection of spells, exactly. More of an analysis of the possibility of removing a soul from one body in order to reside in another. Near the bottom of the page, the names of two demons leaped out at him.

"It looks like our boy might have raised a demon—either Cephrastes of Crete or Articiphus—to remove his soul from his body and place it in another," Richard said.

"So...if his soul was separated from his body, wouldn't it be dead —the soul, I mean?"

Richard continued scanning the text but didn't find anything relevant to Dylan's question. "I would think so, but perhaps he's running some kind of maintenance spell to keep the body going even if no one is home."

"That sounds plausible."

"So, the question is: Whose body is he in? And what's happening with that person's soul? Is it just being pushed aside? Or is Randy just sitting inside his or her brain, watching?"

"New adventures in espionage?" Dylan asked, carefully setting the book on the desk beside the Milton. He then reached for another text that was laying open. "Swedenborg, eh? *Heaven and Hell*. At least it's in translation. Ah always loved Swedenborg." He looked over the page.

Richard looked over his shoulder. It seemed to be a description of a particular neighborhood in Heaven—standard Swedenborgian vision stuff.

"What's he interested in the geography of Heaven for?" Richard asked, moseying back to finish his investigation of the triangle.

"Ah don't know, dude, but this section seems to be describing the downtown civic center area of Heaven."

Richard picked up a cloth crumpled on the floor and shook it out. With a clatter, a cell phone fell from its folds to the floor. "Bingo," said Richard.

"Whatcha got?" Dylan said. He marked places in all three books and put them in his shoulder bag before joining Richard in the circle and kneeling to examine the find. "Oh, it's one of them old LG jobbers—Susan calls them 'Barbie's laptop.' Was it flipped open like that when you found it?"

"Yeah. What does that mean?" Richard asked.

"Well, dude, that means that either he was text messaging someone during the ritual—highly unlikely, as you really don't want to take your eyes off the demon, as you well know—or he was in speakerphone mode."

They looked at each other. "Dyl, he wasn't in this alone." Richard fumbled with the controls. "I'm sure we can see what numbers he called just before the working, but—"

"Dude, if you don't know what you're doing, you'd better let me handle it—or better yet, Susan. Don't want to erase anything accidentally, and this is a pretty weird phone. As Ah recall, the reviews Ah read said the controls were not exactly intuitive. Let's just take it home and pull up a PDF of the instruction manual and get at the info the right way. But yer right, we should be able to see who he called—or who called him. Might even give us the name, if it was a number he called regularly."

"Okay. I think we've got enough for now," said Richard, putting the phone in Dylan's jacket pocket and fastening it. He patted it, and they both nodded—it was safe, and they both knew just where it was. "Let's do one final sweep of the house to make sure we didn't miss anything obvious," Richard said. "But let's take different rooms this time—I'll take the bedrooms and bath; you take the garage and kitchen."

"Check."

Just as Richard emerged from the bedrooms after a fruitless sweep, he waited in the foyer for Dylan and felt a rush of excitement. Between the phone and the books—and the evidence at the scene—they had a lot to go on. As he was musing, Dylan wandered out from the kitchen, an odd and curious expression on his face. "Dude, what's with all the avocados in the fridge?"

17

TERRY ARRIVED at the hospital in full clerical dress. He was always amazed at the nearly unlimited access his priestly uniform afforded him in such places. As long as he was wearing his priest's collar, no one questioned him, no one stopped him, and nearly everyone gave him a deferential nod whenever he caught their eye. Only occasionally did someone look close enough to notice his earrings, and he always enjoyed the double take that precipitated.

He strode confidently to the information desk. "Randall Webber, please."

The young student volunteer set her hand tentatively on her computer mouse like it was a dangerous beast she did not know how to control. "Uh...let me see...Webber...Webber...oh, here he is. Room 2107. The elevators are right through there."

"Thank you."

Terry found the room without any trouble and went inside. He had been curious to see what the magickian looked like. They all seemed to be of a type, in his experience. Randall was no exception, he was not surprised to note. Skinny, malnourished, usually asthmatic. But this magickian was also unconscious. Terry took a seat as he studied him.

With an effort of will, he softened the focus of his eyes and summoned forth his second sight. The web of energy that was what all things were made of became visible to him, and he marveled at the beauty and intricacy of it.

His jaw dropped, however, as his gaze was drawn to the magickian's head. His crown chakra seemed to be spitting blue fire like the back end of a rocket. The force of it seemed positively violent, and Terry wondered how such a stream of energy could possibly be maintained. He saw the drain on the magickian's body but also intuited that much of the energy came from another source. *And not a good one*, he thought.

He approached the body and laid hands upon it, feeling for the presence of some entity within, human or demonic. He was expecting to detect the presence of the magickian's soul, incapacitated by a chakra system blown to shit, like so many exploded fuses from one end of his torso to the other.

What he found made him pull his hands back in shock. What he sensed within was not human nor demonic. He looked again at the blue light and noted a slight violet tinge to it. "Holy shit," he whispered to himself.

Terry laid hands on the magickian's body once more and felt into him with the energy of his own body. The doctors apparently had been quite correct. Except for the deterioration one would expect from a body as sedentary as a computer programmer's, one that subsists almost entirely on Pringles and Coca-Cola, he was perfectly healthy. Terry detected two minor cysts and a few cancerous cells that were, even as he detected them, being adequately defeated by the magickian's immune system. As normal as normal could be.

Except, of course, for the energetic anomaly, and that was quite a thing to behold. Terry felt around for the presence of some entity and was beginning to think that the body was vacant, being kept alive by some sort of demonic life support when he encountered the Sleeper.

It was a subtle presence, almost undetectable. He thought at first that it might be a very weak demon, but the energy was all wrong. He surrounded the Presence with his own energy and examined its nebulous edges, its interface with the body. This, he found, was nonexistent.

Terry was not sure what to do. Should he leave the Sleeper as he was, unconscious and trapped in the magickian's body? Or should he try to connect the two, give the being a chance to emerge into consciousness? The image he got was of a fetus curled into a ball, protected from the wild world in a womb of alien flesh.

Terry hesitated. Who was he to bring forth this life into consciousness? Could he even do it? Should he? Terry considered phoning Richard or Brian, but then he glanced out at the hallway and wondered just how long he had before his presence would be detected, and perhaps challenged. He could hardly justify a pastoral visit to an unconscious patient that lasted more than five minutes. His mind raced—what to do?

He swallowed and made his decision. He laid hands upon the magickian once again and felt out for that place where the seat of the soul connects to the meat of the body. With quick but uncertain movements of his mind, he joined the two and then fell back on his ass as the magickian's mouth snapped open and emitted an overpowering and unearthly howl of pain.

18

KAT LOOKED up from where she was seated at Dylan's computer station and stared for a long moment at Susan, who was up to her eyeballs in a web design project. She admired the older woman's style —full figured yet with an awareness of her beauty, her hair cut short and her glasses set into thick black retro frames. Kat smiled as she realized just how hot Susan would be considered by most of the dykes she knew. In fact, she thought she was pretty hot herself.

Susan sensed her eyes upon her and with effort dragged her gaze from her screen. "What? Do I have spinach in my teeth?"

"No, I'm just...admiring how pretty you are."

Susan scowled at this, an odd compliment coming from a woman nearly twenty years her junior, seventy pounds lighter, and, she was very much aware, much more conventionally attractive than herself. "Uh...thanks, I guess. You able to log on to your email okay?"

"Oh yeah, it's just a Yahoo account. No sweat."

Susan turned back to her screen.

"I'm really grateful," Kat said.

Susan looked up at her again, this time with a real turn of attention. "Grateful?"

"Yesterday at this time, you didn't know me from Adam—or Eve, I suppose. And now, well, I may be trapped in your home, but nobody seems to mind. I feel so welcome, so...strangely at home. It might have been very different. Not everyone would have made me feel so welcome. So...thank you."

"You're welcome," Susan said. She removed her glasses and smiled at Kat with real feeling and sincerity. "It's part of what we are called to do, you know? We were all strangers once, and God makes of us a family. Hospitality is part of religious life. The guys here would hardly be good friars if they didn't welcome the stranger as if he or she were Jesus himself." She stretched. "My eyes are getting crossed, staring at that screen. I need a break. How's about we get some tea?"

They moved to the kitchen, and Susan put the kettle on.

"I've never been to a monastery before," Kat said.

"It's a friary, not a monastery," Susan corrected with a smile. "But it's a common mistake."

"What's the difference?" Kat asked, sliding onto one of the benches at the table.

"Friars live in friaries, so they have a communal religious life, but they work out there"—she pointed out the window—"you know, in the world, side by side with ordinary folks. Monks live shut up in monasteries, by and large."

"So, that's what I am now that I can't leave—a monk!"

"Well, technically, I think you'd be a nun—it's genitalia-specific," Susan giggled.

"Okay, a *friary*, then. Still, I gotta say, I didn't expect it to be anything like this. I mean..." she pointed to an enormous bong on the shelf next to the fridge. "These guys aren't like any priests I've ever met. Not that I've ever actually met any before, to my knowledge, at least. Still, they're not what I..." She trailed off, her face screwing into a look of confusion. "Now, just how is it they are...friars...at all? I mean, some of them are Catholic priests, right? Like your husband?"

"Yup," Susan smiled. She had had this conversation many times, and knew where it was going.

"But priests are supposed to be celibate, aren't they?"

"This order is Old Catholic, not Roman Catholic."

"I've never heard of 'Old Catholic.'"

"Yeah, not many people have. It's the best-kept secret in Catholicism. But there are lots of Old Catholics around."

"And they're allowed to be married? Or gay?"

"Most of them. It depends upon the bishop. It's a pretty chaotic movement in the States. The bishops make the rules. Some bishops are more conservative than Rome, and some are more liberal than Annie Sprinkle."

"Saint Annie!" Kat exclaimed.

"Hey, I'd pray to her!" Susan announced. They had a good laugh. "Really, there are lots of different kinds of Catholics. Russian Orthodox, Greek Orthodox, Anglicans, Old Catholics, they're all Catholic, just not Roman. And the Romans are the only Catholics in the world that require their clergy to be celibate. It's a crazy rule, put into effect in the Middle Ages only to prevent the sons of priests from inheriting the church's property." The kettle began to squeal.

"You're shitting me."

"I shit you not." Susan poured the hot water into their cups.

Kat bobbed her teabag up and down considering this. "You keep saying, 'them.' So, does that mean you're not Old Catholic?"

"No. I'm Lutheran—cradle to grave." She smiled. "I even did my master's in theology at PLTS—that's the Lutheran seminary up on the hill. That's where Dylan and I met, actually."

"And the other spousal unit around here, Brian?"

"He's Jewish."

"But he lives here? He's not a friar, is he?"

"No. Jews don't have friars. He's just married to one."

Kat's head swam but in a delightful, intoxicating way. "Okay, here's what I don't get. When I think of Christians, I don't think of cool people who love gays and smoke doobies. I think of uptight assholes trying to hijack American politics."

"Yeah, so do we, actually. It's kind of a shame."

"So why be Christian?"

Susan squeezed out her teabag and set it down on the table, her face taut with careful consideration. "Okay, you're Wiccan, right?"

"Yeah. Although I mostly work with a Yoruban pantheon right now."

"Okay. Well, know any asshole Wiccans?"

"Who doesn't?"

Susan laughed. "Got that right! Anyway, so what are you going to do? Just walk away and hand over your religion to the assholes? Or are you going to live it the way you think it's *supposed* to be lived, even if you're the only one doing it? If you have this beautiful thing that gives your life structure and meaning, why should you just walk away from it because some assholes are trying to hijack it? Are you going to do that?"

"Fuck no, I'd fight like hell for it."

"Welcome to the front lines, babe."

Kat sipped at her tea and wondered at this. "Okay, so what about Jesus? I mean, okay, I can see how you can ignore all the horrible people doing all this evil shit in his name and all, but what's so great about him?"

"Let me tell you about Jesus—"

Kat never thought she would ever hear those words in a way she would be receptive to, and it surprised her that she was genuinely curious about what Susan was going to say.

"Jesus was a guy who really *got* it. He got that God loves everyone, no matter who they are, how much money they have—or don't—how talented they are—or aren't—or what wonderful or terrible things they've done in their lives. God loves everyone, period. And he lived in a society where everyone divided themselves by their ideas of who's acceptable and who's not—"

"That sounds familiar."

"Yeah, except that *he* treated everyone the same. He sat down and ate dinner with rich people and poor people, with religious people and criminals, with high society ladies and prostitutes. And he loved every one of them, just like God does. And that changed people's lives. The people who had been socialized to feel like nothings, he made them feel like *something*. The ones who felt like people should bow and scrape at their feet, he treated them as equals and pissed them off royally. In biblical language, he raised up the valleys and made the mountains low."

"Oh...is *that* what that means?"

"The vision of Jesus is a simple one: to create the Community of God—or in traditional language, the Kingdom of God—where everyone is welcome, where none go hungry or homeless, where no one is lonely or afraid. Where there are no 'have-nots,' only 'haves.'"

"That's a pretty rocking vision. But it's pretty unrealistic."

"Sure it is, on a global scale. So, we do it in pockets. This house, to the best of our ability, is a little pocket of the Kingdom of God. If you got enough little pockets, then you *can* change the world. That's what churches—or religious orders, or anywhere that people of faith try to live *as if* the Kingdom were already here—that's what they are *supposed* to be about. Not getting people 'saved,' not coercing them to believe exactly like we do but embracing people just as they are and loving each other the way God loves." She stared at her teacup for a moment. "So, yeah. We know this world is a long way from the Kingdom, from the way God wants it to be. But we believe we are faithful to the vision so long as we live *as if* it were already here."

"That's kind of beautiful—and eccentrically quixotic!"

Susan laughed. "It sure the hell is."

Kat looked down, and a reflective hush descended over the room. Susan blew on her tea and gave her the space she needed. Eventually, she cocked her head, looking at Susan through her hair with one eye. "Can I tell you something...well, kind of weird?"

"My dear, I've been filling the air with weirdness for fifteen minutes. Don't you think it's your turn?"

Kat smiled and looked down again. "I saw this place before I came here. I...dream things..."

19

WHEN TERRY GOT HOME, the others were just sitting down to lunch. His hands were shaking as he joined them and picked up his sandwich.

"Hi, Baby," Brian, bustling around the table, leaned in and kissed him. "You okay?"

"I am physically unharmed, Honey, but I am *not* okay."

"What's up, Terry?" asked Richard, taking a bite. Terry looked over at Kat. Her face was ashen, obviously desperate for news. "Your brother's body is in the hospital, but your brother is not there."

Richard nodded gravely as if expecting this news.

"But someone else is," Terry finished.

"What does that mean?" Kat asked.

"Is he possessed?" asked Brian.

"Yes, he's possessed, but not by a demon." Suddenly, Terry realized every eye in the place was on him. "I think there's an angel in there."

"He's possessed by an angel?" Dylan sputtered. "Is that even possible?"

"The angel is not comfortable, and he's certainly not there of his own free will. When I detected him, he wasn't"—he searched for the words—"well, he wasn't hooked up to Randall's nervous system. So...I hooked him up."

Every eye was wide.

"Was that a good idea?" asked Dylan.

"I'm not sure, because he screamed bloody murder for about an hour." Terry felt a little sick.

"How do you know it's an angel in there?" asked Richard.

Terry pointed to the top of his head. "Purple lights. Very rare. Well, not rare for an angel, but you sure don't see it very often."

Kat looked like she was about to cry. "So, he's in pain? We have to stop it!"

Susan reached out and grabbed her hand. "Kat, it's not your brother in pain." She turned to Terry. "What can we do?"

"I disconnected it again before I left. The doctors were not happy about the whole incident. They still want to hold him for observation."

"Is it—he—in any shape to communicate?" Richard asked.

"Well, not when I left. They'd sedated him, and gave me a pretty nasty look, too, as if I'd done something to him."

"Well, dude, you did," noted Dylan. Kat looked alarmed but bit her lips and kept silent.

"How did you guys make out?" asked Susan, turning to Richard and Dylan.

A twinkle came into Dylan's eye. "Waal, he slipped me a little tongue, and we petted a bit," he deadpanned. A collective groan rose from the table.

"We actually did pretty well," said Richard, refilling his iced tea. "We figured out what grimoire he was using—the *Lesser Key of Solomon.*"

"Is that bad?" asked Kat.

"Honey, they're *all* bad," said Terry with his mouth full.

"And we found this—" Dylan set the cell phone on the table.

"That's Randall's phone!" said Kat.

"Yup, that's what we figgered," said Dylan. "Its controls are a little odd. You know how to work it?"

"Yeah, I had one like it. I thought it was too bulky, and so I traded it in," Kat said, examining it.

"Good," said Richard. "After lunch, you pull the numbers off it. We need everything you can find. Numbers in, numbers out, along with times and dates. Also, his whole phone book. Mikael on the road already? Good. Phone him with whatever addresses you can run down."

At first, Kat bristled at being given orders, but nobody else seemed to notice or mind. Then she got it. It was kind of like *Star Trek*. Under stress, the friars seemed to operate in a semi-military fashion, and Richard was like Captain Picard. He wasn't being despotic, but someone had to call the shots or there would be chaos. She was in. "Aye-aye," she saluted and gave him a tired smile.

"So, what do we think is going on here?" asked Susan.

Richard's brow furrowed. "Dylan found a book detailing a ritual for taking a soul and putting it in another body. We've got a magickian with what appears to be an angel inhabiting his body, so that ritual appeared to work. And we've got a major Goetic working, so we know it was performed by demonic means."

"We've also know that Kat's brother was trying to get the lay of the land in Heaven—we found a copy of Swedenborg's *Heaven and Hell* opened to the description of a very specific neighborhood," Dylan added. "So, if you want mah guess, and Ah reckon you do, what we got is an angel in a magickian's body in the hospital, and a magickian in an angel's body in Heaven."

For a moment, nobody said anything. It was simply too strange to take in all at once. "Why would Randy want to go to Heaven?" asked Kat, then realizing how that sounded, qualified it. "Well, who wouldn't want to go to Heaven? But I mean, why work demon magick to do it?"

"Good question, Honey," said Terry. "Let's say we do have a magickian who has snuck into Heaven wearing an angel's body—what's he up to?"

"I think we need to *see* what he's doing," Richard said.

"Can we do that?" asked Kat.

"Well, call me crazy," said Dylan, "but Ah think it has something to do with avocadas."

20

ALAN DANE WATCHED the little girl closely as her mother scolded her. He couldn't hear her words, but he recognized the rage, the hand raised in threat, the blood rising into her face. He remembered his own father's abuse as if it were yesterday. If ever there were a child in need of rescue, this little girl was one.

The girl looked poor, possibly Hispanic or Middle Eastern. Dane's eyes darted from one end of the street to the other. The mother, still pontificating and gesticulating, went back inside an apartment building. The little girl sat on the steps, head in her hands, her face a hard mask determined not to cry.

Dane's heart went out to her. What could this sweet child have done to warrant such a response? It was criminal. He sat patiently, waiting for her to act.

He had been on edge ever since he discovered those priests in his house attempting to subvert his justice. He normally wouldn't need to liberate another child again, not for several weeks. But he had been so shaken by the exorcism that the itch had started early, and started big.

He despaired that there was so little he could do. Saving one child hardly seemed worth the risk and effort when he thought about the statistics—about the millions of children every year that suffer from abuse. *If only I could save them all*, he thought. He shook his head and sighed. *If only...*

The little girl got up and smoothed out her dress. It was olive green, accenting the color of her skin in a most appealing way, hanging almost long enough to reach her ankles. She turned and stuck her tongue out at the door of her house and began to pound defiantly down the street away from Dane's car.

Dane tapped on the glass separating himself from his driver. "When she gets to the corner, pull up, and keep her in sight."

He did enjoy the hunt, though. There was always the possibility of detection, of getting caught. It added spice to what was already a very satisfying dish.

His cell phone rang, a sprightly reggae version of "Somewhere Over the Rainbow." He glanced at the screen—Sweeney. He flipped it open.

"Dane here," he said.

"I got something here, Mr. Dane."

He had called Sweeney less than an hour after the aborted attempt to exorcise the demon from his father. He had been surprised by those priests, and he was damned if he were going to let it happen again. "What did you find?"

"They're real priests, all right. But they're not Roman Catholic." Sweeney's voice betrayed his New York origins, rough from years of cigarettes and Giants games. "They're called the Old Catholic Order of Saint Raphael. Even have a web page. They do exorcisms and shit for a living."

"*Old* Catholic?"

"Yeah, some breakaway group, goes back a few hundred years, apparently. Anyhow, turns out there's an FBI file on them, and not a little bit of dirt."

"An FBI file? How did you get—"

"Mr. Dane, that is why you pay me the big bucks."

Alan Dane smiled grimly and watched as the little girl rounded another corner. He tapped on the glass and motioned the driver to pull up to the next corner.

"Anything damning?"

"Well, not legally. Not to you and me. Not to the cops. But..." Dane could almost hear an evil grin creep over the cell phone. "If you wanted to, you could probably cause these guys a shitload of trouble."

"I'm listening."

"Their denomination is holding their annual meeting this weekend in Texas. If these FBI files ended up in the right hands..."

"I think I see where you're going with this, Sweeney. It's payback, and I like it. Make it happen. What's the score as far as keeping an eye on them? I don't want any more surprises."

"They're holed up in their place in Berkeley for the time being, except for the guy you referred to as Goth Boy. I got Jamison on him now."

"I wonder..."

"What's that, Mr. Dane?"

"I'd like to talk to this Goth Boy. Think we could set that up?"

"Ha! Nothin' like nabbing a fella to put the fear of God into him. Yeah, I think we could arrange that."

"Good. Gotta go." Dane flipped his cell phone closed and watched as the little girl walked into a park.

"Mr. Pell," Dane said, tapping on the glass. "Would that little girl like to help us look for our lost puppy?"

The driver looked from side to side nervously. Dane noticed he was sweating. "I don't know about this, Mr. Dane. I can't do this again. I've had nightmares ever since..." He trailed off and made a vague whimpering sound.

Dane closed his eyes and fought to maintain his temper. He checked to make sure all the windows were closed then spoke in as even a voice as possible. "Is the car in park, Pell?"

"Y-yes, sir. Yes, it is."

"Good." Dane leveled the revolver at the back of the seat and pulled the trigger. He was amazed at how loud it was. He put one finger into his ear and wiggled it back and forth. *Shit*, he thought, *that really hurt.*

He looked through the window to see Pell slumped over and unmoving. "I hate having to do things myself," Dane said out loud to himself.

It occurred to him that there were demons that could drive as well as humans, and they would have no qualms about his activities. Even if they did, they would have no choice in the matter. And he had to employ a new driver, anyway. Well then, a demon it was. He also realized that he could probably get them to do some of Sweeney's surveillance work as well, and for free at that. He pursed his lips and gave a satisfied nod. Then he opened the door of the car and walked into the park, calling for his imaginary dog.

21

Mikael was beginning to think it was not such a bad assignment. He rolled into the Lower Haight at a leisurely pace. A scrap of paper in his lap bore a hastily scrawled address he had just received from Susan. Mornings were always chilly in San Francisco, especially in February, which he didn't mind at all since it meant he could keep the windows up and blast a Black Flag album as loud as he wanted to with impunity to all but his future hearing.

He followed the numbers on the buildings and realized he had another couple of blocks to go. His thoughts kept drifting to Kat, and as he played unconsciously with his long black hair, he imagined it was her fingers running through it. He was excited to discover she was Wiccan, since that was the tradition he practiced, albeit with a Christian spin, and he had found out the hard way that it was always best to date someone he could connect with spiritually.

"Hmm, 2617...2619...there it is," he said out loud to himself. He noticed a parking space on the street across from the target building, which was nothing short of a minor miracle in almost any part of San Francisco. He spun the wheel, completing an illegal Y turn in the middle of a business district and almost tossed a bicycle messenger in the process. "Ope...sorry, guy..." he said out loud again, completing his parallel park. He turned off the engine and surveyed the building. It was a grand but dilapidated Victorian that looked like it hadn't been painted in fifty years. Black felt covered the windows, blocking out every possible scrap of light.

The house was quiet, but any knowledge of those coming in or out could be useful, so he reached in the backseat for his camera, attached the telephoto lens, and settled in for a lengthy wait. "Now, where is that Snapple bottle?" he asked himself aloud.

22

ASTRID HAD SOUNDED groggy when Richard called. And, indeed, she had been taking a nap. He had apologized profusely, and she had called him a cunt. Still, after he explained what they were up against, she agreed to come right over. "I can't stay long, though," she had said. "I have a date at six."

Richard said that was fine, but it really wasn't. He had had a crush on her from the moment they had met at one of the socials hosted by the Center for Gay and Lesbian Studies at the Graduate Theological Union. Astrid had been Andrew at the time, and Richard's interest had not been swayed by her transsexuality. He had never betrayed his feelings, but he was certain that his mooning over her could not possibly go unnoticed. He just hoped it also did not go completely unappreciated.

In the kitchen, Kat found Susan and the friars gathered around a steaming French press of enormous dimensions. She took a place at the table, and soon Susan was sliding a large mug of steaming Italian roast under her nose. "Oh my, that's decadent," she said, waving the fragrant steam into her face.

She looked up to see Richard come in, an oddly mesmerized look on his face.

"What's the scoop, dude?" asked Dylan. "Was Astrid home?"

"Yeah, she's on her way over," Richard said.

"Who is this chick?" asked Kat, a little absently as she was really debating whether to add half-and-half to what was already such a wondrous treat.

"Well, she used to be a dude," Dylan answered. "Ah don't think she's had surgery, so Ah suppose anatomically she still is. Dicky's got a thing for her."

"I do not—"

"Unfortunately for him," Dylan ignored him, "she only dates lesbians."

"Wait, how does that even work?" Kat asked, confused.

"She also used to be a professor at the Swedenborgian House of Studies," Susan swatted her husband on the back of the head, "until her little 'talent' became common knowledge."

"Transsexuality is a *talent*?"

"Astrid is a scryer," Richard said, taking a seat and reaching for a cup.

"You mean like crystal balls and such?" asked Kat incredulously.

"Well, she uses a seer's stone, but yeah, it's pretty much the same thing."

"Why did that get her into trouble?" asked Kat and then thought better of it. "Oh, these are Christians we're talking about, isn't it? Stupid question."

At this comment, every eye in the room locked on her, accompanied by a look of shock and a little hurt. Brian laughed out loud.

"Oh my God," Kat said, covering her mouth and turning red in a rush. "I am so sorry. That was really, really insensitive of me. Please forgive me."

Then the moment passed, and most everyone chuckled. "Why don't you tell us how you *really* feel, Kat?" invited Dylan.

"Actually," said Susan, "the Swedenborgians are technically heretics, so they're not your average Christians. They're pretty cool, by and large."

"The congregational Swedenborgians, you mean," corrected Dylan. "The episcopal Swedenborgians are pretty fundamentalist."

"Wait, this is getting confusing," said Kat. "What the hell is a Sweden...I can't even *say* it."

Brian made an O with his right index finger and thumb and threw his arm back so that his palm cupped the right side of his face, creating a little monocle with spider fingers spread over his cheek. "We. Are. The Sweden-Borg," he said in his best mechanical Stephen Hawking impersonation. "Comprehension. Is. Futile."

Everyone laughed, but Kat was utterly lost.

"Sorry," said Brian. "It's a *Star Trek* thing."

"Emanuel Swedenborg was the eighteenth century's greatest scientist, certainly the greatest Sweden has ever known," Richard explained. "He mastered every one of the sciences in his day, but when he entered middle age, he had a mystical experience that compelled him to drop everything and pursue spiritual investigation full time."

"Yeah," continued Dylan, "he used to go into these trances, and travel to Heaven and Hell and all, and talk to the angels. He wrote about thirty books detailing his conversations with angelic beings. It's pretty trippy shit."

"Swedenborg gave us some very explicit descriptions of the other side, most of which have been corroborated by folks who have had near-death experiences," Richard said.

"And so the Sweden...borgians, they're the people who believe in his writings?" asked Kat.

"Yup," said Dylan, pouring himself some coffee. "But he never intended to start a church—just to reform the old one."

"Where have we heard that one before?" moaned Terry.

"Of course, none of the established churches would listen," Richard picked up the tale again. "Swedenborg was a modal monarchian, which was condemned as a heresy fifteen hundred years ago."

"Do I want to know what that is?" asked Kat.

"Probably not," laughed Susan, "It's one of the pettier, hair-splitting proclamations of heresy that make even conservative Christians roll their eyes."

"Mah theory is that most Christians are modals," said Dylan, wiping coffee from where he had just spilled it down the front of his shirt. "They just don't know what to call it."

"Okay, so why is this Astrid on the outs with the Swedenborg people? Isn't she basically doing the same thing with her crystal ba... stone that Mr. Swedenborg was doing in a trance?"

"Well, yes, exactly," answered Susan, handing her husband a wet washcloth to better tend to his shirt. "And let that be a lesson to you ladies out there in TV land—don't try at home those things that are the reserved domain of Old Dead White Guys."

"Lest you be kicked out on yo' asses," added Dylan, wiping at his shirt.

"Amen," agreed Terry liturgically, and poured himself a final cup from the dregs.

Just then the doorbell rang, and Richard froze. Of course, this was not lost on anyone. "Get yourself together, Lover Boy," Susan said to him, heading for the door. "I'll let her in."

Kat, intrigued, extracted her legs from the bench and followed. Susan opened the door, and Astrid swept into the foyer like a goddess. She was the closest thing to a Swedish Amazon Kat had ever seen, her shining golden hair hanging knee length and her body veiled in enough sequins and gauze to instigate all-out war between Liberace and the gypsies.

"Hey, Tobers," Astrid said, hugging the dog.

"Astrid, meet Kat," Susan said. Kat rose and shook her hand, wondering at its size and also at how anyone could get away with dressing in such a fashion in California.

"Hey, assholes!" she waved through the kitchen door. Kat squinted at Richard—was he drooling? It appeared that he was. Astrid set down a bowling bag. "Where's Morpheus?"

"Mikael's on stakeout," Richard said.

"Got a hot one, huh?" she asked but didn't wait for an answer. "Where do you want me to set up? In the chapel, like last time?"

"That'll do," said Terry, and rushed ahead of her to clear the candlesticks from the main altar to make a space for her. He paused to give her a kiss. She had to lean down to do it. "Hi, you big tranny."

"Hi, faggot. Hey, I'm having a housewarming next weekend. Can you and your bottom half come?"

"We'll look at the calendar. I'll let you know. But we'd love to if we can. Will we be the only testosterone in the room—besides your estrogen-addled self, I mean?"

"You'll be the tokens."

"Bully for us, then."

Richard brought a stool from the kitchen for Astrid to sit on. He set it in the place where he and the other priests usually stood to say mass, and then watched as Astrid opened her bag and took out a large black tablecloth. She spread it over the altar and then removed a leather case. She unlocked it, and Kat saw a flash of red velvet as she opened it. Inside was a shiny black rock, polished flat and smooth on one side until it shone like glass.

Astrid placed the stone in the middle of the altar and turned it so the shiny side was angled toward her face. Then she took another black sheet of cloth and threw it over her shoulders like a stole.

"Okay, Gents, what am I looking for?"

"We think Kat's brother used demon magick to trade bodies with an angel, and he is now roaming Heaven. And he's probably up to no good."

"You're shitting me."

"God's honest truth," Dylan said, settling into one of the chairs on the side to enjoy the show.

"What do you think he's doing?" asked Astrid.

"That's what we called you to find out," said Richard.

"You know for sure he's in Heaven?"

"No. But we found one of his books open to the passage in *Heaven and Hell* where the Borg describes the Akashic records neighborhood."

"He doesn't call it that, dufus," said Astrid.

"No, but you know the general vicinity I mean."

"I know it. That's helpful. Do you know what this angel's body he's in looks like?"

Richard shuffled nervously. "No."

Dylan piped up helpfully. "He *will* be totin' an avocada."

Richard rolled his eyes, but Astrid nodded vigorously. "Good, that's really good. Can't be too many angels carrying avocados around. I'll tune into that." Then she paused, her face screwed up into a puzzle. "Why an avocado?"

"Beats us," said Dylan. "But he had a whole fridge full of the suckers. Gotta be involved somehow."

"Speaking of avocados, I'll go make some snacks. Guacamole, anyone?" asked Brian. A cheer went up all around. Brian smiled and headed for the kitchen.

Astrid turned to Kat. "What can you tell me about your brother's energy?"

Kat considered a moment. "He's got horrendous ADD. He's a computer programmer but can't sit still for a moment. He works at home—"

"'Nuff said," Astrid proclaimed, dismissing her with a wave. "Let's take a look."

She pulled over her head one edge of the cloth draped around her neck until the corners of it met the black cloth covering the altar. Like a hill of bumpy blackness, she quivered beneath the cloth as she entered into her ecstasy.

The others waited breathlessly. Scrying was often a lengthy process. Sometimes access was easy; sometimes it was not. Planetary alignments and the scryer's own emotional equilibrium all must conspire to make a session successful. If something was off, it could complicate or even frustrate the effort. But apparently, neither the astrological orientations nor her excitement over her upcoming date prevented her. Within minutes, a muffled voice called out from beneath the black cloth. "Got something..."

Kat was beside herself with anxiety. She was concerned about her brother but also nervous and a little ashamed of what he was doing. She wanted to help him, she realized, but also wanted to *stop* him.

"What do you see?" Terry had his omnipresent laptop open and clacking as she spoke.

"I see a teeming crowd in a huge city square. Fountains, enormous buildings on every side of the square. We're in the neighborhood, just as Swedenborg described it. A few new additions since his time, nothing dramatic. Lots of angels. Typical sabbath in Heaven."

"Are there people there? Or only angels?" Kat asked.

"According to Swedenborg, people become angels when they pass over," Dylan explained.

"Ah…" she nodded. "Do people become demons, too?"

Dylan looked at Richard, and Kat saw both sets of eyebrows shoot up. "What a good question, Kat," said Richard. "I haven't a clue."

"Yes," called Astrid from beneath her blanket.

"Yes, demons are actually of human origin?" Richard asked.

"Some of them. Some are Nephilim."

"Huh," said Richard. "Who knew?"

"Nephilim?" asked Kat.

"The offspring of God's original angels and human women," Richard explained. "Also known as giants."

"This sounds like myth," said Kat.

"Yeah, and so do angels, demons, jinn, faeries, and a whole host of other allegedly 'mythological' beings we deal with every day around here," said Dylan with a chuckle.

"Okay, I've located the Hall of Records," called Astrid.

"Did you say that was where the Akashic records are kept, Richard?" Kat asked.

"Swedenborg didn't call it that," Astrid said again with an irritated lilt to her voice. "Blavatsky did."

"Whatever you call it, yeah, that's where everything that has ever happened in this or any other universe is stored," Richard answered.

"Makes the Smithsonian pale by comparison," Susan commented.

"What I wouldn't give to browse that place," said Terry wistfully.

"Ah heard that," agreed Dylan.

"Eat your Wheaties, and say your rosary, little boy, and someday you will," Richard grinned.

"Wait! I think I see your guy!" Astrid's voice raised up several notches in excitement. "He's limping—obviously, he doesn't quite know how to work that body he's in. And he's carrying an avocado—very hard to do, I'd imagine given the gross, heavy nature of an earthly object and the subtle form of an angelic body. It's gotta be like lugging an anvil around! No doubt about it, though, this is your guy."

"What's he doing?" asked Kat. "I mean, besides struggling with the avocado?"

"Well, he's not going into the Hall of Records. He's headed toward another building. God! It's hard work. My heart would go out to him if he weren't up to no good!"

"Well, we don't actually have any evidence that he's intending any evil, do we?" asked Kat hopefully.

"You mean aside from the demon-magick conspiracy, the violence to an angel, and breaking and entering Heaven?" Terry asked, mock-bitchily.

"Okay, okay..." Kat trailed off, feeling a little pathetic for her lunge at hope.

"Hey, gang," called Brian, "chips, salsa, and my famous guacamole are on the kitchen table when you need a break."

"Thanks, Honey," said Terry. He leaned over and grabbed Brian's pant leg and pulled him toward him, wrapping his arm around Brian's legs and holding him still as everyone concentrated on Astrid. Brian played with Terry's tonsure and waited with them.

"He's going into another building. It's still large but not *as* large. It's very old, though, older than the Hall of Records, or *as* old at least. I can't see a sign yet..."

They all waited breathlessly.

"Okay, there's one. It's in Enochian, of course. *Aziazior*—that mean anything to you, Terry?"

"Yeah, it means 'forms,'" Terry answered quickly. "A pretty common word, actually, as the angels use it in a number of different contexts. It's synonymous with our words 'likeness,' 'image,' 'archetype,' 'symbol,' 'shape,' 'projection,' and a whole bunch of others, but you get the idea."

"Yeah," said Richard. "Is he going in?"

"It looks like he is...yes, he's headed up the stairs. Not gracefully, mind you. In fact, as I get closer to him, he looks like he's in a lot of pain."

Susan reached over and squeezed Kat's hand.

"But he's soldiering on," Astrid said. "I'm going to try to follow him into the building. Sometimes I can, and sometimes I can't..."

"Do your best," Richard implored.

"So, what is this 'Forms' place?" Kat asked, trying to cap the hysteria that threatened to overwhelm her.

"The Hall of Forms is where the archetypes for all things are enshrined," Astrid called from beneath her cloth.

"Huh?" Kat shot Richard a confused look.

"Ever studied Plato?" he asked.

"I always preferred Silly-Putty, why?" she answered, without a trace of humor.

Brian burst out with such a forceful guffaw that he accidentally farted.

"Good one, dude," called Dylan, holding up his hand to Brian for a high-five.

"Ugh, Brian-fart. Glad I'm under here and properly filtered," came Astrid's voice.

"Wait, how did you know that was even me?" Brian asked, pretending to be wounded.

"Remote viewing of your gaping anus, you voracious bottom whore," said Astrid.

"He is pretty voracious," agreed Terry, smiling up at his partner.

"Not Play-Doh," corrected Richard, ignoring the exchange of barbs, "Plato, the philosopher."

"Oh, *him*," Kat's features betrayed a faint distaste. "I failed Intro to Philosophy. It was the beginning of the end of my college career."

"Well, had you stuck it out, you would have learned about Plato's World of Forms, the place where the archetypes for all earthly things reside. Plato was being typically grandiose—the Forms don't require an entire world of their own. A glorified museum obviously suffices to house them."

"What *are* the Forms?" asked Kat.

"Well, they're more ideas than anything else, but in Heaven I imagine they must have some visible presence. Let's say you come across a spider in your yard. How do you know it's a spider?"

"Uh, because I know what a spider looks like?"

"But you've never seen this particular spider; how do you know it is a spider at all?"

"Because all spiders have eight legs?" Kat suddenly felt on thin ice in this conversation.

"Exactly. You have in your mind a familiarity with the archetypal spider, the perfect spider, from which all earthly spiders draw their form and reality. Because you are acquainted with 'spiderness' when you encounter spiderness in an actual being, you recognize it, even though it may look nothing at all like the last spider you encountered."

"Okay, but isn't that just something in my head?"

"Solipsism alert!" called Dylan, and Terry laughed with him.

"How could it be just in your head when we all share the same archetypal knowledge?" asked Richard, also enjoying the joke.

"Okay, he's in," Astrid called. "I'm going to try to enter... It's dim, but I'm still getting something. Pretty hazy...okay, it's clearing now. He roaming aisles, he's obviously having an attack of wonder. And I don't blame him. It's pretty glorious."

"What do you see?" asked Richard.

"Everything in the hall is in motion, ghostly images, all interacting. It's pretty chaotic...no, there's order, but it's complex. It's like everything here is participating in an enormous ritual. The forms seem to be arranged in symbolic relationships to one another, and they're all moving. It's kind of like being in the middle of a huge clockworks, with everything around you whirring and spinning in a regulated way...wow, it's really, really trippy."

"Did Swedenborg write about this?" Brian asked.

"He called them 'correspondences,'" answered Richard.

"Another fine translation of the Enochian *aziazior*," noted Terry.

"He wrote about them as realities, but not about a hall as such," Richard said.

"You have to go to the apocryphal Swedenborgian writings for that," corrected Astrid, "but it's there."

Richard shrugged, obviously surprised. "Who knew there was a Swedenborgian apocrypha?"

"How could there not be?" asked Astrid.

"Good point," said Dylan. "If you can imagine it, it must exist somewhere."

"God, that's a whole conversation I don't want to have right now," Richard shook his head. "What's the magickian doing now?"

"'The Magickian' has a name," said Kat defensively.

"I'm sorry. What's Randy doing?"

"He looks like he's just trying to get his bearings. I can just imagine the vertigo he's feeling. I feel it, and I'm holding on to a table. He's standing in free space in an alien body with all these ghostly forms whizzing by him. I'm amazed he's still standing up."

"Stay with him," Richard said.

"Don't tell me what to do, Dicky," said Astrid testily. "I'm not one of your minions."

Richard sighed.

"Minions?" Dylan shot Susan an amused look. "Is we minions?"

"I's a *women*ion," retorted Susan, kissing him on the nose.

"Now he's looking around, like he's searching for something specific. There's a whole host of foodstuffs in an orbit around Eva Kadmona—"

"The archetypal human," explained Richard. "The Kabbalists posited Adam Kadmon, but they were wrong. Man isn't the default form of the human; woman is."

"We could have told you *that*," said Susan, winking at Kat.

"Oh my God, oh my God!" called Astrid.

"What?" Kat almost screamed.

"He's found the orbit of the archetypal avocado. He's holding the one he brought with him up into its path..."

"Holy shit!" breathed Dylan. And then they all jumped as a single earthquake jolt shook the house.

"And it's *gone*..."

"What's gone?" asked Richard. "What's *gone*?!"

"The avocado is gone. And so is its form. When they collided, they both...disappeared."

"Like matter and anti-matter," breathed Dylan.

"We just witnessed something huge, gang," Richard said. "That generated a shockwave. I felt it."

"It could have really been an earthquake, you know, a coincidence," said Dylan.

"I don't believe in coincidences," Richard said.

Astrid pulled her head out from under the cloth, her hair wild and tangled. "It was worse in Heaven. Knocked Kat's brother on his ass, and half of Heaven with him."

"Well, now we know what he was up to," Dylan said.

"Yes, but we don't know why," Richard countered.

"Well, you gents have your work cut out for you. And I have a date." Astrid began to pack her things.

Brian eased himself out of Terry's nervous grasp and headed to the kitchen. Everyone else seemed to be lost in a state of bewildered shock.

"Uh, guys!?" called Brian. Everyone looked toward the kitchen, and he leaned his head through the doorway. "I've got bad news. The guacamole—it's gone."

23

MIKAEL WAS BEGINNING to fight the midafternoon nods. Watching a house with no activity is not the most stimulating of chores, and he fought against his own internal rhythms to keep himself awake. He was accustomed to an afternoon nap, and his body, like a faithful dog, did not understand being denied.

He had tried staying awake by girl watching, and indeed, the Lower Haight provided ample opportunity for such an activity. But inexplicably, the appeal of this, enticing as it often was, did not serve to override his body's horizontal drag. He had taken to bending his fingers at unnatural angles until they threatened to snap, using the pain to jolt him back to a momentary state of full wakefulness.

Eventually, he noticed that he really needed to shit. Just down the block was a coffee shop. He knew the place well, as he had once spent a good deal of time there several years ago when he had first come out to California and had been couch surfing for nearly a year.

He opened his kit bag and thought through how to go about this. He could set the burning gall in the planter just to the left of the door. The plant in it was dead, anyway. And he would bring more with him in case someone decided to play good Samaritan and put it out while he was in the can. He could also get a sandwich and a good, tall cup of coffee to help with the afternoon lethargy. It was a plan.

He blew on the charcoal until it was glowing red and then placed the fish entrails on it. Opening the car door, he jumped out and made for the shop door halfway down the block, a noxious cloud of black smoke trailing behind him.

He placed the abalone shell in the planter and then stepped through the door, trying to appear nonchalant. He needn't have worked at it, however. Every eye in the place was glued to the television set.

How odd, Mikael thought, and looked around. The place was a little dingy, half coffee shop, half used bookstore, with tattered living room furniture set at odd angles everywhere. Usually, the place was sprinkled with twenty- and thirty- somethings, huddled over laptops or faces buried in textbooks. Occasionally, a lively conversation would emerge from one corner.

But not today. Today, you could have heard a pin drop were it not for the news commentator's voice crackling tinnily from the tiny television speaker. Mikael set his bag down on the counter and leaned in to listen.

"Seems able to explain the sudden disappearance of avocados worldwide. Food and Drug Administration representatives have not yet issued any statements, and agriculture stocks are plummeting in a shocking upset that utterly blindsided the market. Let's go now to Alison Dana live outside the Tres Marillos Taqueria. Alison?"

"Thanks, Pete. I'm here with the owner of Tres Marillos, Dolores Wang. Mrs. Wang, how will the sudden disappearance of avocados affect your business?"

The obviously hysterical Mrs. Wang could not calm herself enough to respond in English and assaulted the reporter with a flurry of Mandarin.

Mikael furrowed his brow. He remembered Richard and Dylan saying something about Kat's brother using avocados in a magickal working, and a chill descended his spine. This had the ultimate effect of aggravating the urgency of the bulk in his bowels, and he remembered why he was there and headed to the bathroom, completely unnoticed by anyone else in the place.

Bowels once voided, he reminded himself that the burning gall at the doorway would not long be an effective deterrent to any demonic nasties, especially since there were windows and a back door to the place. He made for the counter and waved to get the counter-person's attention. A stocky butch girl behind the counter with a nose ring and a Maori pattern tattooed on her forehead pried her eyes from the screen unwillingly and glanced at him for no more than a split second before returning to the television. "Yeah? What do you want?"

"Barbecue beef sandwich on a sourdough roll, please. And a bag of salt-and-vinegar chips. Oh, and a large coffee."

Silently, without looking away from the television, the young woman went into action. Mikael was impressed with how much she was able to do on complete autopilot.

"What do you think it means?" she said to no one in particular.

He looked around and realized he was the only person she could reasonably be speaking to. "I...I don't know." It wasn't a lie. He probably knew more than most people in the world about it, but he didn't know what it *meant*, philosophically. He hadn't really thought about it. And probably wouldn't. "I'll bet it's a trick," he said with a burst of inspiration.

"What do you mean?" she said, looking at him for the first time.

"Oh, you know, everyone takes avocados for granted. They're nothing special, you know?" Mikael posited, warming to his idea. "So, if you're the National Avocado Board, and you're smart, you know that people don't really know what they have until it's gone. You make all the avocados disappear, and suddenly everyone wonders how they could live without them. You bring them back, and *voilà*! People love avocados like never before."

"So, you think it's a publicity stunt." She said it as a statement, not a question and mulled it over, nodding. "You must be right. It's just the sort of thing those assholes would do."

"Yeah, and it's not hard to see where they got the idea, either,"

Mikael said. "Just look at their acronym, National Avocado Board —eh? Eh?"

"NAB," she breathed.

"Nab those motherfucking avocados," Mikael said with certainty. "I'm just shocked they didn't try something like this years ago."

"You are *so* right."

She put his order in a bag and slid it in front of him. A moment later, she handed him a large cup of coffee. "How much?" he asked.

"My treat," she said. "I think you just solved the mystery of the century." She flipped open her cell phone and began text messaging.

"Thanks!" Mikael said and gave her a wave that went completely ignored. When he got to the door, he found the charcoal still white and spitting, but the gall gone. He placed some more of the slimy innards in the shell, and as soon as the smoke began to emerge, he made for the car.

On the way, he glanced at the house. Nothing. He didn't expect to see any activity. He looked at his watch and realized he was five minutes late checking in with Susan. He set the shell on top of the car's roof along with his lunch and felt in his pockets for his keys. And that was when he noted, to his horror, that they were still inside the car.

Panic swept over him, and he felt a wave of vertigo. He clutched at the roof of the car to steady himself and looked around. No sign of baddies, but then, unless you were Terry, there never were. Demons, like most spiritual beings, were usually invisible unless they chose to be otherwise. He looked back at the keys dangling from the ignition and forced himself to be calm, to think rationally. *Check the other doors*, he told himself, and ran around the car, futilely pulling at all the handles. No good—all were locked.

He considered breaking a window and wondered if Terry's warding would still be effective. He decided it was his best option given the circumstances, and cast around for a rock. As on most city streets, rocks were in short supply. Fighting panic, he looked around up and down the street and tried not to think about what would happen if the sigilic backlash caught up with him. If the demon Kat's brother had employed began to siphon off his own soul, he would be powerless to do anything to stop it.

The urge to cry came over him, but he recognized it as a manifestation of panic and closed his eyes, forcing himself to do a couple seconds of zazen meditation right where he was standing to focus and calm himself. Opening his eyes, he thought, *First things first*, and placed the last of his fish gall on the dying coal. Then, carrying it above his head like the lamp of Diogenes, he marched down the street looking for a large heavy object with which to smash a window.

Suddenly, he saw it. A twisted metal pole about the length of his forearm sticking out of a block of cement that had obviously been recently uprooted from the ground. *Perhaps part of a fence that had been knocked over by a car?* he wondered, and picked it up with resolve.

He marched back toward the car, but before he got there he saw, to his great dismay, an obviously homeless man leaning toward the roof of his car, helping himself to Mikael's lunch. "Goddammit!" Mikael spat. "Hey, you!" he yelled. "Back off my lunch!"

The homeless guy looked straight at him, and noticing the heavy pole and its obvious aggressive potential, backed off from the car momentarily. But then the man smiled, reached up, and grabbed the sandwich.

"You little shit!" Mikael screamed and wielded the pole as if to strike the man. He wouldn't, of course, but he wasn't above using its potential to scare the man. He had swung it under his left arm, which was still holding the now-dormant abalone shell aloft, readying the bar for a feigned blow when a hard, dull pain caught him at the base of his neck and he faded quickly into darkness. He was unconscious before the abalone shell clattered to the ground.

24

EXCEPT FOR ASTRID, they rushed past Brian into the kitchen *en masse*. On the table was a bowl of chips and beside it a bowl with a little salsa in it. Every bit of the avocado that had been mixed up in it was gone.

"Brian, you're sure—" Richard began.

Brian held up a hand to stop him. "Full of guac. Trust me."

"This is tragic," said Richard.

"You got that right," Dylan agreed. "I was really lookin' forward to Brian's guacamole."

"Dylan, this isn't just about Brian's guacamole. If what I'm thinking is right, every avocado on the face of the earth just disappeared."

"Holy shit," said Dylan, staring off into space and contemplating the horror of a world without guacamole. "I need a joint, man."

"Make it a fatty," said Brian.

"Ah heard that," agreed Dylan. He turned toward Kat. "What did your brother have against 'cadas, anyway?"

Kat shrugged and then grimaced a little as she said, "He always hated guacamole."

"No hatred of foodstuffs runs that deep," Dylan countered.

"I don't think this is really *about* avocados," said Richard. "There's too much we don't know. Avocados might actually just be a random choice of fruit for whatever Randy was trying to accomplish."

"Well, it was certainly one he wouldn't miss," offered Kat.

"So, if he had to pick *something*, why not pick something he didn't like?" Richard nodded. "Makes sense. But why obliterate a fruit at all?"

Brian was studying the salsa left in the bottom of the bowl. Wordlessly, he went to the refrigerator and pulled out a tub of sour cream. Grabbing a spoon, he put several dollops into the bowl, followed by a couple dashes of soy sauce, and stirred the mixture. Then he set the bowl back on the table and tried the mixture on the end of a chip. Apparently satisfied, he turned to the sink and started putting dishes away.

Dylan grabbed a chip and tried the new mixture. "Huh," he said, and then tried another, and another.

"This is big," said Terry. "We gotta figure out who's working this side of things, and how to reverse it. Who knows how this might affect the world?"

"A butterfly effect kind of thing?" asked Susan.

"Exactly."

Tobias's nose was touching the bowl of Brian's new dip, sniffing eagerly. Richard pushed it back farther from the edge. "Okay, let's follow up on those numbers we got off Randy's phone. Kat, what did you get?"

"We got about five numbers I don't recognize in the past two days."

"What about calls made around the time of the ritual?" asked Richard, trying the new dip himself. His eyebrows lifted in surprise as the tangy taste registered. He reached for another chip.

"There was one call, over an hour long, at midnight the evening before Kat found him," Susan said. "That was the last call received."

"That's the one, I'll wager," Richard said.

"I used the online reverse directory and got an address. It's in San Francisco, on Haight Street."

"One of mah favorite neighborhoods!" Dylan announced to no one in particular.

"Not the Upper Haight; this is nowhere near Ashbury. It's in the Lower Haight—"

"That's not nearly as cool," said Dylan darkly. "Ah always imagine magickians doin' their thing in really *cool* places."

"I texted the address to Mikael about an hour ago. He should be there now," Susan continued. "Mikael should have checked in about fifteen minutes ago." She checked her cell phone for messages. There were none. She checked the log for missed calls. None. "I'll give him a call now." She punched the numbers with her thumb. "Maybe he just fell asleep."

"He's on a stakeout," said Richard, imploring Heaven with exaggerated arm movements. "*Of course* he fell asleep."

Susan held her hand up for silence, and they all watched her with mounting anxiety in spite of the good sense of Susan's assessment of the situation. He probably *had* dozed off. Still...

A gruff voice answered the cell phone. "What the fuck??" the voice barked. Susan's eyes widened, and she hit the button for speakerphone. "Who the fuck is this?" the gruff voice came again, but this time they could all hear it.

"Who the fuck is *this*?" Richard yelled in the direction of the phone. "Where's Mikael?"

"Fuck Mikael. Don't call me again, asshole." And with a click, the strange voice was gone.

25

BISHOP TOM WAS BEGINNING to worry when lunch came and went and he had not yet heard back from the friars. He had no doubt that Susan had passed on his message, and he wondered what might be going on that was so important that they neglected to call him. He gave his friends the benefit of the doubt, and resolved to keep them updated whether they had time to speak to him or not.

Tom had no trouble that day keeping the afternoon sleepies at bay. Everything in him dreaded the completion of the day's agenda, when the synod would once again take up the matter of the order's excommunication.

But to his great relief, that moment never came. The afternoon's business had been tied up with an argument about liturgy and local variation, which Tom would have found engaging anyway even if he had not been on needles and pins. But by the end of business that day, the argument was still raging, and the matter of the order's expulsion would have to wait another day.

"Let us rise and bless our meal before adjourning to the dining hall," announced Bishop Mellert. The blessing was mercifully brief, and in moments the gathered bishops were stretching their atrophied episcopal limbs and shuffling toward the cafeteria.

Tom was quiet as he picked up a tray and helped himself to what was really quite a sumptuous spread. The Sisters of Mercy apparently took no vows of epicurean chastity, because the meals were uniformly well prepared, healthy, and attractively presented. Tom helped himself to rather more lasagna than his wife would have approved and made his way to a table with a few empty places. He was glad to see that one of people already there was Bishop Jeffers. He took a spot next to him, saying, "Is this taken?"

Jeffers looked up and smiled to see Tom. "Not at all. Please." He motioned toward the empty place. Tom slid his tray into place and pulled up to the table. Bishop Van Patton cocked her head, intending to say something, but waited to swallow first. "Tom," she finally managed, "I was so sorry about what Hammet tried to pull yesterday."

Jeffers bobbed his head in agreement. "That was low. I'm sorry I wasn't more forceful, but coming on the heels of the gay clergy motion—I was a bit shell-shocked already."

"Thanks, Andy, and thank you, Leslie. I quite understand. It certainly took me by surprise." Tom noted that the presiding bishop had taken a seat at the next table, and resolved to keep his voice down. "The thing is, I know my boys," he said in a near-whisper. Jeffers and Van Patton leaned in conspiratorially. "I know what they're capable of, and I know what they've been up to. This whole thing just smacks of another one of Hammet's witch hunts."

"The man certainly needs to have someone to hate," Jeffers agreed.

"More like he has to make someone else out to be wrong so that he can feel like he is right," Van Patton interjected.

"That's just sad," said Tom, remembering to pay attention to the truly excellent lasagna.

Just then one of the sisters made her way across the cafeteria and tapped Presiding Bishop Mellert on the shoulder. Tom watched as he leaned back and spoke to her. A moment later he was folding his napkin and making apologetic gestures. He then followed the nun out of the hall.

"What do you think?" Jeffers caught his eye. Tom realized he had tuned out the conversation.

"I'm sorry. I'm a bit distracted today. What was that, Andy?"

"Is there something else bothering you, Tom?" Van Patton inquired.

"No. Well, maybe. The order...the order in question...should have called me last night after I left a message about what was going on here." He took a drink of apple cider. "I figured they should know what's happening. But they haven't called back."

"That does seem strange," Jeffers agreed. "What do you think it means?"

"I think it probably means they're too busy doing God's work to give much weight to the blowhard speculations of old men in funny hats—and I *do* mean the *men*, Leslie."

She gave him a wry smile, and Jeffers chuckled. "Knowing what I do about that order of yours, I wouldn't be at all surprised if that's exactly on the money." Jeffers slapped Tom on the shoulder.

There was free time after dinner, and Tom considered his options as they filed out of the cafeteria. Several of the bishops were carpooling into Houston for a concert of sacred choral works at the Episcopal cathedral, while some were planning to gather in one of the common rooms to watch a DVD and, no doubt, consume more port than was good for them.

Tom was leaning toward the concert when one of the local clergy, a deacon, approached him. Tom fumbled in his addled brain for his name. What was it? Ah, yes, there it was. Eldritch, of all things. "Reverend Eldritch, nice to see you again." He shook the man's hand.

"Bishop Müeller, the presiding bishop requests a meeting with you. It's urgent."

What now? Tom thought, then he wondered if he had said it aloud. Just in case, he said it again, changing the emphasis. "What? Now?"

"Right now, please. I'll show you to his room." With that, the deacon turned and made his way toward the dormitory. Tom had no choice but to follow. Within a few minutes, he found himself outside one of the doors, exactly like the hundreds of others on the three floors of dorm rooms the convent made available for retreatants and conference attendees.

Bishop Mellert opened the door and waved Tom inside. "Thank you, Eldritch," he said to the deacon. "I won't be needing you for the rest of the evening. Thank you for all your hard work today." He shook the young man's hand and scanned the hallway suspiciously before closing the door and turning to his guest.

Tom was quite impressed with the room. His own could reasonably be described as a cell. It was hardly large enough to turn around in and contained nothing more than a small single bed, a sink, a desk, and a small wardrobe, all in a mere five-by-eight-foot area. But this room was much larger—obviously designed for married couples, the room sported a full-size bed, a bookcase, and enough room to dress oneself in comfortably. *Lucky bastard*, Tom thought.

"Tom, have a seat." Tom did, appreciating the fact that the room also contained chairs, which had never seemed such a luxury before.

Bishop Mellert sat on the bed and sighed.

"What's going on?" Tom asked.

Mellert picked up a FedEx package and handed it to him. Tom took it and peered inside.

"I just picked this up at the front desk, halfway through dinner. I warn you, Tom, it's disturbing."

Tom shook the contents out onto his lap and swallowed. They were an assortment of papers and photos, he noted, all of them either mentioning or showing members of the Order of Saint Raphael— none of them in a good light.

As Tom turned page after page, his face lost color, and he felt a cold sweat begin to break out on his forehead. By the time he turned the last one over, he felt faint.

"It's pretty damning stuff, Tom," Mellert said, though he didn't need to say it. It was painfully obvious.

"Yes. Yes, it is." Tom wiped his forehead with his sleeve. "What... what do you plan to do with this?"

Mellert scowled at him. "That's a very good question. Bishop

Hammet would be champing at the bit to get hold of these," he said. "It would prove his case."

"I'm not sure it proves anything," Tom noted.

"It might be all he needs to stack the deck in his favor, though," Mellert said. "But that's not *my* problem. *My* problem is, what do I do with these?"

Tom's head was spinning. "You can't give them to Hammet! Andrus, promise me you're not even considering that!"

"Why not? I don't have a stake in this one way or the other. It is the business of the House of Bishops to weigh the evidence and make decisions. How can we do that if I deliberately withhold evidence? And why shouldn't Hammet have it for his arguments? For that matter, isn't it equally fair that I give you fair warning, like I'm doing now?"

"You haven't already shown this to Hammet!?"

"No. But *should* I? That's the question." Mellert looked at his shoes and brooded. "What do you think I should do, Tom?"

Tom chewed on his lip and willed himself to relax. "First of all, these pictures don't actually *prove* anything. They are circumstantial, and nothing more."

"And the documents?"

"They don't prove any of Hammet's charges, either."

"So?"

"So, they're not relevant. I think you should shred them."

Mellert's brow furrowed. "I doubt Casey Hammet would see it that way."

"I'm sure you're right about that." He looked Mellert in the eye. "What *are* you going to do?"

"What any bishop worth his salt would do in my position," Mellert said. "Pray."

Tom turned the FedEx package over, and in a moment of clarity, took note of the sender. Committing it to memory, he handed the envelope back to Mellert.

"That sounds like an excellent plan," he said.

26

"WHO THE HELL WAS THAT?" asked Terry.

"Ah didn't recognize 'im," Dylan offered. "Did any of y'all?" No one had. The voice had been low, gruff, and hard.

"I don't think we can waste any time," Richard announced. "I'm not going to believe that Mikael is dead until I see it. Until then, we have one lead. Let's follow it up."

"What do you propose?" asked Terry.

"I say we go to this address, knock on the door, and ask for our friar back," Richard answered testily.

"It's not a subtle plan," noted Terry.

"Fuck subtle. For all we know, Mikael's in danger. Even if he hasn't been physically harmed, he's probably not in a warded environment, which means that whatever happened to Kat's brother—"

"Is happening to him," finished Kat. "Oh God!"

"Dylan, Terry, let's go," said Richard, grabbing a coat.

Dylan gave Susan a peck, and in moments the friars were winding their way through the Berkeley neighborhoods toward I-80. It was a grim and quiet ride, but it passed quickly, and within three-quarters of an hour they were pulling into the Lower Haight.

Terry looked up from the address on the scrap of paper. "It's

2620..." he mused aloud. "Next block." Dylan drove slowly, passing numerous liquor stores, sleeping winos, trendy coffee bistros. "That's it, there." Almost rolling to a stop, the three looked up from the driver's side windows at a criminally neglected Victorian. Its paint—which had probably been a salmon color in the distant past—was peeling, and black cloth adorned the inside of its windows.

"Okay, let's park," said Richard, feeling his heart rate pick up the pace. Dylan jabbed the accelerator to circle the block, when Terry squealed.

"If you must be such a sissy, can you please do it at farther remove from my ear?" Richard complained, shaking his ear canal with his finger.

"It's Mikael's car, look!"

Plainly, it was his battered Tercel. Dylan turned to look both of them in the face, his eyes registering concern. "Don't panic. Just park," Richard said. "Let's check it out."

"There's a place, half a block up, on the left. Quick!"

"Ah, see it," said Dylan, speeding up and whipping an illegal U in the middle of the street. "Thank you, Jesus."

"No," corrected Terry impishly, "Thank you, *Baby* Jesus."

Dylan parked in the narrow space in one try, and Richard silently marveled at his prowess as they jogged to Mikael's car. Terry peered in and squinted. Then he tried the doors, but they were locked. "Holy Christ," he muttered.

"What?"

"Well, the doors are locked, but the keys are inside. See?" Dylan leaned over and peered through the glass. Sure enough, the keys were hanging from the ignition.

"What do you think happened?" asked Richard.

"Well, knowing Mikael"—Terry straightened up and made a face —"I'd say he went to the john and accidentally locked his keys in the car. Then, when he ran out of fish gall, he went into a dissociative state—"

"From the demon activity," added Dylan.

"Exactly. He probably fainted, and, well, my guess is that someone called an ambulance."

"Right." Richard snapped open his cell phone and speed dialed the friary. Susan picked up the phone. "Susan, we found Mikael's car. It's empty. We think he succumbed to the demon, and fainted. Our best guess is that he's in a coma in some hospital. Can you call the emergency rooms in the vicinity of the Lower Haight? Atta girl." He snapped the phone closed and replaced it in his pocket. "She and Kat are gonna cover the whole city."

"Good move," nodded Dylan, still peering into the car. "Terry, these wards still in effect?"

Terry ran a hand along the side of the car, perambulating it with his eyes closed. "They're fading now, but they're intact."

Richard was standing on the edge of the sidewalk, staring across the street at the moldy Victorian. Terry noticed and went to stand by him, taking his arm. "You doin' okay?"

Richard looked down at him and nodded. He returned his gaze to the house, and his eyes narrowed. "We gotta go in."

Dylan joined them, placing his own hand on Richard's shoulder. "Hey, dude, whatcha thinking?"

"I'm thinking of doing some serious hurt to someone."

"Waal, let's find out what we're dealing with first. Maybe we oughta—"

Without another word, Richard strode off across the street toward the Victorian. His long strides had Terry nearly jogging, and Dylan puffing a few steps behind. In a few moments, however, they were all standing on the porch, rotted timber beneath their feet groaning slightly, exposed nails threatening tetanus.

Richard pounded on the door and hopped up and down on the balls of his feet.

"Dude, maybe we oughta think this through a little, first?" Dylan continued. "We can still ditch—"

But then they couldn't. The door swung open, and a young man roughly their own age stuck his head out. His hair was midnight black and as unruly as Mikael's typically was. A scar split his cheek, and his eyes widened at the sight of three tonsured friars in black habit. "I'm sorry," he said, "we don't give to religious institutions." He made to close the door.

Richard thrust his foot in the door, blocking its closure. "We're not an institution," he said, his eyes steely and hard. "We're a mother-fucking force of nature, and you would do well to fear us."

The young man froze, uncertain. Richard took advantage of his surprise and leveled a shoulder into the door, knocking the man backward. Richard didn't hesitate for a moment, but forced his way in, kneeling on the steps by the young man's head, taking his collar in his fists. Dylan and Terry edged themselves inside and closed the door behind them to avoid curious onlookers.

"Dude," Dylan began, but Richard was hearing none of it.

He knocked the young man's head against the painted wooden steps, not hard enough to hurt him but plenty hard enough to get his attention. "I wanna know where my friar is, shit-fucker."

"What?" the young man wailed, clearly scared now.

"We got a novice friar who's been watching your house. He's gone missing. I wanna know *where...he...is*." He punctuated each the final three words by slamming the young man's head against the step in succession.

"Please, I don't know what—who—"

A voice called from the top of the stairs. "You're Richard Kinney."

Richard stopped and looked up. At the top of the steep and narrow staircase, a lone figure hovered. "Who wants to know?"

"I...I never thought I'd meet you. I'm so pleased."

Richard looked at Dylan and Terry. Dylan shrugged. "I didn't know you had fans, dude."

The voice called down again. "If you can find it within yourself to leave off assaulting my *fritter* there, please come up and have a drink. I've been dying to talk to you for the longest time."

Richard released the shirt, and the young man curled into the fetal position to protect himself. Standing up, Richard nodded at Dylan and Terry and took to the stairs.

At the top of the stairs, Richard held the rail and stood still to let his eyes adjust. Gradually, the room came into focus: A motley assembly of threadbare couches and overstuffed Victorian-era chairs stood against the walls, while opposite him stood a tall antique desk, the kind that was raised up about two feet higher than regular desks and required a barstool to sit at it properly. Near the desk, the blacked-out window was adorned with velvet curtains, dusty and faded pink with age.

In a moment, Terry was by his side. He squinted. "Whoa, good thing I've got Molly Maids on speed dial."

Sitting so still Richard did not notice him until that moment, a thin, tall figure unfolded from one of the chairs. He strode across the room with the grace of a cat, despite his height. In sharp contrast to the shabbiness of the room, he was nattily dressed, a fine-featured man in his late fifties with a kindly face and eyes gleaming with excitement and intelligence.

He extended a hand to Richard. "At long last. I have looked forward to this for a long time, sir."

Richard shook his hand and introduced Terry. A moment later, he introduced Dylan, who had just reached the top of the stairs and was puffing audibly.

"I am Stanis Larch." He paused to see if there would be a reaction, and smiled to see the gleam of recognition in Terry's face.

"Larch? Where do I know that name?" Terry snapped his fingers. "Wait! You're Ourobouros93!"

"Really?" Richard said, a new appreciation transformed his face. "I loved your essay on Kazantzakis's *Saviors of God* as a companion testament to *The Book of the Law*—'He Croucheth in Our Bones,' I think it was called. What was that, ten years ago? Fuckin' great paper."

Larch made a little bow. "The very same." He then waved toward the furniture. "Please, make yourselves comfortable."

Closer up, Richard could see that the bookshelf was packed with paperback Weiser editions and, on the lower shelves, ancient-looking tomes bound in leather. No titles adorned their spines, but Richard could guess what they were: grimoires. Just then, he noticed the hand-painted plaster Baphomet staring down from the top of the bookshelf. "Howdy to you, too," he winked at the statue. *Yup*, he thought to himself, *this is a magickian's den, no bout a doubt it.*

Richard ignored the smell of mold emanating from the armchair, and forced himself to sit. Terry and Dylan took places beside one another on one of the couches, and Larch planted himself in another armchair directly across from Richard. Just then, the shock-haired young man who had answered the door emerged from the stairwell, holding the back of his head and grimacing. "Oh, it seems you've met Frater Charybdis."

"Sorry about the head-thing," Richard said, without any real remorse.

"Fuck you," said Charybdis.

"Frater, some tea for our guests, if you please."

Charybdis sneered but turned and limped toward what Richard assumed must be the kitchen.

"Richard Kinney," Larch shook his head. "My, my. You know, I've been reading your posts since the early WELL days."

"Then we've been mutual admirers," Richard returned, a real smile emerging.

"Well?" asked Dylan.

"A very popular computer bulletin board in the Bay Area back in the '90s," Terry explained. "The first real internet community for most of us."

"Just so," smiled Larch. "I still remember how you put those Temple of Set bastards in their place on the Ceremonial Magick list."

Richard couldn't help a smile himself. "Oh yeah. That *was* intense." Despite himself, Richard found he was warming to Larch. He told himself it was the result of intentional flattery and to stay on guard. "Listen, Mr. Larch, we're here on business."

Larch's smile lessened somewhat but did not disappear. "And pray, what would that be?"

"One of our friars has gone missing. We want him back."

"And you think he might be here? Why?"

"He was staking out your house earlier today."

Real surprise registered on Larch's face. "No. My God, no. Father Kinney, you may feel free to scour every inch of this house. I'm sure you and your companions are familiar with the paraphernalia of the magickian's craft; it will hold no surprises for you. Your friar is not here."

"Then where is he?"

"I'm as clueless as you seem to be, I'm afraid."

"We'll see about that. Look, we have one of your brothers."

Larch's eyebrows shot up. "You know where Randall Webber is?"

"I do. He's safe, but we're not disclosing his location. You want him back; we want our friar back."

"You're holding him hostage?"

"Not at all. He's gravely ill, and his sister is tending to him." It wasn't exactly true, but Larch didn't need to know that. "She has employed us to find out what happened to him. In the course of our investigation, our friar disappeared."

Terry passed Larch an iPod, a photo of Mikael grinning stupidly on its screen. "That's Mikael Bloomink, a member of our order," Richard said deliberately. "You sure you haven't seen him?"

"I swear to God, Father Kinney, I have not."

Richard looked at Terry and gave an almost imperceptible nod.

After a few moments, Terry rose. "Excuse me, may I use your restroom? You only rent coffee, you know."

"Oh of course. Through this door here"—Larch indicated with a wave—"down the hall, to your left."

"Thank you," Terry said and excused himself.

Richard stared at Larch. An uncomfortable silence stretched out between them. Finally, Richard cleared his throat. "Mr. Larch, we inspected Webber's house. We saw the sigils. We know which demon was summoned, and we know what he did."

Larch looked at them with admiration and wonder. "Do you really?"

"Really. What we don't understand is *why*."

Larch cocked his head. "What part of it don't you understand?"

"Why avocados?"

Larch grinned and let a few chuckles fall into his lap. "Well, the avocados aren't the important thing, obviously."

"I'm certain there are a few thousand avocado growers and probably thousands more migrant workers that would disagree with you there."

"What I mean to say is that we have no real interest in avocados. It was...an experiment. To see if it could be done."

"Well, congratulations, I suppose."

"Don't expect me to thank you fellers for depriving the world of guacamole," Dylan sniffed.

"I'm missing that a bit myself, I must admit," Larch feigned a pained look.

"So, what's this really about?" Richard asked.

Just then Charybdis came through the door with an antique tea tray, hastily arranged with yellowed and cracked china. He set the tray down on a cracked fiberboard coffee table and then turned and walked back to the kitchen, letting the door swing behind him.

"Please excuse Charybdis's rudeness." Larch reached over and filled the four cups. "And just to put your minds at ease, I'll drink whichever one you gentlemen don't choose."

"Thank you," said Richard with a nod. He did not reach for a cup. "What was the experiment intending to prove? Why did you do it?"

Larch's eyes narrowed. "Come now, Mr. Kinney, as you well know, every group has its secrets."

Richard *did* know about that, and in lieu of responding, he picked up one of the cracked china cups and swirled tea in its stained and ancient bowl.

Just then, Terry emerged from the hallway and winked at Richard. Richard took a sip of the tea, momentarily amazed at how good simple things can be, especially when one is not expecting them.

"Mr. Larch—"

"Please, I'd always so hoped we could be friends. Call me Stanis, won't you?"

"Let's work up to that, why don't we? Yes, we're on a case. But what's more important to me—to us—is our friend being missing. We want him back, and we will stop at nothing to get him back."

"Why, Richard," Larch said with a smile, "that could be taken as a threat."

"Take it any way you like. Finding Mikael is our priority, but second on our list is the whole missing avocados thing. We know you and your lodge mates are up to something—something dangerous, something that got your friend hurt very badly. What I don't understand is why you're not more concerned about him."

Richard watched Larch closely as Terry slid back into his seat beside Dylan.

"I think you misjudge me, Richard..." Larch paused and looked away, pausing to think through his next words, or perhaps to master his emotions. When he looked back at Richard, he was master of his features.

"I love Randall as much as you love your order mates. You don't need to believe me. I don't care what you think...well, not much." He looked down at his tea for another thoughtful moment. "Tell me, Richard, have you ever put yourself or one of your order mates in danger to achieve something important? Something you believed in? Maybe to save someone, to save a lot of people?"

Richard nodded. *Of course I have. Almost every fucking day*, he thought.

"Then you know. You know the risks, you know what can be at stake. You know how you must keep a stiff upper lip. You know how you must maintain the pretense of having it all together because you're the leader."

Terry snorted. If he had been drinking milk, it would have sprayed. Richard pretended not to notice. "I'm not so good at the last part, but yes, I know what you mean."

"There are no such things as acceptable losses, Richard, but there sure as hell are *losses*." He stared back down at his cup.

"What are you trying to do that could justify such a loss?" Richard asked, finishing the tea in his cup.

"Saving the world, of course."

"From what?"

"From the greatest tyrant it has ever known. From the cause of every evil, every blight, the source of all disease and pain."

"Satan?" asked Dylan.

"No, not Satan. Satan's the fall guy, the patsy, the dupe, the straw man. He's the one that was set up to take all the heat off the real perpetrator."

"And who would that be?" asked Terry.

Larch stared at him for a long moment before responding. "Why, God of course."

27

As Dylan drove back over the Bay Bridge, stony silence ruled over the car. Terry worried silently, while Richard's face was set with grim determination. Not until they reached Emeryville did one of them speak.

"Any idea what Brian's got cooking?" asked Dylan with exaggerated brightness.

Terry ignored him, but Richard took the break in the silence as a cue to wonder aloud. "I fucked up back there."

"How d'ya figger?" asked Dylan.

"I shouldn't have tipped our hand about Kat's brother."

"No, it was good," Terry said. "It's a balance of power thing. Did you sleep through the Cold War?"

"But we were bluffing. That would be fine if we actually had him in our care. We took a gamble even bringing him up. We've got to bring him home. Tonight."

"I have something that will make you happy," said Terry.

"Threesomes are out."

Terry leaned through the bucket seats and presented a flash drive as if it were the Holy Graal.

Dylan glanced over at it. "Yer shittin' me. What did'ja get?"

"I'm not sure. There was a running Mac in what looked like a holy wreck of an office. I just plugged in the drive and dragged a bunch of miscellaneous stuff over to it as fast as I could. I know we got a lodge roster, I made sure of that. We'll have Susan sift through the rest of it when we get home."

Dylan sighed, elated. "Well, dude, you just rock."

Richard managed a "Good job" but otherwise kept his thoughts to himself. As they entered the house, Kat pounced on them at the door. Her eyes were ringed and red, as she grew less able to master her distress. "What did you find? What happened?"

Richard gave her the CliffsNotes version of their meeting as the friars shed their coats and washed up for supper.

"This stew is going to be mush if it stays on the stove any longer." Brian appeared in the hall, his hands on his hips. Given his hunched back, this was a more menacing pose than it might otherwise have appeared.

Seated at the table, they said a quick blessing and began tearing at the bread and helping themselves to the pot of stew steaming in the middle of the huge oaken table.

Susan walked in from the office and gave her husband a peck, settling in next to him. "Guys, Bishop Tom just called."

"Ah shit," said Dylan. "Ah was hopin' that if we just ignored that whole business it would just go away."

"Not happening," Susan said. "In fact, it's worse. A whole file full of damning materials just landed in the presiding bishop's hands today."

"How damning could they be?" asked Terry. "We've got nothing to hide."

"From liberal Berkeleyites, maybe," Richard agreed. "But from assholes like Hammet? I can think of a lot of things about what we do I wouldn't want him and half of the Christians in Texas to know about."

"Like what?" asked Dylan, licking the ends of a joint.

Richard stared at him hard.

"What? What did I say?" Dylan implored.

"No smoking at the dinner table." Brian grabbed the joint out of Dylan's hand and threw it on the shelf behind the portly priest's head. "Jesus, I thought I had you trained."

"Who sent it, that's what I want to know," Richard said, reaching for the bread.

"You'll be so proud of Tom," Susan said. "Because he gave us a name and address on that."

"Go, Tom!" Terry shouted and turned to Dylan for a high-five.

"Turns out it was sent by a private detective agency here in San Francisco."

Kat added pepper to her stew. "So, your enemies are local," she said. "Who would have it in for you?"

"Try anyone we've stopped in the past fifteen years," Dylan said, coming out of his pout.

"I'll keep working on it," Susan said. "But how about you guys? What kind of luck did you have?"

Richard repeated the CliffsNotes version for the benefit of Susan and Brian.

"So, what do we do?" asked Kat. She had placed a couple of ladles' worth of stew in her bowl but couldn't bring herself to touch it.

Brian noticed and pointed at her bowl. "Show some fucking respect. Eat."

She looked at him with her mouth open, incredulous. Terry laughed at her shock, and softened the moment by rubbing Brian's hair. "Every order needs a Jewish mother."

Seeing Susan smile, Kat relaxed but instantly looked back at Richard for guidance.

"What's the plan, Kemosabe?" prompted Dylan.

"The first thing we've got to do is get Kat's brother. I led Larch to believe that we have him, and I want to make sure that we do."

"How will we do that if I can't even leave the house?" asked Kat, her voice rising in panic.

Richard looked lost for a moment, but Susan filled the void. "As soon as we're done eating, Kat, you should call the hospital and explain that you can't come get him because you're ill, and instruct them to release him into the care of...well, whoever is going to get him. Then we'll draft a letter to the same effect, which you will sign, just in case. That should do it."

Kat nodded, eager to get it done. "But first things first," said Susan. "Pass the rice, please."

Ten minutes after clearing the table, Kat had finished on the telephone and was signing the letter Susan had hastily prepared on the computer.

"Dylan, why don't you stay here and give Brian a hand with the kitchen cleanup," Richard said, his face a stony mask. "Susan, I have a feeling we could really use your diplomacy here. Do you feel up for a trip to Alameda?"

"I always love an excuse to go to Alameda. Let me grab my coat."

Kat was biting at her fingers. Richard noticed the strain on her face and put a hand on her shoulder to comfort her, realizing that having a job to do would make the waiting easier on her. "Why don't you move your stuff to Mikael's room and get the guest room ready for your brother? Dylan'll give you a hand."

She nodded, gritting her teeth against the worry.

Susan reappeared in the foyer and handed Richard and Terry their coats. "Let's roll," she said.

28

TERRY DROVE while Richard stared out the windshield and bounced his leg for most of the way. Susan noticed and, leaning her cheek against the back of Richard's seat, felt a wave of compassion for him wash over her. She was worried sick about Mikael, and certainly concerned about Kat's brother, but she knew how heavy the weight of leadership was on Richard, especially coming so close on the heels of being dumped. He wasn't just worried; he also felt *responsible*, and it was obvious that it ate at him.

She distracted herself by watching the dusk settle over one of her favorite places in the Bay Area. Alameda was one of its best-kept secrets.

She always considered it surreal to be in downtown, urban Oakland—as gritty as anywhere in New York or LA—and then, after a forty-second tunnel ride, emerge in Mayberry RFD. Alameda, a tiny little island off the coast of Oakland, evoked a sleepy and wholesome time long past. Webster Street, on the poorer end of the island, exuded small-town charm with plenty of specialty shops and restaurants.

Terry turned left on Central and headed toward the ritzier side of the island, and the hospital.

"Do you think we'll have any trouble breaking him out?" Terry asked no one in particular.

"You talk like he's in prison," Susan complained.

"You ever been in the hospital?"

"Point," she conceded. "Kat talked to the admissions people, and they didn't indicate there would be any trouble. They're expecting us."

She placed a hand on Richard's shoulder. He didn't look back but reached up and squeezed hers in place. Terry looked over, noticed, and smiled. "Here we are," he said, pulling up in the visitors lot.

Like the rest of Alameda, the hospital exuded quaint charm and at the same time was clean and efficient.

The three of them made their way to the admissions desk, and Susan cleared her throat. An octogenarian volunteer had nodded off and was drooling on her intake papers.

Susan reached down and stroked her hair gently. "Hey, pretty lady," she said. "Can you give us a hand?"

The woman jerked upward with a start. "Who the hell are you?" she snapped. Then she looked around and remembered where she was and, it seemed to Susan, what she was there to do. "Excuse me," she said to Susan. "How can I help?"

Susan stifled a laugh and put on her all-business face. "We're here to transport Randall Webber for home care. His sister, Catherine, called about a half hour ago."

"How many of you does the man need?" The woman was looking behind her at the two friars.

"There's only three of us."

"And two more upstairs."

Richard felt a trickle of ice water down his spine. He stepped up. "What two? What are their names?"

"I don't take names, young man, I just give out visitors' badges. Do you want one?"

"No need," Richard said, "Clergy. C'mon." He set off toward the elevators at a panicked trot.

Susan had the presence of mind to stay put and ask for the room number. The woman scrawled it on the paper, and Susan snatched it from her hand and willed her ample frame to catch up to Richard and Terry before the elevator arrived.

While they waited, Richard took charge. "Everyone got cell phones?" Terry nodded, but Susan shook her head. "Terry, stay here, and watch the lobby in case we miss them."

"Check, boss." Terry stepped back just as the elevator arrived, and Richard and Susan stepped on.

"2107," she told him. He hit the button for the third floor and bounced up and down on the balls of his feet.

"Easy, boy. We're going to find him."

He ignored her and continued to bounce until the door chimed and opened onto a nondescript hospital corridor.

They stepped out of the elevator and oriented themselves. "This way," Susan said, pointing at the red sign affixed to the wall at the corner, indicating room numbers.

No one stopped them—indeed, they hardly saw any staff as they jogged toward the room. Richard was breathing heavily as they crossed the threshold. He tugged at the privacy curtain and visibly relaxed as he saw the unconscious man in the bed.

"He's fine, Dicky," Susan said, putting a hand on his arm. "You stay here with him—I'm going to the nurses' station to get the release."

Richard nodded and watched her walk out of the room. He closed his eyes and slumped in the chair. In seconds, all of the accumulated stress of the day rose in his throat until he choked up. *I really need a good cry*, he thought, but he knew this was not the time or place. Instead, he ran his fingers through his hair and breathed deeply several times, willing himself to be present with his body, feeling the aching in his feet, the pressure in his head. He felt the panic drain out of him so vividly that he would have sworn that a pool was collecting on the floor.

After a few minutes, he was able to redirect his focus and take in the room around him. Alameda Hospital was clean, but older than

many hospitals he had visited, and its age was reflected in the shabbiness of its rooms.

This wouldn't be a place where he would want to spend any
significant time. *At least Randall is unconscious*, he thought. *Or the
angel*, reminding himself who the current occupant was. He stared at
the body, its chest silently rising and falling, an occasional tic
twitching a cheek or an eyelid. *Funny*, he thought, *he doesn't look much
like Kat*. Sure, his hair was black like hers, but that's where the resemblance stopped. Still, that's the way it was with some siblings.

Just then, Susan's voice rose above the quiet humming of the
room's monitors. It was hard to fluster Susan, so he was instantly
concerned. He rose and followed her voice to the nurses' station.

"Problem?" Richard asked her, approaching the counter at
her side.

"They just changed shifts," Susan said, holding her forehead in
both hands, "and the last shift didn't tell them we were coming."

"They didn't write anything down?" Richard inquired.

The corpulent African-American woman seated behind the
counter narrowed her eyes at him without deigning to answer. She
exuded an air of arrogant superiority that would not suffer these
fools or any others.

"Did you show her the letter?" Richard asked.

"Of course I showed her the letter."

The nurse cocked an eyebrow as if to say, "I am sitting right here,"
and then turned back to her computer screen.

"So, no problem. Call Kat, and have her explain it again."

Susan nodded and grabbed Richard's phone from his
outstretched hand. Content that Susan had things under control
again, Richard wandered back to the room where the chair was
calling to his aching feet like an orthopedic siren.

It wasn't until he sat down again and allowed himself a relieved
moan that he was seized once again by panic. The bed was empty.

29

MIKAEL AWOKE, sick and disoriented. His head felt thick and woolly, and no sooner had he gained consciousness than the contents of his stomach chose that very moment to seek release.

That was when he noticed that his wrists were bound, as well as his ankles. Unable to turn his body, he whipped his head around as far as it would go and heaved. He grimaced as the vomit ran down his cheek. He could see the steam rising from it, his first clue as to the cold that surrounded him.

As soon as his throat was clear, he began a more careful survey of his environment. It appeared to be a stone room—*Perhaps a cellar?* he thought, seeing tiny tendrils of roots worming their way through where the ceiling and walls met. He was lying on something not soft but not stone, either. He decided it was probably an old mattress thrown on the floor. Iron rings affixed to the wall at his feet provided security for the ropes that held him there, and he assumed that a mated pair held his hands.

To his right, the room extended a good eight to ten feet. Yellow light flickered and guttered at the whims of the draft, throwing unruly shadows on the ceiling.

Not long after coming to, Mikael found himself fading in and out of consciousness. The sleep was a relief, but it was not restful sleep.

After a couple of hours of on-again, off-again lucidity, he came to, but the quality of it was different.

The thick-headedness was gone, and in its place, a chilly numinousity that seemed to crackle with the dancing candle flame. Then Mikael noticed that his perspective was different. Instead of staring up from the mattress, he was staring down from above.

He smiled as he saw himself. *Handsome fucker*, he thought, and he watched his mouth smile in response. He saw his spiky jet-black hairdo, his piercings, the scar to the left of his chin left over from childhood when he had driven his tricycle off the roof.

He was surprised that the overwhelming emotion he felt was not criticism, as it usually was when he looked in the mirror, but compassion, even pity. He saw not a rebellious fuckup but a noble man in unfortunate circumstances. Instead of fear, he felt a calm assurance. He heard Julian of Norwich's words as if whispered to him out of the void, "All shall be well, and all shall be well, and every manner of thing shall be well."

He relaxed even further and enjoyed the floating sensation. Just then, a squeak and a thud broke the stillness, and a door he had not previously noticed opened onto a darkened hall.

With calm disinterest, Mikael watched a man enter the room and close the door behind him. A bolt slid into place, and the man turned toward Mikael's body resting peacefully on the mattress.

From his vantage point on the ceiling, Mikael could not see the man's features, but he found he just didn't care that much who it was. Even in his detached state, his own lack of curiosity seemed odd to him, but he did not dwell on it. Instead, he turned his attention back to the man, now leaning over the Mikael body, now stooping to wipe the vomit from his cheek. Then Mikael realized the man was speaking. He paid closer attention to the words, which slowly became intelligible.

"Sick. There, that's better. I'm really very sorry for all this unpleasantness. I'm not at all sure what to do with you."

A nag of recognition pulled at Mikael. He knew that voice, but from where? He beamed beatifically at the top of the stranger's head, wishing nothing but peace for him.

The man grabbed a blanket from a pile in a dark corner and spread it out over Mikael's body. "There, that's better, isn't it?"

The man sighed and squatted beside the unconscious friar. His thumb worried at the ring on his right hand, and Mikael suddenly knew who it was that was tucking him in—Dane the Younger.

"I wish you would wake up—I have so much I want to ask you!" Dane sat back on his haunches and seemed to consider. Then, apparently thinking aloud, he said, "But maybe I can still ask...what if you're not sick, but plagued? Hmm..." He rose and paced the room's meager distance.

He stopped and raised his right hand, which sported a large red jewel set into his ring. "I hold this dread ring, and I command its power. I do not wish to use it, but I will if I must. Therefore, if there be any demon associated with this man's condition, I command it to appear to me now, or face your doom!"

Dispassionately, Mikael watched the air ripple, and as if projected on the wall, the image of a dragon appeared. The dragon coiled and resolved into the visage of a man, half-beautiful, half-scarred and deformed.

"*Who dares summon me?*" It was an odd voice. Mikael knew that under normal circumstances he would be terrified, but he felt oddly comforted as if he were watching the whole scene on television from the safety of the friars' couch.

"Noble demon, welcome. I bid you come—and behave yourself. Let no harm come to me or to this man, lest harm befall you through the power of this ring."

"*You speak well...yet you are no magickian.*" The infernal Duke eyed him suspiciously. "*How came you by such power?*"

"I will ask the questions here, demon. What misfortune befell this man? And how are you involved?"

Mikael marveled to hear the demon's description of the magickal working wrought by the Lodge of the Hawk and Serpent. Apparently,

Dane found it equally fascinating, as a look of wonder and barely restrained excitement flashed across his upturned face. He grinned broadly and asked the demon more pointed questions about the location of the lodge and the identity of its members.

Amazingly, the demon spoke not with contempt but with patience and respect. Whatever power Dane wielded, it commanded more respect than Mikael thought it possible to summon, especially when it came to demons.

Dane thanked the demon and dismissed him. Mikael watched as the face faded and the serpentine coils of the dragon slithered off the sides of the wall as if absorbed by the corners of the room.

Dane paced excitedly, barely containing his joy. He even did a little hop before turning. "Well, Mr. Monk, it seems you may have led me to my deepest desire. What to do with you now? Prudence dictates that I kill you, I suppose. But you see, I'm not an ingrate, nor am I a murderer. I'm a *savior*. I know, I know, it's sometimes hard to tell the difference."

Mikael could only see the top of his head, but he imagined the man smiling with sad compassion as he said this. Mikael gave him a similar expression, that must have been reflected on his physical face.

"What is this look?" Dane asked, almost laughing. "Are you waking up? No...maybe not." He pulled a syringe out of his pocket and tested it, sending a golden stream into the air for a brief second. "Well, this can wait, then, I suppose." He set the needle down out of reach of Mikael's body.

"Still, you are kind of cute, you know. And so long as you are unconscious..." Dane began to rub at himself. He lay down on the stone floor beside Mikael's body and undid his own belt. Lifting his hips, he slid his pants down and pulled at his penis until it stiffened. As the candle danced, he allowed himself a small moan of pleasure.

From his vantage point on the ceiling, Mikael had no interest in the man's erection, nor did he feel any revulsion or disdain. Nor did he feel any when Dane swung around on his knees, and climbed up on the mattress. He planted his knees near Mikael's head and shuddered visibly as he felt the stubble on Mikael's cheek graze the sensitive skin of his scrotum. Again and again, he rocked himself over the unconscious man's head, feeling the ecstasy of the prickly and scratchy beard against his balls.

Mikael watched the scene feeling an overwhelming compassion for the man. The friar did not see what happened next, for his attention was diverted. Above him, a hole seemed to have formed where the stones had been, an ectoplasmic whirlpool that sucked at Mikael's consciousness like an undertow. At the center of it, he saw a child—a little girl dressed in what appeared to be a long, olive-colored dress. She looked frightened and uncertain, and stared straight into what would have been Mikael's eyes had he been using physical senses. Moved by compassion, he held out his hand to the little girl and moved toward her into the eye of the vortex. He did not panic as he was drawn up into it, nor was he reassured that all would be well.

30

KAT PUT the few things that she considered "hers" into a laundry basket and carried it to Mikael's room. She placed the basket on the bed and sat down beside it. She tried to muster the energy to unpack it, but instead she just sighed and looked around her, seeing little.

The room was small. At one time it had been a veranda—perfect for sleeping out of doors on hot, muggy nights. But such nights were rare in foggy North Berkeley, and at some point in the house's long history, the veranda had been enclosed. The result was a long, funky room with more windows than wall space.

The room was not wide enough for anything but a single bed. Kat smoothed the covers, imagining what it would be like to try to sleep in it with Mikael. It would be crowded, she knew. *No, it would be cozy*, she thought.

And at that, her face crumpled, and she heaved a sob so fierce she fell to the comforter and buried her face. She sobbed for Mikael, whom she barely knew, but who had already snagged at her heart. She sobbed for her brother, for his stupidity, for what he had done to himself, to that poor angel, and maybe to others as well.

After a while, the wave of grief passed, and she gulped at the cool, good air like a drowning man. Her mind went blank for a brief moment, and she *enjoyed* the sensation of simply breathing.

She looked around for something to blow her nose on. She didn't see any Kleenex boxes—did she really expect to, in the cell of a punk-rock-musician-cum-friar?

Then her eyes lit upon the little altar set up by the window farthest from the door, by the foot of the bed.

Atop a short bookcase, a scarlet altar cloth had been draped. On it the stub of a candle stood, unlit but obviously much used, if the melted wax at its base was any indication. Directly behind the candle was a Byzantine icon of Christ Pantocrator, his right hand held up in a mudra of absolution and blessing.

"Fat lot of good you're doing," she said to the icon. "You've got a lot of people around here who really love you, you know. Although I'll be damned if I can figure out why, because you sure as hell don't seem to be doing anything for them."

The face of the icon stared at her with eyes that radiated compassion and judgment at once, a disturbing gaze that was hard to focus on for very long.

"Stop looking at me like that, goddammit," Kat raised her voice at the icon, but the eyes did not look away. They bored straight into her soul, and it scared her.

"Look, I'll make a deal with you, okay?" The icon's eyes did not blink. "I've never met people like this before. I've always just assumed that the people who followed you were self-deceived assholes. And, I know, the folks who live here can be assholes, too, but it's different when someone can actually say, 'Hey, I fucked up,' or 'I was really being an asshole,' you know, and these people can *do* that. They might be hypocrites, but at least they're not pretending they're *not* hypocrites, and that really *means* something. At least it does to me."

She couldn't tell if the icon was smiling or not. There was a slight curve to its left lip that reminded her of Elvis, an ambiguous expression that seemed to change depending on one's own mental state.

"You save Mikael and my brother," she said, haltingly, "and I'll follow you. Like the friars do here. Hell, I'll *join* them."

The words hung in the air as if a reverb chamber were keeping them afloat. She was surprised by the surreality of the notion. *I'm a fucking witch*, she thought. *There's no way they would have me. There's no way* he *would have me.* She looked at the icon again, and she knew that it wasn't true. What was it that was written above the giant icon in the chapel? *This man eats with fuckups and sinners.* No, he would not turn even a witch away. She wouldn't have known that three days ago, but she did now.

"I'll join this fucking order," she said, just to hear it again.

"You don't have to do that," a soft voice came from the doorway. Brian stuck his head in and smiled at her, his close-shaved head bobbing at an odd angle due to the hump on his back. He also limped a little when he walked, and he dragged his left foot into the doorway with the rest of him. "I'm sorry. I wasn't eavesdropping, really. I came to see if you needed any help." He laid a small bundle on the bed beside her. "Fresh linens."

She was relieved to see him, and scooted over on the bed, an unspoken invitation to join her.

"What do you mean, I don't have to do it?"

"You don't have to make bargains with God."

Her lip trembled as she fought back another wave of tears. Brian reached out and put his hand on top of hers.

"I'm just so...so scared. For Randy and Mikael."

"I know," Brian said, "And good old Yeshua over there knows it, too." He pointed at the icon. "And it's very tempting to want to exert any kind of control we can when we feel like we have so little. But God isn't going to intercede just to trap you into making some commitment to him. God already *has* you."

"But I'm a witch!"

"And I'm a Jew! So what?" His eyes softened as he looked at her. "God doesn't give a rat's ass about your religious affiliation, or how you like to worship, or in what form you imagine the Divine. God isn't going to help us because we're on 'the right team,' whatever the hell that means, but because we're trying to *do the right thing*. And God is going to do that, with or without your signing any loyalty oaths—especially those that you might regret later."

She looked at him, and then away at the icon, and then back to Brian. "I just feel so..."

"I know...helpless. I feel that a lot myself. Especially when I know Terry is up against something nasty. But that's a time for faith, not bargaining. Listen, do you know the story of Jephthah's daughter?"

"No," she said, wiping her nose on the back of her hand.

Brian noticed and pulled a clean handkerchief from his back pocket. He handed it to her. "It's from the scriptures of my people. Jephthah was a general in the Hebrew army, and it looked like they were going to be wiped out. So, he made a deal with God. If God would let the Jews win, Jephthah would sacrifice the first living being he saw upon returning to his house."

"So, did they win?"

"You bet your ass. And what do you think was the first thing Jephthah saw when he got home?"

"Not his dog. Don't say his dog."

"Worse. His daughter."

"No."

"Sad but true. So, he told his daughter what he had done, and she asked for some time to party with her crew first. And then he killed her."

"That's a horrible story."

"Yes, but instructive." He touched her cheek and whispered. "God doesn't need any more sacrificed daughters on his hands."

She threw her arms around his neck and cried again. She realized after a few moments that her nose was dripping on Brian's hump, but it didn't matter. He was a lovely man.

After a few moments, she let go and drew back again. "But if Mikael gets back, I *want* to...to join. To be here. I want to have a chance."

"I don't think that will be a problem no matter what religion you are. Look, the friars are Catholics, but Dylan's married to a Lutheran, and she lives here. Terry's partnered with a Jew, and I live here. Who's gonna care if Mikael's girlfriend is a witch?"

She shook her head and blew her nose again. "I can't believe how weird you guys are."

Brian laughed at this, and even Kat smiled. But it was just a reprieve. Her breaths soon came again in deep, short spasms. "Oh, Brian. I'm just so scared. Tell me it's going to be okay."

He put his hand on her shoulder. "I don't know if it's going to be okay. We're dealing with some dangerous stuff here. I'm not going to lie to you. I'm scared, too. I'm pretty fond of Mikael's skinny goth ass myself."

They sat for a moment in silence before Brian continued. "But I can promise you one thing. Whatever it is we have to face, we're going to meet it together. You're not alone in this, Honey. I'm here, Dylan's here, Terry's here, Susan's here, Richard's here. Even Tobias is here." It was true, Tobias had just padded into the room and pushed at her hand for a pet. For some reason, this show of canine affection unleashed another round of grief, and she leaned over and buried her face in the lab's golden fur. Tobias licked at her face, tasted the hot and salty tears, and licked some more, with even greater vigor.

"And you're not going anywhere?" she asked, leaning over the side of the bed, her back toward Brian.

"Nope."

"And I don't have to go anywhere if I don't want to?"

"Nope."

"Maybe I shouldn't be so demanding with my prayers..." she trailed off.

"Oh, go ahead, be demanding. But don't doubt one thing—God will not abandon you, and neither will we."

31

RICHARD CLUTCHED at his head and wailed. "Shit!" he yelled. "Shit shit shit!"

Susan ran into the room moments later. "What? What's wrong?"

"He's gone," Richard sat down on the bed heavily. "God *damn* it!"

"Okay, let's think," Susan tried to be calm. "No one could have wheeled him out; we were right down the hall. We would have seen him coming or going."

"But we wouldn't have noticed someone simply *walking* down the hall. There's lots of people here."

"But he *can't* walk," Susan complained. "He's unconscious."

"Yeah, Randall Webber is," said Richard, suddenly seething. "But that Serpentine masquerading as him, the one who was lying in this bed mere moments ago, wasn't."

Susan's mouth dropped open. "But why a decoy?"

"Maybe he wasn't intending to be a decoy. Maybe he was clearing out Webber's stuff when he heard us coming and jumped in the bed."

"He did have the covers pulled all the way up to his neck," Susan remembered.

"Maybe they're not out of the building yet," Richard said, an idea germinating quickly. He fished in his pocket for his cell phone and speed dialed Terry.

"Coast is clear, Boss," Terry's voice was professional but relaxed.

"Terry, they've stolen the body."

"Where have we heard *that* one before?"

"No, seriously. Someone made off with Webber. We need to find him before they leave the hospital, if we're not too late already."

"Jesu, you're serious," Terry breathed. "Okay, what's the plan?"

"You remember how you reconnected the angel's will to Webber's nervous system?"

"That's not exactly what I did, but yeah."

"Do it again. Now!"

"But he's not in front of me!"

"Do you absolutely need proximity to do it?"

"Well…" He stared off into space, wondering about it himself. "I'm not really sure."

"It can't hurt to try. Do it, and quick!"

The line went dead, and Terry's head swam. He wasn't at all sure it would work, but he raced over to a waiting room chair and sat so that he wouldn't fall over and hurt himself while in trance.

Terry shut his eyes and reached out into the ether for the violet light of the angelic subtle body. Dimly, he thought he saw it. His perception had nothing to do with physical, geographic space, he knew. He was in the realm of the spirit, of metaphor, of the imagination. In his mind's eye, he seized upon the flash of purple and willed himself toward it at great speed. The closer he got, the surer he was he had found his target. What worried him, however, were the ghostly wisps of red light hovering around it. Not demons but trails of demonic energy. People who do demon magick often leave such signatures on the astral plane, so he was sure he was on the right track.

In his imagination, he stopped as close to the violet light as he could. The light was strong now, and he could dimly see the energy field of the magickian's body.

Just as he had done before, he reached out his hands—or imagined that he was reaching—and with a couple of careful strokes adjusted the connection between the angelic spirit and the meat puppet of Webber's body.

No sooner had he done that than a banshee wail ripped through the hospital lobby. The sound was so shreddingly loud, so pain-riddled, so ghastly, that it reached to nearly every floor, stopping people cold in their tracks in the hallways.

Terry jumped up and made for the sound, doubling back when the wail became muffled, and having to nearly hold his hands over his ears as he made ground.

Then he saw them. Two men were on the ground, their faces grimacing against the magnitude of the unearthly wail. The body, mouth opened in a continuous scream, sat bolt upright on a gurney, halfway in and halfway out of a service elevator.

Not sure what to do, Terry saw movement and turned to see Richard and Susan running toward him. He gulped his relief and, hands still affixed to his ears, strode toward the gurney.

He leaned his head in to touch it against the head of the screaming angel, and once again disconnected the angel's spirit from the body. As if a switch had been thrown, the screaming stopped, and the body fell into a prone position as if it had been dropped.

Security was not far behind, the officers pounding down the hall toward them, their hands fumbling at their service revolvers. Richard nodded at Susan, and they both sat down on the men still writhing on the floor.

"Just in time, gentlemen," Richard said breathlessly as the security guards tripped to a halt at the elevator doors. "These men were kidnapping a patient."

Sure, now that the man he was sitting on wasn't going anywhere but to the police department for questioning, he stood and peered down at Webber's apparently sleeping face.

"Now *this* guy looks like Kat," he said to Susan as she stood and joined him. "He looks so peaceful."

"Anything but," Terry corrected him. "The soul in that body is in so much pain he may never be right again. And since angels don't die, that's a significant danger."

Richard nodded, and clapped Terry on the arm. "Good job, Freak Show."

"I'm just glad it worked."

Richard nodded, very much relieved himself. "Let's get this puppy home."

32

GETTING the angel up the narrow stairs of the old farmhouse was not easy, but they eventually managed it. Richard and Dylan settled him gently into the bed, and Terry and Kat undressed him and got him into an old pair of Dylan's pajamas. If he had been standing, they would have been comically large draped over the magickian's wire-thin frame. But lying down it made little difference. With a supply of clean blankets and pillows, they made him as comfortable as humanly possible.

Kat had cried out when she saw him, not sure he wasn't simply dead. "He's so limp," she said. But she felt at his face, and it was warm. Soon, she was all business.

Before long it appeared as if he were sleeping peacefully, and Kat took up vigil beside him, chewing at her nails and stroking his hand.

"Well, I've got a husband to tend to," Terry said. "I'm going to head out for the cottage."

"Thank you, Terry," Kat said, grabbing his hand and holding it to her cheek. Terry smiled, and in moments they heard him clumping down the back stairs.

Richard had already disappeared, though he hadn't said anything to anyone. Dylan and Susan paused at the door to the guest room. "Just call us if you need anything," Susan said. "Honestly, anything."

Kat nodded, so overwhelmed with their generosity that she couldn't speak.

"Want to make some cocoa, Baby?" Susan asked her husband as they approached their room.

"What Ah need is a doobie," Dylan replied. "It's been one fucked-up day."

"Why not have both? Chocolate and Mary Jane—sounds like a winning combination to me."

"You don't even smoke."

"Well, it would sound good to me...if it sounded good to me." She grinned and kissed him. He touched her cheek so she wouldn't pull away, and cherished the intimacy for a long moment. "How did Ah ever get so lucky as to meet you, Baby?"

"That makes two of us," she said, grabbing his hand and leading him down the front stairs.

"Ah think Ah got the better end of that deal," he said, smiling.

Once in the kitchen, Tobias ran to Dylan, tail ablaze. He sat down at the table and gave the lab a good rub while Susan lit a burner under the saucepan.

She poured in some milk, and Dylan grabbed the old cigar box from the bookshelf that held his stash and began rolling a joint.

He did it lovingly, with quick and practiced movements. Tobias was not content with so little attention and flipped at Dylan's hand with his snout, sending a shower of cleaned weed over the table.

"Oh dear," said Susan, noticing.

"No harm done," said Dylan, brushing the weed into a pile. "Ain't gonna hurt to smoke a few breadcrumbs."

Susan added the chocolate, and as she stirred she wondered aloud, "I'd give anything to know where Mikael is tonight."

Dylan's head sagged at this. "Ah know what you mean. It could have been any of us, though."

"Don't talk as if he's dead!"

"Ah'm not. Ah'm just sayin' that any of us could be missin' right now. It's a soberin' thought." He lit the joint and took a deep drag. He felt the warm roughness in his chest, and in a few moments felt the soft blanket of the drug descend over his brain, soothing and calming as it did.

"Ah, that's the stuff," he said.

"And here's the other stuff, Sweetie," Susan said, pouring two cups of cocoa and walking them to the table.

"Sure you don't want a power-hit?"

"Not tonight. Ask me when I get my period, though."

"O' course."

"I'm worried about Mikael, but I'm also worried about Dicky," Susan said, once she was seated.

Dylan took a sip of the strong, sweet chocolate and drummed his fingers on the table. "He's havin' a rough time, but he's holdin' it together. Ah'm just glad Ah'm not callin' the shots in this order."

As if on cue, a wail went up from the front porch, vaguely reminiscent of a tomcat. Tobias's ears stood up on end.

"Speak of the devil," Susan said. "You'd better go talk to him."

Dylan took another deep drag on his joint and put it out. "Any more of that?" He pointed at his cup.

"Here, take mine to him. I'll make more," Susan said, sliding her cup toward him.

"Wish me luck," he said.

"See you in bed, Baby. I'm heading up."

"Okay. Ah'll try not to be too long."

Susan went back to the stove, and Dylan got to his feet with a groan. Tobias shadowed him to the door. "Stay here, big boy," Dylan said, and shut the door.

Richard was sitting in one of the porch swings. Dylan could tell by his breathing that he'd been crying. Dylan sat in a folding chair near him and placed the cups down on the rail of the porch. "Susan made cocoa."

Richard reached out and topped off one of the cups from a flask of whisky. He then sipped at the cup without a word.

"Dude, it's gonna be okay. We're gonna find him."

Richard swung for a good long time before replying. "We haven't got a clue."

"Not true," Dylan said. "Clues we got. We just don't know what they mean yet. But we will. We always figger it out. Ah believe in us, man. Hell, Ah believe in *you*."

At this, Richard buried his face in his hands and sobbed.

"Ah, dude, don't do this to yerself."

When the jag subsided, Richard fished for a handkerchief and dirtied it. "I'm not the right guy for this job."

"What the fuck are you talking about?" Dylan asked indignantly. "Who the fuck do you think could do it better?"

"You."

"Fuck that. Ah'm no leader. You gotta be born a leader. People follow you, or they don't. The only place people follow me is to the dinner table. You, though…Shit, man, any one of us would follow you into Hell and back. Fuck that; we *have*."

If Richard's head were hanging any lower, he'd be licking his own nipples, Dylan thought as he slurped at his cup and centered himself in the marijuana's glow. Before he could say anything else, Richard was talking again.

"I have done nothing but fuck up the last couple of days. I fucked up my relationship—"

"Yuh didn't necessarily do that *in a couple of days*," Dylan pointed out helpfully, but Richard ignored him.

"I fucked up the Dane exorcism—"

"Dude—"

"I fucked up the assignments and got Mikael nabbed by God knows who. And if I understand the messages from Bishop Tom, I've even fucked things up with the denomination. I gotta face it, man, I'm a total fuckup."

"Jesus loves fuckups, dude," Dylan reminded him.

"Sure, but he'd be an idiot to put them in charge of anything."

"There goes Peter, I guess."

A smile tempted Richard's mouth but faded before it fully materialized.

The two sat in silence for several minutes. Then Dylan spoke gently. "Dude, Ah'm sorry for the tough love here, but Ah need you to do a couple of things for me—for us."

Richard sat still, waiting.

"First, Ah need you to go see your spiritual director. Not at the end of the month. Like, tomorrow. And I'm not, like, asking you. You fuckin' *need* to do this."

Richard waited as a momentary rage ruffled through him. Then, calmly, he answered. "I'll call her tomorrow. I'll go as soon as I can get an appointment."

"Good boy."

"What's the second thing?"

"Ah need you to promise me you won't quit until this thing is over. We got to get Mikael back and get Kat's case sorted out. You gotta hang in there until that's done. And then, if you wanna go off on your own after that...well, that would be a bummer, but Ah'll support ya. But not fuckin *now*, you hear me?"

"But I'm fucking everything—"

"Fuck you, asshole. This isn't about you. It's about Mikael an' Kat an' her family. It is not about you and your angsty ass feeling sorry for yerself. Ah don't care how bad you think you're fucking it up, you are gonna stay here until the job is done. You get me, motherfucker?"

Richard was staring straight ahead. Dylan was sure he had dissociated, so he reached over and, putting a hand on his neck, pulled him over so that their heads touched.

"Got it?" he said again.

"Got..." but Richard trailed off as his throat swelled again.

Dylan reached out and took the flask from him. He stood. "Ah'm gonna head for bed, dude. You should, too. We'll get a fresh start on things tomorrah. It'll be different. You'll see." Then he turned and headed back into the house.

33

LARCH DRUMMED his fingers on the arm of an overstuffed and threadbare chair as he considered his companions.

"So, what you're telling me is, you lost him," he finished Charybdis's sentence.

"We *had* him," Charybdis said sheepishly. The diminutive magickian looked at the bookshelf, at his shoes, anywhere but at Larch. "But then we lost him."

"It was an excellent plan, Frater," Frater Purderabo volunteered. "It should have worked. We had the man on a gurney and halfway to the exit before he—"

"Before he *what*?" Larch asked.

Turpelo swallowed. "Before he waxed ithyphallic and began screaming bloody murder."

"Are you saying you were foiled by Randall's raging erection?" Larch's eyes narrowed.

"Pardon my obfuscating turn of phrase. No, sir, I mean he sat bolt-upright before he began to assault our eardrums."

"And do you know *why* he chose that exact moment to *spring* out of his coma?" Larch closed his eyes, struggling to maintain his composure.

Frater Eleazar raised his hand. "There was a monk and a woman. He came into Randy's—"

"Magickal names, please!"

"Fine—into Frater Benedict's room just as I was gathering his stuff together. I jumped in the bed and pretended to be asleep." He leaned in and whispered. "I think they thought I was *him*."

"A monk, you said."

"Yeah."

Larch rolled his eyes and sighed. "Describe this...monk."

"I don't know," Frater Eleazar said, looking at the ceiling. "Tall, tall as you. Brown hair, balding, kind of Irish looking. Looked like a nice guy."

Larch continued to drum his fingers. He did not own a gun, but the fantasy of pulling one out and blowing a hole in any one of his brothers at this moment was an enormously satisfying one. "He *is* a nice guy," Larch said. "And obviously much smarter than the lot of you."

He rose and paced to the window. When he spoke again, it was with his back turned to them. "Get out of my sight, all of you. I'm disgusted with you."

"But Frater Khams is making bean dip," Frater Charybdis protested.

"Out!" he said, without turning around.

Out of the corner of his eye, he could see them rise, heads hung low in shame, tottering to the kitchen to put things away. He closed his eyes and breathed deeply, counting to seventy-five.

The doorbell rang. Larch glanced at his watch. *Who the fuck could that be?* he thought. *It's nearly eleven.*

Most of the brothers were filing downstairs, but just as the last of them descended out of sight, Frater Charybdis emerged again with a stranger in tow.

He was tall, lithe, and carried himself with an arrogant and exaggerated grace that was just a tad bit fey. He was also handsome enough to be a model—with sculptured cheekbones and wavy black hair that seemed to defy gravity.

He was also young. About half Larch's own age, he estimated, and yet he carried himself with an authority far beyond his years. An authority, Larch guessed, that was purchased rather than earned.

"I'm so sorry to have disturbed your evening," the young man said, offering his hand. "I am Alan Dane."

"Dane?" Larch looked at him again. "Of the San Francisco Danes?"

"The same. May I have a seat?" He looked at the seating options and seemed to have immediately regretted his request, but Larch waved him into one of the less objectionable options and took his regular chair for himself.

"Well, I'm delighted to meet you, Mr. Dane," Larch managed a smile. "To what do I owe this pleasure?"

"I understand you and your...friends"—he smiled, apparently realizing he was ignorant of the proper nomenclature among magickians—"have succeeded in a most ambitious feat."

"What feat would that be?" Larch stopped smiling.

"A feat that resulted in the disappearance of a large amount of fruit."

"It could be that you heard something of the sort," Larch said cautiously. "But from where?"

Dane smiled. "Let us just say a little bird told me."

"A bird?"

"Yes. A bird named *Articiphus*."

Larch's mouth sprang open, and he felt a little queasy. In a few moments, the initial shock had passed, and the ability to speak English was restored to him. "Articiphus—the *demon* Articiphus—told you about what we have done?"

"He did." A bored smugness settled over Dane's face, but it was so obviously affected that instead of inspiring awe, it only made Larch angry. Still, he was confounded, not at all clear on the powers or the dangers of the man before him. "I find that...extraordinary, Mr. Dane. But I am unclear why it should interest you."

"Oh, but I am very interested indeed. You see, I have dedicated my life to a philanthropic endeavor that I have assiduously pursued in my own small way, saving one life at a time. Your...experiment has inspired me. With your assistance, I see the promise of helping millions."

"That's very noble, Mr. Dane, but we are committed to our own project of...world change."

Dane grinned. "I love a good game of dueling euphemisms, don't you? I suggest that our ends are not mutually exclusive and that by advancing my agenda, you may advance your own." Dane looked down at his hands, a minute dropping of the guard, an intimation of confidence. "Of course, I have no way of knowing what your ends are, but I would not be surprised if they might not be easier to achieve with some funds at your disposal. I dare say your...headquarters, or whatever you call this place, could use some work." He glanced up at Larch. "No offense intended, I assure you."

Dane rose and sauntered over to the bookshelf, feigning interest in the titles. "What I am suggesting, Mr. Larch, is becoming your patron. Magickians often had patrons in ages past, no? They did work of interest to the patron, but the support also allowed them to pursue their own research as well, isn't that right?"

Larch hated himself for it, but he was interested. Very interested. Many of his brothers were, indeed, very concerned about the state of the Lodge house, and certainly they would advance their work much more quickly if they could dispense with their day jobs. Larch rose and joined Dane by the bookcase. "Just what sort of patronage are we discussing? I mean, in dollar amounts?"

"I suggest 100,000 dollars for three months, with an option to renew for the same amount at the end of that time."

Larch nodded. "And what sort of...work would you like us to pursue?"

Dane smiled a satisfied smile. "Well, fruit is all well and good, but I'd like to make something a little larger disappear." He held up a cautious hand. "But I want to make sure we get it right. I suggest another experiment."

Larch nodded. "Yes, just what we were planning. Perhaps our goals are compatible after all. Suppose we try something...a little larger?"

34

SUSAN SURFACED from the soft sea of sleep to the bouncing of the mattress. Dylan was snoring beside her, and she rolled over to make room for Tobias, who often climbed up on their bed in the middle of the night to claim his favorite spot between them.

She was about to drift off again when she noticed the reek of whiskey. A little startled, she wondered how Tobias had gotten into the liquor, and she turned on her bedside light.

There, nestling into the space between her and her husband, was Richard, fully clothed and apparently drunk into near oblivion. She reached over him and tapped her husband on the head until he opened an eye. Dylan didn't move, but his eye rolled about, taking in the situation.

Richard turned, threw an arm over Susan's waist, and leaned his head on Dylan's chest. Dylan looked up at his wife and chuckled. "Ah guess a little guy just needs some snuggles sometimes."

Susan put her hand to her mouth to stifle a chuckle of her own. "Oh, Richard. You really *do* need someone to hold you right now, don't you?" She looked at her husband again. "What should we do?"

"Ah think we should turn off the light and go to sleep."

"And Richard?"

"So long as he doesn't puke in our bed, Ah'm good."

Susan's face registered a complex mixture of pity, worry, and incredulity. Then, it resolved into compassion as she leaned down and kissed Richard on the top of his head. She did the same for her husband, turned off the light, and pulling Richard's hand closer into her tummy, went back to sleep.

SUNDAY

35

THE NEXT DAY, Kat joined the friars for Sunday morning mass. She seemed grim and distant but there just the same. Dylan didn't think it was a particularly inspiring service but reminded himself that they all had a lot on their minds.

As soon as the service ended, Brian came to the door to announce that breakfast was served. Except for some quiet grunting, few words were spoken until they were all seated.

Brian placed a large steaming bowl of scrambled eggs on the lazy Susan before them, followed by a tray of still-sizzling bacon. Biscuits followed, with apple butter and honey in small matching bowls.

The sight of such beautiful food had an analgesic and enlivening effect on the whole house, and even Tobias begged with renewed vigor.

"Susan," said Terry, his mouth full of biscuit, "have you had a chance to look at that flash drive?"

"Yeah. You've got a couple of articles by that Larch guy—actually fascinating stuff, although it looks like he's still working on them—on chaos magick and Whiteheadian process theism."

"Really?" Richard's first word of the morning. "Can you print that out for me?"

"Good morning, sleepyhead. Welcome to the conversation! Yes, of course I will."

"What else? Was the roster intact?"

"Yes," said Susan, selecting a piece of bacon. "Only five names, though. Still, it's something to start with."

"Hey..." Kat was staring into space but waving her hand for attention.

"What's up?" asked Dylan, scooping a mountain of eggs onto his plate. He made to scoop another spoonful, but Brian reached over and slapped his hand.

"I had this dream..." she scowled, trying to bring it back up.

"Is this a *Dream* dream, or just a dream?" Susan asked, guardedly.

"I'm not sure. I was in a field, and there were lots of holes in the ground—snake holes. And I was digging them up, because there was treasure buried in them."

"The group your brother belonged to was the Lodge of the Hawk and Serpent," Richard offered.

Susan blinked. "Maybe we should be looking for treasure!" She giggled, and then stopped mid-gig. "Wait, maybe we really should be looking for...money?"

"What good would that do?" asked Brian.

"Well, we don't know what the Lodge is up to," Susan thought out loud.

"We know they have it in for God," Richard interrupted and related some of the cryptic conversation he had had with Larch.

"Well, *lots* of people have it in for God," Susan noted, "but we still don't know *why* they were willing to do something so dangerous in order to rid the world of avocados. It seems so senseless."

"Larch made out that it was an experiment."

"Okay, so what are they *really* trying to accomplish?" Susan asked. "What are they going to do when they're *not* experimenting? What is the real thing?"

"You mean, what's gonna happen when it's not about avocados?" Dylan interjected.

"Exactly," Susan nodded slowly.

Richard's head swam with momentary vertigo.

"Wait, I'm still lost," Terry was shaking his head. "What's that got to do with money?"

"Well, I don't know," Susan said, "but let's see if they're working alone or with someone else. If they're working on someone's behalf, I'll bet there's money involved. If we can figure out who that is, we might have another clue as to what they're up to." She looked at Richard for approval.

He was staring off into space, thinking. Then he noticed them all staring at him. "Uh, yeah, good idea. Let's do it."

They looked at each other, a little worried. Dylan muttered an "Okay..." obviously disturbed at how much wind had gone out of Richard's sails.

"So...assignments?" asked Terry, prompting Richard.

Richard shook his head to clear it. "Right. Well, obviously, Susan should get to work on the money thing—"

"I can help," Kat said. "I used to work for Wells Fargo's online banking department."

"No shit," said Richard, impressed. "Okay, the rest of us...the rest of us...um, Terry, why don't you work with the angel, and see what you can figure out. I'll do some research on the sigil we found at Randy's place—see what we can find out about the demon he employed to make the body switch."

"And me and Brian?" asked Dylan.

"We need groceries," Brian said, "and need I remind you, I don't drive."

Richard smiled weakly, "Well, you can't feed an army without food. Grocery shopping it is. Any objections?"

Dylan scowled at him, but said nothing.

"Don't take it so hard, Boobie," Brian said, kissing Dylan on his bald spot. "I'll get you ice cream while we're out."

In spite of the teasingly patronizing nature of the remark, Dylan brightened.

"That's my man," Susan said, patting his hand as she rose from the table. "Let's get to work," she said.

36

Bishop Tom lazed in the shower longer than he normally did. Sleep had proved evasive last night, and he was having a devil of a time waking up. Every time it seemed he might drift off, his thought returned to that damnable FedEx package and the fate of his friars hanging on the whim of Andrus Mellert.

Mellert was a good man. Quiet, but even. Tom had never felt much affection for him, but he liked him well enough. He was a moderate, dismissive neither of tradition nor of the novel pastoral situations that were presenting themselves of late.

Tom tried to trust Mellert. He tried to trust God. In the end, though, he had to admit that he just wasn't feeling that *trusting*.

Clad only in his bathrobe, he padded along the linoleum hallway back to his cell, his slim toiletries case in hand. He fished in it for his key and opened the door.

Then he grinned. For there, in his path, was a FexEd package. He picked it up and shut the door behind him. A Post-it note was stuck to the underside, reading, "I prayed. No answer. You decide. —A.M."

Tom felt the anxiety rush out of him. He hugged the package to his chest and exhaled two great lungfuls of pent-up angst. Then he threw the package on his tiny desk and set about dressing for breakfast and morning mass, feeling for all the world like he had just dodged a bullet.

37

TERRY PEERED in the door of the guest room and saw the body of Randall Webber resting quietly. He pushed the door open wide and, entering the room, placed a small stack of books on the floor near the bed. Then he opened the blinds and the two windows overlooking the fruit trees that adorned the backyard.

The guest room was small but comfortable. Webber lay on a twin-size bed, a wine-crate nightstand beside him. Terry picked up a glass of water from the night table and carried it down the narrow, winding hallway to the bathroom, where he emptied it and filled it again with fresh water. Then, taking a bottle from the medicine cabinet, he went back to where the sleeping angel lay.

He placed the water glass on the nightstand and removed two of the small orange pills from the bottle. With his thumbnail, he crushed the tablets on the nightstand, and then carefully transferred the powder to the water glass using his fingers. He cursed himself momentarily for not doing this more scientifically, with a mortar and pestle and warm water, but he was too busy to indulge himself. The powder dissolved into the water readily enough despite its temperature, and Terry lifted the glass to the magickian's lips and slowly and carefully emptied it.

Checking his watch, he noted the time and went to the bathroom, both to have his requisite morning shit and to kill some time. Having finished, and read several pages of the current *Christian Century*, Terry returned to the room. Satisfied that nothing had changed, he sat down on an empty space near the foot of the bed. Tobias passed in the hall then doubled back and sniffed at Terry.

"This is likely to be scary, Toby. Better go downstairs."

Tobias panted and licked at Terry's hand. "Go, get!" Terry said, more emphatically. That, Tobias understood, and he dutifully made his way out of the room. In moments, Terry heard the clack of his nails on the back stairs.

Terry sat for several minutes centering himself. He watched the trees out the window sway lazily against the bleak gray sky of the Berkeley winter.

It had been twenty minutes since he had given the magickian the Valium. He waited a few more minutes just to be on the safe side. Ten milligrams of Valium was nothing to sneeze at, but he wanted to make sure the drug was at its optimum power before taking any action.

At the half-hour mark, Terry sucked in his breath. "Okay, here goes." He reached through the slit in his cassock and pulled a pair of foam earplugs out of his pants pocket. Fitting them in his ears, he shut his eyes and reached out in his mind's eye toward the strong, brightly luminous violet ball before him. As he had already done several times, he carefully connected the energy source—the soul of the angel—to the central nervous system of the magickian.

Once again, the result was immediate, and violent. The mouth of the magickian opened wide, and a wail fit to wake the dead filled the air.

DOWNSTAIRS, Susan looked up at the sound of it. "Houston, we have contact," she said. Then she reached out and touched Kat lightly on the cheek. "Stay here," she said, reading Kat's body language. Kat was poised to rush upstairs, to comfort, to protect, to...just *be* there. "We have work to do here, and he's in good hands with Terry. Besides, Terry needs time and space to work with him without...well, distraction." Her look was apologetic, but Kat understood. Just then, Tobias, who had been licking himself by the back door, lifted his head and howled in sympathy.

Susan laughed at the cacophony and squeezed Kat's shoulder. Blinking back tears, Kat returned her gaze to the computer screen. Susan knew she was only faking paying attention to what she was doing, but it was all right; she would be able to focus again eventually, Susan was sure. With another glance toward the ceiling, she looked again at her own screen.

TERRY GRITTED his teeth and waited out the scream. It was a formidable howl, and despite the earplugs, painful. But Terry knew that what he was feeling was nothing compared to the pain the angel was experiencing. He was sure that the magickian had had trouble adjusting to the angel's subtle body, and it would have been very uncomfortable indeed, but it was nothing compared to the anguish this angel must be experiencing trying to interface with such a gross, heavy, and lethargic body as humans have. Terry imagined it must be like performing surgery with sandpaper instead of a scalpel. The analogy made him cringe, but to hear the angel's howl, he imagined it was apt.

After about five minutes, Terry saw the bunched muscles of the angel's neck relax, and the howl softened into a painful moan. Terry moved closer to the magickian's body and felt his forehead, now red with exertion. At his touch, the moan relented momentarily. Terry cocked his head and touched him again, this time running his fingers around his face. The eyes blinked open, and the angel worked at the unfamiliar mouth, smacking and swallowing at nothing perceptible. As soon as Terry withdrew his fingers, the moaning increased. Terry kept one hand running around the outlines of Randall's face and with the other speed dialed Richard on his cell phone. "Hey, Dicky. I'm making progress."

"Yeah, well, the foundations of the house aren't rattling anymore —I'd call that an improvement."

"Listen, can you bring me some things up here? I need to stay in physical contact with him to keep him calm."

"Okay, what do you need?" Richard said, already climbing the stairs out of the basement library.

In moments, Richard appeared at the doorway, carrying a tray laden with hand towels, a bowl of hot water drawn from the tap, and a glass of orange juice.

Terry cleared the nightstand and motioned for him to set the tray down. "Need me to stay?" Richard asked.

"Probably a good idea, just in case he lashes out."

"I'm sorry I didn't think to come up sooner—"

"It's okay; I didn't think of it either. But I'm glad you're here." He smiled at his superior. "Look, as long as I'm touching his face, he's calmer. Can you wet one of those hand towels?"

Richard did and handed it to him. Terry laid it like a wreath around the angel's face. At the touch of the moist, hot fabric, the angel stopped moaning altogether and smacked his lips again.

Gingerly, Terry placed the glass of orange juice to the angel's lips. At the first taste of the sweet, tart liquid, his eyes opened wide, and his lips extended almost comically toward the rim of the glass. Terry stifled a laugh and helped the angel drain the glass.

Terry handed the glass back to Richard. "Let's bring the whole bottle up. Looks like he's thirsty."

"Or he's just never experienced the nutritious goodness of California Sunshine-brand orange juice."

"That, too," Terry grinned.

Richard sat in awe of what was before him until Terry broke his reverie. "Orange juice, Honey Pie, chop chop!"

"Oh, sorry," Richard jumped up.

"And grab my laptop while you're down there!" Terry called after him.

In a minute or so, Richard returned with the jug of orange juice in one hand and the laptop in the other.

"Can you set up and transcribe?" Terry asked.

Richard nodded and planted himself in the room's only chair, opening the laptop and creating a new file.

Terry continued to bathe the magickian's face in warm water. The angel smacked his lips and made small whimpering noises.

"Hey, I'd like to talk to you," Terry said softly to the angel. "Can you understand me?"

The angel smacked his lips but otherwise did not reply. The magickian's eyes did not focus on him but stared straight ahead.

"It looks like he's blind," Richard noted.

Terry nodded and, concentrating, closed his own eyes and made his way into the ball of purple light in his imagination. Summoning it, he led the light to the optic nerves of the magickian's body. Briefly, Terry told Richard what he was doing. "It's not like I'm connecting him to the eyes but pointing out a connection that he hadn't noticed yet."

"Got it," said Richard, typing furiously.

Terry knew he had been successful when the angel gasped and his whole body jerked. Terry opened his eyes, and locked them on the magickian's. There was light in them now, and they were flitting back and forth in a panicked, desperate manner.

"It's okay," Terry said soothingly. "You're safe here. The body you're in was the one made for Adam. It is a Good Thing. You just have to get used to it." He smiled at the angel, and his eyes softened with compassion. "You don't understand a damned thing I'm saying, do you?" The angel's eyes were wide and frightened.

"Okay, I'm a little rusty, but it's time to break out the Enochian." Terry reached for a book on the floor, where he had marked several pages with Post-its.

"*Ulcinin aaoim Enoy Heripsol*," he said in passable Enochian. "Greetings, Lord of Heaven."

The angel jerked his head at the words. Apparently, he had found the nerves to his ears on his own. "*Quiin zirdo?*"

"He wants to know where he is," Terry said. "*Caosg*," he told him, "On the Earth."

The angel looked around him, a little puzzled. He spoke a few words quietly in Enochian. Terry laughed.

"What did he say?" asked Richard.

"He said that Earth is small." Terry pointed to the window above the angel's head, where a strip of gray sky was visible. The magickian's mouth gaped in the angel's wonder. The angel spoke again.

"He says he never thought he'd see it—the Earth, I think he means."

The angel then began speaking a long, fast string of words.

"*Ge mel-f,*" Terry laughed. "I'm telling him to slow it down—I can't translate that fast. Besides, I have to look up a lot of words."

The angel spoke more deliberately, using fewer words and shorter sentences.

"He's asking why he's here," Terry's mouth tightened, not sure how to answer him.

"Just tell him," said Richard. "Anything he can tell us can help."

"Okay, here goes." In halting Enochian, Terry related their adventure thus far—what they had discovered about the demon magick Randall Webber had been involved in, the switching of their bodies, and the magickian's sojourn in Heaven, culminating in the sudden disappearance of the world's avocados.

The magickian's eyes widened as the angel registered what had happened to him, and the minor but significant evil perpetrated on the world.

Terry couldn't think of a time when he had witnessed such acute sorrow. For not knowing how to work the body of flesh, the angel was proving to be a fast learner.

The angel spoke again, in a voice so sad, Terry had to pause to appreciate the pathos. "He wants to know if he is our prisoner." Terry met Richard's eyes, which were wet with emotion.

"No, Honey. *Ag. Ag. Rit nonca. Gil zacam noncf, aala eoan ofekufa Peripsol.*" Terry sighed. "I told him we saved him, and we want to help him get home, and back into his own body, back to Heaven."

"Can you ask him if he can help?" asked Richard.

"How?"

"Well, is he trapped in the body, or can he extricate himself from it and, you know, roam around?"

Terry's brow furrowed, but he put the question to the angel in halting Enochian. The answer, when it came, was long and full of digressions.

"Well, I'm not going to translate all of that, but the upshot is 'no.' All creatures, even spiritual creatures, need a body as a vehicle for consciousness. He would need his angelic body to move around unseen on this plane. He's stuck, I'm afraid."

Richard nodded. "Is he in pain?"

Terry asked the question. "Like you wouldn't believe," he said, grimacing. "But it's better. I think it's just a matter of adjustment."

"Does he have access to Randall's memories?"

Terry's eyebrows shot up, but he asked just the same. "He doesn't know," he answered after the two had conversed for a while in Enochian, "but he's going to root around and see if he can find them. Personally, I think they're there, he just has to figure out how to open the filing cabinets in the old cabeza."

"Will he want to see Kat?"

"Why would he want to see Kat? He's never met Kat."

Richard nodded. Of course he hadn't. "But would Kat want to see him?"

"Okay, but let's make it a short visit. I think he ought to rest soon."

Richard nodded and headed downstairs. In a couple of minutes, he had both Kat and Susan in tow.

Kat was barely holding back tears. When she saw the angel sitting up in her brother's body, saw the light in her brother's eyes, heard the voice from his mouth, she cried out with relief. With tears streaming down her cheeks, she fell upon the bed and pressed her breast to her brother's.

The angel started and gasped. Terry touched her shoulder and gently pushed her back. "Honey, it's your brother's body but not his spirit. The consciousness behind the machine doesn't know you. He's friendly, but he's not your brother."

Kat blinked back tears and sniffed. "I know that. I know that. I'm just...He's alive."

"Yes, he's fine," Terry said.

"Oh, Terry, thank you!" she said, hugging him across the bed.

"Shucks, ma'am, all in a day's work." He winked at Susan and Richard.

Then, unexpectedly, the angel's eyes began flitting back and forth. He spoke excitedly in Enochian.

"Wait up, gang. It seems that seeing Kat has triggered something. He thinks it's Randall's memories. This is a really good sign!" Terry listened for a while and turned to Kat, smiling.

"He says he remembers a time when you were fighting. There was snow on the ground. You were being mean to him. He wants to know if you remember how he got revenge."

"Damn straight," Kat, said, overjoyed. "He peed all over my stuffed animals!" She laughed aloud, both at the memory and with heartfelt relief.

Terry noted that even the angel was smiling. The angel said something else and smacked his lips. "He says that peeing is going to be strange if Randall's memories of it are any indication. But he's figuring he'll need to soon because he wants more orange juice." Richard poured him another glass and handed it to Terry, who held it to Webber's lips to the angel's obvious delight.

"Did you ask him why he did it?" asked Kat. "Did you ask him why Randall made the avocados disappear?"

"He didn't have access to his memories before he saw you, but we can ask him now." He did.

The angel thought for a few minutes, and then his face screwed up into a defiant scowl. His answer was angry, filled with short, staccato syllables.

"Holy shit," Terry said, the blood draining from his face as he listened.

"What is it? What is he saying?" asked Richard.

"Well, as we found out from the lodge, the avocado was just a test. There's something bigger afoot."

"And that is?" Susan prompted.

Terry gulped. "The overthrow of Heaven."

38

THE MORNING SYNOD meeting was duller than Bishop Tom had feared. The last discussion before the break for lunch concerned educational requirements, the exceptions to those requirements, and who got to say who would be accepted and why. Tom was powerfully tempted to remove his socks and, using them as puppets, perform parodies of the seemingly endless and inane discussions.

Eventually, Bishop Mellert threw in the towel and rose, offering a prayer for their meal, and the bishops scattered as if fleeing a sinking vessel.

Very quickly after eating, Tom felt the inevitable tug of afternoon gravity, measurably two or three times as strong as other times of the day. He glanced at his watch and estimated he could get in a thirty-minute power nap before the afternoon session commenced.

He set out immediately for his room, taking the stairs in great, loping strides, two at a time.

He was halfway up when a voice called to him from below. "Oh, Tom!"

Tom groaned inwardly. He could tell by the voice that it was Bishop Demitrio, an oily Greek suffragan bishop from Idaho, unemployed and living in his mother's basement. He was at synod sitting in for Bishop Maggie Tills, who was, God willing, giving birth to healthy twins any moment.

The problem with Bishop Demitrio wasn't the viscosity of his hair, however, but the glacial pace with which his conversations inevitably unfolded. "Demi, hey, can this wait?"

Bishop Demitrio seemed flustered, and he glanced at the top of the stairs nervously. "Not really, no," he said.

Tom groaned and resentfully descended the stairs, one at a time. "What's so important it can't wait a half hour?"

"Well, as you know—as I'm sure you do, most of us do, although it is interesting—I was talking to Van Patton and she didn't know, which surprised me, because you know, she always seems so...on top of everything, you know what I mean? Maybe you don't. Well, there was that time in Springfield when she was absolutely clueless. All of the rest of us knew what was going on. That was the first gay vote, I believe, in 1999. You weren't there, I don't think, or were you? I can't recall. Anyway, Van Patton—"

Tom's head was spinning already, trying against all odds to hold on to the original topic of Demitrio's monologue. "Wait! Demitrio, wait! Listen to me. I have to take one powerful shit, and if you don't get to your point pronto, I'm going to deposit my offering at your feet. You have thirty seconds. Go."

"Oh," the little man seemed genuinely lost. He looked toward Heaven, and, seemingly seeing written in the air his original point, began little hopping motions as he spoke in staccato syllables. "Mellert's term is up at our next synod, and we ought to get him something nice."

Tom's eyes darkened. "Isn't this something that could be handled by email?"

Demitrio looked at his pigeon-toed feet. "Yes, it could. But Mother turned off my DSL."

"Put me down for fifty dollars, whatever you decide get him," Tom said, heading to the stairs. "And now I'm going to take my nap."

"I thought you were going to take a shit," Demitrio called after him. "Uh, Tom..."

"You could use a loudspeaker next time," Tom called over his shoulder, ignoring his further entreaty. In mere moments, he had gained the second floor and was headed toward his room.

He stopped a few feet shy of his door. It was slightly ajar. Cautiously he advanced, and as he got closer, he could see that the wood around the lock was splintered. He pushed the door open and gasped. His suitcase was thrown into a corner, and his clothes were scattered across the floor. His papers, once piled neatly on the desk, seemed tossed to the wind, and covered every surface of the room.

Panic swelled in his chest, and his heart beat so hard it hurt. Frantically, he began sorting through the papers. He looked under everything that wasn't bolted to the floor, to no avail. The FedEx package was gone.

39

BRIAN AND DYLAN returned from their shopping shortly after noon, and Brian quickly had sandwiches made, and lemonade on the table.

Richard filled them in on the progress Terry had made with the angel, and despite the sense of gloom they had all felt since Mikael's abduction, a light and hopeful mood permeated the kitchen. The sun had finally burned through the morning fog, and light poured from the window above the wide double sink.

Dylan sat at the table with a loud "oaf" of relief. Terry joined them momentarily, and Brian whistled for the women to join them. Susan and Kat emerged from the office with Cheshire catlike grins on their faces. Kat was still elated and relieved about the well-being of her brother's physical body, but it was clear something else was up.

After a quick blessing over the food, Dylan, knowing his wife well, nudged her. "Okay, li'l lamb, spill it."

"Did you find something?" asked Terry, reaching for mustard and slathering his sandwich with it.

Brian watched him with disdain. "You're not going to taste anything but fucking mustard!" he complained.

"I like fucking mustard!" Terry winked at him. "That'll be my new nickname for you."

"We found it," said Kat.

"Found what?" asked Richard.

"We found a money trail," Kat elaborated.

"Well, we actually found a couple of them," Susan added. "And you're not going to believe where they're coming from."

"Try me," said Richard.

"First, we looked for a lodge account. No dice, not with any of the major banks, anyway."

"Was...this all legal?" asked Dylan.

Susan ignored him. "So then we started looking at private accounts. Those guys are either working under assumed names, or they are as poor as church mice."

"You mean Satanic temple mice," Terry corrected.

"They're not Satanists," Richard said with a slight note of exasperation.

"Do Satanic temples even have mice?" Dylan asked Terry, ignoring Richard.

"Bats. I think they'd have bats."

"Go on..." Richard encouraged Susan.

"So, I went back to the flash drive. I found a spreadsheet that very conveniently listed an account number. We traced it to a free business account from Providence Savings and Loan. *That* account just had a major influx of cash that posted at 10 a.m. this morning, to the tune of $100,000."

"Holy Christ," Richard whistled. "That's a small fortune for guys like that."

"That'd be a small fortune for *us*," Dylan added.

"We *are* guys like that," Terry admitted.

"Okay, so our suspicion was right," Richard thought out loud. "This isn't entirely the Lodge of the Hawk and Serpent's doing—they have a confederate. The question that strikes me is whether what the client is after is the same as what the lodge is after."

"Do yah mean we maybe should just step back and wait for them to duke it out among themselves?" asked Dylan.

"No, their purposes would have to be congruent up to a point. Susan, who is it? Who is their funder?"

"Well, the deposit was made from Cougar Properties in El Cerrito, which is owned by—are you ready for this?"

"Just fucking spill it, Honey," said Terry, wiping his mustard-stained hands on his napkin.

"Alan Dane."

"You're shitting me," said Richard, the color draining from his face.

"Hey, Dicky," Terry asked, his face contorting comically, "when you were sucking his cock at the Jizz Factory, did you think to ask him whether he was planning a coup in Heaven?"

Richard's color returned, and then some.

"That was mean," Dylan said.

"I *can* be a catty bitch on occasion," Terry said, reaching for the chips. "Sorry, Dicky, I couldn't help myself."

Kat had known nothing about Richard and Dane's sexual encounter, and her eyes were wide. Richard noticed. "I didn't know him from Adam. And it was months ago."

"What's the Jizz Factory?" asked Kat.

"It's a gay sex club here in Berkeley," Susan answered.

"AIDS factory is more like it," Terry said, a note of anger entering his voice. "You sure as shit have better been using protection—"

"All right, calm down," said Richard, now completely flushed with shame. "Of course I was careful. I'm always careful."

"Going to a sex club is never my definition of careful," Terry added.

"Did Philip know about this?" Susan asked.

"We went together," Richard said.

She looked horrified. "I will *never* understand gay men."

"That makes two of us, Sweetie," said Brian, rising to get a bowl of fruit for dessert.

"Can we get back on task?" asked Richard.

"Oh, by all fucking means," answered Terry, still miffed.

"Dane is a businessman. What kind of business would he have with the lodge? Where do their interests intersect?" Richard mused.

"Maybe he's a magickian," Kat suggested.

"Maybe," said Terry, "but we've never heard of him in occult circles, and we've heard of most of the serious practitioners in these parts."

"Mebbe he's taken out a huge insurance policy on his family's avocado plantations?" Dylan offered.

"Good, that's good," Richard said. "Susan, can you check out the kind of businesses they own?"

"Will do," said Susan, reaching for a pear. She leaned toward her husband. "Split this with me?" He nodded.

"Here's what I'm thinking." Richard steepled his index fingers. "Dane is using the lodge, and the lodge is using Dane. It's a marriage of convenience at the moment, but I wouldn't be surprised if they clash somewhere down the road."

"What makes you think that will happen?" asked Kat.

"Because, Honey"—said Terry, getting up from the table—"We know occultists. You get two of them in a room, and you've got three opinions, and they'll both end up psychically attacking each other before the evening's done. They're like fucking wolves."

"That's not exactly fair," noted Dylan.

"It's pretty fucking accurate from what I've seen," said Richard, "and I've been friends with occultists for a very long time."

"We all have," said Terry. "It's true."

"Hey, Independent Catholics are no better," Dylan pointed out.

"Well, at least we don't throw demons at each other," Terry protested.

"Nah, we just *pray* for each other," Dylan answered.

"In other words, we throw angels?" Terry smiled. "Hey, if I had to have my choice which one I'd have lobbed at me..."

"Ah heard that," Dylan said.

"So, anyone up for hearing about the other major payment we found?" Susan teased.

"Ah can't wait," Dylan said.

"Are you all sitting down?" Susan said. Anyone could plainly see that they were, but her words had the intended effect. Richard braced himself for the news. "Last night at 6 p.m. a payment for $20,000 was posted from the Cougar Properties account into the private checking account of a Mr. Casey Hammet in South Fork, Texas."

"Fucking A," Terry breathed. "Bishop Hammet is in Dane's pocket!"

"He already has it in for us," Richard noted. "But with Dane's resources at his disposal..." his voice trailed off.

Silence reigned for several minutes. Finally, Dylan completed the sentence. "We're toast."

"Toast," said several voices together, almost liturgically.

"So, what are we going to do?" Susan asked. She looked at Richard. They all did.

He momentarily shrank back but then he raised his head and squared his shoulders. "This has gotten personal, folks. I think it's time to see what Dane is really up to. Who's up for breaking and entering?"

40

BISHOP TOM SAT rigid through the afternoon session; his jaw was set tight and anger burned in his eyes. For most of the afternoon, he simply glared at Bishop Hammet, barely noticing the business at hand as the excruciating minutiae rolled on hour after merciless hour.

If Hammet noticed his staring, he made no show of it. Instead, the Texan bishop appeared relaxed, cooler than the stuffy room allowed, exhibiting the almost superhuman grace known only to those who possess great power.

Tom did note, however, that, in contrast to Hammet, Presiding Bishop Mellert seemed scattered and unnerved. He, too, seemed to be glaring at the Texan prelate, and the possibility formed in Tom's mind that, perhaps, his room had not been the only one ransacked.

At around 3:30, the current business was wrapped up, and the time had finally arrived. "Bishop Hammet," the presiding bishop said in a careful, deliberately even tone, "You may now present your...*evidence*..." he spoke the word with obvious venom, "against the Order of Saint Raphael."

Bishop Tom could see that many other bishops were suddenly

looking more awake and interested. Bishop Hammet rose and addressed his fellow bishops in a commanding tone. "The day before yesterday, Bishop Stolte quoted our Lord as saying that 'A house divided against itself cannot stand,' and I agree with a whole heart. My brother bishops, we cannot abide in a church where the friends of God and the enemies of God both dwell. 'What has light to do with darkness?' asked Saint Paul, and I ask you the same question. How can we allow a so-called religious order to exist within our fold when it is made up of drug addicts, faggots, and Satanists? We cannot!"

Bishop Stolte spoke out of turn. "And just what evidence do you have against these friars, Casey?"

"As to the charge that they are drug addicts, I present these photos." He passed a stack of 8x10 glossies around the room. In that moment, all of Tom's worst suspicions were confirmed. Those photos had been in the FedEx package.

"In this photo," Hammet continued, "you will see one Fr. Dylan Melanchthon, whom I understand to be the sub-prior. As you can see, he is walking into the so-called Compassionate Care Club in Berkeley, California."

"What is Compassionate Care Club?" asked Bishop Van Patton.

"It is, dear lady," Bishop Hammet acknowledged her existence, perhaps publicly for the first time since her consecration, "a euphemistic phrase indicating a marijuana dispensary, allegedly set up for medical patients." He handed around another stack of photos. "In this next photo, you can see him walking out of the club, shame-lessly dressed in full habit, with a brown paper bag containing his purchase. Please note the *size* of the paper bag."

Tom put his head in his hands and stifled the urge to moan.

"In this next photo, note the prior of the order walking into the Jizz Factory, a gay bathhouse, also in Berkeley, California. Note the time marks on the photos, gentlemen. Father Kinney was in that bathhouse for an hour and a half. What was he doing in there, do you think? Handing out condoms? Witnessing to the patrons, hoping to sway them from their reprobate urges? I think that unlikely. You all know what he was doing in there, and so do I, and it makes me sick. It should make you sick, too."

Bishop Tom barely glanced at the photos as they passed by him. He had seen them already. It was damning evidence, that was for sure, and he knew there was more of it coming.

"The worst of it, gentlemen, is this." He threw a stack of collated papers down in front of him and then handed half of it to each of the bishops to his left and right. "This is a record of selected postings to an online bulletin board specifically for Satanists. Do you see the 'handle' EnochianBitch on many of these pages, ?" He pronounced it with obvious distaste. "This handle belongs to Fr. Terry Milne, a half-breed Japanese. He is another member of this so-called order, who, by the way, lives in an open and unashamed relationship with another man, a Jewish man, besides, who shares his room at the friary."

Tom felt the urge to correct Hammet, to inform him that, actually, Terry and Brian inhabited a small cottage in the backyard, but as the information wouldn't do any good, he let it slide. Instead, Tom turned his attention to the stack of papers once it arrived in his lap.

"It's a lengthy discussion, so allow me to fill you in on the high-lights," Hammet said condescendingly. "In it, Father Milne is having a friendly discussion with an official of the Ordo Templi Orientis, a Satanic organization founded by that notorious enemy of the faith Aleister Crowley! As you can see, Father Milne is not trying to sway the OTO official from his error or trying to rescue anyone from the Satanist's attacks. In fact, far from it. If you will look at the high-lighted portion on page fourteen, you will see that Father Milne asks the Satanic official if he were free to come to the friary for dinner a week hence, and would he like to bring his girlfriend as well?"

He let that sink in and then continued. "On page twenty-five, Father Milne argues the veracity of a twelfth-century grimoire with a member of the Temple of Set, another Satanic organization. Note again the highlighted portion. Father Milne knows the grimoire is authentic because he has tried it, 'and the magick works.'"

Bishop Tom skipped to the page Hammet indicated and read for himself. It didn't *exactly* say that. EnochianBitch had written, *I've performed numerous experiments utilizing information from the grimoire, and it is my opinion that the magick will work.* Tom knew that "performing experiments" and "doing magick" were not precisely the same thing, and he trusted the friars were not, in fact, performing magick, black or any other variety. Still, he was not sure that he could make the subtle distinction clear to the assembly of bishops without sounding like he was splitting hairs.

But, it seemed, the time for considering his options was over. With a flourish, Bishop Hammet relinquished the floor and stared expectantly at the presiding bishop.

Mellert fixed Bishop Hammet with a steely gaze and spoke deliberately, his voice tinged with acid. "Leaving aside for the moment the question of how you came to possess this evidence—and I do mean *for the moment*—it is only fair that we hear the other side of the story. Bishop Müeller, as the person designated to provide episcopal oversight to the Order of Saint Raphael, how do you answer these charges?"

Tom felt a wave of dizziness pass over him as everyone in the room turned to him. Shaking, he rose to his feet. "Um...gentlemen... and ladies...I don't know what to say. I have visited the friary many times, and my opinion of the friars is that they are sincere servants of Jesus Christ." He looked at their faces and saw that they wanted more. But what to say? He ran his hand through his remaining hair and opened his mouth, hoping something intelligible would fall out.

"Do some of them have substance abuse problems? Sure. Half of the people in this room have, at one time or another." A rumble rippled through the assembly, and he saw a wry smile break out on Bishop Van Patton's face. Emboldened, he opened his mouth again, hoping for similar success.

"If Jesus didn't use sinners, there wouldn't be a church, and none of us would be sitting here. Now, about whether the friars are perverts, as Bishop Hammet calls them, I suppose that is a matter of opinion. Father Milne is gay and is in a monogamous, committed relationship with a Talmudic scholar, and yes, they live together on the friary grounds. Father Milne's partner is a part-time librarian at the Graduate Theological Union, and does much of the cooking for the order. I'll admit that his Turkish enchiladas are wicked, but he is not."

Tom picked up the picture of Richard going into the bathhouse. "This piece of evidence is circumstantial at best. I don't know exactly what Father Kinney was doing in that bathhouse. But let's say it is what you allege. I won't defend him. It is, at best, indiscreet. It is, at worst, self-destructive and sad. I don't condemn Father Kinney, but I do feel sorry for him. I feel sorry that he is so desperate for love and affection that he has to go to a place like this to get it. I do know that he struggles with his sexuality. I wish he loved and accepted himself enough to settle down with a partner as Father Terry has. But that is his path to walk, hard as it is, not mine. And not yours, either, Bishop Hammet."

Bishop Hammet opened his mouth to protest, but Tom was on a roll, and continued. "Now, let's consider this last bit of alleged evidence you've presented..." He paused. What *was* he going to say? He picked up the bulletin board log. "I'm afraid Bishop Hammet has fed this synod some misinformation that is unfairly coloring this material. The Ordo Templi Orientis is not a Satanic organization, as Bishop Hammet declares. It did not originate with Aleister Crowley but with a German lodge in the Masonic tradition, which Crowley happened to join. Do we have any Masons in our midst?"

No one volunteered any information. "Well, it is a secret organization, isn't it? I happen to know that several of you are Masons. I even know that one of the lady bishops in our midst is a Co-Mason. Now, did Crowley move the lodge away from the Masonic mainstream? Sure. Is it Satanic? It is not. Call it a mystery religion, call it Gnostic, call it a cult if you want to, but it is not Satanic. Father Milne has taught several classes at the OTO lodge in Oakland, one of them on biblical literacy. The order has friends in the OTO. Why should they not invite them to dinner? Have any of you ever been 'guilty' of being friends with Baptists? Ever invited a Jew for dinner? Have any relatives that are New Agers? Do you tell them they are not welcome at Christmas dinner?

"As for the correspondence with the gentleman from the Temple of Set, I see it as a cordial debate among scholars. I do not see how you can assert conclusively that Father Milne, or any of the friars, have been practicing magick. Only that experiments have been performed. I think it would be unwise for us to leap to any conclusions without consulting Father Milne further on the exact nature of these experiments."

"Thank you, Bishop Müeller—"

"Please, I'm not finished." No one had ever heard him speak this way before. He had always been such a lamb. Now, a bit of lion's mane was beginning to peek through the wool. "I'd like to ask a few questions of Bishop Hammet. What is the cause of this witch hunt, Bishop? What harm have my friars ever done to you? Is this your own initiative, or has someone put you up to it—perhaps someone for whom the Berkeley Blackfriars have become an inconvenience? What evil are you being unwitting party to, Bishop? And most of all, I would like to know how the good bishop came by his 'evidence.'"

The ball was in Bishop Hammet's court, and all eyes turned to him. Yes, the eyes seemed to say, *Why are you so interested in these friars? What is driving such an effort?*

Bishop Hammet tugged at his clerical collar in an attempt to loosen it. Then he poured himself a glass of water. After a leisurely sip or two, he set the glass down and responded cautiously. "A couple of months ago, one of our volunteers uncovered the bulletin board conversations. The photos...sort of fell into my lap, very recently."

"Bishop Hammet," Bishop Tom seethed, "didn't it occur to you that perhaps someone is out to get the friars? That you are most likely being used? That perhaps, we all are?"

A murmur unsettled the room, and the presiding bishop rose, looking at his watch. "As fascinated as I am personally with Bishop Hammet's answers to these questions, I promised this synod we would not run over, and I mean to keep that promise. We will continue this discussion after completing our agenda tomorrow. Let us pray."

Bishop Tom heard not a word of the prayer. He felt proud of having stood up to Hammet, whom he considered an oafish bully. But he knew the fight had not been won. It had, perhaps, only begun.

41

THE FOG ROLLED IN EARLY, obscuring the late afternoon light as the last of the magickians arrived. Larch watched the Lower Haight from the window of the lodge, internalizing the gathering gloom of the approaching dusk.

"I brought snacks," said Frater Parsons, clearing the stairs. He was a tall and bony man, barely thirty but already balding, with thin wisps of blond hair listing where they would as he moved. He set a paper grocery bag on the coffee table and claimed the last seat. Larch took one of the overstuffed chairs, leaving Frater Charybdis scowling from the sofa at the soda pop and spinach dip Parsons unpacked. Frater Turpelo sat beside him, a man of multiple chins and hyperaffected graces.

Larch, whose own magickal name was Frater Babylon, called the meeting to order. "We have had an eventful couple of days, Brothers. We have cause to celebrate...and to grieve. The experiment was a success. I honestly didn't think it would work," he confided. He looked at Frater Parsons, who was wrestling a cork out of a bottle of champagne.

"I'm not sure Frater Benedict did either," said Turpelo with exaggerated pomposity, "or I doubt sincerely whether he would have attempted the working."

"None of us has ever worked with Articiphus before," agreed Charybdis. "He was an unknown quantity. And, for a demon, amazingly compliant."

"That remains to be seen," Larch said darkly, reaching for a bagel chip and scooping it in the spinach dip. "The working was effective, yes, but it is only half-complete. Frater Benedict is still in a coma, for all we know. And there is the other side of the equation, our failure to liberate Frater Benedict from the Alameda hospital." Larch scowled.

The others hung their heads at this. They had almost gotten arrested last night trying to retrieve him, and they had failed.

"We have to fix that, somehow," said Parsons, "but how can we ever try if we don't have access to him?"

"We have a good idea where he is—with the Berkeley Blackfriars," said Larch, "and I'm certain he's as safe with them as with us. I'm also reasonably sure they'll work with us to bring him back once we've figured out a strategy to do so."

"Any ideas?" asked Charybdis.

"The magickal operation was carefully planned," Turpelo insisted. "Frater Benedict would not have forgotten a reversal command."

"Let's assume for the moment that he did not forget it," Larch said, taking a methodical approach to the problem.

"Champagne?" asked Parsons.

"I'll pass just now," Larch waved his hand. "What could have gone wrong?"

"Could be a time thing," Charybdis suggested. "It could be that the reversal is coming, but Randy was not specific about the timing of it."

"Magickal names only, if you please!" bellowed Turpelo.

"Sorry."

"Yes," Larch spoke deliberately, thinking it through. "That is certainly possible. Very sloppy magick on Benedict's part, and it would be just like a demon to fuck with us that way. It's not as if they *like* to be bound to our will."

Turpelo sniffed at a bagel chip. "I have never known a demon *not* to make things as difficult for a magickian as possible. That is why we must be *precise* and *comprehensive* in our instructions."

"All right," said Larch. "What about the other possibility? What if Benedict did everything right? What could have gone wrong?"

"The demon cannot simply disobey," Turpelo opined. "They are bound to obedience."

"So, it may be that Articiphus was not unwilling to effect the reversal of souls, but *unable*."

"It is conceivable," agreed Turpelo, holding out a glass for some champagne. Charybdis filled it.

"What could have interrupted the operation?" Larch wondered aloud.

"It could be the order was countermanded from higher up the demonic lowerarchy."

"Possible," Larch agreed, "but unlikely."

"It could be that the angel is resisting the operation," Parsons suggested. "Who knows how powerful that angel is?"

"Well, we've got to figure that one out, and that right quick," Larch rose and strode to the window, his hands behind his back. "Not just for Benedict's sake but for ours. As of last night, gentlemen, we have a patron, who was very impressed indeed with our little experiment. A very well-paying patron, I must say, who wants to help us further our work."

The brothers looked up with excitement. "Who?" they all seemed to ask at once.

Larch stood and finally snatched up a glass of champagne. Holding it aloft toward the kitchen, he announced dramatically, "Gentlemen, I now present to you our illustrious patron—and one of the wealthiest and most powerful men on the planet—Alan Dane."

A collective gasp rose up as Dane pushed past the swinging door of the kitchen and presented himself with a flourish. "Good afternoon, gentlemen. I trust you are all well?"

Dane's dashing good looks lent him an air of power and prestige that he used to his full advantage. He took a stool from against the wall and forced his way into their circle, causing Parsons to move his chair back in order to create room.

"Gentlemen, your leader and I have struck a bargain," he said and smiled beatifically at the group. "I have made a gift of $100,000 to your lodge"—he paused to let that sink in for a moment and then continued, "and in return I only ask that you pursue your...experiments with all haste. The avocados were a stroke of genius, but as Mr. Larch—"

"You mean Frat—" Parsons began but stopped when Larch shot him a withering look.

"As Mr. Larch here agrees, next time we must try something a bit larger." He basked visibly in the glow of their appreciation.

Larch could almost see the increased production of saliva in his brothers' mouths. He allowed himself to enjoy their moment of recognition—it had been so long in coming, after all.

Dane broke the spell of mutual admiration like the dropping of a bomb. "I'd like to begin the next experiment immediately."

Larch opened his mouth to respond, but Charybdis beat him to it. "But we can't yet!" he protested. "We don't know what went wrong yet."

Dane raised an eyebrow, the very picture of testy patience.

"Mr. Dane, surely you can see our dilemma," Turpelo was calm reason personified. "Ill has befallen one of our number. We daren't try the operation again until we have discovered where we have erred."

"Magick is an art more than a science," Larch attempted to smooth over what seemed to be a minor snag. "We are dealing with creatures of vast power, beings who are easily misunderstood, even by those who are as experienced as we are."

"Allow me to remind you gentlemen that as of this morning when $100,000 was credited to your account, we have a partnership of sorts," Dane said, his smile unwaning. "As far as I am concerned a little...collateral damage is to be expected."

The magickians looked at one another nervously, not sure how to answer him. Larch coughed into his hand and stood, leaning on his chair. "Mr. Dane, we fully expect to hold up our end of our arrangement; we are only saying that we need to figure out what went wrong before we can proceed. We want to *succeed*, for the sake of all of us."

Dane's smile soured into a sinister sneer. "Sit down, Mr. Larch, and listen to me carefully." Larch obeyed, clearly annoyed about being ordered about. "I don't care, Mr. Larch, if each and every one of you ends up in a coma by the time we are done. I have paid you for a service, and I have a right to expect prompt delivery of it."

"Mr. Dane, we're just asking for a little more time to troubleshoot the operation."

"And I don't want to wait." Dane stated simply, almost petulantly.

"Please, Mr. Dane, you must understand the forces we're working with here," Larch said as forcefully as he could muster.

"Oh, I understand them more than you assume." Dane rose and began to circle the magickians. "You see, I have lived with a demon for nearly fifteen years."

The magickians' eyes grew wide. "My father was possessed, by his own invitation. The demon granted him almost unlimited power to obtain his fortune, and in return..."

"In return, the demon got to enjoy carnality," Larch guessed.

"Precisely so," Larch agreed. "Until my father grew too old to provide much enjoyment."

"But surely, Mr. Dane, *you* are not possessed. We are all of us here experienced enough to know that when we see it," Turpelo reasoned. "What prevented the demon from continuing his incarnation through your willing or unwilling vehicle?"

"You're saying that the demon is still inhabiting your father?" Charybdis was equally perplexed. "Why would he do that?"

In answer, Dane drew a small object from the pocket of his vest. He held it up for them all to see: a large, ornate golden ring with an enormous red stone in an ancient setting. "Because, gentlemen," Larch said, the smile returning to his face, "the demon, like you, has no choice."

42

THE MIST HAD GROWN soupy by the time the friars arrived at the Dane mansion. After parking, they stood on the sidewalk outside, and Richard marveled at the enormity of the house, and of their task.

"Well, compadres, how d'ya wanna do this?" Dylan asked. "You two've been here, so yer one up on me."

"Well, I don't think we should just break in," Richard said, drawing his habit closer to him against the chill of the fog. "Terry, you remember the garden outside the elder Dane's room?"

"Yeah, of course."

"Take Dylan, and wait for me there. If all goes well, I should open the door for you from the inside in about five minutes—ten at the most."

Dylan put a hand on Richard's shoulder. "You sure you wanna do this part of it alone—I mean, right now, with all that's been going on?"

Richard put his hand over Dylan's and squeezed. "I'm okay."

Dylan did not look completely convinced, but he nodded and he and Terry set off around the house to look for a garden entrance.

Richard closed his eyes and breathed deep. Images of everything at stake for him flashed through his mind in an instant: the howling angel, duplicitous lodge members, Kat, and most of all, Mikael. His resolve quickened, and he marched to the front door and rang the bell.

It was several minutes before an answer came. The door swung inward, and a middle-aged woman in green scrubs looked down at him. A nurse, obviously, but not Nurse Stahl.

This woman was short with a pageboy cut and a no-nonsense air about her. She did not smile.

Richard did. "Good evening. I'm Fr. Richard Kinney—"

"We don't give handouts."

"I'm not here—"

"And we already give to nonprofits. Good day." She went to close the door, but Richard put his foot in it, deciding to take another tack.

"Excuse me, ma'am, *who* do you think you *are*?" Richard said, with feigned outrage. "I am the elder Mr. Dane's priest, and I have come to hear his confession and bring him communion. And you are?"

The woman was taken aback and looked Richard over from head to toe more carefully, clearly flustered. Richard fixed his stare straight into her eyes, and then he smiled again. "Ah, but I see that you're new here." He pumped up the charm. "Of course, you would not have seen me before. Ms. Stahl, the last nurse here, knew me well. She even brought me tea—no need to bother yourself about that, dear. But if you don't mind, I have other pastoral visits to make tonight..."

Richard did not wait to be invited in, but charged forward, trusting that, like the Red Sea, the way would be opened before him. It was.

Richard was pretty sure he could remember the way—his display of confidence would, after all, lend credence to his subterfuge—and made directly for the elder Dane's sickroom.

Looking increasingly uncertain, the nurse followed behind. Richard glanced back at her and made small talk. "When did you begin? What happened to Nurse Stahl? I'm sorry, I didn't catch your name."

The woman looked worried, and stammered a reply as she scurried to keep up through the long, ornate hallways. "I don't know what happened to Ms. Stahl. I started yesterday. My name is Alice Stout."

"A beautiful house, isn't it, Alice? So nice to meet you." And then he was there. Richard waved his arm, in an *after you* motion to Nurse Alice, and stood back.

A little uncertain still, Nurse Alice opened the French doors and waited for Richard to walk through before shutting them again.

The room was just as Richard remembered it from two days before. Old man Dane lay quietly, an IV drip affixed to his arm and a gob of spit hanging from his chin. Richard smiled beatifically at the nurse. "Thank you so much, Alice. I'll call if I need you."

"Oh, I don't think I should leave him alone with you—"

"Oh, but you must. A confession is a private matter, my dear." Richard was all slimy pomposity at this point, and part of him, he realized, was enjoying it.

"But I don't think he's conscious."

Richard glided over to the hospital bed and touched the old man on the chest. Dane's eyes snapped open, fiery red and moist with mucus. Not Dane's eyes, Richard knew, but Duunel's. "Things can be a little odd around here," Richard said in a conspiratorial tone. "Perhaps you've noticed?"

Her eyes darkened and narrowed, a look that told Richard much. He smiled solicitously. "You'll adjust to it, I'm sure. Now, please, if you will..." He waved toward the servant's quarters.

Warily, Nurse Alice walked to her room and shut the door behind her. Richard lost no time making for the double French doors leading to the garden and undid the latch. He held his finger to his lips as Dylan and Terry tiptoed in.

"We have to make it quick. That nurse knows more than she's letting on." Richard motioned toward the doors to the hall. "Remember, anything that will give us a clue as to what Dane's up to."

Terry nodded curtly and set off with Dylan in tow. As soon as the door was shut again, Richard walked to the bedside.

"So, Duunel, how's tricks?" he asked.

"Have you come to torment me again, Christian?"

"Not at all. I thought maybe we'd chat."

"I have nothing to say to you."

"Well then, we can sit here and stare at each other."

And that's what they did, for several minutes.

"Here's what I don't get," Richard said finally. "Why are you holding so tenaciously to this body, Duunel? It can't be any fun anymore. You've got to be feeling just as much pain as old man Dane. Why stay in him? Why not inhabit the young Mr. Dane? Or someone else of wealth or power or rampant hedonism? Why stay here?"

"You are more ignorant than I thought," Duunel hissed. "I do not stay here of my own will, you idiot."

"Then whose will compels you?" Richard had been just passing time with Duunel while Dylan and Terry did their thing, but now he was intrigued.

"The younger Dane's," the demon's voice was raw with rage.

"But I don't understand. Is the younger Dane a magickian? He doesn't look the type. Too *GQ* for the hairball magick set."

"He is no magickian. Magickians I can...deal with."

Richard was becoming more curious with every second. "So how can he possibly compel you?"

"Did you really not notice...the ring?"

Richard thought back to when he had seen Dane burst into this very room just two days ago. His hands were wet, his eyes wild with rage, his shirt cuffs open and flailing, and on his hand...a huge, ostentatious red stone. Yes, he had noticed it, but he'd simply taken it for a token of the rich man's vanity.

But what sort of ring could compel demons, especially if the bearer was not a magickian? And then it dawned on him—the greatest treasure of the ancient Middle East.

"That ring...is the *Ring of Solomon*?" whispered Richard.

"The same," Duunel hissed.

Richard caught the side of the bed to steady himself. To have been so close to an artifact of such magnitude was almost too much for him. His mind staggered at the thought of how much power its bearer could wield and the danger to the world should that bearer be the wrong sort of man—which it always, invariably, was. Only one sort of man sought out Solomon's Ring—those drunk with power and intent on no good.

Richard got a grip on himself and turned back to the demon. "To what end does he hold you here? Why? What possible good is it doing him?"

"Hatred. Revenge," came the otherworldly voice from the wizened lips. "So much does he hate the old man, that he compels me to inhabit him so that he will continue to draw breath. So that he will—"

"Continue to suffer," Richard finished.

"Yessss…"

"Evil fucking bastard."

"No shit, Priest."

"Duunel, listen, we think Dane—the younger Dane—might have something to do with the disappearance of one of our friars. Do you remember Mikael?"

"Goth boy. Newbie. Three nipples."

Richard arched an eyebrow. *How in hell did Duunel know about that?* "Er…yeah, that's him. He's gone missing, and we're sure he's undergoing demonic oppression from one of your colleagues. Can you tell me where Mikael is?"

"Do I look like I get out much?" Duunel narrowed one eye at him menacingly.

"Just asking." Richard puckered his lips and thought.

"Besides, why should I tell you anything?"

Richard thought about that, too. Finally, he spoke solemnly. "Because we can help you. We're no friends of the younger Mr. Dane. If we can find a way to stop him, whatever it is he's up to, we will. And when we do, we'll liberate you from your prison. You have my word."

"And is your word good, Priest?"

"Better than most."

The demon stared at him in silence, clearly weighing the options. Finally, he spoke. "I don't know where your friar is, but I do know that there is a set of catacombs beneath this house. The younger Mr. Dane goes there often. That is all I know."

Richard felt a stab of hope. "And how do we reach these catacombs?" he said, whipping out his cell phone and speed dialing Terry.

43

"STAY HERE," Richard said to Duunel. The demon scowled at him as he ran from the room.

In the hall, he turned left and, following Duunel's instructions, made for the hidden entrance to the catacombs. Cursing himself for being so out of shape, Richard was panting heavily by the time he spotted Dylan and Terry. They had pried the door open and, Richard noted, done a great deal of damage to the wall in the process. *So much for a subtle operation*, he thought but then dismissed it. If Mikael were here, if there were any way to retrieve him, he would rip this mansion down with his bare and bloody hands.

Panting heavily, he nodded at his companions, and Dylan went in, holding his lighter aloft. *That's why you need a pothead in your pack*, Richard thought, and followed Terry down the narrow, winding stone steps into the dark.

It seemed a long way down, and Richard fought hard against the claustrophobia rising up in him. It triggered the emotions he had been fighting over the past several days—the frustration of being in a situation he couldn't find a way out of, his overwhelming feeling of shame, his suspicion that he simply wasn't adequate to the task. The cold and the dark seemed to amplify his feelings with every step, and he began to sweat. He fought the panic and willed his mind to fix on Mikael rather than his own fucked-up self.

It helped, and before long the panic subsided, just as the narrow staircase emptied out into a long hallway cut into stone. It, too, was narrow, but there was more room to move about.

"Shit!" Dylan cursed and the lighter went out.

"What happened?" Terry asked, fighting his own rising panic.

"Burned mah damned fingers on the lighter. Wind changed when we left the stairs."

Richard paid attention, and it was true. There was a discernible draft coming from behind him.

"Want me to hold it?" Terry offered.

"Ah will when Ah find it," Dylan said. Then both he and Terry said "Ouch!" simultaneously, and Richard's mind painted on the velvet black field of his lightless eyes a comic scene of Dylan and Terry on their hands and knees, bumping heads.

"Found it!" Terry said. In a moment, leaping yellow light flooded the hallway again.

Richard noted the many holes cut into the stone, all up and down the hallway. Each opening was about a cubit square, one on top of another, about four holes from floor to ceiling. Each stack of holes was followed by another about every four feet. Richard whistled. There were literally hundreds of holes. "Terry," Richard called and grabbed Terry's arm to shine the light into one of the holes. There was something in there, and it appeared to be wrapped in linen.

"It's a body," breathed Dylan.

"Of course it's a body," Richard said, "these are catacombs. Probably been the Dane family resting place for a hundred years."

They continued on, looking for a door, or for the hallway to branch out into a room—anywhere Mikael might be.

"Oh God," Dylan breathed. "D'ya think...?" he pointed to one of the burial holes.

"No, I don't," Richard said, marching doggedly after Terry. "I *can't.*"

Just then, Dylan froze in his tracks. "Terry, bring the light." Terry stopped short near where Dylan was crouched. Although in his black cassock, he was especially hard to see. Terry had almost tripped over him.

Dylan stood up and held something to the light. A red Hello Kitty purse, about the size of a small Chinese take-out box.

A chill ran down Richard's spine. "This. Is not good."

"What does it mean?" asked Terry.

"It means we gotta get Mikael out of here, pronto, before he ends up stuffing one of these holes."

Richard raced ahead of his companions. He was beyond the reach of the light, but he didn't care. Only when Dylan reached out and held him back did he slow down at all. He let Terry take the lead again, and they followed the sputtering light into the bowels of their own fear.

The passage turned to the left and then abruptly ended. "Shit!" said Richard.

"No, look, dude, the wall here isn't solid. These are fake rocks, plastic. This is a door." Dylan scratched at the end of the passage, and his nails made a sound like they were running over a gallon milk jug.

Richard allowed himself a brief flood of hope. "How do we get it open?" he asked.

"Be prepared," Terry said, reciting the Boy Scout motto. He reached through the slit in his cassock to his jeans pocket and drew out a black leather case.

The lighter went out briefly. "Dylan, you have to hold this again."

Dylan yowled in pain as the hot metal of the lighter touched his hand. "Suck it up, you big baby," Terry said.

"Dude, that is so unkind," Dylan complained and raked his thumb along the lighter's flint wheel. Blue sparks shot out, then the yellow flame danced again.

Terry knelt by the door and withdrew lock picks from the leather case. He held back the plastic flap covering the keyhole and began to work at it with the slender silver instruments. In a few moments, Richard heard a click, and the door swung inward.

They were met by a blast of rank air, smelling of excrement and sweat. Richard ignored it and followed Dylan into the chamber without hesitation. Terry, showing the better part of valor, kept watch in the hall. "What do you see?" he called into the chamber after them.

At first, Richard thought that the chamber was empty, but then he saw a dark form in the far corner. Tugging on Dylan, he drew him over. As they grew near, they saw that the floor was covered by a thin mattress, spotted by water—or worse. On the mattress, covered by rough army surplus wool blankets, was a slight figure. Richard knelt on the mattress, which, he noted, was wet and stinking, and drew back the edge of the blanket.

It was Mikael. His wild hair was matted, and he looked more bone-thin than usual. Richard placed two fingers on his neck. Yes, there was a pulse, however faint. Richard slapped lightly at his face, but Mikael did not budge.

"We found him!" he called to Terry. "And he's alive!"

"Thanks be to God!" Terry called back from the doorway.

Richard took one of Mikael's arms and threw it over his own shoulder. He motioned for Dylan to do the same. Dylan did. The lighter went out momentarily, and Richard felt a flash of panic in the pitch blackness, but as soon as they had lifted Mikael between them, the flame sprang to life once more.

As soon as they were through the door, Terry took the lighter and led the way. Mikael's feet dragged behind them, and Richard worried that they were hurting his arms in their haste, but he put it out of his mind. He didn't care if they dislocated both of Mikael's shoulders, so long as they got him out. They could fucking pop his arms back into their sockets later.

Richard wasn't really concentrating on where they were going, and he collided with Terry when the shorter man stopped in his tracks. "Oh shit," he heard Terry whisper.

Richard looked up and added his own expletives. Coming down the narrow stone steps was a flaming figure, so bright that Richard had to squint against it until his eyes adjusted.

When they did, however, he wished again for the relative coziness of the dark. Descending from the final step onto the hardpacked earth was Alice Stout, transfigured by an orange luminosity emanating from her eyes and from balls of light affixed to two of her four hands.

In the other two hands, in constant motion up and down, were curved blades that flashed and reflected the light like razor-sharp mirrors.

Beneath her page-boy haircut, beneath the orange balls of fire that were her eyes, a tongue hung twisting obscenely from her gaping jaws, much longer and more prehensile than a human tongue had any right to be.

But that was because, it was obvious to the friars, this creature was not human.

"I *knew* there was something about her," Richard breathed. He quickly but gently lowered Mikael to the floor. "Terry, the rite. Dylan, something cruciform, quick!"

Instantly, Terry began to recite from the Rite of Exorcism, pausing only briefly to allow his memory to fill in the gaps: "Holy Lord! All powerful! Eternal God! Father of Our Lord Jesus Christ! You who destined that recalcitrant and apostate Tyrant to the fires of Hell; you who sent your only Son into this world in order that He might crush this Roaring Lion. Throw your terror, Lord, over this Beast. Give faith to your servants against this most Evil Serpent, to fight most bravely—"

Dylan had a harder time of it, finally grabbing at Richard's belt, tying it to his own to form a makeshift equilateral cross. Once he had it crudely assembled, he stepped in front of his colleagues, holding the talisman before them like a shield. Richard fumbled at the fanny pack beneath his cassock and withdrew a vial of holy water, blessed at the last vigil of Easter.

The demon was noticeably subdued by the recitation, and at the sight of the cross she shrank back a couple of steps, turning her fiery gaze away.

Richard stepped forward, flicking holy water at her, and the sound of water crackling against a hot frying pan echoed off the stones.

In the dim and failing light of her flailing palms, they could see smoke rising from where the water had struck her. The friars moved in on her as one.

She retreated a couple of steps but was not undone. Screaming with fury, she lashed out at them with the scimitars, lunging toward them, so close that Richard felt the wind of the blades.

He swung the holy water vial furiously, sending streams of silver beads arcing through the air toward the faltering demon, great gushes of steam issuing from where they landed. Howls of pain unnerved the friars as they strove to hold their ground.

Richard flung another arc of holy water, and then the stream ceased. The vial was empty. Richard shook it and tried again, to no avail. Sensing the worst of it was over and that victory was near, the demon advanced again, forcing Richard to step back to avoid the slashing blades. He tripped over Dylan, and both men went down with a groan. The demon raised her blade over her head in an act of ritual victory before taking off their heads.

Just then, Terry ceased the recitation and began a chant. "*Keshava klesha-harana, narayana janardana, govinda paramananda, mam samud-dhara madhava...*"

The demon stopped short, dropped both blades, and shrank back, holding her various hands to her head to block out the sound. Richard noticed, and although he did not know the chant, picked it up as best he could and added his own voice. Dylan did the same with his deep baritone, and the hallway was soon thrumming with the insistent, even militant cadence of the chant.

The demon fell to the floor, and the lights in her palms guttered out. With a final cry of anguish, the friars found themselves engulfed once again in clean darkness and cold silence.

"Thanks be to God," Richard breathed.

"Ah heard that," Dylan agreed.

The feeble flame of the lighter sprang up again, and Dylan and Richard lifted Mikael to their shoulders. Following Terry, they stepped over the demon's carcass toward the stairs.

44

ONCE IN THE CAR, Dylan threatened to break the land speed record for San Francisco. "Better back off," Richard advised. "We don't need to explain why we have a friar passed out in our backseat, reeking of shit."

"Oh I dunno, dude, that's not so hard to explain. We friars are notorious fer bein' drunken louts thanks to Tuck." But he slowed down just the same, trying to maintain a steady five miles an hour over the posted limit as he made for the Bay Bridge.

Terry checked as many of Mikael's vitals as he could unaided by any instruments. When he finished, he held the unconscious man's hand and looked out the window. In the strobe of passing amber streetlamps, Richard could see tears trailing Terry's cheeks. Terry noticed him looking and forced a smile. Richard smiled back, grimly, and turned back to face the front.

"Terry, Ah wanna know how you knew to do that Hindu chant. Ah thought we wuz gonners fer sure. How the hell did ya pull that one out o' yer ass?"

Terry sniffed, but Richard could hear a note of pride in his voice. "It was obvious from her iconographic form that the demon was Indian. She reminded me of Putana, the first demon that Krishna defeated as a child. Her thing was murdering babies, and she used to gain access to their rooms by posing as a nurse. She used to smear her breast with poison, then when the baby went to suck, boom! Dead baby. But when she tried it with Krishna, it was she that keeled over. Anyway, I assumed that since the demon was native to the Hindu paradigm, an invocation of the Hindu pantheon would be more efficacious. Since Jesus is considered by Hindus to be an incarnation of Vishnu, I decided to invoke the most popular incarnation of Vishnu—Krishna. And since the demon reminded me of one Krishna had defeated anyway, it seemed like confirmation that it was the right thing to do."

"Well, praise fucking Krishna," Dylan said with genuine awe, shaking his head. He then shot Richard an inquiring look. "So, dude, did ya get any useful information out of Dane's demon while we was chasin' our tails?"

Richard's silence told him that he had. "Well, spill it, man!"

"What did you find, Richard?" Terry called from the backseat.

"I learned how Dane is controlling these demons without being a magickian."

"Ah jus' figgered he *was* a magickian," Dylan shrugged.

"Nah, wrong type," Terry commented. "He's the playboy, an' *I don't want to work any harder than I have to* kind of person. Magickians work their asses off."

"That's true," agreed Dylan. "It takes a high level of geek proficiency and commitment."

"More than Dane could ever muster," Richard added. "So, he found a workaround."

"I can only think of one magickal artifact that could provide that," Terry said.

"Would it be something involving a red stone in a gaudily ostentatious setting?" Richard teased. "Like the ring Dane was wearing when he interrupted our exorcism the other day?"

Richard looked over his shoulder to see Terry's reaction. The smaller man's eyes were wide. "Solomon's Ring? The man has the fucking Ring of Solomon? Where the hell...?" And he trailed off, incredulous.

"Think about it," Richard said, "The man has almost unlimited wealth. He could get his hands on just about anything."

Above Terry's head, Richard could see the headlights of the cars behind them. They had just pulled onto the Bay Bridge, and the merging cars typically got a little too close for comfort, but as Richard watched, the car behind them did not back off.

"Okay, Dylan, don't panic, but the car behind us is really eating our ass."

Dylan's eyes flicked back and forth between the road and his mirrors. "Shit, he is *not* backin' off, is he?"

In fact, Richard noted, the car was closing the distance. He grabbed the headrest in both hands against the impact, but even so, when it came, he was not ready.

It was only a tap, but it rattled his teeth in his head just the same. "Shit!" Dylan exclaimed, correcting the swerve caused by the rear collision.

Richard looked closely at the car behind them. In the dim fluorescent light of the bridge's undercarriage, it appeared to be a black town car, with tinted windows such that he could make out none of the occupants.

"Fifty bucks says that if we ran those plates, we'd find Dane somewhere on the other end," Dylan said through clenched teeth.

"I'm bettin' you're right," Richard nodded.

Dylan accelerated, trying to put as much distance between them and the car behind as he could.

Richard watched as the car fell behind but then picked up speed again, heading for their bumper without any hesitation, and this time with a lot more speed. "Hold on," Richard warned.

This time, the impact pitched them all forward. Mikael's head struck the back of Richard's seat, and Terry swore. Dylan fought the fishtail, steering into the swerve and accelerating.

They hit Treasure Island doing about eighty miles per hour, the car behind them toying with them like a cat does a mouse. It came closer, then backed off, then came closer as if to ram them again.

"What does he want?" Terry asked.

"My guess is that he wants Mikael back probably because if he comes to, he can put Dane away for kidnapping."

"But why did he take Mikael in the first place?"

Richard didn't know, but he didn't have time to speculate. The car behind them was threatening another ram.

"Well, dudes, this is only likely to get uglier once we get off the bridge," Dylan said, gripping the wheel so hard his fists were white. "What are we gonna do?"

"I have an idea," said Terry.

"I wuz hopin' you would say that, little buddy," Dylan's voice betrayed his relief.

"We have to slow down when we get near the toll plaza—too many CHP around. He'll play along, I'm sure. About a hundred yards past the toll plaza, you have to let me out—to the left, not the right, so I can make for the protection of the median divider."

"Okay..."

"Then you take the first exit to your right—to the Oakland docks. Circle around to the toll plaza—stick to the left and just turn into the parking lot before you hit the toll booths. Zoom through the parking lot and pick me up."

"Just make a loop, yer sayin'?"

"It'll give me just enough time to set some wards."

Dylan looked at Richard for approval. Richard shrugged. "I don't have a better plan," he said.

Dylan nodded and swerved into the left-hand lane. The off-ramp for the bridge was just ahead of them, and Terry got ready. "Don't stop; just slow down. I'll roll out, and then you step on it again."

"Aye-aye," Dylan affirmed.

The black car behind them backed off as they slowed, cautious of being observed by the highway patrol near the toll station, as Terry had predicted. Terry opened the door just enough to lower himself out and then rolled as he hit the pavement.

"Shit!" he swore, as his funny bone took a jolt. A wave of pain coursed through his arm, straight to his head, so severe he was certain he would vomit.

But he didn't. In a moment, he stopped rolling, and, cradling his elbow, he sat up and looked toward the East. He was hoping that it was dark enough that the pursuing car would not have noticed, but perhaps that was hoping too much. At least, he noted with relief, the car continued to follow their own.

He knew he only had about three minutes to work, so he lost no time. Orienting himself to the four directions as accurately as he could, he picked up four stones and began in the East. Placing the stone on the shoulder of the highway, he held his hands over it and began the invocation. "In the name of the Lord of Heaven I entreat thee, Raphael, archangel and healer, guardian of air and the East, set thy seal upon this stone and rise up in thy wroth against all evil that seek to trespass against us. Come, Raphael, guard and protect us."

Quickly, he did the same for the North, invoking the archangel Uriel. Then, taking his own life in his hands, he dashed across the freeway to the other side of the road, narrowly escaping death-by-motorcycle. Once safely across, he took a deep breath, centered himself, and set the wards for the West and the South, invoking Gabriel and Michael.

It was just in time.

Terry breathed a sigh of relief to see the friary's Geo bearing down on him. He waved them to go on and started running after them as fast as he could humanly manage.

Moments later, Terry's suspicions were confirmed. He had suspected the driver might be a demon. If not, his plan would have been useless. But as it was...

The car hit the warding, and the air was filled with the sound of shattering glass and twisting metal. The impact tossed the car like a Tonka Toy, and Terry stopped in wonder to watch the slow, ethereal aerial ballet as it spun in slow motion above his head, in its own way a thing of beauty. It reached the top of its arc and began an equally slow descent, turning in free space and reflecting from a thousand shiny parts the floodlight glow of the toll plaza.

Then, with an impact that nearly knocked Terry from his feet, the town car smashed onto the concrete median separating the two halves of the freeway.

Time having regained its accustomed tempo, Terry sprinted once again to where the friars' Geo had pulled to the shoulder. He jumped in and slapped Dylan, "Go, go, go! Before the CHP starts asking questions!"

"Ah heard that," Dylan said, and gunned it.

45

IT WAS NOT YET DUSK when they pulled up to the friary. Terry rushed in to rouse everyone and to get Mikael's bed ready while Richard and Dylan debated the best way to move him.

"I'm afraid of doing any more damage to his arms," Richard said. "Why don't I get him 'round the chest and you get his feet?"

Dylan nodded. "That'll work."

They pulled him from the car and gently laid him on the pavement. Then Richard raised him up and, crouching behind him, got him in a barrel-chested bear hug.

Dylan picked up his feet, and they started moving toward the house with Richard walking backward.

That was when Dylan noticed their neighbors sitting on their front porch, staring open-mouthed at the sight of an unconscious man being transported by two habited friars sporting full tonsures.

"Drinking," Dylan called to them, then tsk-ed. "It's a terrible habit, and he's goin' right into rehab."

Richard rolled his eyes but kept moving, taking the stairs cautiously as he climbed them backward.

They stopped to rest twice but eventually got Mikael up the broad front staircase and into the bathroom. From the moment they crossed the threshold, Kat had trailed them, wringing her hands.

Terry already had started the water going in the tub, and the others set about undressing him.

The stench was awful, and it wasn't clear if the excrement caked into the clothes was Mikael's or—Richard shuddered—if it belonged to former occupants of the room in which they had found him. Using scissors and working rapidly, they cut away his shirt and pants—his cassock had been lost before they found him, apparently.

Out of the corner of his eye, Richard saw Kat cringe at Mikael's shit-smeared skeletal frame. Then her face registered more curiosity than horror. "Has he got three nipples?" she asked no one in particular.

"According to the Pawnee," Dylan offered, "That's a sure sign of a great spiritual nurturer."

Richard turned Mikael's body in order to free the last vestiges of what had once been his shirt, revealing a latticework of red and white scars on his back. Kat cried out at the sight of them. "What happened to him?" she asked. "What did he *do* to him?"

"Ah don't think Dane did this, Darlin'," Dylan said in a soothing voice. "Them's some old wounds."

"How did it happen?" Kat insisted.

"That's one story Ah don't know," Dylan admitted, a little sadly.

Richard cut away Mikael's briefs, exposing his nakedness. Kat's jaw dropped at the sight of it. "Holy God," she breathed. "Is that real?"

Terry sidled up to her and admired Mikael's endowment himself. "He certainly made out like a bandit." He winked at her. "Play your cards right, my dear, you will be one very lucky woman."

"Very sore woman, you mean." Her face was a complex mixture of concern, dread, admiration, and amusement.

"Okay, Dyl, one more time," Richard said, taking Mikael by the torso and lifting. They shuffled with him dangled between them into the bathroom and lowered him gingerly into the tub.

Susan appeared from the back stairs and took in the scene. "Oh Jesus," she said. "Is he all right?"

"He appears to be in a coma. My guess is demonic dissociation—the very thing we were trying to avoid by quarantining him and Kat."

"How do we fix it?" she asked.

Richard met Dylan's eyes but said nothing.

"Okay, guys, news flash," Terry interjected. "We are all *filthy*."

Dylan and Richard looked at their own cassocks. It was true. They pulled them over their heads and piled them on the bathroom floor. "Look, why don't you guys go shower," Terry suggested. "Kat and I will wash him, and then I'll take my turn."

Richard nodded and followed Dylan to the shower in the master bedroom he and Susan shared. "You go first," Richard said to Dylan and went to collect a clean cassock from his room.

In the quiet of his own room, the last light of the day filtering through the blinds, Richard allowed himself a moment of repose. Everything was still—especially, most unusually, his own heart. He breathed deep and felt his awareness expand. He felt every ache in his bones, felt his weariness, saw clearly the toll the stress of the last few days had taken on his psyche, his stamina, his soul.

He breathed again and spoke aloud. "Thank you." Thanks be to God they had Mikael back...if not completely *back*. He felt the worry and anxiety drain from him, sure that if he looked at his feet he would see a pool of water spreading outward. He closed his eyes and prayed again the only two words that mattered in the whole of creation: "Thank you."

46

Showered and changed, Richard met the others downstairs for supper. Tobias begged beside the table as Brian unveiled his nut loaf with cranberry gravy to the instant Pavlovian salivation of all who had experienced it before. Kat, however, said, "What the hell is that?" Then she covered her mouth and blushed.

"That, my dear, is dinner. Eat it or starve," Brian barked at her, with mock annoyance.

The lazy Susan was quickly loaded with mashed potatoes and ginger spinach. Dylan said a simple grace, and the little Susan started spinning.

The big Susan was eyeing Kat with worried caution. Richard noticed and directed his question to her. "Kat, is Mikael all set?"

She froze at the question, not sure how to answer it. Terry leaped in. "He's resting comfortably in his own bed. He's as good as he can possibly be under the circumstances."

"The question is, how do we change those circumstances?" Richard asked.

Brian sat down and unfolded his napkin. "Let's go over what we know. We know a specific demon, Articiphus, is involved. We know that residual effects from Kat's brother's soul exchange have removed Mikael's soul, but we don't know to where, or how, to get it back."

Susan perked up. "Dylan, what about a soul retrieval?"

Dylan scowled. "Wal, dependin' on where his soul has got to, it *could* work. It's worth a try."

Kat blinked. "A soul retrieval? You mean, like in shamanism?"

"Exactly," Susan said with a reassuring smile. "Shamanism is Dylan's specialty." She gave Dylan a proud wink.

"It can't hurt," Richard said. "When should we set up?"

"Wal, the longer we wait, the harder it's gonna be. Ah say, let's do it right after supper. Ah mean, after dessert."

"Does that get you out of cleanup duty?" Terry narrowed one eye.

"Ah sure as shit hope so," Dylan said, scooping up some mashed potatoes.

"Why did he do this?" Kat wailed. Her outburst of emotion stopped everyone for a second.

"Who?" Terry asked, "You mean Dane?"

Kat nodded. Richard put down his fork, and as he spoke his shoulders sagged. "I'm not sure. My guess is that after our unsuccessful exit job, he had us tailed, probably by professionals, or even by demons—"

"Like the one that followed us across the bridge," Terry interjected.

"Exactly."

"Well, if he kidnapped Mikael because he was *annoyed*, what the hell is he going to do *now*?" Kat asked, a note of helplessness in her voice. "How do we stop him—and the lodge—before they...do something else?"

"We can't," Richard said. "Dane is unstoppable."

Susan's mouth dropped open. Terry nodded. "Tell them," he said.

"About what?" asked Susan.

"Dane has the Ring of Solomon," Richard announced.

"That sounds ominous. What's this ring?" Susan asked.

"The Ring of Solomon was wielded by King Solomon in ancient

Israel," Dylan explained. "Y'all correct me if I get any of this wrong—"

"You're on target so far, Honey," said Terry.

"It gave him the power to command any demon whatsoever, even against the demon's will, even against the demon's self-interest."

"*That's* what made him the most powerful man in the world," said Brian, reaching for a slice of toast.

"Yup," confirmed Dylan. "It's kind of like the Holy Graal for Goetic magickians. It's been lost, but there are always rumors that it's surfaced somewhere or other. Like most things involving demon magick, though, it's hard to control and usually ends up backfiring on whatever unfortunate fuck tries to be King of the World, and before you know it the ring has disappeared again. You might be able to command them demons, y'know, but they don't like it, and you gotta sleep sometime."

"That certainly fits Dane," Richard said. "He is without a doubt the kind of guy who wants to be King of the World, and what with all the corporations he's running he's got a good start on it already. And he's certainly got the wealth to pursue this thing to the ends of the earth. I'm not at all surprised he was able to procure it."

"How do we stop it?" Susan asked.

"We don't. We can't. It's indefensible." Richard answered.

"So, what, are we just giving up?" she demanded.

Richard looked at Dylan then at Brian. Brian cleared his throat. "That ring has a lot of lore behind it. Richard's right. It's unstoppable. Giving up would be the most prudent thing to do."

Susan was indignant. "Who are you people, and what have you done with our friars? That is *not* the way we do things around here! We don't just give up; we find creative workarounds!"

Dylan placed a hand on her arm. "Now, Darlin', think about this. We got Kat's brother back, and we might still be able to restore him given time. We got Mikael back, and we're gonna do what we can for him, too. Nobody's givin' up on that. But savin' the world's avocadas, wal, maybe we jus' gotta cut our losses."

"I never thought I would hear you say those words," Susan stared at him, incredulous. "Especially where guacamole is concerned."

"Tough times make for tough decisions," he agreed.

Tobias barked and ran out of the kitchen toward the living room.

"If we back off now, Dane may leave us alone," Richard said. "We can ward the house more heavily and hole up for a while—"

"I'm going to go stark raving crazy in here!" Kat shrieked.

"You just have to hang on," Richard said. "You don't want what happened to Mikael to happen to you, too."

Kat looked at her plate. She had barely touched it. Brian noticed. "You know," he said, "you *will* hurt my feelings if you don't try the nut loaf."

Just then, an earthquake jolted the building, lurching everything in sight one hard tug westward.

"Okay, *that* was a big one," Susan said warily, waiting for an aftershock. Everyone held their breath, but nothing happened. Slowly, they returned to their meal.

Terry placed his elbows on the table. "Friends," he said evenly, "let's do what we can for Mikael tonight and sleep on what further action to take. We've had a hell of a day, and right now may not be the right time to decide."

"That sounds like the fuckin' voice o' Wisdom," Dylan pronounced.

"Dylan, why don't you get together what you need to do the soul retrieval?" Richard suggested. "Give it your best shot."

"After dessert, you mean."

"Ah...yes, after dessert. Terry, you and I can clean up and say evening prayer. Sound good?"

"Sounds like a plan," Dylan agreed, relieved to be off the hook. He looked around for Tobias to give him his scraps.

"Anybody see Toby?" he asked.

No one did. "He was just here a minute ago," Susan noted. "He just ran into the living room." She rose and left the room in pursuit. "He's not here," she called back.

With more alacrity than anyone would have expected of him, Dylan leaped to his feet and ran to join Susan in her hunt.

Richard rose quickly and went to the back door off the kitchen. He scanned the backyard. "Toby!" he called. Just then he spied one of their neighbors, Myra Koss, peering over their shared fence.

Richard ran out the door, down the steps, and across the yard to where she stood, her hair in rollers, dressed in a stained muumuu.

"You boys seen my Mimi?" she asked, working at her cigarette in a state of near panic. "She's never run away before! She loves me! Tell me you've seen her!"

Richard shook his head. "Myra, I'm sorry. I'll ask the others, but I haven't seen her. But we can't find Toby, either."

Her eyes went wide. "We've got a neighborhood-wide dog-napper!"

Richard frowned. "Maybe we do. Listen, Myra, I've got your number. I'll call if we see any sign of Mimi. Will you do the same if you see Toby?"

"Of course, Sweetie. What kind of evil person...?"

Richard placed a reassuring hand on her shoulder and turned back to the house. He paused at Toby's doghouse and looked in. Empty, save for the wadded blanket and a couple of large beef bones.

Others were scouring the yards by now, too, but none had found Tobias. Richard walked to the front, and found Dylan standing in the middle of the street, talking to other neighbors. Seeing Richard, Dylan excused himself and trotted off to meet him. "Dude, this is *not* good. The Mayers' dog is missing, too."

"So is Mimi."

"No shit! What the fuck?!"

Richard looked back at the house and saw Kat staring at him from the window. She mouthed "What's up?" He held up an index finger, asking her to wait a minute.

Just then a siren wafted its way to them. Down the street, they saw a fire truck appear and then fade as it grew more distant.

"Ho. Ly. Shit." Dylan breathed.

"What?" Richard asked.

"Listen," Dylan's eyes were closed.

"I don't hear anything but the siren," Richard said.

Dylan opened his eyes and fixed a severe gaze on him. "Exactly. Do you hear one dog in this whole neighborhood howling?"

Dylan was right. A shiver of fear ran up Richard's spine. The dogs were gone. All the dogs. Tobias was gone. Richard felt faint; he felt sick. He steadied himself by clutching Dylan's arm and noticed that Dylan needed steadying, too. Tears of panic were welling in his eyes. "That wasn't no earthquake, dude."

Richard nodded, "I know." He cupped his friend's cheek in his hand and raised Dylan's eyes to his own. "I'm willing to bet that wherever in the universe those avocados went, Toby has gone there, too."

If Tobias was especially bonded to anyone at the friary, it was Dylan. He was, technically, the "house" dog, but Richard thought of him as Dylan's, and indeed, it was Dylan who saw to the specifics of his care. Dylan nodded, frantic. "We gotta get him back."

Richard swallowed. "Were we talking about giving up, just now? What the *fuck* were we thinking? Dylan, Dyl, listen to me. *Fuck* what we said before. Dane may not be beatable, but that doesn't mean we're not going to fight him. We're going to find Toby, or we're going to die trying. I promise you." He drew his friend into a hug and held him as the options clicked through his mind.

47

KAT TURNED to him as he stepped inside the door. "It's not just Toby, is it?" she asked.

"No." Richard said.

"It's all of the dogs, isn't it?"

"It looks that way."

"In the whole world," she said, her lower lip trembling.

He fought back the anger rising like bile in his throat. "We don't know that for sure, but I think it's a safe bet."

She turned back to the window, and Richard saw that her arms were shaking. The look on her face confirmed that it was rage more than sadness that moved her. "Goddamn my fucking brother and all those trolls he hung out with. You know what I thought?" She turned on Richard again. "I thought they were harmless, like little D&D-playing *puer aeternus*—or whatever the plural of that is in Latin."

Terry entered the living room from the chapel. "*Pueri aeterni,*" he said. "Count me in on that one."

"I don't think you want to be included in this particular group of *pueri aeterni*—not with Kat around," Richard said.

"Think we should finish our meeting?" Terry suggested.

Richard nodded. Terry lifted his hand in the *hang-ten* formation to his mouth and whistled so loud that Richard picked at his ear to see if there was any blood coming from it.

"I really, really hate it when you do that," Richard said. "A little warning next time?"

Kat tapped on the glass and motioned to Dylan, and within minutes they were all assembled again, this time in the comfortable environment of the living room.

As Dylan sat, Richard looked at his own hands, marveling at how they were shaking, how *his* hands could be so beyond his control this way.

"I don't think there's any doubt what just happened here," Susan said. "Avocados was quirky—it didn't really hurt very many people, farmers and Taqueria owners aside. But this...this hurts the whole world."

"At least the dog-people half," Brian added.

"I don't think there are going to be very many cat-people sleeping soundly tonight," Terry countered. Brian nodded his agreement.

"First things first," Richard said. "Dylan, I know you're in a lot of pain over Toby right now, but we need you to pull it together and see what you can do for Mikael."

"I don't know, dude, I'm pretty scattered—"

Kat hovered over the sofa and put her hand on his shoulder. "Please, Dylan," she said.

Dylan hung his head, and a long silence passed. "Ah'll try it," he said at last.

"Kat, can you monitor the news on the web? We probably know more about what's actually happening than anyone else in the world, but one of us should be monitoring how the world is responding and what people are saying."

She straightened up and cocked her head. Richard realized he had just said "one of us" in reference to her. He smiled.

"Oh. Yeah. Okay," she answered. "I'll do that. I need to give Randy a sponge bath tonight some time, but I can do that, too. Um, not at the same time, but...yes. Sir." She apparently realized that she was officially coming across as an idiot, and shut up.

A hint of a smile crossed Richard's face. "The rest of us—including you, Susan, if you feel up to it—we have some major grief counseling work to do right here in our neighborhood. Let's pace ourselves, and each of us take a different direction."

"Ah'll need someone to drum and watch for mah journey," Dylan said.

"I can do that," said Brian.

"Dude, you drum too fast," Dylan said warily.

"I'll be careful," Brian smiled.

EVERYONE SCATTERED, and Brian and Dylan climbed the stairs. They split up briefly, Brian to fetch a drum from the spare bedroom and Dylan to snag a sprig of sage to cleanse the area.

Once they met in Mikael's room, Brian closed the windows against the noise in the street. Dylan tried to focus as he lit the sage and began a Lakota chant. He was, in fact, one-sixteenth Lakota, not enough to see in his stocky Melungeon features but enough to claim headrights, he knew, should he ever choose to do so.

Fragrant smoke curled up from the sage and gradually charged the room with Beauty. Using a feather, Dylan blessed himself with the smoke, then the skinny, prone frame of Mikael, and finally, Brian, who sat erect on a stool, cradling a Native-American drum. Laying the unburned sage in an oil-glittery abalone shell half, Dylan also laid aside the feather and stretched out on the twin bed next to Mikael.

Dylan nudged him over a little and eventually got comfortable. Lying faceup, his hands at his sides, he winked at Brian. "Let's get going."

"How long?" Brian asked.

"You're gonna hate me."

"How long?" Brian scowled.

"Gimme an hour and a half under and a half an hour return."

"Oh...my hands are going to *so* hurt."

"Ah told you, you wuz gonna hate me."

"Just get going," Brian said, with mock irritation.

"If Ah can surface early, Ah will."

"Deal."

Brian began to pound on the drum with clean, slow, even beats. Dylan allowed the concern about Toby to be there but chose not to focus on it. Instead, he concentrated on the rhythm, and in his mind's eye he traveled down a wooded path, deeper and deeper into an alternative reality that is the Middle World.

Soon, the imaginal realm had solidified, and he began to experience it not as a phenomenon of consciousness, not as a world viewed through his mind's eye, but as a world as solid and real as any in waking life.

As he walked toward a clearing, all traces of normal reality were left behind, and the sunlight, so bright he almost had to look away, shimmered in the heat of an afternoon that was definitely *not* cold, gray Berkeley in winter.

No sooner had he hit the clearing than he became aware of a large, luminous presence padding along beside him. "Hullo, Jaguar," Dylan said, reaching out to touch the mottled black fur of the great beast at his side. He watched as the sunlight played upon the solid ripples of muscle just below the pelt. His spots, velvet pools of midnight, were separated by highlights of gold—the same color as his brilliant eyes.

Jaguar said nothing but kept pace with him, looking about warily. "Good to see you, dude." Dylan didn't expect a reply to this. Jaguar was a fiercely loyal animal guide—emphasis on fierce—but he was not much for small talk or pleasantries. In fact, of all the creatures Dylan had ever met in the Otherworld, Jaguar was hands down the surliest.

Dylan remembered back to the time he had first begun doing shamanic journeys. It must have been his second foray into the Lower World when, near the close of the journey, he had called after Jaguar, "Hey, dude, why are you so surly?" The enormous cat had stopped and faced him and without a hint of irony answered, "Because the world is hard," and then turned and stalked away. Dylan shook his head, remembering the scene.

"Dude, Mikael's in a bad way. He got caught in a magickal cross-fire, kinda, and his soul has been separated from his body. We gotta get it back, stuff it in him, make it all better."

Jaguar looked at him, comprehending but silent.

"So, where should we look?" Dylan prompted.

Finally, the great cat spoke. "For what?" Although the sentence was slight, the rumble of his voice was felt in Dylan's belly.

"For his soul," Dylan answered, with an implied "of course" in his diction.

"How should I know?" asked the Jaguar.

Dylan stopped and faced the creature. "Uh, I don't know, dude, because you're, like, a magickal dude, and you know...everything?"

The Jaguar padded on without him. "You're an idiot," he threw over his shoulder.

"Ah'm not an idiot, and Ah'll remind you to be civil when we're working together. Ah don't mind what you say behind mah back to all the other celestial menagerie-folk, but to my face we're gonna have some respect. Am Ah clear?"

Jaguar stopped. "Of course. I'm sorry. I don't know where Mikael's soul is."

"Can you think of any likely places?" Dylan asked.

The great cat thought, wind playing on his fur as he sniffed at the dry yellow grass of the clearing. "He was not the target of the magickal working, was he?"

"No, it was residual energy from sighting the sigil used in a working."

"Which means he probably wasn't intentionally *carried* anywhere. He probably just got separated, and got lost."

"So, he'd be...what, wandering around Pier 39?" Dylan grabbed at straws.

"Perhaps hung up in a pocket of the pain body."

"Yer thinkin' he would have gravitated naturally toward a locus of primal wounding," Dylan considered.

"It won't hurt to look," Jaguar suggested.

"We can even do some retrieval of those parts of his soul that got split off from that wounding, and integrate them with the larger soul later."

Jaguar nodded.

"Well, all right then, Jagger, let's root around in Mikael's cellar, shall we?"

48

KAT TROLLED the web for a few minutes but so far wasn't turning up much. The most mentions of the disappearance of dogs she was able to find weren't on the web at all but on CNN, where they were—she could hardly believe it—joking about it. They weren't fooling her, she told herself; the anchorwoman looked pretty fucking rattled.

She began an mp4 capture of CNN and gathered her things for her brother's bath. She put a large dish tub in the kitchen sink and drew it half-full of warm water, adding just enough dish soap to make a generous supply of suds. "Soap is soap," she said to herself. "No need to go in search of different kinds." From the linen cabinet she got a clean washcloth and started up the back steps, holding the tub like an offering in front of her as she went.

She set it down on the nightstand in the guest room and shut the door to ensure her brother his privacy. Then she turned down the bedclothes and placed a loving hand on his chest...his very, very *cold* chest.

Her eyes wide with horror, she drew back, startled and panicked. Catching herself, she struggled to have the presence of mind to proceed logically. She placed two fingers on his neck and felt for his pulse.

None. The skin was already ashen. She could see that now. His mouth, which she had always thought was dorky due to his overbite, drew no air, and his jaw hung slack.

Tears welled up in her and spilled out onto the cold bedding. She had already felt he was lost to her, and was, in a way, already prepared for this. Yet now that it was here, she marveled at the surreality of the moment, the unreality of it. She shook her head and squeaked, "No, no, no..." Then she laid her head on his chest and sobbed.

It was dark when she picked her head up. She turned on the light but couldn't bring herself to look at the body. Instead, she paused at the mirror and drew the mussed strands of hair back over her ears, fighting hard not to cry again at the sight of her swollen eyes.

Oddly, a faint blue glow obscured her chin in the mirror. She thought it was a trick of the light, but as she moved, she found that it remained where it was. She reached out and touched the glass, but it was set back a couple of inches. If it had been a reflection of something, it would have been hovering about three inches in front of the mirror, but instead it seemed to be hovering *behind* it. She turned off the light, sure that whatever it was would be extinguished with nothing to reflect. But the blue-violet glow endured.

49

RICHARD CROSSED Cedar and headed up windy Arch Street toward the backside of the Pacific School of Religion. He wasn't sure what drew him, but he followed his instincts, exercising a well-honed professional skill of getting out of the way and letting God work. God seemed to want to wander up Arch Street, and Richard did not argue. A wail went up, piercing the air, and Richard headed toward the sound. He walked toward an open garage, and there, on the floor, beside a steel cage, a familiar figure sat, keening and rocking back and forth.

It was Mr. Kim, the owner of the Gallic Hotel. Richard stopped short, assessing his feelings. Mr. Kim was far from his favorite person in the world. Once he had even tossed Richard out for not having enough money for another cup of coffee, shouting that he had taken up space in his shop long enough. He had also uttered a few choice anti-gay epithets in Richard's direction on more than one occasion. Mr. Kim was not someone Richard particularly felt like ministering to. But as he took in the scene, his heart softened, and he saw not an intolerant businessman but a man bereft of someone he truly loved.

Richard entered the garage uninvited, and sat down on the floor next to Mr. Kim. The balding man's face was flushed as he almost choked on his emotion. He continued to rock back and forth, apparently oblivious to the friar's presence. Richard put a hand out, and laid it gently on Kim's arm, giving it a light squeeze and then releasing it. The man choked on his words. "I heard...on radio...but I didn't believe it until...until...she's gone. My baby is gone..."

Richard looked around for signs of what sort of dog "she" must have been. It was a large cage, so that told him something. The water bowl might have held half a gallon, and there was a femur lying in the cage that might have belonged to a rhino. She had been a good-size dog, he reasoned.

For a brief moment, Richard struggled with what to say. He tried "It's going to be okay" on for size, as well as "There, there," but they both seemed so outrageously lame that he bit them back and kept his silence.

And it was silence that was the proper thing. There was nothing to say because, Richard realized, he had nothing to promise. All he had to offer was presence, empathy, and support, and he gave those things without reservation, and without words.

He didn't know how long he sat on the floor beside Mr. Kim. Until the other had stopped crying and lay on the floor, the cold concrete of the garage cooling the businessman's fiery cheek. He sat there until the sun was long down, until Mr. Kim finally rose, pulled him to his feet, hugged him briefly, and went inside his house.

On the way back toward the friary, Richard felt as if he were slogging through tar. He thought of Toby and was just beginning to recognize his own grief at the loss of the dog— "their" dog. He multiplied that grief by millions and millions of Mr. Kims, and realized that no evil of this magnitude had been visited upon the planet since the Angel of Death had swooped over the Egyptians.

Wandering down Spruce, he heard a small crowd of men cursing loudly in Spanish. He crossed to the east side of the street and followed the voices. As if in a dream, Richard walked through a gate into someone else's backyard, where several large, angry Latino men were arguing. Richard didn't understand the Spanish, but he did understand their confusion and their rage. An empty collar attached to a chain lay on the ground, illuminated by a blue porch light.

An enormous, muscled man with his head shaved bald and tattoos adorning his neck was still yelling. He noticed Richard, and yelled at him for a while. In an almost dissociated state, Richard reached up and touched the man's cheek. "I'm sorry, *miho*," he said. The man's face went through many rapid changes, from rage to confusion to fear, to remorse. "Who, Padre, who did this evil thing? My Feo! He's gone! Who took my Feo?"

Richard didn't think about it. If he had, he never would have done it. It was as if he were watching someone else's hand pull out a pen and a scrap of paper; someone else scrawling an address to a house in the Lower Haight. "Here," he said, handing the paper to the man. "The people at this address—they did this."

The man looked at the paper, back at Richard, and nodded. "*¡Vamanos!*" he cried, and a small army of Latino men and boys paraded to the front yard, to waiting cars, armed with garden tools and baseball bats.

50

EVEN THOUGH HE was walking through a clearing with Jaguar, Dylan knew that his body was lying on Mikael's bed, and he could make use of that proximity energetically. "Jes' a minnit, Jag," he said and closed his eyes, concentrating on the body he knew was only six inches away. He reached toward it with his mind and sought out places of concentrated energy. Oddly, he was drawn to Mikael's back, and holding on to Jaguar with one hand, he entered into it in his mind. When he opened his eyes, he was in another place altogether: a shabby apartment with a stained orange shag carpet. The television was on, and Bob Barker was telling someone to "Come on down!" Flies buzzed at the windows, and dishes were piled high beyond the rim of the sink. Dylan stepped over plates of wet cat food, scattering more flies, and made his way over to the couch. The room was oppressively hot even though the windows were open and a generous breeze blew through.

On the couch, apparently unconscious, was a woman in her thirties. Dylan hovered over her—he could see a resemblance between herself and Mikael. She was missing several teeth, and the skin of her face was wrinkled beyond her apparent years. A pool of what appeared to be dried vomit had accumulated on the fabric of the couch. Dylan heard a rustling from another room, and then a shrieking voice, "Hold still, you little shit!"

It was an old woman's voice, and Dylan followed it into the bathroom.

The door was shut. He tried the knob—it was locked. He turned to Jaguar. "I can't get in," he said.

"You don't *want* to go in," Jaguar countered. "To go in, all you've got to do is walk through the door."

Dylan steeled himself and walked forward, expecting to smash his nose on the door. But instead, a shimmer passed his peripheral vision, and he passed through the door.

There he stopped, his eyes widening at the sight. Standing in the tub, his fists held out before him defiantly, was a young Mikael, maybe ten years old. He was dressed only in a ratty pair of white briefs, and his face was pocked with scabs and bruises.

He was tiny, as a boy, betraying none of the size he would later accumulate. But the defiant hook in his nose was already in place, as well as the piercing look in his eye.

Facing him was an enormous woman, three times his size, gnarled and obese. In her right hand she held a steaming saucepan, and the other was waving in the air, making swipes at the young Mikael.

"You gonna mind your nana!" she shouted at him, making another grab at the boy, blocking his escape with her enormous frame.

"I hate you!" he shouted.

"Jesus said to kill boys who don't respect their elders," she hissed. "But I'm not gonna kill ya, 'cause I love you, Booby-boy. And it's only 'cause I love ya that I gotta discipline ya. I wouldn't be no kinda Christian if I failed you in my duty. Now hold the fuck still!" She made another grab and this time caught a handful of wild black hair. She pulled at it until he cried out, forcing his head down toward the tub. Once his back was exposed to her, she raised the saucepan over it and poured a stream of whitish, viscous fluid down on his back.

As soon as it hit his skin, he screamed. Steam leaped from his back into the air, and white streams flowed slowly down his back until it stopped, clinging to his skin in hardening sheets.

"Ahhhh!" the boy screamed, twisting around to break free of her grip. "You fucking witch! I hate you, hate you, hate you!"

With a jerk, he leaped back and pulled her forward, pulling her off balance. Seizing his opportunity, he leaped out of the tub and ran under the arm holding the saucepan. Not to be undone, she swung the pan down and around, catching him in the back of the head. Without another sound, the young Mikael went down like a dropped rag doll, lying facedown at the threshold to the hall.

"Oh, Booby-Boy, you are such an evil baby." She dropped the pan, now empty of scorching wax, and, with difficulty, picked the child up in her arms. Tenderly, she brought him to the bedroom, laid him on the bed, and shut the door.

Dylan debated whether to enter the bedroom. What he had seen already was bad enough—did he really want to see more? He looked to Jaguar for help.

"What do you think, Jag-meister? Do we go in?"

"You're not here to make yourself comfortable. You're here to find Mikael."

Dylan was confused. "I don't think the adult Mikael is here."

"No." Jaguar swished his tail. "But the young Mikael is."

"Ah can't just leave him here like this," Dylan said.

"If you do, he'll be here forever," Jaguar said, raising a back leg and licking at his privates.

Dylan nodded and, like a ghost, walked through the door. The bedroom was no improvement on the rest of the house. A full-size mattress lay on the floor, with a wad of bedding to one side.

On the other side of the mattress was the little boy Mikael, unconscious, his head to one side, with a mat of blood visible on the back of his head.

Crouching over him, his grandmother rocked back and forth, tears streaming down her face as she cried out, "Oh Jesus, Oh my Jesus, come into this child and cast out the willful spirits of evil that cause him to disobey his nana! Oh Jesus, oh Jesus, come, Jesus..."

And she shuddered and covered his body with her own, apparently attempting to breathe the Holy Spirit into the child with her own wet and sloppy jowls.

Without another second of hesitation, Dylan knelt and picked up the child, apparently unnoticed by the old woman, who remained poised over an empty spot on the mattress.

Adjusting his grip on the boy, Dylan nodded to Jaguar. "Lead on, O Kinky Turtle," he said, humming "Lead On, O King Eternal" as they exited the hovel.

51

RICHARD RETURNED to a house awash in funereal spirit. Kat was inconsolable over her brother's death—or, rather, the death of his body, which, Richard thought, pretty much amounted to the same thing. There was, after all, no way of getting her brother's spirit back with no body to put it in. No, he was gone, and Richard's heart went out to Kat as she wept in the chapel. He sat next to her and put a tentative arm around her shoulder. The tentativeness faded quickly as she curled up and clung to his chest, wetting the front of his cassock with her tears. He held her tightly to him and stroked her hair, saying nothing, not knowing what to say. As with Mr. Kim, it seemed enough to simply be there.

As he held her, Richard was amazed at the quantity and magnitude of grief surrounding him on all sides. The very world was grieving, and in the magnified world of the friary the grief was even greater. It seemed to him as if he were watching it at a distance—almost like a movie. He was able to bear it because the grief was not his—but he knew that wasn't true. He loved both Mikael and Toby, and they were both gone. He marveled then at his own detachment, as if he were watching himself from afar, from outside his body. And in that moment, it was the lack of emotion he felt that was grievous to him. He desperately needed to sob the way Kat was doing now. He *wanted* to feel his feelings, to connect with the sadness that was, now more than ever, the common lot of humanity. He wanted, he realized, to feel connected to *others*. At this realization, he hugged Kat even closer and buried his face in her hair. It was not enough, he knew. He wanted more, and more intimate contact than Kat could provide. The urgency of his need rose up in him with the suddenness of a tide. It scared him.

Just then, Susan appeared in the door leading to the kitchen, a mug of what Richard guessed to be hot chocolate in one fist, a yellow Post-it note stuck to a finger on her other hand. She hesitated upon seeing them, huddled in the dark, rocking back and forth slowly. Richard met her eyes and smiled at her encouragingly.

He patted the back of the chair on the other side of Kat, and hesitantly Susan took it, leaning into Kat and nuzzling her as she let out a deep and sympathetic breath.

After a few minutes like that, Susan straightened up and passed the Post-it to Richard. In the sanctuary lamp he could just make it out: *Spiritual Direction tomorrow, 10 a.m. Mother Maggie says,* 'Be there or you're a Cathar.' Richard smiled an annoyed smile. Damn Susan and Dylan, making good on their threat to get him an appointment ASAP. But he wasn't angry. It was probably, he realized, a good thing. His mind wandered back to the note. The Cathar leaders were called perfects, weren't they? About as far removed from how he felt about himself as he could possibly imagine.

They sat in the dark, huddled together in a pile for a long and timeless space. In the distance, the boom boom boom of Brian's drumming brought a feeling of primal majesty to the chapel. Richard watched the play of light upon the patchwork Jesus, the leaping flames bringing his features to life, making them appear to move in a kaleidoscopic, swirling pattern that reminded Richard of window-pane acid.

Behind them the front door opened, and Terry walked in. He paused a moment to let his eyes adjust and then walked toward the others. In the flicker of the candle, Richard could see concern, confusion, and weariness on Terry's face. He sat down next to Susan and laid his head on her shoulder. "What's up?" he asked.

"Randall died," she whispered.

Richard expected another jag of sobs from Kat when she heard that, but she seemed to be cried out.

Terry reached over Susan and touched Kat on the arm. He didn't say anything else, though. He had just spent two hours comforting those who had lost other loved ones, and he was exhausted. A touch of sympathy was all he could give, and, fortunately, it was all that was required.

The drum filled the air with sacredness despite the grief and fear. Then, suddenly, it stopped. Richard was startled when it did. It had been comforting, like a mother's heartbeat or the wheels of a train. He had taken it for granted, and when it was gone it was as if something lovely and holy had been sucked out of the world.

"Dylan must be back," Susan said.

"Let's hope Mikael is, too," Terry added.

Richard did not have a good feeling about it, but he held his tongue and pulled Kat's hair back from her face. "You okay?" he asked gently. "We're going to go see about Mikael."

She wiped her nose on her sleeve and nodded. "I'm coming with you," she said, uncurling her legs to get to her feet.

Like a mournful medieval procession, they made their way past the foyer, through the living room, and began to climb the wide front stairway.

Richard brought up the rear and paused on the last step as Terry poked his head into Mikael's room. Soon they were all crowded around the doorway, watching as Dylan, kneeling over Mikael's body, cupped his hands and blew into his mouth. He did it again, mumbling prayers only heard by himself, his power animal, and the Divine.

Then he sat back on his haunches and discovered he had an audience. "Well?" asked Brian, rubbing his wrist. "Tell me I didn't just aggravate my carpal tunnel for nothing."

"We were able to retrieve a significant chunk of Mikael's soul, split off when he was a kid," Dylan said, his voice cracked with exhaustion. "But no, we didn't find *him*-him."

The small amount of hope in the room deflated like a knifed basketball. Richard put his hand on Kat's arm, wondering how much more she could take.

When she spoke, though, it was with such strength and clarity that he was taken aback. "That's it? You're just giving up?"

Dylan sighed, and Richard could hear him carefully control his annoyance, buffering it with compassion despite how little he had left to give. "No, Darlin', Ah'm not givin' up. But Ah *am* gonna go ta bed. T'marra Ah'll give it another try."

She lowered her head. Dylan had gently put her in her place, and if she resented it, she made no show of it. Without another word, Dylan rose and made his way to the bathroom. "Goin' ta bed, now," he called down the hall.

"More cocoa," Susan said, and slipped down the front stairs.

"Ready for bed, Baby?" Terry sidled up to where Brian was seated and pressed his belly against his partner's face. Brian pressed back into the belly and nodded. "Ass-thoo-fud," came Brian's muffled voice.

"Huh?" asked Richard.

"Cats to feed," Terry translated.

Richard was impressed but said nothing. Kat sat down on the bed beside Mikael and stroked his wild black hair. Terry touched her on the shoulder. "You going to be okay sleeping here?"

She nodded and lay down, spooning against Mikael's unconscious form. Wordlessly, the three men filed out of the room and down to the kitchen, where Susan was poised over the stove.

"Someone has to call the coroner," she said to them, not looking up.

"Can't we do that in the morning?" Brian asked.

"I don't know; aren't there laws about these things?" Richard asked.

"I'll do it," Susan said. "I'll just call the police and tell them we can wait until morning if they can. Their call. If they want to come tonight, I'll let them in. I'm a little wired tonight anyway."

Terry kissed her on the cheek. "Thanks, Sweetie," he said and, holding Brian's hand, led him out the back door to their cottage.

When she and Richard were alone, Susan offered, "Chocolate?"

"Nah. I need to get some air."

"Where are you going?" she said, a little concerned.

"I don't know," he answered, but it was a lie.

52

As he often did, Dane had ordered his driver to pull up near a playground. He knew it would probably be too late to see any of the children, but there was something about such places that soothed him. He would often come here to watch the little ones. He loved to "read" them, to discern what kind of homes they lived in, which of them had mommies and daddies worthy of them. In other words, he liked to see which of them was suffering the most.

Then he would fantasize about liberating them. How he would do it, what it would look like, feel like, how it would smell. He often got so swept up in his fantasies that he lost track of time. Sometimes the fantasies were enough, and he went away satisfied. Sometimes, they were merely antecedent pleasures leading up to that glorious time when he, their savior, would deliver to them their salvation.

Happily for him, it often turned out that the children who were most abused were those with the least amount of supervision. Some of them simply gave him their hands and walked with him directly to his car. They were, he knew, the ones who needed him most. He loved them more than any of the others because they came willingly, offering their worship with a glad heart.

Tonight, however, there were no children at the playground. It was late, and then there was the disappearance of the dogs, which no doubt contributed to the lack of teenagers—a playground's normal nocturnal residents.

He would have to come back soon, though. Perhaps tomorrow. He would need another child, and this one would be special. A sacrifice to end all sacrifices—the giving of a single life for the salvation of many. But there were no likely candidates at this park, on this evening.

He stewed in what was, after all, a petty disappointment. He reminded himself that there would be other opportunities, other children, other days of reckoning. Soon, he promised himself, *soon*.

Just then, the vibration of his cell phone interrupted his musings. He flipped it open and pressed it to his ear.

"Dane," he said curtly. The speaker was talking too fast—he could barely understand him. "Slow down, I can't...oh, it's you, Larch. I'm glad you called—very nicely done with the dogs, sir. You are to be congratulated. So now we know it can be done for a living creature of that size—"

Larch was screaming at him now. Dane squeezed his eyes closed and struggled to maintain his composure. "I don't give a rat's ass if your man is in a coma. You knew that would happen...What? No, *you* idiots are the demon experts; *you* find a way to reverse it or prevent it. That's not my job. My job is money. And power. And I have both, and you will not forget it. You work for me—" He held the phone away from his ear until Larch had finished his rant. "Larch, you will speak to me calmly and respectfully, or a hit squad of demons will teach you how to show such respect. Am I clear?"

The phone was silent as Larch apparently considered his words. "Beat up? What do you mean you were beat up?" Dane asked, amused by the notion. "What, all of you? Baseball bats and chains? How did they... You didn't have to open the door for them, you numb-skull." With a lighter spirit, Dane listened to the rest of the story of the lodge's assault, more delighted at the surprising turn than concerned.

"Look, only one of you is in the hospital, so consider yourself lucky. No, Larch, there you are wrong. One of you *will* carry the final package. This is what we have all been working toward. Yes, well, you have your agenda, and I have mine. A deal is a deal, sir. Tough. You don't have to do the ritual yourself—this is one of the perks of leadership—you get to delegate the dangerous work to the plebes...just pick someone competent. You can knock yourselves out trying to fix them later." Dane listened to Larch's feeble protestations and finally, irritably, interrupted him. "Tomorrow night at midnight. I will be there with the package. And you will be there to make sure your magickian goes through with it. You've done good work for me so far, Larch. If you want to live to see your precious revolution, *don't blow it.*"

He snapped the phone shut and breathed a long, irritated breath. He tapped on the glass, and his demon driver turned and showed him his fangs. "Where to, sir?" the creature said, with perfect British diction.

"I need to unwind, Clive. Take me to the usual place."

53

It was Richard's favorite kind of sex—anonymous and sweaty. He wasn't feeling picky that night. His partner was an annoyingly nelly bear he had found at the Jizz Factory bar—not usually his type, but Richard wasn't really paying attention. Worry invaded his mind, and he wondered whether Dylan would have better luck in his next attempt to find Mikael's spirit. A pang of regret mixed with guilt shot through him, a frustration that he met with renewed violence in the thrust of his hips.

"Oh God, yeah!" squealed the bear, who, Richard was mildly horrified to note, was sucking his thumb between verbal outbursts.

His mind wandered to Kat, and he felt his heart move within him. He had done everything he could, hadn't he? What had he missed? What might they have done that would have avoided his death? And now, for her to face the prospect that Mikael might never wake from his coma—it was too much to ask of anyone. Richard simply didn't know how to comfort her. *I barely know how to comfort myself*, he thought.

Banging the bear with hard, relentless strokes, Richard wondered momentarily at how outrageously packed the Jizz Factory was that evening. Of course it would be busy tonight. It made perfect sense—

the grief experienced by the largely childless gay community would far outweigh that of the straight, where pets were accorded their "normal" station in life. For many of Richard's gay and lesbian friends, though, their pets *were* their lives—their children. And here was the evidence—half the gay population of Berkeley converging in one place to bang their butts out—literally—to deal with their grief. *Just like me*, Richard thought, and the flash of empathy, insight, and solidarity caught him momentarily off balance. It made him feel vulnerable, which was no surprise, lately, but it was also oddly, comfortingly, human.

He simply could not believe that the eradication of the canine species had been Dane's ultimate objective—or the lodge's, for that matter. It had to be another experiment. Start with something small, an avocado, then try something bigger, a dog. But in preparation for what? What was the ultimate target of Dane and his clueless magickal employees?

Richard was still mystified as to Larch's antipathy for God—presumably, a dislike shared by his lodge as well. This was not unusual—many people go into the occult because of a negative reaction to the religious abuse they had suffered at the hands of so-called Christian conservatives. But Richard could not understand how making fruit or pets disappear could possibly undermine the Kingdom of Heaven. Then again, he didn't know what they were going to try next—and he shuddered at the thought.

"That was cool, do that again!" shouted the bear.

"Do what again?" asked Richard, not slowing down.

"That shaking thing with your body—it was *niiiice*."

Just then Richard felt himself pushing over the edge. He ground himself into the bear's guts as a shock of white lightning lit up his brain. Richard panted and pushed and cried out loud until the spasms slowed.

Catching the end of the condom in one hand to hold it in place, Richard pulled out before he got too soft. "Thanks, man, that was great." He kissed the bear on the cheek and turned away toward the showers.

Turning the knob of his combination lock, he fairly radiated relief, noting the almost complete lack of tension in his limbs. He was just pulling his T-shirt over his head when he heard a voice that froze him in his tracks.

"You're too cute. Does your bigness match your cuteness?" Richard paused to be sure, but there was no doubt. It was Alan Dane's voice, using the exact same line he had used when Richard had met him so many months before in this very place.

Holding his breath, Richard leaned against the lockers, listening. Quietly, he made his way to the end of the row of lockers and peeked around to the next row. He drew back quickly. Dane had been standing in front of an open locker, facing away from him, toward the showers, flirting with a guy several lockers down.

Richard listened to his own heart nearly beat through his chest as he waited. After what seemed like an eternity, Dane shut his locker and snapped a combination lock into a hole in the handle. Richard heard the click as it locked and continued to listen as Dane's voice slowly diminished with distance.

Richard's mind raced. There was no way Dane would leave the Ring of Solomon at home—especially after being burgled by the friars. He had to have it on him. It was also doubtful whether he would wear it into the baths—too easy to lose it—even easier to have it stolen with a dozen anonymous hands pawing at you.

No, he decided, *it must be in that locker.*

He peeked around the corner again to make sure that Dane was out of sight, and then, as nonchalantly as he could, he made for the front desk in search of an idea. Could he tell the guy on duty that he'd forgotten his combination, and could they please cut the lock off? What would he say when it opened and the thing was full of clothes—when Richard was already wearing clothes? They might make him prove the contents were his, maybe look at the wallet? *Too risky*, he told himself. "Shit!" he breathed and willed himself to be calm. He may not have viewed himself as a *good* man, but Richard knew what he loved, and there was way too much at stake to blow this. At the end of the foyer was a Dutch door, the upper half of the door wide open and the lower half slightly ajar, with soiled towels piled on its ledge. Glancing back at the front desk, Richard saw that it was mobbed with people either trying to get in or complaining about someone's behavior in the baths. Three employees were trying to expedite things, and none, fortuitously, were taking any notice of him. He ducked through the Dutch door and, casting about with barely controlled panic, found himself in a utility room. A free-standing tool chest on rollers was pushed to one side of the room, almost obscured by towels. He leaped to it and jerked open the lowest and largest drawer. Inside there was only a very large crescent wrench and some rusted pipe. He tried the second-largest drawer and nearly fainted from relief—a pair of short-handled bolt cutters.

Acting quickly, he found a stack of clean towels and wrapped one around the cutters. Then he made for the door.

He had just entered the hall when a voice stopped him. "You! What were you doing in there?" A man in a dark blue polo shirt with the Jizz Factory logo was staring right at him and glaring. "Yeah, you? What were you doing in there?"

Richard hesitated just a moment, his brain nearly short-circuiting with panic. He held up the cutters, wrapped in the towel. "You're short on towels. I was looking for one."

"Goddammit. Will someone go and stock the fucking towels?" The man turned away from him, and Richard continued, swallowing hard and willing his heartbeat to slow.

Turning the corner into the row of lockers where Dane's effects were housed, Richard approached the locker and turned his back to the men dressing or undressing several lockers down. He held one corner of the towel and let the rest of it fall, making sure that its length still obscured the cutters, but now only one layer thick so that the tool was still operable through the fabric. To anyone else on the row, he hoped it would look like he was holding a towel while fiddling with his lock, when in reality, he was cutting it off.

It would have been an impossible deceit, but fortunately no one was paying him any attention, and no one seemed to notice when the lock broke off with a satisfying but too-audible-for-comfort "snap!"

Richard laid the cutters on the bench in front of him, making sure to cover them with the towel. Then, stealing one more glance behind him, he raised the lever on Dane's locker and swung wide the door.

Inside was the sort of suit Richard had seen him in just days before. His heart raced as he felt at the pants pockets. Nothing.

He reached past the trousers to the suit jacket and felt at the inside pocket. A comb. Lowering his hands, he felt at the large outside jacket pockets—and there was a likely bulge. He fished inside the pocket and pulled forth an enormous golden ring with a gleaming red stone.

He stared at it with his mouth agape, in wonder at the historic and mystical treasure in his very hands. This was the stuff of legends, and its appearance did not disappoint. It looked exactly as he had expected it to, and he trembled and quailed at its power.

Then, suddenly, he realized where he was and what he was doing. He stuffed the ring into the front pocket of his jeans—he had, wisely, left his cassock in the car—and began closing the door to the locker. A shine of black leather caught his eye, and he bent to investigate. Sitting on the bottom of the locker was a black leather bag, kind of like an old doctor's kit but deeper. Without thinking, he took up the bag in his left hand and closed the locker door with his right. He left the bolt cutters where they lay and, trying to appear as nonchalant as he possibly could, strolled out the front door into the frigid Berkeley winter night.

MONDAY

54

WHEN THE BELLS sounded for morning prayer, Richard hissed and covered his eyes like a vampire allergic to the sun. He'd only gotten a few hours of sleep, but the events of the coming day loomed heavily over him, and his pulse was already pounding beyond the possibility of sleep.

He threw on his cleanest cassock and stumbled down the front stairs, yawning as he took his place in the choir.

He was amazed that he'd made it with a couple of minutes to spare. Either Brian or Terry rang the bells ten minutes prior to the commencement of all the daily offices, which was usually enough time for the friars to wrap up what they were doing and get to the chapel.

He listed, trying to focus his eyes, when Dylan entered and sat next to him, dropping a newspaper in his lap. The headline screamed in 135-point type: DOG RAPTURE ROCKS WORLD!

Struggling to see the smaller type of the story more clearly, he read about the "mysterious disappearance of canines all over the planet." The writer even linked it to the disappearance of the avocados, Richard was pleased to see. He was particularly interested in the mention of breakaway evangelical cults that had arisen in the past day, interpreting the disappearance as an actual Rapture. "The Lord has chosen to take the purest in heart first," said the Rev. Spike Malloway of Calgary, Idaho. It made Richard smile.

"Did yah see the bit about the UFO cults?" Dylan asked.

"No, not yet," Richard chuckled.

"Y'know, it's weird bein' the handful of people on the planet who actually knows what's goin' on," Dylan mused.

"I'd feel a hell of a lot better about it if we actually did know what was going on," Richard countered. "I'm just waiting for the other shoe to drop."

"Why do we have to wait for them to act; why not stop 'em now? A preemptive strike, y'know?"

"What are we going to do? Have them arrested? With what evidence?" Richard answered, turning the page. "Are we going to kill them? Bad ethical form there. What exactly do you propose we *do*, Dyl?"

Dylan pursed his lips and rocked back and forth slightly. Before he could think of an answer, Terry and Kat had found their places, and Dylan rang a Tibetan bell to mark the start of the service.

They sang the canticle and sat quietly as Terry recited the readings. Afterward, none of them had a "word from the Lord" to share, so the homiletical portion was observed in silence. They moved on to the prayers.

Richard offered prayers for all those grieving the loss of their pets. Dylan offered prayers for the soul of Kat's brother. Terry offered prayer for Mikael's restoration. Then Kat exploded.

"Fuck you!" she screamed at the patchwork icon of Jesus. "Fuck you, you motherfucking son of a whore!" She stepped into the middle of the room and threw her coffee at it. The cup smashed into the icon's chin, and a brown spray covered the lower half of his face. She pointed her finger at it. "Fuck you and everything you're trying to do! How could you..." Then she collapsed to her knees and buried her face in her hands, making soft whimpering sounds.

The friars, moved, spontaneously applauded. "That there's some good fucking prayer," Dylan noted with approval.

"Let 'im have it, Sister!" Terry cheered encouragingly.

Kat looked up at them, horrified. Richard could not tell, however, whether the horror was in response to her own outburst or to their response. "Well done," he said, and smiled at her.

"What the *fuck* are you talking about?" she shook her head, incredulous. "I just ruined your prayer."

"Nah, Ah think ya saved it," Dylan said. "That was the most honest prayer Ah've heard in ages."

"Hear, hear," agreed Terry. "You don't have to worry about swearing at Jesus. He's a big boy. He can take it. All he wants is to know how you *really* feel anyway."

"Do you have anything else you want to say to him?" Richard asked her. "We're still doing the Prayers of the People, you know."

She shook her head, apparently a little dazed.

Terry sang the benediction, and they rang the big bell again, bringing prayer to a close.

Kat's outburst had had a revivifying effect on them all, and whereas they had all stumbled in feeling defeated and morose, they closed their prayers feeling invigorated and hopeful.

Dylan paused to consider the stain on their icon. "Y'know," he said to Terry, "Ah think the coffee stains give him a more handsome, rugged appearance. It's the five o'clock shadow, sensitive-but-macho Jesus." Terry bobbed his head back and forth, uncertain about the new look.

Richard knelt by Kat. "You okay?" he asked.

"You are the weirdest fucking people I have ever met," she said, looking up at him uncertainly.

"We aim to please," Richard smiled down at her and offered a hand up.

She took it, and they both headed toward the kitchen.

"No Susan?" Brian asked, skillet in hand.

"She was up late with the paramedics and the police," Dylan said. "Ah'll put a plate in the fridge for her for later."

"You'll need to, 'cause I have to work this morning," Brian said, emptying the skillet of its bacon onto a paper towel-lined bowl on the lazy Susan.

Fresh-squeezed juice was on the table as well, along with fried potatoes and blueberry muffins with jam.

"Every meal around here is nothin' but fucking food porn," Dylan said admiringly.

"How could it be porn?" Terry asked, scrunching his brows together. "It's the real thing, not a representative of the real thing."

"The signifier co-inheres with the signified," Dylan quoted, and Richard recognized it from a sacramental theology text he had read years ago.

"Dylan, you are *so* talking out of your ass," Richard accused.

"Mah ass can also play the trumpet," Dylan grabbed a handful of bacon, "although the spit valve is not pretty."

"When your ass can shuffle cards, call me," Terry said, giggling.

"You know," Kat said, her face ashen and grave, "someone did die yesterday. And millions of people lost loved ones."

The friars looked down at their plates. "Perhaps we have *not* met the morning with sufficient gravity," Richard said, by way of apology.

He helped himself to a muffin. "Brian, did you say you were going in to work today?"

"Yup, ten o'clock." Brian worked part time as a research specialist at the Graduate Theological Union Library.

"Well, while you're there, see what you can find out about this," and with slow, dramatic flourish, he placed the Ring of Solomon on the table in front of him.

"What the fuck?" asked Terry. "That's not—"

"It is."

"Ho. Ly. Shit," breathed Dylan. "Have you put it on?"

"Are you fucking nuts?" asked Richard. "I don't know what it does or how it works."

"That's what you want me to find out, then?" Brian asked, slapping Dylan's hand. "Save some bacon for Sue."

"Exactly," Richard said. "We know that demons have to obey it, but we don't know how or why. We don't want to break our vows out of ignorance any more than we do from volition." Nods all around confirmed their commitment.

"What good is it if we don't kn—can't use it?" Dylan asked, scowling at Brian.

"At least Dane doesn't have it," Terry said. "And hey, how the hell did *you* get your hands on it, anyway?" Terry asked.

Richard blushed, his eyes skittering back and forth like a cornered cat. "You didn't..." Terry looked at him with his *disappointed* look. "You whore," he said.

Kat's brows knitted as she attempted to follow the conversation. "What am I missing?" she asked.

"Simple. Richard went to a sex club last night because, oh, I don't know, his friends weren't *enough* support for his fragile self-image, apparently." Terry glowered at him.

Richard betrayed no other visible sign of shame besides his color, which was now approaching chartreuse. "Dane was there. I stole the ring while he was boinking," he explained. "I also took this." He set Dane's leather bag on the table. "Unfortunately, it doesn't appear to contain anything of import. I thought maybe you could have an energetic look at it just to be sure, Terry."

"I'm tempted to say 'good job,' but I refuse to encourage you," Terry said.

"Why is it that monogamous gays are *way* more judgmental than monogamous straights?" Richard asked no one in particular.

"'Cause we've seen more people die of AIDS up close and personal, you asshole." Terry threw down his napkin, grabbed the leather bag, and stormed out of the kitchen toward his cottage.

"Ya struck a nerve, dude," Dylan said. "He's right, too, *and*"—he patted Richard's arm—"good job."

"Assignments for the day," Richard announced, grateful to have thought of a change of subject. "I have a spiritual direction session at ten, no thanks to you." He nodded at Dylan.

"Ah'm gonna have another go at a soul retrieval this a.m. Then Ah have a baptismal rehearsal for little Jamie this after."

"I'll work on the ring at the GTU," Brian said.

Kat was tempted to say, "What about me?" but she held her tongue. She had something to show Terry.

55

KAT WAS SQUEEZING water from a sopping washcloth into Mikael's mouth when Dylan and Susan entered the room. She forced a smile for them and made way for Dylan to lie down.

She had heard about shamanic journeys before but had never seen one. "What went wrong yesterday?" she asked Dylan, as the rotund friar wiggled his way into place.

"Nothin' went wrong, exactly," Dylan said, getting comfortable. "We jes' wasn't lookin' in the right place. Today, we'll look somewhar else."

"We?" Kat asked.

"Me and Jaguar," Dylan said. "He's mah power animal."

"Does everybody have a power animal?" Kat asked.

"Oh, they do, yeah. But it never turns out to be what you think it's gonna be. Me, Ah'm a dog person. Ah always assumed it would be a dog. Imagine mah surprise when this enormous cat shows up."

"What's your power animal like?" she asked, more and more curious. Susan was taking her place beside Dylan, tapping at her drum.

"He's a surly motherfucker," Dylan answered. "But he's *mah* surly motherfucker. Ready there, Honey Pants?"

"Ready, curly buns," Susan replied. "Going up or down?"

"Up this time. Need to get some guidance."

"How long?"

"Give me an hour, then a half hour return."

She nodded and with an encouraging smile at Kat, began to beat the drum.

Kat sat still and listened to the hypnotic pounding of the drum—plain, regular, fast, and utterly without deviation. Within minutes she could feel herself getting sleepy and wondered at how Susan was able to drum for so long. A minute later, she got up and moved to the guest room. There she leaned against the wall and looked at the empty bed, where her brother had lain just a few hours ago.

It seemed almost like a dream, it was so grotesque. An alien being inhabiting the body of the boy—no, the man—she loved so very much. She fought back tears and swallowed. She thought back to how much she had cried in the past couple of days, and fought against an overwhelming feeling of shame. Her behavior had been so at odds with how she had always seen herself—strong, indomitable, resolute. But the events of the past few days had completely undone her. She never would have believed any of it if it had not happened to her. She wasn't sure she believed it *now*.

She turned and looked back at the open door to Mikael's room, still held in the trance of Susan's otherworldly rhythm. Love at first sight was something she had always sneered at, never imagining for a moment it would fall on her. She wasn't ready for him. Mikael had just *happened*. And at the most inconvenient time imaginable. And now, now he was the most important thing in the world—this skeletal goth boy that she barely knew.

Being trapped in the house did *not* help matters, either. At least the house was big—it didn't prevent her feeling claustrophobic, but it sure as hell helped. It felt good to have been able to help with the web research—she just wished there was more she could do.

She turned around again and saw the mirror. With the bright sun filling the room, she saw nothing in it that was unusual. She cupped her hands around several sections, but it was no good. Should she bring Terry up here? What would he see if she couldn't even see anything? *He'll think I'm an idiot*, she said to herself. And pursed her lips. She could take it to a darker place, she reasoned, and with that thought she lifted it off the wall and started down the narrow back stairway.

Carrying the mirror under her arm, she went out the back door of the kitchen and crossed the yard to the cottage. She hesitated for a moment—she didn't really know Terry all that well, and if she were honest, his mercurial extroversion scared her a little. But she breathed deep and knocked.

He answered the door moments later dressed in a lavender leotard, wearing white pancake makeup with neat little circles of rouge painted onto his cheeks.

"Do I need to explain this to you?" he asked her with the tiniest intimation of prickliness.

"You do not," she assured him, mildly amused.

"Please come into my fairy castle, fair princess," he waved his hand in a grand gesture bidding her to enter.

"Why, thank you, I think." She smiled, a little nervously. The cottage was very small but was painted with such bright colors and was so devoid of clutter that the size did not seem oppressive. The furnishings were elegant, modern, and spare. A couple of scented candles gave the room a yellow warmth on what was otherwise a gray and gloomy day.

"What's up?" Terry asked, stepping into the kitchenette. "Tea?"

"Sure," she said. "Anything."

"Whatchagot there?" he asked.

"It's a mirror," she said.

"No shit," he said, plugging in the electric kettle. "That's the one from the guest room, isn't it?"

"Yes. I wanted to show you something. Can we—um, go into the bathroom? It kind of needs to be dark."

His eyebrows rose dramatically, and he signaled her to follow him. They squeezed into the tiny bathroom together, and Kat pushed the door until it was only ajar a few inches.

Terry gasped. She had hoped to hear such a thing, and the tension in her shoulders lessened somewhat.

There, in the mirror, a dim violet light about the size of a golf ball hovered.

"It's him, isn't it?" she asked him. "Not my brother, I mean. It's the angel. I'm sure it is."

Terry was nodding, and she watched as he reached out his hand and attempted to touch the radiance. But it seemed to be several inches *into* the mirror, on the other side.

"Probably got trapped there once his body...expired." He looked at her with soft eyes. "At least he's *somewhere*."

"What would happen to him if he weren't...in there?" Kat asked, opening the bathroom door again.

The kettle was whistling, and Terry skipped ahead of her to turn it off. "I'm not sure. Spirits need to be in bodies, even subtle bodies like angels have. If they're not, they...dissipate. Then they're *really* dead, because they're just *gone*."

"That's scary. I think that's scarier than thinking Heaven or Hell is real," Kat said, her brow knitting.

"Well, some people prefer the idea of annihilation to the survival of the soul, but I'm with you—I think it's pretty scary, too." He poured them each a cup of tea and set out a couple of oat cakes.

"So, what can we do for him? The angel, I mean," Kat asked.

"Well, I'm not sure," Terry sat down and gave her a serious look. "What we *need* to do is to get him back to Heaven, to his proper body."

She hadn't thought of that. Fear seized at her chest. "And what will happen to Randall's soul when that happens?" she asked.

Terry didn't look at her. But he did, in a way, answer her. He leaned over and blew out a candle.

WHEN HE OPENED his mind's eye, Dylan saw the tree. It was the same tree he always climbed when he went to visit the Upper World, and he climbed it with an alacrity impossible in the conventional world.

Not bothering to look down, he felt the wind on his face and the slight sway of the tree as he reached higher and thinner limbs. Soon he climbed through a cloud, and once above it, he swung down.

He was still in the clouds, only now he was standing on one. An arm reached out to help him find his balance.

"Hullo, Arnault. Good to see you, dude," Dylan shook his head and beamed. Arnault was a slight, elderly man wearing a vaguely Roman-style toga. He was cordial, but never exactly friendly. Dylan wondered why everyone in the Otherworld was so...not depressed, exactly, but not happy about things, either.

"Good morning, Father Dylan," Arnault spoke with a stiff British accent, too, which was just a little too cliché for Dylan's comfort, but who was he to complain? It was his Otherworld, after all. If he wanted to people it with the cast of *I, Claudius*, he bloody well could.

Soon, Dylan saw Jaguar padding over the clouds toward him. He waved at the big cat and raised a friendly hand to pet his muzzle as he approached.

"To the Grandfathers, please, Jaggy." Dylan supposed he would be able to find his way by himself, but Jaguar didn't do much when he came to the Upper World, usually, so Dylan thought it was a kindness to give him a job.

He waved goodbye to Arnault, whose never-ending, never-wavering occupation seemed to consist entirely of helping people down from trees. As he and Jaguar walked toward a deep green valley, he wondered what crime Arnault had committed to be resigned to such petty work.

Eventually, wisps of cloud gave way to rolling green hills, and Jaguar led them over a knoll toward a ring of tepees beside a thin, winding river.

It was a familiar sight, as Dylan often approached the Grandfathers to solicit their wisdom. Seven small tepees were gathered in a circle around an enormous one in the center. No one met or questioned them as they approached the flap on the largest of the skin structures.

Without hesitation Dylan ducked his head into the tepee, and Jaguar followed him inside. There they saw a large circle of Native-American men and women, some sitting quietly as if waiting for him, and some talking and joking in low voices. He and Jaguar found gaps in the circle and filled them. Dylan sat cross-legged, close enough to the Grandfather who seemed to be in charge to hear him plainly. Dylan called him Old Leatherface, though not to his leathery face. The elderly Indian rocked back and forth, a gap-tooth smile playing on his ancient and weatherbeaten jowls.

He didn't seem to notice Dylan or Jaguar but did start to hum after they had been seated for a while. His humming seemed tuneless, almost random, but it did have a rhythm to it, more or less matching the beat Susan was pounding out, still audible, though distant.

When he finished his song, a deep silence descended on the room. No one spoke, although Dylan could see a lot of smiles on the twenty or so Native faces.

"I think last time you were here we named you Sleeping Bear," said the old man, and chuckles spilled out into the room from the other Grandfathers and Grandmothers.

"Yeah, Ah've put on a few pounds, even since Ah saw y'all last." Dylan also thought the name apt because he would really like to be taking a nap about now.

But there was business to tend to, so he forced himself to stay awake and alert. Grandfather seemed to notice. "Sleep, if you want," he said. "We're in no hurry. Not our way."

Dylan knew all about their "way," and it was precisely because of this that he had sought their council. If there were a path, a "way" to Mikael, he wanted to know it.

"Ah'm sorry to take up your time, Grandfather, Ah just don't know who else to ask about this stuff."

"First, let us have a smoke," the old man said in a tone that left no room for negotiation. A peace pipe was produced and filled with sacred tobacco. It was passed around the circle. When it came to him, Dylan noticed that it was packed with sticky green bud, not tobacco at all, apparently, just for him. He took a deep hit and exhaled slowly, passing the pipe to his left, where it once again inexplicably seemed to be filled with tobacco.

It was a kindness that Dylan appreciated, and he felt his muscles relax as the THC invaded his nerve-addled brain.

Once the pipe had made its way all around, the Grandfathers and Grandmothers sat silently, apparently waiting for him to speak.

"Grandfathers, Grandmothers, I come seeking your help," Dylan began. Many of them were smiling slightly and nodding, giving him their rapt attention.

"Mah friend Mikael got waylaid by a demon—he viewed the sigil, see. The demon had been summoned to switch the magickian's body with an angel's, and now Mikael's body has been...well, abandoned by his spirit. Ah attempted a soul retrieval, but Ah couldn't find a large portion of his soul. It don't seem to be in the Middle World. Ah'm hopin' you can give me some clue as to where Ah can find 'im."

Dylan looked at Jaguar, but the great cat's face revealed nothing.

"What makes you think he wants to be found?" Old Leatherface asked.

"He didn't leave his body willingly," Dylan said, "At least, Ah don't think he would've. Ah haven't known Mikael all that long, but from what Ah've seen, he's a life-lovin' kind of dude."

"Demons are bad news," said one Grandmother. Dylan resisted the urge to say "No shit, Grandma" in response and waited for her to continue. Her face was wrinkled like a dried apple, and ringlets of smoke-black hair hung into her eyes. She ran her tongue over her few remaining teeth. "If he were scared, he would go someplace safe." She nodded at him.

He thought about that. What is a place that Mikael would consider safe? The grove where his Christo-Pagan Craft Circle did their rituals? Maybe. The Montague Sommers Memorial Chapel at the Friary? An equal chance, but it didn't strike Dylan as much of an aha. He looked at Jaguar for help, but the cat was licking its ass with no apparent self-consciousness whatsoever. In fact, he really seemed to be digging for gold.

Dylan made a face and turned back to the elders. "A safe place, Ah get that," Dylan said. "Can you be more specific?"

This was the problem with help from the Otherworld, of course. You could always count on them for input, but it was almost always so cryptic as to be maddeningly unhelpful.

One old man pointed at Dylan and laughed. "What?" Dylan asked, checking his nose to see if there was a booger hanging from it. "He is doing what he loves most! It brings him comfort." The old man smiled a toothless smile and nodded his head.

"Sleeping Bear has his answer. Time to go," said Old Leatherface.

"What are you talking about?" Dylan asked. "You're just tossing me out? But Ah still don't know where he is."

"Yes, you do. He is safe, doing what he loves. Go there." And then the Grandfather began humming again. The audience was ended.

57

CEDAR STREET in north Berkeley was buzzing with students from the University of California and young mothers pushing prams, yet Richard saw no one. On autopilot, he steered himself toward All Saints' Episcopal Church and opened the door to the offices.

He did not bother to straighten what was left of his windblown hair but merely plopped down in a chair in the large hallway. He fought a moment of resentment toward Dylan and Susan, but knew it was all for the best. He didn't like being ordered around, but his spiritual director's perspective was always valuable, if not completely welcome. In a few moments, Mother Maggie poked her head into the hallway. "Hello, Padre. Are you ready?"

Maggie was a diminutive dumpling of a woman who seemed to Richard unmoved by age, illness, or any variety of trouble. Her gray hair and wrinkled features suggested she had seen plenty of it, but her zeal for every endeavor, and indeed, everyone she met left no doubt who had been victorious. Richard admired her, and her matronly attention persuaded him to open up to her. She was, in fact, the only spiritual director he had ever been able to be completely vulnerable with. Mother was an unusual nickname for an Episcopal priest, but it fit her. He sometimes referred to her as his true *alma mater*, the mother of his soul.

"Thanks for the short notice, Maggie," he said. "Even if it wasn't entirely my doing."

She nodded. "What are friends for?" He wasn't sure whether she was referring to herself or to Dylan and Susan but decided it didn't matter. They sat for a few minutes in silence together. Once they had centered, Maggie lit a candle on the table beside her. "Let this serve to remind us that there are three of us here." The statement jolted him, and Richard caught a note of profound sadness in her voice. Usually, Maggie's dog, JoJo, was lying in her bed in the corner. Maggie's usual invocation was, "Let this serve to remind us that there are four of us here." The new formulation only served to point out that JoJo was gone. Richard's eyes lit upon the little blue dog bed, void and lonely in its familiar place.

Then they sat in silence some more. When he first started seeing her, Richard had found Maggie's methods unsettling, but he was used to it now. To be alone with another person and not speak was profoundly countercultural, and yet now that he was used to it, it seemed to him almost obscenely intimate.

When he finally did speak, he was surprised to find that it was not in words but sobs. They had started as words, but they had never made it. Crossing the threshold of the throat, they swelled with emotion and choked him. He folded over and surrendered to an accelerating rush of pent-up feelings scrambling to get out through the hacking, snot, and tears.

When he was conscious of his surroundings again, he found Maggie's cheek resting on the top of his head, hovering above him, her hands caressing his shoulders. When she noticed the storm within him subsiding, she kissed the bald top of his head and took her seat, nudging the Kleenex box closer to him.

She didn't ask, "What was that about?" She just waited, and the silence spoke for her.

When he finally did speak, his voice sounded to him like a child's. He told her all about what had happened, about being dumped by

Philip, about the avocados, about the dogs, about the confrontation with the lodge, and about Kat's brother. Through it all she sat silently, giving him the gift of her attention and her presence. When, finally, the story lay as if open on the floor between them, she asked him what seemed to be a most irrelevant question. "And how do you feel?"

Without pausing to think, he blurted out, "I feel damned."

She nodded as if expecting this answer. "By whom?" she asked.

He opened his mouth to say, "By God, of course," but he knew before it had come out that that was not right. *Damn her*, he thought, *she always knows just the right questions to ask.*

He knew what the wrong answer was to the question, but not what the right one was. "I don't know," he finally breathed.

"Bullshit," she said with an affectionate smile. "'I don't know' always means 'I don't want to say.'"

"But I really think I don't. It's just a feeling."

"Okay," she said, "Why don't you tell me how you feel using other words?"

His gaze wandered off and became unfocused as he rooted about inside. "I feel completely fucked up inside."

"That's more like it," she said. "What feels fucked up? I'll make a list." She held up her clipboard in a gesture of helpfulness.

"I don't deserve to lead this order."

"Why not?"

"I feel like a fake, an impostor. Like I'm just playing at being the prior. I feel like a friar—I just don't feel like a leader. I'm not...holy. I'm fucked up."

She bent her head and scribbled with hands misshapen by arthritis. She looked up. "What else?"

"You aren't going to try to talk me out of it?"

Her eyebrows shot up. "Should I?"

He scowled at her. Her methods always caught him off guard.

"I hate being bisexual."

"Why?" She looked at him with real affection. It unnerved him.

"Because I don't know who the hell I am. I don't understand myself. I can't seem to commit to men *or* women. I feel..."

"Don't say 'damned'," she warned.

"Okay, I feel..." But there wasn't another word. "Set up? I feel set up by God. For failure."

She wrote. "Good, good. This is all good. Anything else?"

"What—?" *In what way was this good?* he wondered. He teetered on the brink of exasperation with her. But he gave in and continued to play it her way. "Yes. I drink too much. I worry about myself. About being an addict."

She looked up from her clipboard, and Richard could see the emotion in the corners of her eyes.

"Let's pray!" she announced, grabbing his hand.

Richard resisted inside, hating at that moment the roller coaster ride that every session with Mother Maggie turned out to be. Yet for being such a workout, they were almost always transformative, and it was with great effort that he tried to get his ego, fears, and resistances out of the way. Not that there was any way to stop her. She had already turned her face to Heaven and parted her hands, her misshapen palms held upward in entreaty to God.

"Lord of Heaven, we give thee joyful thanks for the gifts thou hast given Father Richard, thy servant, in the form of these icky feelings. We thank thee for his feelings of damnation, for because of them he will never presume himself to be superior to anyone. He will not think he is special, or elect, or somehow favored by thee over another. We thank thee that he feels like a fake, for then he will never assume that he knows what he is doing, and will never make bullshit pronouncements about what you allegedly want. For these gifts of humility we give thee hearty thanks—"

Ouch, Richard thought.

"We thank thee for his bisexuality, for his confusion and struggle, for thou hast given him the special gift of being able to love all peoples, regardless of their genitalia—"

Richard winced painfully but restrained himself from interrupting.

"And finally, we thank thee for his troubled relationship with alcohol, for the longing for transcendence it represents. We thank thee that he can empathize with all those who fight against the unseen forces of addiction, and that he is brave enough to speak it aloud, to himself, to me, and to thee. And we thank thee for Richard's vulnerability, that he is fully human, even as the rest of us are, and we ask thee to comfort him, to see himself as the blessing to the world thou hast made him to be, even in the midst of his petty afflictions. Amen."

"Fuck you, Maggie. Sometimes I really hate you."

"The truth is often painful." She patted his hand lovingly. "But it's good to take everything to God in prayer."

"Have you ever been reported for malpractice?"

"My insurance is paid up. And you're deflecting."

He slumped in his chair.

"Do you want some advice?"

"Do I have a choice?" he asked.

"This insecurity of yours is a form of arrogance—"

"What are you talk—"

"Shut the fuck up, and listen to me, you little coward."

Richard sat up as if he had been punched in the gut. Maggie continued, smiling beatifically. "If you think your puny sins—or even your worst ones—are powerful enough to invalidate or over-power the love of God, then you are as full of shit as my composter."

She leaned in until her red and pudgy face was almost touching his. "You can choose to love yourself as God loves you, or you can suffer. Your choice. But as long as you fight your demons, you. Will. Be. Fighting."

"Okay," he said, trying to back even farther into his chair, "that's obvious."

"Not really. Lots of people think if they just ignore their demons, they'll go away. But they never do," she leaned back and sat comfortably in her own chair again, restoring the comfort of Richard's personal space.

"So, if I can't ignore them and I can't fight them, what do I do?" he asked her.

She hummed to herself and gave him a wicked little grin. "As soon as you embrace them, you know, they'll stop tormenting you." She leaned over and whispered, "Just like you, they only want to be loved. Why don't you invite them to dinner?"

58

RICHARD OPENED the door of the friary uncertainly. He dared not hope. He removed his rain gear and rounded the corner into the kitchen. The sour faces at the table brought the news before any words were said.

Dylan, Susan, and Kat sat with the collective energy of deflated balloons. They stared at the table and didn't even bother to look up when Richard entered the room. "Okay, I'm guessing not much movement on the Mikael front?"

Dylan shook his head, obviously lost in thought. Terry, at least, kissed Richard on the cheek, and then turned to resume his sandwich-making activity. For several minutes no one spoke.

"So, what happened?" Richard asked as Terry set a platter of sandwiches on the lazy Susan before them.

"Well, we went to see the Grandfathers and Grandmothers, to ask their advice," Dylan said, reaching for a sandwich.

Terry slapped at his hand. "Grace," he said. "Just because it's a hard day doesn't mean we have nothing to be grateful for. You're the offender; you can say it."

Dylan scowled at him. He had tried to be the hero, not the

offender. But he realized Terry was just channeling Brian in his partner's absence.

"All right. Let us pray. O Lord, we give you thanks fer this food, and fer the pesky hand what made it. Amen."

"Thank you. I think," said Terry, placing a jug of apple cider on the table and sitting down.

"And what did they say—the Grandfathers and Grandmothers?" Richard asked, reaching for a sandwich of his own.

"They said, 'He is safe, doing what he loves. Go there.' Wherever the fuck *there* is. Where he feels the *most safe*. Damned if Ah know where that would be."

Terry and Richard locked eyes, and Richard sat up straight as if he were hit by lightning. He thought back to the elder Dane's unsuccessful exorcism. Mikael had been nervous, and Terry asked him about the place where he felt the *most safe*.

"Dyl, hey," he laughed. Everyone at the table—except Terry—looked at him like he had suddenly turned into cream cheese.

"We know where that is," Terry said.

Just then the doorbell rang. "Ah, shit, they're early!" Dylan whined. "Hold that thought, dude!" he said, pointing at Terry. He rose from the table like a man propelled. "And bag a couple o' them sandwiches fer me, will ya, Ter?"

"Who is it?" Kat asked.

"It's the Swansons, here for the baptismal rehearsal. Five minutes, that's all Ah ask, five minutes for a fuckin' sandwich..." But then he was at the door and swinging it wide with a broad smile. "Come in! Welcome!" The Swansons entered, little Jamie in her daddy's arms. "Hello, Boopsi!" Dylan touched her nose. She wrinkled it and turned a sad face into her father's shoulder.

"Uh-oh, li'l Darlin', what's the matter?"

Her father set her on the floor, and she looked at her shoes. Dylan held his hand out to her, and finally she spoke, barely audible. "Sammy went to Heaven."

Dylan looked up at her parents, who were themselves looking

pretty sad. "Is Sammy your puppy?" Dylan asked. The little girl nodded. Dylan sat on the floor next to her, cross-legged, and without prompting she sat in his lap and threw her arms around his neck. Surprised, Dylan took a moment to adjust to the sudden outburst of affection and smiled, hugging the little girl to him and rocking. "Oh, Ah know, Darlin', Ah know. Ah lost mah puppy, too. His name was Tobias—remember him? Ah miss him so much I feel like dyin'." He did, too, and tears sprang to his eyes thinking about him.

She drew back and looked at his face. She reached out a finger and touched one of the tears on Dylan's broad cheek. "I didn't know grown-ups could cry," she said, amazed.

"Ah'm not really a grown-up," he said in a conspiratorial whisper. "Ah'm just a little kid *pretendin'* to be a grown-up." She looked at him in awe. "You pray for Sammy, okay? 'Cause God can do amazing things, an' ya never know."

"Will God make Sammy come back?"

Dylan put on his serious face. "Well, ordinarily Ah'd say no, but this is a pretty special case. Now sometimes puppies die, and they can't come back. But Sammy and Toby, they're not dead. So, it's hard to say. All Ah'm sayin' is, it don't hurt to pray, okay?"

She nodded. "Do I have to take a bath?"

Dylan laughed. "Not exactly, li'l one. We're gonna put some water on your head, but it's not as icky as taking a bath. It's kind of like a play, so it's a lot of fun. What do you think? Do you wanna be in a play?" He nodded excitedly and was relieved when she nodded back.

Dylan scooped her up and, standing, shook her father's hand, then her mother's, and took their coats. Mrs. Swanson gazed through the door into the kitchen, and they all waved at her. "Oh, I'm sorry to have interrupted your meal," Connie said.

"S'no problem," Dylan said. "Sandwiches keep. Now, let's all have a seat here in the chapel and talk through the ceremony."

Terry shut the swinging door to keep the kitchen talk from spilling out into the chapel. But no sooner had he resumed his place than the doorbell rang again.

"Grand Fucking Central!" he threw down his napkin again.

"I'll get it," Richard said and pushed past the kitchen door. He caught Dylan's eye as he passed through the chapel, and pointed at the door.

Dylan mouthed, "Thank you," and turned his attention back to the rehearsal.

Richard opened the door partway to see who it was. The face that met him was badly bruised and swollen, and it took him a moment to realize who it was.

"Larch?" he asked.

"Yes, it's fucking Larch. I need to speak to you."

Richard shot a worried glance back at Dylan, but the rotund friar wasn't looking. Richard stepped out onto the porch and bade Larch sit.

He didn't protest but painfully lowered himself into one of the lawn chairs at the far end of the porch. Richard watched him grimace, and he felt a pang of compassion for him.

"What happened to you? Demon get you by the scruff of the neck?"

Larch relaxed, and some of the pain eased from his face. In a moment, it was replaced by contempt. "Did you send a band of Latino thugs to beat us up?"

Richard froze. He had forgotten all about that little stroke of genius. And in the moment, he didn't know how he should respond. He decided to deflect. "Did you make our dog disappear? For that matter, did you make *every dog on earth* disappear?"

Larch looked at his own feet, and shifted uncomfortably. "We didn't *want* to do it."

"I thought it was part of your grand scheme to overthrow Heaven," Richard accused snidely. "I just wasn't aware that canines were such an important part of the celestial infantry."

"They're *not*," Larch said quietly, for some reason dignifying Richard's jab with an answer.

"No shit," Richard said.

"Look, the avocado thing, yes. We...we wanted to see if we could do it. We'd been talking about it for weeks; we even had a running bet with the guys at the Evil Eye that we could pull it off."

Richard knew the shop. It was a hole-in-the-wall occult arts store on Divisidero in San Francisco. The place held regular salons for serious ceremonial magickians. Terry had even been engaged to lecture there on Enochian magick more than once.

"So, let me guess: Dane is there, wearing his smoking jacket and drinking Earl Grey, overhears your bragging, and makes you an offer you can't refuse."

Larch nodded. "No, he wasn't there. Maybe he heard about it there, who knows? I don't know how he found out about it, but that's beside the point. The lodge roof is on its last legs, so to speak. It was either take his offer or let the place go. I, for one, am all for a 'new-paradigm' magickal lodge that meets mostly in Second Life, but there's a couple of our brothers that have a deep sentimental attach-ment to the place."

Richard wondered how off a person would have to be to have a sentimental attachment to a rat's nest like their Victorian on Haight, but he held his tongue.

"So, you made a deal with the Devil—oh, excuse me, that's what you *do*, isn't it?" Richard jabbed.

"I wish we hadn't. Now we've got two of our brothers in a coma—"

"One," said Richard.

"What?"

"You've only got one Lodge brother in a coma. Randall Webber died."

Richard watched as the horror descended on Larch's features. His mouth was agape, and his lower lip trembled. "Oh God, no..."

"I'm sorry. But I'm mostly sorry for Kat, his sister. And I mostly blame you and your 'brothers.' Dane's a force of nature—he's going to do whatever will serve his greed. But you're smarter than that, Larch. I know you are."

Larch did not reply but only stared at his hands, still in shock. "Is there no way to save him?"

Richard wasn't sure whether Larch meant Webber or the

magickian still in a coma, but it didn't really matter. He waited until Larch could speak again.

"Kinney, I beg you; you've got to stop him."

"Who?"

"Dane."

"*You* stop him. Or better yet, just stop working for him."

"You don't understand. We...don't have a choice."

"You always have a choice, man."

Larch looked him in the eye. "No. No, we don't. He's going to make us do it again. He's going to put another one of our brothers into a coma. You've got to help us."

"I don't see how *your* cowardice translates into *my* problem."

"It's not going to be dogs this time," Larch snapped.

"That would be hard given that there are no dogs to make disappear anymore. So, what's it going to be?"

"I don't know. I won't know until tonight." He stared at his shoes again. "The ritual will be tonight. Midnight. Please. You have to stop him...us."

Richard was moved. It took a lot of courage to come here, to be so vulnerable, and he could see the man's desperation. He weighed whether to break the news that he had stolen Solomon's Ring. Surely, that was the power Dane was holding over his head. But he hesitated. Maybe Dane had *not* revealed the source of his power. Perhaps it was something else he was holding over their heads. And besides, with all that was going on, the last thing Richard needed was a pack of desperate magickians plotting to steal the thing from him. He decided to keep quiet about it.

When he looked at him again, Larch's eyes were locked on something across the street. Richard followed his gaze and saw a black limousine rolling to a halt near the park entrance.

"I'd better be going..." he said and rose to his feet, a little shakily. "Say you'll help us." He met Richard's eyes again.

"I won't help you. But we sure as shit are gonna stop you."

"Good enough," he said and limped off the porch.

"Wait—" Richard said. Something else was nagging at him—he

had to find a way to get the demons to back off. If Kat and Mikael were ever going to find a way to have a normal life—assuming they could get Mikael back safe, that was—then they'd have to break the power of that sigil somehow. Something Maggie said in their session tugged at him. *Why didn't he invite his demons to dinner?* "I need a favor from you first." he said.

59

DANE NOTED WITH A GRIM, satisfied grin that Larch had seen him and was walking toward him, though apparently not without some pain and difficulty.

There was no humor in that grin, though. He felt at the empty pocket of his jacket, where the ring had previously been, and fumed. He had originally thought these friars to be a humorous diversion, a bunch of bumbling incompetents that would add comic relief to his drama, but they were turning out to be a royal pain in his ass. The Ring of Solomon had taken him years to locate, and was the only power he had over demons and magickians alike. He panicked at the thought that they might tell Larch they had taken it, but he willed himself to be calm and cross that bridge if he came to it. Until then, he must pretend that all was normal. No one had ever needed to be *persuaded* by the ring's power, after all. The mere sight of it—the threat of it—had been enough. Only half a day until the final ritual brought his heroic plans to fruition—he could bluff that long, surely.

All he needed now was a child. One child to be the ransom for many. One lucky little boy or girl to save all children everywhere from the evil that he himself had known all too well.

As Larch approached, the demon who was acting as chauffeur got out and opened the door for him. The magickian nervously slid into the car, facing Dane. He seemed pale and shaken.

"What's the matter, Larch? You look like you've seen a ghost."

"Webber died, damn you."

"Don't blame me; the avocado experiment was *your* idea."

"Yes, but *you*—" he looked away and mastered his anger. "Two more of us wouldn't have to."

"I'm not so sure about that," Dane said, silkily. "You had a pretty ambitious program planned before we started...working together. There's no telling what your ambition might have driven you to."

"Yes, okay, we have plans, but you're the one pushing us forward before we have the kinks worked out of them. We would never have tried another eradication before getting Webber back, safe and sound. If you hadn't strong-armed us, we would've, too, dammit."

"Too bad your *friar* friends couldn't save him, eh?"

Larch's eyes narrowed, and he fumed silently for a minute. "*They* don't know the demons intimately as we do. They don't make contracts with them, and they don't know how to control them. Not really."

"So I've gathered," Larch said, remembering the lack of success they had had with his own father. Something approaching a real smile touched his lips at the thought of it.

"Can you tell me, Larch, what in hell you are doing here?"

Larch froze. He had been expecting this question from the moment he saw the car across the street. He tried to appear more relaxed than he really was. "I wanted to see Webber. I didn't know that he was...dead."

Dane nodded, apparently satisfied with this answer. "After tonight, I will release you from your...obligations. You may devote yourselves to retrieving your fellows without molestation—from me, anyway."

Larch felt slightly relieved at this news, though he wasn't sure he could trust him. He also shuddered at the prospect of eradicating another species, be it plant or animal. "What is the...target?" he asked, finally.

Dane stared at the friary, and watched as the front door opened and Father Dylan walked out. He shook hands with a young couple and knelt down to shake hands with their little girl. He smiled to see the little girl grab at the husky priest's neck and give him a squeeze.

"Her." Dane said simply. Even from a distance the little girl exuded joyous innocence. And Dane was damned if he were going to stand by and let life tarnish that innocence. "The target is *her.*"

60

AFTER LUNCH, Dylan and Susan consulted with Richard and Terry and decided not to waste another moment. Susan began drumming, and Dylan went deep, and fast. He headed for the Middle World, and Jaguar came almost immediately upon his arrival there. Wordlessly, the companions walked side by side.

It seemed to Dylan that they had been walking for nearly a mile through nothing but fog. Jaguar padded silently beside him, but he could see little. Then, the glow of a yellow streetlamp passed overhead, reflecting a radiant gold off Jaguar's mottled black fur. Dylan admired the taut, bunched muscles moving with silky efficiency beneath the cat's skin, and he shuddered at its power. *Thank God he's on mah side*, he thought to himself.

Another streetlamp passed, and the fog began to thin. It was clear they were on a street in industrial West Berkeley.

They crossed the street, and Dylan stepped over trash gathered against the gutter. Their approach seemed to startle an apparently homeless man picking through a public trash receptacle, hoping to add empties to his collection piled high in a shopping cart. He stared at them with barely restrained ferocity, perhaps daunted by the sight of an enormous black jaguar.

Dylan wondered for a moment about the objective reality of such people. Were those who populated his journeys aspects of himself? Where they manifestations of universal archetypes? Were they real souls—or portions of souls—that had somehow "gotten lost" and were awaiting a shaman such as himself to intercede on their behalf and reintegrate them?

No matter how long he studied the occult arts, including his own specialty, he never came close to having his questions answered. For no matter how much he knew, the information only brought with it more questions. Religion was a bottomless pit of mystery, and better men than he had gone crazy trying to plumb its depths.

A train whistle cut the air in the distance, and straining, Dylan could hear its passage. He headed toward the sound instinctively, and before long, another sound arose.

It was faint at first, but as Dylan and Jaguar walked the rain-soaked streets in perpetual twilight, it gradually became clearer.

It was music, Dylan realized, and it made him smile. As the volume steadily increased, it became clear that it was not, after all, the kind of music Dylan liked. It wasn't the folk or blues or roots rock of his idols, but that didn't matter. His grin widened when he recognized the genre, pop-punk, the kind made famous by Sleater-Kinney and Green Day—the kind of music Mikael loved and played.

Loves, Dylan corrected himself. *Plays. He's not dead. God help me; he's not dead.*

The music got louder and louder until he could make out some of the lyrics—something about a trashy girlfriend in the afterlife. The music was a joyous, major-key stomper that contrasted nicely with the macabre words. Soon it became clear that the music was coming from a squat, cinder block structure advertising a caning shop on one side. Shiny bronze numbers announced the address—924—but no other signage testified to the nature of the business.

It didn't need to, however, because 924 Gilman had a legendary status in Berkeley's musical heritage. It was ground zero for the East Bay punk scene, and still attracted capacity crowds every weekend.

There was no one manning the entrance as they approached. No one asked them for payment, or for tickets, or questioned the wisdom of allowing an apparently wild Jaguar to enter the place. They just walked in.

There was more light inside than out, so it was easy to see. Dylan had been inside the club a couple of times to watch Mikael and his various bands play, but he had never seen it so sparsely populated.

The air was smoky, which was odd since Berkeley had been a smoke-free city for some time now. Dylan reminded himself that this version of 924 Gilman existed more in the Otherworld than in conventional reality, and maybe smoking was still allowed there. He dismissed the thought as a distraction and began a systematic surveillance of the place.

The walls were black, adorned with concert posters and silver graffiti. A different band seemed to be playing now, and their energy could only be described as soporific. They seemed to be going through the motions, the beat slow and their performance dissociated, more akin to Pink Floyd than Black Flag.

Nobody seemed to mind, however. Several people stood around, swaying slightly, staring at their shoes or sitting cross-legged on the floor. "Not a high-energy crowd, here, Jaggy." Dylan pursed his lips with worry and kept looking. No sign of Mikael. Just then he heard a crash behind them, and with a concerned glance at Jaguar, they both sprang toward the back door.

Dylan pushed it open recklessly, and it hit the wall as it sprang open. On the sidewalk, Dylan stood still and listened. He heard a scuffle to his right behind the building and, waving Jaguar to him, he ran toward the rear of the building.

A large parking lot sprawled out behind the club and the cane shop, surrounded by a high chain-link fence, topped by razor wire. And there, on the other side of the fence, a skinny scarecrow of a man with big, mussy black hair was getting the shit beat out of him.

"Mikael!" Dylan shouted, but Mikael didn't look up. One of the thugs, a large man with a shaved head, stood behind him, holding his arms as another skinhead pummeled his abdomen with his fists. Mikael cried out as a third punk swung a two-by-four at his head.

Dylan heard it crack as it connected and watched in horror as the man behind Mikael let go and the skinny youth plummeted to the ground, hitting his head as he did so.

Dylan tore at the fence, but it was no good. He jammed his toes into the diamonds of the fence and clambered to get up, but halfway up lost his footing and landed hard on his knee. "SHeee-it!" he swore, holding his knee with both hands. "Jaggy, don't just fucking sit there, do something!!"

The Jaguar looked at him dispassionately for a long moment, and then, almost leisurely, he swiped at the fence with his claws, opening a wide swath in it. The portion of the fence fell forward, and with all the eloquence of a queen, the great cat stepped through and padded toward the thugs.

With one claw, he swiped at the kid with the two-by-four and removed a large section of skin from his face. The youth grabbed at his flayed cheek and, screaming, dropped to his knees, writhing in agony. Sinking his teeth into the skinhead who had held Mikael, Jaguar shook the young man like a rag doll. Dylan could almost hear his bones rattle and watched in wonder as the great cat flung him into a heap several yards away. The last kid seemed frozen in his tracks when Jaguar roared. Seeming to snap back to reality, he turned tail and ran as fast as he could.

Dylan stepped through the fence and knelt beside Mikael. The back of his head was bloody, but he seemed to be breathing. Dylan looked up at Jaguar, who sat on his haunches and licked his paws patiently. "Can you do anything for him?"

The cat just looked at him.

Dylan cradled Mikael's head in his lap and pulled his wild hair away from his face. "Hold on, there, Mikey-boy, you're going to be all right." He rocked back and forth slowly as he thought. Ruminating out loud, he addressed Jaguar. "Ah can't really take him back like this, can Ah? Ah mean, he's gotta be conscious, or Ah got nothin' to carry."

Jaguar said nothing but only swished his tail. "We're gonna have to wait until he wakes up, then, and Susan can't drum all night. Ah'm gonna have to come back fer him later, give him time to rest, recover, come to. Yeah, that's it…" he said it loudly as if trying to convince himself of the right thing to do.

"Jaggy, I want you to stay right here and guard him. Can you do that?"

The cat just looked at him, his tail swishing back and forth like the end of a whip. "Goddammit, Jaguar, answer me!"

"I will stay here. I will guard him. Come back tomorrow."

Dylan scratched at his head. "Really, tomorrow?"

"Come back tomorrow."

Dylan stood and straightened out his cassock, flicking the dust off the black fabric. "All right. But don't you go nowhere." He knelt again and touched Mikael on the shoulder. "You, either."

61

Kat jabbed at the magazine with her scissors, cutting out faces of people far, far happier than she felt at that moment. Sitting cross-legged on the floor of the chapel, she tore out whole pages showing fields of wildflowers and other beautiful places that *she could not visit* because she was fucking quarantined in this fucking house.

Just as she was attacking the picture of a dumpy little girl dressed as Harry Potter (*fucking magickians*, she thought) her fingers slipped and she cut her knee.

"Goddammit!" she said, wiping the blood away with her thumb and putting it in her mouth. She took a scrap of a magazine and held it to the wound until it stuck and picked up the magazine and the scissors again.

This time, she found a picture of a radiant African-American woman in a dark blue jogging suit. She clipped her out and, snatching up a glue stick, pasted the woman into the beard of the huge patchwork icon of Jesus. She considered its placement, admiring the effect.

Why am I doing this? A little voice nagged at her. "Because I'm sooo fucking bored," she said out loud and, flipping a page, found a photo of a kangaroo. She wondered about the theological implications of adding animals to the icon and decided to ask Susan about it later. In the meantime, she kept turning pages. A little girl astride a tricycle...perfect. She reminded Kat of the little girl Dylan was going to baptize tomorrow. She clipped the photo out, tricycle and all.

She wasn't sure how she felt about that baptism thing. It seemed unfair to make the little girl a part of a religion without her really knowing what she was being inducted into. Not just unfair, it seemed *wrong*. But one thing she had learned since she had been, well, *captive* here was that she wasn't always in possession of all the puzzle pieces. She decided to make a list of things to discuss with Susan. She pulled out a pen and wrote baptism and animal Jesus, hoping she could figure out what the heck that referred to later.

She glued the little girl just above Jesus's upper lip, forming part of his mustache, roughly along the line of the coffee stain.

I know why I'm doing this, she thought, *I'm doing it to burn time because I don't want to think about Mikael.* How long had it been since he'd eaten? What had he endured in Dane's dungeon? How did he get those scars on his back? Did he really have three nipples? She smiled as that question occurred to her. She'd looked it up and it was a sign of witchcraft—most appropriate for the order's Wicca expert but also—as with the Pawnee if Dylan were right—a sign of nurturing and sensitivity. She wasn't sure that it indicated any such thing in real life—*how many murderers were there with three nipples*, she wondered; *there must be thousands*—but she liked to think it was true in Mikael's case.

She flipped through a couple more pages and found a photo of a young punkish couple in Belfast. It reminded her of herself and Mikael, and she went to work on it, pasting it on Jesus's chin.

Okay, the truth is I'm doing this because I feel guilty for damaging the icon. She sighed, depressed at the thought, but it rested more easily in her breast than the others. That was the whole truth of it, and it was okay.

What was also true was that the icon fascinated her. Not only because of how oddly it was constructed but by what it suggested, what it meant. She *loved* the icon, although she would be hard pressed to articulate exactly *why*. It touched her in some deep and ineffable place—it *spoke* to her.

She threw the magazine onto the discard pile and took up another, this one a *Woman's Day*, that she couldn't imagine anyone at the friary reading. Nevertheless, she picked up the magazine-of-spurious-origin and began to leaf through it.

Several pages in, her breath caught in her throat, and she sat up as if slapped. On the left-hand page was an ad for California avocados, and facing it on the right a golden retriever hawking flea medicine.

She stared at them for a long time without knowing why—if kangaroos were suspect sources for Jesus's facial features, surely dogs and oily fruit were, too.

But she cut the pictures out just the same. Just to have them. Just to remind herself what an avocado or a dog looked like when, twenty years from now, she began to forget. She carefully placed the pictures within the pages of the book she was reading to keep them safe and flat.

62

THE LATE AFTERNOON sun cast a rosy glow through the kitchen window as Richard entered to find Dylan and Susan at the dinner table, munching away at two sides of the same ice cream pop. "Sorry," he said, shielding his eyes. "I didn't realize I was wandering into an outtake from *Lady and the Tramp*."

"That's okay, dude," said Dylan, licking his lips, "Just so long as we're all agreed that Ah'm Tramp." Susan reached around the pop and kissed her hubby on the lips. "Nuthin' weirder than kissin' a cold mouth, Darlin'," he told her.

"Where do we stand with Mikael?" Richard asked. Kat overheard the question and stood in the doorway, listening. Susan scooched over on the bench and patted the seat beside her. Kat took it.

"Waal, he's alive, but beat up pretty bad. Jaguar is guardin' him, and Ah've been instructed to come for him tomorrow. That's where it stands." He looked more sad than worried. "Honestly, Ah think he's gonna be fine. His spirit is tough, and it's going to take more than a little out-of-the-body roughin' up to endanger that guy. The most important thing is that we found 'im, and Ah know where to go to get 'im."

"I don't understand why you can't just bring him back *now*," Kat complained, a petulant note creeping into her voice.

"Ah can't just carry 'im out. He has to be conscious, and he's gotta want to come. Ah can't explain why; that's jus' one of the mysteries of shamanism," Dylan explained.

Kat seemed satisfied with Dylan's answer though not so much with the situation.

Just then, Richard's cell phone rang, the air filling with the triumphant strains of "Rise Up, O Men of God." He checked the screen. "It's Brian," he said. "Kat, can you grab Terry?"

Kat narrowed her eyes. Who was he to give her orders? She stayed in her place but reached out and clanged the dinner bell. Richard winced at the noise. "I could have done that!" He flipped open the phone and glowered at her. "Hey, Brian, whatcha got?"

"Hey," came Brian's voice. Richard could hear cars passing. "I've only got fifteen minutes on this break, and I'm five minutes in and I gotta use the loo."

"So, shoot," Richard said, turning on the speakerphone option and placing the phone on the table. Terry came in through the back door, a toothbrush sticking out of his mouth.

"Two things. First, the demon we're dealing with here is Artici-phus, a Middle Eastern blood demon specializing in bilocation and soul transference."

"That makes a lot of sense," Dylan nodded.

"What makes him a *blood* demon?" Kat asked.

"Well, different demons thrive on different substances," Brian's voice came through, strong but tinny. "Some feed on souls, some on sweat, some, like succubi, on semen. Blood demons—"

"Eat blood," Kat looked aghast. "I get it."

"What else you got, Brian?" Richard asked. "Please, God, tell me you've figured out how this damned ring works."

"Well, yes and no. What I've been able to glean so far is that it isn't activated just by putting it on. It also isn't activated by touching it to something else."

"Then how *does* it work?"

"You have to put it on and *then* touch it to something else. Here's the problem though—whatever it does, it doesn't just do it to the thing you touch, it also does it to *you*."

"Talk about a rebound effect," Richard said, concerned. "So what, exactly, does it *do*?"

"That's what I don't know," Brian said. "I've got a lead on a Sumerian manuscript in the National Library in Alexandria. I've got a call in to a friend at the American consulate there, and he's promised to email me a scan as soon as he can access it. He should be able to help translate it as well. Meanwhile, I'm following up a couple of other leads, too."

"Good," said Richard, "because according to Larch, tonight at midnight is the next ritual, and unless anyone else has any bright ideas on how to stop them, we may have to use Dane's ring against him, so long as we can do it without violating any of our vows. And we can't know if we can do that until we know what the fuck this thing *does*."

"Don't worry, Dicky, I'm not going anywhere until I crack this thing."

"Good to hear it, Bri. Thanks." Richard straightened up and pulled at his chin, thinking. "Okay, if it does the same thing to the wearer as it does to the target, how did Dane survive it?"

"My guess," said Brian's tinny voice, "is that he's been bluffing. The demonic folk are so terrified of the ring that they'll obey right out of the gate. I'll bet that all Dane had to do was to put it on and flash it around."

"If that's the case," Richard mused, "We can bluff, too."

"I gotta go; break's up."

"Go, then, and thanks."

"Sure thing."

Richard looked at Terry and back at the floor, thinking. Terry looked at Kat, and she nodded. He looked back at Richard. "Uh, Dicky, we've got something to show youze guys." Without explanation, Terry turned and went back to the cottage. In a moment, he was back, holding the mirror.

"It's our mirror," Dylan said. "From the guest room. So?"

"Everybody follow me," Terry said and led them into the chapel. Once there, he drew the curtains, and an instant gloom settled over the room. He placed the mirror on the altar, and Susan gasped. There, clear to all, was the violet circle of light.

"I think I know what that is, but I want to hear you say it," Richard said, looking at Terry with wonder.

"It's our friend the angel," Terry said. "When Kat's brother's body died, the angel's spirit should have just dissipated. But, luckily, there was a mirror nearby, and his soul got caught."

The purplish light radiated steadily, casting the room in a faint rosy hue. "Which means he's not gone," Richard stated, hesitantly.

"He's not gone, but he can't really go anywhere, either. Not without a body. And I'm not sure how long he can stay trapped there without, you know..."

"Dissipating," Kat finished.

"Yeah."

"Okay, guys," Richard said, taking a deep breath. He had been wrestling with something, unsure whether to bring it up. Unsure even whether he should think about it, let alone speak it aloud. Oddly, it was as if he were at a distance, watching as his mouth moved, "I'm going to suggest something, and you're going to think I'm crazy. But short of hiring another band of neighborhood thugs, I don't see another way out of this."

Dylan sat up straight, and Terry cocked his head. Susan looked at him warily, and said, "Uh-huh. I have a feeling I'm going to hate this. What is it?"

"I'm going to suggest we invite our...enemies for dinner."

63

BISHOP TOM barely noticed the business discussed that morning. He had talked to several of the other bishops privately, and although many of them had been personally encouraging, the dry Arizona wind was not blowing in an auspicious direction.

He sank into his chair for the afternoon session with an air of resignation. That many of the other bishops avoided his eyes was *not* a good sign. Bishop Mellert called the meeting to order, and once the hubbub had died down, he leaned over his folded hands and addressed the assembly with more gravity than Tom had previously seen in the man.

"My brother and sister bishops, this is the final day of our synod, and we have before us this afternoon only one final piece of business —whether or not the Order of Saint Raphael will continue under the auspices of the Old Catholic Synod of the Americas. In other words, this is a question of *communion*, and whether this order will remain in communion with this body. I do not need to remind any of you the importance of this question. For us to allow the order to continue in our communion will be to say that we approve of their corporate life and ministry. To decide otherwise will be a permanent mark against them, from which they may have trouble recovering. Make no mistake about it, we are passing judgment upon them—which none of us should take lightly." Dead silence reigned in the room. Mellert took the time to look each of them in the eyes. Finally, he leaned back and asked, "Are there any final statements to be made before we take a vote?"

"I have a question, not a statement." Bishop Van Patton stood.

Mellert nodded.

"I think it would be impossible for me to approve of the lifestyle of the Blackfriars," she said. "But on the other hand, I can think of things about each and every one of you that I don't like. No offense intended, of course." She smiled, and several of the bishops guffawed. "My point is that I don't approve 100 percent of anyone's lifestyle—my own included. But that doesn't mean that I don't acknowledge the validity of our ministries. Why do we not allow the same grace for the Order of Saint Raphael?"

She sat, and Tom nodded, looking hopefully at the assembled prelates. Bishop Hammet rose and waited to be recognized. "My dear girl," he said condescendingly, "it is not as if we are straining at gnats, here. We are all sinners, of course, but we are talking about a matter of *degree*, aren't we? The Blackfriars exhibit a *magnitude* of heresy, apostasy, and licentiousness that cannot be ignored or suffered to continue. We are not talking about godly but misunderstood misfits, but willful and open rebellion against the most foundational moral standards required by the Gospel of Jesus Christ."

Bishop Tom rose at this, immediately, and almost as quickly regretted it. Mellert nodded to him, and Hammet yielded the floor, but Tom had absolutely no idea what to say. "Uh...I..." he stammered, thinking, *Think, you idiot!* and wiping his sweating palms against the seat of his pants. "Begging your pardon, Bishop Hammet, but you are wrong. We are, in fact, talking about sincere ministers who are indeed misunderstood and, admittedly, misfits. And we are not talking about a group that exists solely to undermine the work of God in the world, as you see fit to paint them. I know each of them personally and intimately. I have served as their confessor and their counselor. Every member of that order obsesses about his own personal integrity and is sincerely committed to his ministry. They intend to do good in this world, and I can personally attest to the fact that they are successful in this. Do they have problems? Yes. More than Bishop Van Patton? Perhaps. More than Bishop Hammet?" He leveled a severe eye at the Texan prelate. "That is not for me, or any of us, to judge."

He looked away and swept his hand around the rest of the room. "Do they have more problems than anyone else in this room? I have gotten to know most of you in the last couple of years, and I don't believe there is a single person here with feet made of any more precious substance than clay. Our Lord said, 'By their fruits ye shall know them.' I say look at the Blackfriars' professional track record. Look at the literally hundreds of successful exorcisms they have performed—at the people that have been restored to their lives, to their loved ones, to their faith.

"Look at the trust placed in them by our sister communions. Do any of you oversee ministries that your local Roman Catholic arch-diocese employs? Or the local Episcopal diocese?" Tom watched the bishops slunk into their seats, looking for the first time a little sheep-ish. "No? Instead, they look upon us with pity, often contempt for our little parishes and—to their way of thinking—insignificant ministries. But the Order of Saint Raphael is routinely called upon by the Roman and Episcopal authorities in the San Francisco Bay Area, because they are *good* at what they do. Because they are effective. Because they get results. Because there is no one else of any commu-nion that does it better. No, when the Roman Archdiocese comes to the Berkeley Blackfriars to perform an exorcism, it comes to a ministry of the Old Catholic Synod of the Americas to meet their needs. I'm proud of the order. And I want you to think twice about expelling the most effective, the most celebrated, and the most *needed* ministry in our communion. And the next time you or the people you care for come to you with a demonic disorder, ask yourselves, where you are going to go for help? To Bishop Hammet? I'd like to see him facedown a demonic host without making water in his pantaloons." With that, Tom sat down and crossed his hands, meeting Hammet's acid gaze with one of his own.

Bishop Mellert could not disguise a slight smile at someone putting Hammet in his place. "Any further discussion?" he asked, trying to appear professional. "Then I suggest we take a vote—by private ballot."

Index cards were passed around as Mellert made the necessary clarifications. "This is a yes or no vote on the question: 'Should the Old Catholic Order of Saint Raphael be excommunicated?' Yes or no. No other answer will be considered. Now, vote."

Tom stared sadly at his index card. With a sinking heart he wrote *No* on it and folded it in half. Deacon Eldritch circled around the room collecting the cards and, having received them all, sat back down next to the presiding bishop to count them. In a few moments, he had divided the cards into two piles. He looked up and addressed Mellert. "Seventeen for, six against."

Tom crumbled in his seat, covering his face with his hands. "The synod has spoken," Mellert announced. "The Old Catholic Order of Saint Raphael is hereby ex—"

"Wait!" Bishop Tom stood up, his folding chair once again shooting out from under him and clattering to the ground. But he did not hear it. A righteous rage had gripped him, and he could not let the excommunication just happen, not without a fight. "This is an unjust action, and I will not stand for it!"

Mellert's eyebrows rose, and Hammet smiled evilly over his steepled fingers. Mellert spoke slowly and cautiously. "And just what do you intend to do about it, Bishop Müeller?"

Tom was breathing hard, and he looked around like a caged animal. "If the Blackfriars go, I go."

"Really, Tom," Mellert said, shaking his head in distaste. "That kind of threat does not become you."

"It is no threat!" Tom announced, and before them all he removed the episcopal ring from his finger and placed it on the table before Mellert. Then, amid the sound of gasps and protests, he strode out of the room.

64

TERRY HAD BALKED, of course. "I am not summoning any demons! It is against our rule, and a danger to everyone in the house!"

Richard had thought all of this through. He patiently explained that issuing an invitation on the astral plane was not the same as summoning—the demons were not *compelled* to come, after all. He didn't bother telling them he had asked Larch to issue his own invitations, since Richard had no idea how compulsory *those* would be. He also explained that, yes, they would have to remove the wards surrounding the house, which would be especially dangerous to both Mikael and Kat, since Articiphus, the very demon that was oppressing them, was at the top of the guest list. "All we need to do," Richard had explained to universally gaping mouths, "is to ward Mikael's room. Everyone can hole up there until dinner is over. I'll be the only one at risk."

Terry had called him "fucking nuts," and Dylan had said worse. Susan was livid, and Kat was incredulous.

"Look, so far we've just been reacting to things—we need to begin ordering them," Richard had argued. "Even if we do get Mikael back, he's nothing better than a prisoner. Kat, too. We need some options, and we need to start making them for ourselves. I'm not exactly sure what's going to go down here, but it sure as hell beats sitting back and waiting to get hit again. Does anybody have a better idea?" he had asked. Silence had reigned in the chapel, and so he started handing out assignments. They were all too angry, and too scared, to grumble. Richard didn't blame them.

At six o'clock sharp he opened the front door and pricked his finger. He squeezed a drop of blood on the threshold, and continued squeezing, leaving a trail of red drops all the way to the kitchen table, where he took a seat and waited.

After a few moments, he began to intone. "Come, Articiphus, noble duke, ruler of two score legions of demons. Come, Malack..."

Night came early in February, and Richard drew his habit closer about himself against the cold. Candles on the kitchen table guttered, and shadows danced about the walls. Richard took a deep breath and willed himself to relax.

He heard the door creak, and he broke off his chant, listening. *It's just the wind*, he told himself, and continued. "Come, Talin..."

As if his eyes were adjusting to a light not previously seen, he watched with mounting anxiety as a wispy shape floated into view of the kitchen. Richard's voice caught in his throat, but he fought the fear and continued his droning invocation.

He continued even as the great lizard loped into view, the traditional mount of the demon Batheliel. In ghostly procession, the lizard pawed into the foyer, past the chapel, and into the kitchen. The doorway was too narrow for the beast's great frame, but the parts that were too wide simply passed through the walls at either side of the door. Richard's intonation halted as soon as he saw the rider astride the great lizard. Bearing a goshawk on one fist and reins in the other, he sat erect and proud. A robe of satin and ermine hung around his broad shoulders, but within the hood he saw the kindly face of an old man.

No sooner had he passed into the kitchen than the next guest arrived. Richard's eyes widened at the sight of the massive wolf with the tail of a serpent. From his great jowls he vomited fire, blue-black flames that froze the air and made the winter's cold almost unbearable. This, Richard knew, was almost certainly the infernal Marquis Talin.

Once more, Richard saw movement in the hallway and steeled himself against the next apparition. This one had the shape of a man, in a long black cloak. Richard almost breathed in relief until he looked into the hood of the cloak and saw the face—not of a man but of raven, its cruel beak clacking open and shut in rapid, inhuman movements. Its black eyes were soulless and seemed to look past him. *Malack*, Richard whispered to himself, naming the one that governed forty legions of demons.

As these three dignitaries took their places at the table, yet another figure stirred and entered, gliding through the doorway and past the walls. This was the most horrible and glorious of them all. Seated high upon a dragon, so high that his crowns poked through the ceiling, another great duke of the infernal realm took his place. He held a serpent in one hand, and his face on one side was a beautiful youth, while the other was most horribly scarred. This was the one he had been waiting for, Richard knew. This was Articiphus, the duke of Hell that had stolen Mikael's spirit from his body and had delivered two magickians to the Beautiful Gate.

Richard watched in awe as Articiphus descended from his mount and took a place at the large oaken table.

Richard cleared his throat and tried to appear confident. "Greetings, nobility of Hell, and welcome to my home."

Talin's wolf-head growled, but Batheliel spoke gently. "Yours is a strange hospitality, Priest. It has been a very long time since I have been made welcome by one such as you. It makes me...suspicious." He grinned a leering grin.

Talin was staring straight at Richard's head and drooling. Malack turned his head so that one eye looked directly at him. "Feed us," said the wolf.

Almost wilting beneath his menacing glare, Richard nodded and drew out several teacups from a bag sitting on the bench next to him.

Then he retrieved a knife and, holding the blade carefully in his right hand, made a neat, shallow incision on his left forearm.

A stream of blood pumped forth, and Richard, struggling to keep his arm from shaking, held the wound over the cups and drained a goodly portion of his blood into each one of them. *Thank God only four answered my call*, he thought to himself.

That being done, he placed a cup—each with about three thimbles full of blood—before each of the demons. He bowed as he set each cup down, showing what he hoped would be appropriate deference.

Malack dipped his beak into the cup before him. He didn't seem to be drinking it so much as soaking in it, or even *communing* with it. Richard was fascinated to see the others do similarly. Only Talin seemed to actively lap the blood up with his tongue. Batheliel sniffed at it, apparently savoring the aroma, while Articiphus placed his finger in the cup, and seemed content with whatever nourishment he was able to draw from it that way.

However odd the means of ingestion, Richard was relieved to see how pleased they seemed. He wasn't sure how eagerly an offering of live blood would be received, but he was gratified to see that his intuition had been on target.

Finger still in bowl, Articiphus turned his attention to Richard. The beauty on half of his face contrasted with the horror of the other half, creating an unsettling effect, yet his voice was mellifluous and dignified.

"Surely, you have not simply invited us here to feed us, Priest," he began. "Why have you summoned us?"

"I didn't summon you," Richard corrected him, only too late realizing how dangerous it might be to do so. "I invited you, and it was good of you to come."

"Goodness is not a virtue to which most of us aspire," Batheliel smirked. "At least, not as our Enemy defines it."

"Then let us say I am *grateful* that you have come," Richard said, only beginning to realize the verbal landmine he had so blithely walked into. "I seek your counsel and ask your favor."

"Why should we favor you?" asked Talin with a growl. "You are the sworn man of our Enemy."

"Let us not hold that against him, Talin," Batheliel counseled. "He only knows what he has been told, and he has not been told the whole of it."

Richard frowned at such cryptic talk and wondered whether to inquire further. He decided to stay on point. "Thank you, noble Dukes, for your indulgence. Indeed, there is much I do not know, and I beg your patience." He put a Band-aid on his arm and then continued. "Your majesty Articiphus, your sigil, used in a magickal working, was inadvertently glimpsed by two people in this house, Kat Webber and Mikael Bloomink. As a result of this, Mikael's spirit was removed from his body."

"That *can* happen, yes." Articiphus said with cool indifference.

"I'd like to ask you to exempt these two persons from your oppression."

"Magick is like a river," Articiphus said as if to a child. "Once set in motion, it flows where it will. It only takes great effort to control it, not to make it."

"I know this is a great favor that I ask. Won't you please curb the... flow, in this case?"

"Why should I exert the energy? I have regions to run, hosts to oversee. Why should I trouble myself with two careless humans? From the goodness of my heart?" He chuckled at that, and an outburst of humor rocked the room, Malack cawing loudly.

"Because...because I know you are being bound by magickians of the Lodge of the Hawk and Serpent, your majesty. I intend to stop them, to put an end to your servitude to them. I am hoping you will assist me in kind."

"Out of some human sense of reciprocity, no doubt," Articiphus sniffed.

"Something like that, yes," Richard said.

The princely head pursed its lips and stared at Richard intently, apparently considering his offer. "And how about them?" He pointed to his colleagues. "Why did you invite them?"

"On a hunch," Richard said, hoping that honesty and transparency would be the most efficacious route. "I have another favor to ask, and since each of you are demons that specialize in 'carrying,' I am hoping I can enlist your assistance."

"You need something carried?" Betheliel sneered. "I saw an ad for two dykes and a truck—I can get you the number."

"Unfortunately, they cannot go where I need the delivery made."

"And what, pray, is the package?" asked Batheliel.

"An angel's soul, trapped in a mirror. I'm certain that there is now another angel trapped in the body of one of the lodge magickians—that would need to go as well. If you can bring back the magickian's soul, so much the better."

"You are asking us to breach the Enemy's gates," Talin snarled. "Do you think we are idiots?"

"Quite the contrary," Richard said, gaining confidence. He looked directly at Articiphus. "I know of one of your number who has already breached Heaven—twice."

They all turned and looked at Articiphus. "Against my better judgment," he admitted. "But I had no choice. The magickian compelled me, and I was bound by Great Magick to obey."

Richard thought for a moment that he caught a note of sad resignation and understanding on the faces of the other demonic dignitaries. Richard thought about how it must be to have such wealth, power, and honor among the infernal spirits and yet be reduced to slavery at the whims of magickians. It was cruel and undignified, even for a demon. Richard felt a passing moment of pity for them.

"And if we say no?" asked Batheliel, smiling with a saccharine sweetness. "Will you then compel us?"

"I am no magickian," Richard said, and the raven-headed demon made a strangling sound, which must have been a kind of laugh. "So I will work no magick against you."

Slowly and deliberately he took the Ring of Solomon out of his pocket and placed it on his finger, setting his hands on the table before him so that the ring was clearly visible to all.

A collective gasp rose from the infernal dignitaries, and they all leaned back reactively.

"It is not our way to coerce or compel," Richard explained. "That is why I asked you here politely, and why I have also asked you for your assistance. Willing cooperation is always superior to coercion. Don't you agree?"

The demons looked at one another. They looked at him. They looked at the ring. They were each of them profoundly uncomfortable to be in such close proximity to it.

The threat was implied, and they had all gotten the message. Articiphus spoke. "I want to eat the soul of the man who compels me."

Richard shook his head. "I will not feed him to you."

They were clearly rattled, but none of them were budging. Richard began to sweat despite the extreme cold.

"Then promise me this, Priest," Articiphus said. "That you will intercede in the impending ritual, and that when you do, you will destroy my sigil and free me from the magickian's thrall."

Richard nodded. "With a whole heart, that I will do."

"And promise me that you will never compel me by means of this ring," Articiphus met his eye.

"Is my word good to you, then?"

"I know your reputation, Priest. In spite of your...eccentricities, you are known to be worthy of trust."

The friar thought for a long moment. "So long as you threaten no one in my care," Richard said finally, nodding slowly. "I promise I will not compel you, with this ring nor by any other means."

"A drop of blood will seal our agreement," Articiphus flashed him a wry smile.

Greedy fucking bastard, Richard thought, but he reached for his knife just the same.

65

KAT WATCHED Mikael sleeping and played with one of his many stray locks. Terry sat next to her, Dane's leather bag in front of him. He seemed to have emptied it of Dane's mundane effects and filled it with the books, journals and internet printouts he had been studying.

Dylan and Susan occupied folding chairs near the door. Susan was knitting, and Dylan was hunched over a bowl of water, a liturgy book balanced on one knee and a salt shaker next to his ear on a bookshelf.

Kat watched him as he did his own sort of magick. "I exorcise thee, creature of water, by the living God, by the holy God, by the omnipotent God, that thou mayest be purified from all evil influence, in the name of the Holy One who is master of angels and of men, whose majesty and glory filleth the whole Earth," he prayed, reading from the liturgy. "O God, look upon this thy creature of salt and water, pour down upon it the radiance of thy blessing and hallow it with the dew of thy lovingkindness that wherever it shall be sprinkled and thy holy name shall be invoked in prayer, every noble aspiration may be strengthened, every good resolve made firm and the fellowship of the Holy Spirit vouchsafed to us who place our trust in thee; thou who with the son livest and reignest, in the unity of the same Holy Spirit,

God throughout all ages of ages. Amen." He finished and set the liturgy book aside. The bowl of water, however, he kept in his lap, as ready defense against demonic forces.

"So, that's holy water now?" Kat asked.

"It is," Dylan answered.

"I thought it would be more...ornate. The ritual, I mean. Or, like, something a cardinal or something had to do."

"Waal, technically, a cardinal can be a layperson, so there's been some cardinals that can't make holy water. But any priest can do it. Ah wonder if deacons can. Ah'll have to look that up."

A sudden gust of wind buffeted the converted porch, and the temperature plummeted within a few heartbeats.

"Ah shit," said Dylan through his teeth. "We got company. This is *such* a fucking bad idea."

"Calm down, grasshopper," Terry said, not looking up from the book he was reading. "Wards are set. Dicky is the only person here in any real danger."

"That's supposed to make me feel better?"

"You know, the weird thing is," Kat mused, "a week ago, I didn't even believe in demons."

"Most Wiccans don't," Susan said. "It's just not part of that paradigm. What's really odd is that most Christians don't either, and it *is* part of ours."

"What was it C.S. Lewis said?" Dylan asked. "Something about Satan's greatest trick was convincing the world that he don't exist?"

"That's a paraphrase if I ever heard one," Terry said, turning a page. The lights dimmed as if some large appliance had just turned on. After a moment, they came back full strength.

"What was that?" Kat asked.

"Can't really say, but mah guess is more demons. Jes' a different species."

"Demons have species?" Kat asked.

"About seventeen hundred documented varieties," Dylan answered her. "'Course some of those are just tribal variants, nothing scientifically distinguishable."

"Where do they come from?" Kat asked.

"That depends on what mythology yer askin'," Dylan said, shifting in the folding chair, obviously uncomfortable. "According to the Christian mythos, they all started off as angels, but when Satan rebelled, one-third of the angels joined his rebellion. Ever since then, they've either holed up in Hell or been causin' havoc here on Earth."

"Where do the Hindus say they come from?" Kat asked.

"Waal, according to the Hindus, the demons used to be the gods. And the gods used to be the demons. It ain't about who's morally superior fer them but about who has the most power."

"Is that really true?" asked Kat, unsure.

"Cross mah heart and swear to Kali," Dylan crossed himself.

Kat frowned. "That seems weird."

"Ain't much about Hinduism that isn't fucking gloriously weird, in my opinion," Dylan affirmed.

"Hear, hear," Terry, said, raising a hand in the air. He turned the last page, scanned the final paragraph, and slammed the book shut.

He looked up. "Are the demons gone yet?"

"Mah guess is that they're still having appetizers," Dylan answered.

Just then, his cell phone blared out the staccato horn part from "Tenth Avenue Freeze-Out." "Father Dylan, here," he answered it, all business.

"Dylan?" the voice was tinny and slightly garbled.

"Tom, dude, is that you?"

"It is. Listen, Dylan, I take it Richard is not there? He's not answering his phone."

"Dude, Richard is feeding demons his own blood at the moment," he said as if it were an everyday event. "But can I help you?"

"Egad," Tom said. "Well, at least I tried for the proper chain of command. Dylan, I have bad news."

"This would be that famous third tragedy we've all been waiting for, Ah'm guessin'."

"I'm not sure what you mean, but yes, it's bad."

"Waal, Ah'm sittin' down, so do yer worst."

"The synod just voted. Dylan, the Order of Saint Raphael has been...excommunicated."

"Aw shit. Are you shittin' me? That means we don't have a bishop. And that means we have no power over the forces of darkness." He sighed. "An' just when we have a house full o' demons, too. Couldn't be better fuckin' timing."

He looked up and saw the wide eyes of everyone in the room, breathlessly hanging on his every word.

"No, Dylan, that's not what it means," Bishop Tom said gravely. "You see, the moment they ousted you, I quit. I walked right up to the presiding bishop and handed over my episcopal ring. So, you still have a bishop. You still have me. So maybe we're a very small church right now, but Jesus said, 'Wherever two or three are gathered, I am there among them,' and we are many more than two or three. The forces of darkness do not have the upper hand yet, my friend. We stand together."

Dylan's throat swelled, and he swallowed hard to clear it. He wiped at his eyes and sniffed. "Dude, that damn well makes up for it. Thank you for sacrificing...thank you for believin' in us."

"I do believe in you, Father Dylan. I'll want to talk to Richard later, when he's finished...feeding. I don't think I want to know. Anyway, blessings to you, my friend." And Bishop Tom ended the call.

Dylan sat frozen, staring at his cell phone for a few moments.

"What?" Susan demanded. "What did he say?"

Dylan related the substance of the conversation and watched with satisfaction as Susan and Terry responded with nearly as much emotion as he had.

Kat said, "I never in my life thought I would like a Catholic bishop, but Tom sounds like a *really* wonderful guy."

Susan nodded. "He is. And it was a huge sacrifice for him. We have to invite him for a visit soon."

"And pay his way," added Terry.

For several minutes they all sat in silence, too stunned and moved to speak. Finally, Terry sighed. "Should have warded the potty room."

"You in bad shape yet?" Dylan asked. Susan took up her knitting again.

"Nah, I can hold it. Ought to start cleaning this mess up, though." He gathered the book and the papers spread out in front of them and lowered them into Dane's satchel. An odd look came over his face as he did so.

"What's up, Terry?" Susan asked, looking up at him and noting his expression.

Terry stood up and lowered his left hand into the satchel. Then with his other hand, he touched the bedspread. He looked back and forth from one arm to the other. There was no doubt about it. His left arm was bent at a more acute angle than his right.

"Well..." he said slowly, thinking aloud, "Either my right arm grew shorter overnight, or the bottom of this bag isn't the bottom of this bag."

Susan's needles stopped, and her mouth dropped open.

Terry turned the bag upside down and dumped everything out onto the bed, and partly onto Mikael as well. Then he put both hands into the bag, feeling at the seams around what he had previously supposed to be the bottom. Concentrating, his eyes looked toward Heaven and moved back and forth as he felt.

"Got something," he said and, grasping a slight leather tongue between his right thumb and forefinger, gave it a pull. He heard a dim click from within the bag, and the tongue gave way. He pulled it up and out of the bag. Attached to it was a false bottom, which he set on the bed beside him.

"Holy shit," said Dylan. "So, what the fuck is in there?"

Terry reached in again and felt. There seemed to be lot of small pieces of cardboard, almost like—"photos," Terry said. He pulled up his hand and deposited a handful of photographs on the bedspread.

"I'm almost afraid to look," Kat said, but she reached for one of them anyway. As she pulled it toward her face, she winced.

"It's a little boy. He looks like he's in a cave. His eyes are all puffy, like he's been crying. He's got bruises on his face." She swallowed and looked up. "I don't think I've ever seen anyone who looked as sad as this." She passed it to Susan.

Terry was looking at another. "This one's a little girl. She doesn't look any happier." He started flipping through them more rapidly. "They're all kids," he said.

Susan handed her photo to Dylan, who peered at it intently. "Ah know where this is," he said. "You, too, Ter."

Terry nodded. He looked up and met Dylan's gaze. "These kids are in the Dane catacombs."

"Damn straight," Dylan said.

No one spoke. Susan's mouth tightened and she struggled to keep her composure. "So, I know this is an obvious question," she began, "but what the hell did he do to those children?"

"I shudder to think," Terry answered, a chill running up his spine that had nothing to do with the demonic presences.

"The other question," Kat added, "is *why*."

"Do you think he killed them?" Susan asked, reaching for another of the photos.

"Ah'd bet my head on it," Dylan said. "Ah jes' hope that's *all* he did to them."

Just then Dylan's cell phone rang out again. "Jesus, no more bad news, please—we've had our three!" He looked at the number on the screen and scowled. Focusing his eyes on his wife's he flipped open the phone. "Father Dylan, here."

His face fell as he listened, concern degenerating into shock, and then despair. "When?" he asked. "Did you call the police?" He nodded, still holding Susan's eyes. She put out a hand to comfort and steady him. "Yes, of course Ah will pray for her. Please let me know if you find out anything, or if Ah can help in any way. Y'all take care of each other. Bye-bye."

Dylan's face was ashen as he closed the phone. "It was the Swansons. Ah was supposed to baptize their little girl tomorrow, Jamie. She's gone missing. They think she was kidnapped." He picked up one of the photos and spoke through angry and gritted teeth. "Ah'll bet mah balls Ah know where she is."

66

Climbing the steps, Richard felt dizzy and weary. "Too much adrenaline, for too long," he muttered to himself. He knocked on Mikael's door and opened it a crack. "All's clear," he called and opened the door wider.

Everyone seemed to be sitting stock still in stunned silence—not quite the response he was expecting. "Um...we should maybe do a banishing, just to be on the safe—"

"No time," Terry said, finding his momentum. "We have to move. Now."

"Dude," Dylan said, a little shakily, "we know what the third disappearance is gonna be."

It was a question that had been nagging at Richard for days. "What? And how do you know?" Wearily, he leaned on the door frame for support.

"Li'l Jamie—the girl Ah'm supposed to baptize tomorrow—she's gone missing. Ah don't think it's any accident."

Richard's head reeled with the implication. "Children," he breathed. "Dane's going to make all the children disappear? That's just crazy!"

"No, it isn't," Kat said, throwing a stack of photos in his direction.

Richard picked up the stack where it landed and studied the bleary Polaroids.

"Looks like he's already been making children disappear," Susan said. "Although only God knows why. He's just going to do it on a much larger scale."

"Shit," Richard uttered, and kept repeating it.

"We thought the dogs was the new plague of the Egyptians," Dylan commented, "but that was just the warm-up. This is the real deal."

Richard felt a wave of inferiority rise up the back of his brain, but he forced it down with an act of will. Pushing off the door frame, he stood tall and addressed them commandingly. "Let's mobilize, gang. We've got work to do."

He turned toward Kat and the comatose Mikael. "I worked out an...arrangement with the demon that has been oppressing the two of you. It should be fine. You can leave the house."

"It should be fine?" Terry repeated. "*It should be fine?* You mean you don't know?"

"Look, we made a deal—"

"Great," sneered Terry, "deals with devils often work out well for everybody."

"Look, Kat, it's your choice. If you want to be absolutely safe, you can stay here with Mikael. The room is warded, and we can re-ward the house. I'm just saying I think you're safe."

She nodded, taking that in and weighing the danger.

"We know what we gotta do," Dylan said, "but where are we doin' it?"

Richard sat on the edge of the bed and felt at the stubble of his beard, thinking. "When I asked Larch that this afternoon, he didn't know. But I think we have three likely locations. It could be at Kat's brother's place in Alameda—it's pretty much set up for this working. Who knows, the dog working might have been done there as well. Another possibility is the lodge house in the Lower Haight. We didn't see any circles of invocation, but then we didn't roll up any oriental carpets, either. The last possible place is one that I really don't want to visit again," Richard said, looking at the photos. "I doubt he has any permanent casting circles there, but it wouldn't take long to spray paint one."

"Plus, he's got the kid right there," Terry said. "I'll bet she's locked in his dungeon right now," he said, waving his hand toward the Polaroids.

"Plus, Dane could control the environment," Susan said, her brow furrowed in thought. "He took Polaroids of these kids—what do you want to bet he'll want a souvenir of *this* event?"

Richard exhaled. "You're right. It all points to Dane's place. Should we split up and cover the other places just in case?"

"Well, dude, Dane's place is the farthest away. We can check these out and then head over as soon as we've verified that nothin's going on."

"Okay," Richard said, "that sounds like a plan. Dylan, you take Kat's car, and go to her brother's house right now. Terry, you take Mikael's sorry excuse for a car and head to the Haight. I'll pack the kits and head out for Dane's place in the Geo. If it turns out that they're at your places, speed dial the rest of us, and we'll join you pronto. Otherwise, we'll all meet up at Dane's in just under an hour." He looked at his watch. It was ten o'clock. They would have plenty of time.

"What about me?" Kat asked. "Or Susan?"

Susan waved her away. "Our rule when we got married is that I do *not* fight demons. I do graphic design and, when needed, some internet research. I've given up enough to be part of his crazy life; I'm not willing to give up *my* life as well." She nodded toward Mikael. "I'll stay with him."

"Do you want to stay here?" Richard asked Kat.

"Are you fucking nuts?" she belted back.

"Oh yeah, dude, you should know," Dylan added. "We got excommunicated."

KAT DROVE HER OWN CAR, and Dylan tuned in KFOG on the car stereo. "If the world is goin' down in flames," he opined, "we might as well have decent tunes for it."

She cut due west, up Gilman, toward I-80. Dylan looked at 924 Gilman in the real world as it whizzed past. "That's where Mikael is," he said, pointing behind them.

"Where? The Gilman? What do you mean?" Kat asked, concentrating on the road and keeping an eye out for cops. "Mikael's at the friary."

"No, Ah mean his spirit. He's at 924 Gilman. It's okay, Jaguar is with him."

Kat felt her eyes moisten and swallowed hard. "We only had a few hours together, Dylan," she said. "And I already know, you know?"

He smiled at her, a sad and sympathetic smile. "Ah do know. It weren't like that fer me and Susan, not at all. Ah had to woo her fer years. But Ah know it happens. And Ah know he was gaga fer ya."

She smiled and took comfort in that. She turned left and gunned it for the freeway on-ramp.

The drive to Alameda was short and uneventful. The tunnel was nearly empty, and in what seemed like no time they were pulling up in front of her brother's house.

Something in her heart sank when she saw it. An eddy of grief lapped at her soul, and she shuddered and clutched her hands into fists against the emotional tide.

"You okay?" asked Dylan. She didn't look at him but nodded, her eyes fixed to the dark house, looking lonely now, even abandoned. *It's my house, now*, she thought, but it didn't feel like hers.

"Don't look like much is goin' on, here," Dylan said, opening the car door. "But let's have a look-about, just to make sure."

She opened her own door, and together they walked up the drive to the front door. She unlocked it, and it swung open into a house filled with shadows. She felt for the light switch and narrowed her eyes against the glare.

"Looks clear," Dylan said. "Ah'll just check the bedrooms," and he pushed past her. "All clear," he said and then strode into the living room.

There he stopped. She noticed and caught up to him. "What is it?" she asked.

"Waal, it's not how Ah left it." His brow furrowed. He pointed to the credence table. "See that? It's been cleaned up. In fact...it looks like another ritual has been done here since Dicky and I checked it out."

Kat knelt in a small circle near the far side of the circle of invocation. "Dylan, there's hair here."

Dylan joined her and picked up the strands. "That's not hair, that's fur. Looks like they came back here to do the dog ritual."

"So, doesn't it make sense that they would do the next ritual here, too?"

"Does to me, but magickians don't think like normal folk. Mah guess is that this next ritual is Dane's big night, and he's gonna want to cater his own party." He brushed his hands on his cassock and stood. "Ah don't think anything is goin' down here tonight. Ah say we hightail it to the city."

Kat nodded, moved to resolve by the anger welling up in her. How dare they do a magickal working in her house, after all? "Let's go get the bastards," she said.

68

It had taken Richard nearly fifteen minutes to pack the kits, even with Susan's help. It would have been longer had he had to confect holy water, but Susan happily indicated that Dylan had already done up a bowl while they were waiting for the infernal diners to finish their repast. It was more than enough to stock all the vials. Each kit also contained a weapon, appropriate to each friar's ability, which, he prayed, they would never have to use again. Liturgy books and an anthology of the most popular grimoires also went with them into battle, along with ceremonial crosses. Richard checked the batteries and bulbs in the flashlights and restocked each kit with two bottles of water and three packaged oat cakes.

He took two of the kits out to the Geo while Susan followed with the third. She kissed him on the cheek. "God be with you, Dicky," she said, meaning every word.

He squeezed her hand and climbed into the car. It roared to life, and he headed down Cedar, past All Saints' Episcopal, toward San Pablo, Gilman, and the freeway.

Once underway, he speed dialed Brian on his cell phone.

"Brian," came the crackly voice from his speakerphone.

"Please, God, tell me you know how this damned thing works," he said, fingering the ring in his pocket.

"I wish I could, Dicky, but my friend in Alexandria didn't come through," his voice sounded tired, and Richard's heart sank. "What's going on?"

Briefly, Richard filled him in on the plan. Brian whistled. "My advice is, if you have a couple of minutes of down time, try it out on yourself. I wish I could think of some other way, man, but I can't. I've been racking my brains, and uncovering every stone in that damned ring's five-thousand-year history. There's *lots* of stories about it, as you know, and instructions for use. One interesting tidbit is that among the Arabs it is called 'The Eye of God,' which is a cool name, but I'm not sure it actually tells us anything. Certainly, it doesn't help us figure out what it actually *does*. You'll just have to take the plunge and find out."

Richard did not like the sound of that. He felt a shiver roil up his spine to the top of his head.

"Brian, don't give up—"

"I don't have any choice, Dicky. They're locking up here. I can go home and do some web trolling, but that's it."

"Okay, okay. Thanks for trying. Call me if you find anything." He snapped the cell phone shut and made a left turn onto the on-ramp.

69

TERRY SLOWED as he passed the lodge's Victorian in the Lower Haight, but he couldn't see anything. He found a parking space around the block and quickly climbed the hill back to Haight Street. Puffing slightly and cursing how out of shape he was, he wound his scarf around his neck again, pleased with the effect of the rust fabric against the black of his habit.

He stood outside the Victorian and noted the light of a single candle in the highest window. All else seemed quiet. He tried to find a way to the back, but in true San Francisco style, the houses were so close together that even a rat would have a tough time wriggling between them. Terry knew he was lithe, but even he could not squeeze through.

There seemed to be no way in except the front door, and so, with resolve, the friar mounted the steps and rang the doorbell.

There was a pause of several minutes. Eventually, though, he heard steps on the stairs, and stood back.

The door creaked open just a crack, and Terry recognized Charybdis's unfriendly gaze. "What do you want?" the magickian snapped.

"I'm hankering for a good demon summoning, and I heard you

might have just that sort of shindig going down here tonight," Terry said cheerily but watching him like a hawk.

"Not here," Charybdis suddenly looked defeated, sad, even tired. "There's nobody here but me—and Parsons. But he's..." the magickian glanced behind him.

"Let me guess," Terry said, his smile fading, "in a coma."

Charybdis nodded, not meeting his eyes. "I heard Randy...died."

"Yeah," Terry said, softening toward him despite himself. "Day before yesterday. I'm sorry. We did everything we could."

"Did you learn anything that might...you know, help Parsons?" Charybdis did look at him now, but there was little hope in his gaze.

Terry shook his head. "But I promise you one thing, we won't let it happen to another of your brothers. Not if we can help it."

The magickian nodded, taking courage from that.

"Just tell me where the ritual is being held. Is it Dane's?"

Charybdis nodded, looking frightened.

Terry reached out and touched the man on the shoulder. "Hey, we're going to do everything we can."

"Wait," Charybdis said, running back up the stairs. "I'm going to come with you." In a moment, he had grabbed a coat and was locking the door behind him.

"What about Parsons?" Terry asked.

"He's not going anywhere, is he?"

Terry didn't answer but headed back down toward the car. He wasn't quite sure about having Charybdis along. He didn't trust him at all, but he certainly felt for him.

"I don't see how you think you can possibly stop him," Charybdis said. "He has every demon in Hell in thrall to him."

"Had," Terry said. "You didn't hear? Dane lost the Ring."

Charybdis stopped, his mouth open. "How, when?"

"Last night," Terry said smugly. "As for how—let's just say some fellas ought to know when to keep it in their pants."

Charybdis's eyes lit up. Possibility positively shone from him. "The demons don't know that, though," he said.

"They do now," Terry said. "Our prior just had a summit, with the noble Duke Articiphus as the guest of honor."

"No shit," Charybdis said.

"That's right. The only one who can compel him now is...well, your lodge brothers. And they don't *have* to." He scowled at the magickian as they reached the car. He unlocked the driver's side. "Never did have to, until Dane got involved." It was an accusation, and Charybdis caught it.

"You don't understand. We're trying to do something good, here." He waited as Terry ducked in and unlocked his door. Opening it, he slid in.

"Ordinarily, 'demons' and 'good' don't fit naturally into the same sentence," Terry noted.

"That's because you don't understand them," the magickian explained.

Terry started the engine but then turned to face Charybdis. "Oh, wait. Let me get this straight. Demons—the variety that come from Hell, yes?—aren't so much *evil*, they're just *misunderstood*?"

"Well...yes."

"You are more full of shit than the 9/11 report."

"Maybe now isn't really the time to explain," Charybdis offered an olive branch.

"You think?" Terry spat. "Look, let's concentrate on saving your brothers' asses, and then you can make tea for us again and explain how we've got the demons all wrong."

They rode in silence for a while as Terry made his way west through the city.

"We're going to have to be careful getting in," Charybdis said, finally breaking the silence after ten blocks or so. "Last I heard, he's got Howlers in place, ever since you guys broke into his house last."

"Are you shitting me?" Terry asked, whipping out his cell phone. "Why didn't you say so?" He speed dialed Richard, whispering a prayer that he wasn't too late.

70

RICHARD PARALLEL PARKED about a block from the Dane mansion. In the dense, soupy San Francisco night its silhouette loomed, enveloping the horizon, threatening to swallow all.

I should wait for the others, he thought to himself, but the urgency of the situation compelled him. As he got out of his car, a bird shrieked, foreshadowing the grieving wails that would engulf the planet if they did not succeed. Richard felt bowed under the weight of it. His shoulders drooped, and his breathing came in heavy gasps as if, in his anxiety, he gulped at hope and, finding none, gulped all the more desperately. Why had this fallen to him? To them? Who the fuck were *they*?

There was no question of their worthiness. None of them were worthy of forbearance, let alone this kind of trust. Everything Bishop Tom said they had been accused of was, he realized, absolutely true. They were addicts and perverts and dabblers in dark things, completely undeserving of this kind of responsibility. Richard fought an urge to claw at his own eyes. *That* was what he deserved. Instead, he stared at his hands.

From some far recesses of his brain, the gem of Eastern Orthodox spirituality, the Jesus prayer, leaped into consciousness. Without being aware of choosing to, he spoke the words aloud, "Jesus Christ, Son of God, have mercy on me, a sinner." He said it again, and again. As he did so, the mantra crowded out the obsessive self-condemnation. He didn't feel worthy, but he didn't need to. He felt better.

Taking advantage of the renewed energy, he decided not to sit and continue to stew but to walk around the block, a reconnoitering. He needed to confirm that, yes, the ritual was indeed taking place here. He might even be able to tell in what room it would happen by the lights.

He shut the car door, set his cell phone to vibrate, and set out toward the Dane mansion, the Jesus prayer continuing to provide a much-needed emotional analgesic.

Richard stared at the house as he walked. From the front, he saw few lights. The porch light was on, of course, and lights above the curved drive. But none of the windows betrayed any life within.

He rounded the corner. A hip-high stone wall contained the yard, rough dark stones covered with moisture that glistened in the amber streetlight.

This side of the house sported one light outside, and a distant glow in the second-floor window.

"Have mercy on me, a sinner..." he breathed rhythmically, and in a few moments, he was rounding the corner again. This time, most of the house was obscured by a high hedge.

He stopped and got his bearings. He was walking north now, and at the far end of the yard was the entrance to the elder Dane's room. Richard wondered if the younger Dane had bothered to replace the nurse, and if so, with what species.

It took Richard a moment to orient himself in the neighborhood, but, squinting into the fog, he caught sight of a street sign, and everything clicked. The historic Swedenborgian Church was about a block and a half northwest of him, and he smiled to think of it. An oddly beautiful structure, it was the closest thing to holding church in a hobbit hole he had ever experienced. Somehow knowing where he was on the map grounded him, and his panic receded by another small measure.

But as he turned to continue his northward perambulation, he froze as he heard a slathering all too near his ear. The temperature dropped almost instantaneously, and an icy gust stabbed at his cheek.

With renewed panic screaming in his ears, Richard turned to face the slathering. The being that confronted him was half again as tall as a man, its long black trench coat dangling above its waist. Its shoulders were rounded and bulbous, too-long arms poised and ready to snatch at him, its bunched, powerful thighs coiled and prepared for the lunge.

Oh shit! threatened to overtake the Jesus prayer, but Richard mentally clamped down on the panic and began to recite the prayer aloud. "Jesus Christ, Son of God, have mercy on me, a sinner," he spoke as he raised his head to look into the face of the creature that had so rudely interrupted his walk.

The face was an inky pit devoid of features but surrounded by a stiff, hoary mane that erupted from its neck.

It loomed over Richard, apparently savoring his fear and the universal rush of power that every hunter feels at the moment of overwhelming its prey.

"A Howler," Richard said aloud, forgetting the Jesus Prayer altogether. He was paralyzed, whether by his own terror or by some occult device of the Howler demon he could not tell. *So, this is it, I'm just waiting to die*, he thought, as the ebony void through which the demon devoured its prey descended upon him.

Richard hit the sidewalk and rolled. Frantically, he tore at his fanny pack and felt for his metal crucifix. His fingers closed around it, and he jerked his hand out just as the Howler, with a massive stride, caught up to him and began to lower the void that should have been any earthly creature's face.

Richard felt the icy sucking of wind as the void came closer, threatening to vacuum his soul into Sheol. Just as the Howler's hood came within arm's length, Richard thrust the crucifix up into the void.

It felt like plunging his hand into a glacial stream. The cold bit at his fingers, and he set his face in determination.

It didn't last long, however. The Howler demon, caught off guard, gave an excellent demonstration of its name, sending up a screech that could have awakened the dead, and perhaps did. As if on fire, the demon thrashed around, clawing at the void of its face and spinning away from Richard.

As Richard rose to his feet, the Howler demon was leaning against the stone garden wall of the Dane mansion, whimpering and spitting in his direction.

Richard heard footsteps pounding behind him and turned to see Dylan and Kat running toward him full-tilt. He waved, and in a moment they caught up to him. "Dude, you all right?" Dylan asked, placing a concerned hand on his shoulder.

Kat was staring at the demon, who seemed to be staring back at her. "What the hell is *that*?" she asked. Richard could almost see her goose bumps through her jacket.

"*That* is a Howler demon," Richard said.

"We heard 'im howl all right," Dylan nodded.

"Is he dangerous?" she asked, still staring at it.

"Does it look dangerous?" Richard laughed. "Shit, yeah, they're dangerous. They're stupid, though. Low-level thugs. You've got to defend yourself from them, but they're not, generally speaking, the ones you've got to watch out for."

Dylan looked around, "Yeah, but the problem is the howl generally brings more demons. We're gonna need artillery. Ya got the kits?"

Richard nodded and led the way to the car. Kat followed, still looking over her shoulder at the wounded Howler.

Richard opened the trunk and began to unload. He gave two bags to Dylan and lifted the last one out himself.

"Aren't you scared?" Kat asked no one in particular.

"Shit yeah, we're scared," Dylan answered. "You think we're crazy?"

"Just because it's scary doesn't mean it doesn't need to be done," Richard said. "And that's the definition of courage—being scared and doing it anyway."

She nodded, looking around for more Howlers.

"I take it Webber's place was a bust?" Richard asked.

"Yeah," Dylan answered. "Empty. But at least now we know where the dog ritual was performed. So, we came straight here. Any sign of Terry?"

As if on cue, the little engine of Mikael's Tercel spluttered into earshot, its one working headlight spearing the sooty fog. Richard waved him in but was surprised to note there was a passenger.

He was even more surprised once they'd parked to discover the rider was Charybdis. As Terry and his passenger walked toward them, Richard could see that the magickian was ashen and distracted. His surly demeanor seemed to have completely dissolved into nervous anxiety.

Richard preferred that side of him. It was, at least, honest, and therefore an improvement.

"Dude, you brought company," Dylan stated the obvious.

"He was nursing a lodge brother back there that was as much of a turnip as," Terry noticed Kat's brows bunching, "as a turnip."

Before he could continue, Charybdis interrupted. "Look, I know we're not going to see eye to eye. And I'm sorry I was so rude to you guys last time we met. But I've lost two lodge brothers to this stupid plan, and I don't want to lose another one. Especially Larch."

Richard whirled on him. "You're saying Larch is doing this working? I was certain he would delegate it. He's..." he wanted to say he was too important but realized that Charybdis might find that offensive.

"No," Charybdis said. "He's opted to put himself in harm's way before asking any of us to do it. Regardless of what you all think of him, he's not a bad guy."

He turned and looked straight at Richard. "By the way, did you send a bunch of Latino guys to rough him up?"

Richard ignored the question. "Just stay out of the way. We don't want you getting hurt, too. And Kat, same goes for you." He grabbed a kit bag from Dylan and tossed it to Terry.

Both Terry and Dylan got to work. With practiced efficiency, they dropped to one knee, undid the bags, and began to stock their belts and pockets with whatever they might need to meet the dangers of the next hour.

"How about us?" Kat asked. "How are we supposed to defend ourselves?

Richard opened the trunk again. He took out a smaller bag and pulled out two crucifixes and a couple of bottles of water.

"Is that holy water?" Kat asked.

"It soon will be," Richard said, dropping to one knee himself and fishing around in his kit for his liturgy and salt.

In a few minutes, they were ready to go. "Time?" Terry asked. Richard looked at his watch. "Eleven. Still plenty of time, unless they start early, that is."

"Midnight's a pretty auspicious time for working demon magick," Terry pointed out.

"Yeah, but Dane might want to beat us to the punch," Richard countered. "I say we shouldn't tarry." He turned to Charybdis. "Best way in?" The magickian shrugged.

"Ah say let's go over the wall and through the hospital room."

"Don't you think the old Dane will raise the alarm?" Terry asked.

"Not with me holding Solomon's Ring, he won't," Richard said, leading the way toward the hedge. A random muscle in his belly began to shudder involuntarily, and he tightened his diaphragm and willed it to be still. The voices in his head were gaining volume, reminding him of all the reasons that he shouldn't be doing this: because he wasn't worthy, because he was a fake, because he was a sinner, because the demons would eat him for a midnight snack. He ignored them all and put one foot in front of another.

As they approached the hedge, the Howler hissed at them, still curled into a protective ball near the wall. Richard aimed a kick at the side of the monster's head, and enjoyed a surge of satisfaction to feel it not only connect but bang into the wall behind it as well. The demon roared, but Richard kept marching, followed by the others.

At the far end of the hedge, Richard positioned himself, dropped his bag, and intertwined the fingers of both hands to give a leg up to whoever would go first.

Terry stepped up without hesitation. Hoisting his elfin frame was effortless, and in moments Terry had spread his own jacket over the broken glass and barbed wire at the top of the fence. He jumped down and called a quiet "All clear."

Richard helped Kat up next. "Shit!" she whispered as she jumped from the wall.

"What?" Richard called.

"Cut my hand on that damned glass!" she practically moaned.

"Careful," Richard said to Dylan. To Charybdis he said, "Help me with him."

"Thanks, dude," Dylan said, sarcastically, but didn't refuse the extra help. With not a few grunts and groans, he cleared the wall and jumped to the other side with an "oaf!" that was just a little too loud for Richard's comfort.

"It's okay," he told himself as he helped Charybdis up, "if they're doing anything really dangerous, they're not going to notice us anyway."

Once Charybdis was over, Richard, taller than the rest, jumped and grabbed the barbed wire through Terry's jacket. Once he secured a grip that wouldn't rip through his flesh, he swung his leg up, caught the edge of the wall, and rolled over the top of it, almost landing on Charybdis's head on the other side.

"You're supposed to move out of the way," Richard said, kind of by way of an apology for almost flattening his skull. "You guys don't do a lot of this kind of stuff, do you?"

"You mean breaking and entering? No."

"It shows."

Terry tried the door, which, not surprisingly, turned out to be locked. Terry reached into his kit and pulled out a crowbar. "No time for subtlety," he muttered, and with a single swing shattered the glass door. Terry reached his hand through, unlocked the door, and opened it. Without another word, they followed him inside. Richard brought up the rear but was momentarily irritated to discover that the group did not progress once inside. Soon, he found out why.

The elder Dane sat erect in his bed, unnaturally, without support.

The old man's eyes were bloodshot and wide. His thin slit of a mouth was drawn back into something halfway between a smile and a grimace. Thin wisps of hair floated above his head by some sorcery of static electricity, creating the appearance of an old man peering at them from beneath the waves.

Dane the elder ignored all but Richard. He speared the prior with the sharpest of glares. "My son is in the great hall," the otherworldly voice sprang from the old man's lips. "I trust, Priest, that you will not forget our agreement?"

All eyes turned to Richard, who kept his focus on the demon in the old man suit. "I remember," he said. "I'll be true to my word. Anything else we need to know?"

"Probably not," the old man sank back into his bed with a wheeze that itself sounded lethal. "I could say, 'Watch your ass,' but you won't survive it anyway."

"Thanks for the vote of confidence," Richard said, taking the lead and striding out into the hallway.

"Okay," Terry said, trotting on his shorter legs behind him. "Exactly how many devils did you make deals with? And is this something I need to be worried about?"

"I promised him dibs on my complete collection of '60s-era *Playboy*s if I croak, so see that he gets those, will you?"

"Uh-huh," Terry said. "Remind me to give you the brushoff next time you ask me an important question."

The hallway was dark, and their feet moved soundlessly on the thick carpet. Their eyes were restless but diligent, keen for any sign of opposition.

They hadn't long to wait. Rounding the corner, Richard froze. Terry ploughed into him, but the others took note before adding to the collision. "Holy shit," Richard breathed. Without looking behind him, he spoke quietly but evenly, just loud enough for them to hear. "Back away. Don't let them see you. *Back the fuck away.*"

But Terry had already seen, and his crowbar slipped from his hand to the floor with a ringing clang that guaranteed they would not escape detection.

One by one, the others disobeyed Richard's instruction, stepping out around the corner and halting, either dropping their jaws, wetting themselves, or both.

Richard felt his flesh crawl under his cassock. The temperature had fallen to below zero, and breath issued forth from his mouth in a frosty haze that obscured the terrible scene before him.

He blinked and struggled to take it in. The massive dining room, which could easily accommodate nearly a hundred diners, was filled to standing capacity with a grand assortment of demonic hosts.

Moving his eyes from left to right, he took them in: Brush demons, with their sandy, scaly skin, flicking their tongues, observing him with their multiple stalked eyes; Howler demons, like a host of tall explosions frozen in time, leering down at him and screaming; Painter demons, capable of shooting streams of inky blue poison hundreds of feet from glands on their gilled necks; Gunthers, diminutive imps that were about as intelligent as dogs but far more antisocial and dangerous, named for the eighteenth-century German occultist that had first summoned them from the pit and set them loose upon the human world. These and many other species too numerous to catalog faced him, barring his entrance to the Great Hall, heralding the end of his sad, sorry struggle to survive.

"Jesus Christ, have mercy on me, a sinner..." Richard began, as the front line of the demonic horde, composed mainly of Howlers, began to close the meager yards that separated them.

Richard, panicked, spun his head to one side and then the other, looking for an exit. He could always turn and run back the way they had come, but he knew the Howlers would close the distance in two quick bounds. A door to the kitchen was directly to his right, about fifteen feet away, but one of the Sand demons was already headed for it, anticipating this strategy.

The yards had quickly closed, and Richard could feel the chill of the demons' breath. "Ideas?" he called over his shoulder.

"There aren't enough crucifixes in the fucking Vatican to keep this crew at bay!" Terry cried. "Now is probably a really a good time to pull out that ring."

"But I don't know what it will do—to me or to them!" Richard argued.

"I can tell you for sure what's going to happen if you don't use it," Terry countered, "and it's going to happen quick!"

Maybe I can just show it to them, Richard thought. *Maybe that will be threat enough.* He stuck his hand into his pocket and pulled out the ring, even as one of the Howlers hovered above him.

He plunged his right index finger into the ring and held it up for all the demons to see. The Howler recognized it at once and took a step back. Even the Sand demons hesitated. But to the Gunthers it meant nothing. Capable of only rudimentary thought, it was as inconsequential to them as any other piece of clothing.

They appeared not to have noticed that the larger demons had stopped advancing, and soon Richard saw a wave of Gunthers scrambling over their larger, more intelligent kin, closing their distance fast. A group of three of them in the lead, moving almost in formation, leaped the final three yards.

Richard saw them coming and crouched. "Shit!" he shouted and at the last possible moment punched at the flying Gunthers with his right hand, the red glow of the ring piercing the dim light of the room.

He wasn't sure what to expect. Perhaps an explosion, perhaps the terrible rending of his soul, but it was nothing like that.

Time froze. The universe deconstructed. He saw himself, at a great distance, arm upraised as if greeting the Gunthers, a frozen tableau in a museum of the occult arts. But he took little notice of himself because all that is was also frozen in time before him. Every creature, every interaction on Earth, was visible and immediate to him. Other worlds were likewise on display, with all their myriad inhabitants, their situations and dramas. His mind nearly snapped with the magnitude of it, but some grace touched and contained him, and his perception took on even greater dimensions. What lay before him was not simply all of space but all of time as well—the hard record of the past and all the malleable, possible futures spread out like a million strands of yarn secured to the single point of the present and exploding into infinity.

There, clearly visible, was his own past and uncountable futures, possible loves, a thousand possible deaths. He witnessed these without concern, as one tiny part of a whole so vast he could literally feel himself teetering between comprehension and madness.

As he breathed into this new revelation, another facet of experience assaulted him—an overwhelming attack of compassion. He did not witness all of time and space as a distant observer but as a participant, for even the sensations of the tiniest microbe were experienced as if they were happening to his own body. Every joy, every tear, every grievous sigh, every cruelty, every sting of pride or hatred or envy, every prick of pain, every ache of longing or love or loss that ever was and ever could be, he felt as if it were his own. Indeed, it *was* his own.

Amid the cacophony, without effort, he felt his own insecurity and despair, his crushing sense of unworthiness. And he loved it. He loved all of it. Every creature, on every world, every rock, every sensation, every potential future he loved. His heart swelled within him, but this heart was larger than the universe—it contained it, indeed it held it, protected it, sustained it, caressed it, married itself to it, worlds without end.

His love for all that is, was, and ever would be pierced his consciousness like a lightning strike, becoming the single-pointed source and end of all of being, a point that exploded with the ferocity of a billion orgasms.

71

RICHARD BLINKED, unable to assimilate what he was seeing. Terry seemed to be hovering over him, floating in free space. Then Dylan's face drifted into view, followed by Kat's. He grinned warmly and broadly at them, wondering if perhaps he were in Heaven, or dreaming. Then he saw Charybdis's face, and it all came rushing back—the demons, the danger, the vision, and now, apparently, him lying on the floor in a pool of his own piss grinning stupidly at the ceiling. *And he was fine with it.* He knew that only moments before, he would have found his situation humiliating, disconcerting, even untenable. But now it just seemed right and proper. Of course he would fall to the floor. Of course his friends would be staring down at him in concern. Of course he would have voided his bladder when blessed with a glimpse of unmediated Reality.

His brain seemed to still be in shock from the vision, unable to fully contract to the limited field of perception afforded by his senses yet no longer receiving the information that had, only moments ago, lit up every receptor in his brain simultaneously. Although the vision had been withdrawn, the memory of it continued to shake him. He had seen the universe as God sees it; had seen all things held in love; had seen himself utterly embraced in grace, without condition, without even a hint of the judgment that he feared and so mercilessly applied to himself. He had seen only beauty—in himself, in the world, in every creature. Even in the demons.

The Eye of God, indeed, he thought. And he laughed. He laughed for all the pointless years he had carried around all that guilt and shame and anger and self-loathing that had so marred his life and his experience of the world. With great explosions of joy and relief he doubled over, laughing at all the wasted time and energy, at all the prejudice and bloodshed and hatred that had so seared the troubled world of men.

"What a waste!" he cried aloud, staring up at his friends.

Kat exchanged confused and concerned looks with Dylan and Terry. "What's a waste, dude?" Dylan asked him, hesitantly.

Richard didn't answer him. Overall, two things remained to him —a sense of almost infinite insignificance, coexisting simultaneously with the awareness of being loved powerfully and without reservation. He rose, light of heart and afraid of nothing. For he knew in his very bones that, despite all that was happening, nothing at all was amiss that could not be set right; that "all will be well, all will be well, and every manner of thing will be well."

Staggering slightly, Richard surveyed the damage. The room was literal pandemonium. The three Gunthers that had come in contact with the ring were twitching and immobile at his feet. The Howlers were climbing over each other to jump out the windows—anything to put distance between themselves and the ring. The Sand demons and others were cowering in confusion, bringing up the rear of the Howler's escape.

Richard knelt by the Gunthers. "Hey, little guys, it's okay." They seemed to be breathing, but their eyes were glassy and sightless. Richard felt sad in his soul for them. For all of them. He stood and addressed them, even as they tumbled out the tall windows.

"Where are you going? God is out there, too! Where can you go to escape him? What are you afraid of? Everything is fine! Everything is going to be okay! You're going to be okay! I'm not going to hurt you. The ring won't hurt you! No one is going to hurt you!" He had walked right up to them, gregarious, pleading, and unafraid. The closer he got, the more they cowered, the more frantically they scrambled over one another to get out of the windows.

Rather, what once *had been* windows—they were now shambles. Broken glass spilled out onto the lawn outside, and great chunks of the wall had been taken out where two largish demons had refused to take turns exiting.

Richard walked to the wall and switched on the lights. "No need for all this gloom," he said, to no one in particular. By now the last of the large demons was gone, and the smaller ones were trailing out.

Richard walked back to where his friends were standing. They were still huddled together, mouths open, and Dylan was shaking his head. "Dude, you got fucking nuts the size of a monstrance."

Terry broke from the pack and rushed up to him, taking his hands in his. "What happened, Dicky? What did you see?"

Richard stopped and looked up, remembering. He smiled. "I saw everything. I saw it as God sees it. And I loved it. All of it." He turned and looked at the damage left by the fleeing demons. "Even them." He turned back and poked Terry on the nose. "Even you," he said, and leaned over, kissing Terry on the top of the head. Terry raised one eyebrow so high it looked to Richard as if his forehead might snap.

"Dude, do you think you're mentally stable enough to continue?" Dylan asked, walking over to Richard and placing a hand on his arm.

Richard looked him in the eyes and beamed with sincerity. "Dyl, I have never felt better in my entire fucking life. Let's go tell these magickians just how much we love them," and he set off toward the doors leading to the Great Hall.

"That was not exactly mah plan," said Dylan, looking nervously at Terry and Kat. Charybdis stood with his hand to his mouth, uncertain whether to follow. But as the others walked away, he looked around and, eyes widening at the sight of all the destruction, trotted to catch up to them.

Richard took the lead with his head held high, his shoulders broad and square, and his eyes shining. Dylan and Terry were close behind him, kit bags over their shoulders, flourishing crucifixes with vials of holy water at the ready.

Richard paused momentarily at the doors to the Great Hall. With both hands he gripped the large pewter door handles and plunged them down as he pushed.

Nothing happened. The doors wouldn't budge. Richard called over his shoulder, "I think someone has bolted the doors from the inside."

"What if the five of us rammed it?" Dylan asked.

"Worth a try," Richard agreed.

They backed up about ten paces from the door. Standing shoulder to shoulder, Richard counted down. "On three. One, two, three!" As one, they rushed the enormous oaken doors and threw all their weight upon them.

"I heard something crack," Terry said.

"That was mah shoulder," Dylan moaned.

"Again!" Richard called.

Once again, they lined up and rushed at the door. Once again, they threw their shoulders against it in unison. This time, the cracking was even more audible, and the doors swayed inward before they caught and held.

"Again!" Dylan shouted.

Once again, they regrouped, and once again they battered the door. This time their shoulders met the wood, and with a great, reverberating snap the threshold opened before them.

They weren't expecting to meet such little resistance and almost lost their balance inside the door. Within a few seconds, however, they found their feet and took in the scene.

Lit by pewter candle stands as tall as a man's shoulder, the hall was festooned with a score of flickering flames. Red LEDs betrayed the presence of at least three video cameras, set at the periphery of the room on tripods. Richard noted that a giant circle had been inscribed on the hardwood floor in chalk—a circle of summoning, ornamented by Latin phrases and sigils of arcane origin.

Within the ring, a circle of safety had been inscribed but a larger one than usual, for this one protected not just the magickian—Larch stared at them in dumb horror as they entered—but their patron as well. Dane's eyes were shining with what must have been tears of joy before his ritual had been so rudely interrupted. Now his watery eyes were fierce as he stared at the friars, and a blood vessel protruded from his forehead so pronounced that Richard could plainly see it even across the room.

But that was not all, he noted. Outside the circle of safety was the circle in which the demon was circumscribed. As Richard expected, a credence table had been set, with the small paper triangle containing the sigil of the demon to be called—in this case, it was plain to see, Articiphus. This circle, too, was larger than that of a normal opera-tion, for contained within this circle was another creature, looking very small, vulnerable, and frightened.

"Jamie!" Dylan shouted, just now recognizing the rag doll form on the floor. "Hold on, Honey, we're coming to get you!"

Richard could see that they had crashed the party at the crucial moment of the ritual. The air before the child was shimmering, and the fiery aspect of the demon was resolving into a ghostly dragon, the mount of Articiphus. And astride him, just now shimmering into focus, the great duke of Hell himself, his scarred visage severe, his crown catching the glow of the score of candles that dotted the room.

The dragon coiled and shot out its tail, planting its massive but weirdly weightless feet far too near Jamie's cowering form.

"What the fuck do we do now?" Terry called. "We're outside the circle of protection. There's nothing stopping that demon from eating us right where we stand!"

Richard looked at him with calm benignity. "They'd better not. We made a deal."

"A deal with demons? Forgive me if Ah'm lackin' in confidence."

"Point. But here goes." And with that, Richard strode into the room, directly for Dane.

He walked with resolution, but he did not hurry. He saw the coiling body of the infernal Duke's mount, but he ignored it. He saw Larch's mouth moving, miming "no, no, no" and waving him away, but it meant nothing to him. His eyes were fixed upon Dane, and bearing a visage that was both terrible in justice and soft with compassion, he steadily closed the distance between himself and the scion.

Dane's face was screwed into a mask of frustration and fury. The demon had arrived, was ready to do the magickian's bidding, but Larch was distracted. The rich man screamed at Larch, but Richard did not register the words. He did register the fact that, as he crossed the boundary of the great circle, Dane pulled a revolver out of his jacket pocket. He screamed something at Richard and waved at him menacingly with the gun. Richard did not falter but, placing one foot after the other, continued his advent.

As if in slow motion, Dane screamed something else at him, his long black locks flailing in the candle light, flecks of gold sweat spinning into the gloom as his head whipped from side to side. His mouth moved slowly, a curse, it seemed, as he raised the pistol and took aim, directly at Richard's head.

Richard's face revealed not anger or fear but only pity. Nor did he hesitate. Richard saw the muzzle of the pistol blaze momentarily, and felt the rush of wind and the pinch of his flesh as the bullet grazed his temple.

Richard paused momentarily and put a hand up to the side of his head. Looking at it, he noted without panic the blood that covered his fingers, appearing wetly black in the dim light. He looked up at Dane again, shook his head, and took another step.

72

LARCH HAD HIT the floor the moment he heard the first gunshot. Careful to stay within the protective circle, he curled up in the fetal position and closed his eyes.

Dylan, throwing every ounce of caution to the wind, dashed to the child's side and hugged her to him. She buried her face in his habit and held on for dear life. Dylan clamped his left arm around her protectively, and in his right brandished a crucifix in the direction of the infernal worm and its rider.

Terry made directly for the object of summoning—the paper triangle on which the sigil of the demon had been inscribed. Along the way, he grabbed one of the candles off its holder and strode quickly to the credence table where the triangle was placed before a smoldering incense burner. The winding, scaled body of the dragon blocked his way, but Terry set his jaw and continued walking. As he expected, he passed through the apparition with naught but psychological resistance.

Arriving at the credence table, Terry bent and held the flame of the candle to the tiny paper triangle. It flared, and a curl of flame leaped and danced above it. In moments, the paper was consumed.

Satisfied, Terry straightened and turned around, expecting to see the noble duke Articiphus wink out of sight.

He was disappointed. Instead, he watched in horror as the great, cowled demon dismounted. His dragon slithered off into mist as Articiphus gathered himself to his full height. Even afoot, the demon towered above Terry, an effect heightened by the stack of crowns that adorned his head.

Terry felt paralyzed as the infernal prince surveyed the scene. The two halves of the prince's face—beautiful and scarred—turned toward the confrontation between Richard and Dane for a moment then lit for a moment on the cowering shadow that was Charybdis in a heap near the door. Terry then watched as the crowned and faceless head turned to Dylan and the little girl.

Terry sprang to place himself between the duke and his friend, raising a crucifix and reciting from the Liturgy of Exorcism.

Apparently unconcerned, however, the dark prince waved his left hand away from his body. The space to Terry's immediate right seemed to disappear, either obliterated or sucked into another dimension. To cope with the vacuum, Terry felt the ground he stood on lurch to the right to fill the void, leaving him standing three feet from where he had been only moments before.

No sooner did he realize what had happened to him than the demon was already passing the spot where he had been, bending toward the screaming girl and Dylan, who was desperately waving his crucifix toward the Duke.

About two feet from the reach of Dylan's outstretched arm, the demon halted. Terry could feel the temperature in the room continue to drop and noted without reflecting on it that his breath was now issuing in visible puffs.

"I will not harm her," the demon spoke, no steam issuing from the visible, beautiful half of his face. "There will be no more slavery this night."

"You're supposed to be gone!" Terry shouted at him. "I destroyed your sigil!"

The demon straightened and turned toward Terry. "You destroyed the instrument of my compulsion, yes, Priest. But I am here now of my own free will."

Dylan continued to cradle the child. His arm was beginning to tire, and eventually he let the crucifix drop, balancing it on his knee, still pointed toward the demon.

The demon turned away and began to walk toward the center of the room. As it did so, Dylan fished in his kit bag for a pocket knife and began to saw at the little girl's bonds.

DANE RAISED his pistol for another shot. Richard did not flinch, did not hesitate, but slowly and deliberately closed the distance between himself and the rich man. He did not fear death. Indeed, even though the full force of the vision was even now receding, he did not fear anything. He watched with dispassion as Dane's finger contracted.

The gun did not fire, however. From his peripheral vision, Richard saw a dark shape spinning into the circle from behind Dane. He smiled broadly when he recognized it as Kat. She had grabbed one of the tall candle stands and was spinning with it, gathering speed, and with a practiced agility he did not know she possessed, he watched her connect the candle stand with the back of Dane's head. It made an audible crack. Dane's head lurched forward, his eyes wide, his mouth open. He pitched forward and caught himself on his hands and knees.

"That's for my brother," Kat said.

Richard was about to object that her brother did what he did without Dane, but it was pointless—she was already in motion. She whirled the candle stand around her head and brought it down again upon Dane's spine with an impact that Richard felt. "And that's for the dogs!" she spat, her black hair flying at all angles. She spun around again, twirling the candle stand above her head and planting it with force once more on his spine. "And that's for Mikael!" She held the candle stand to his back and twisted it.

Dane was still conscious but obviously in a world of pain. He writhed on the floor, uttering mangled cries of mixed pain and rage.

Richard saw the mighty Duke Articiphus approaching and moved back. Kat, eyes wide, did the same. The demon bent over the scion and touched his bunched and straining brow with a skeletal finger.

"So, tell me, Priest," his infernal majesty addressed Richard, "who here is under your protection?"

Richard froze. He looked around the room then at Kat, candle stand poised like a baseball bat ready to swing; at Dane, writhing and cringing at the demon's feet; at Larch, uncurled now but paralyzed in fear; at Dylan cutting at the rope binding the feet of little Jamie; at Terry, madly flipping through a liturgy book; and the cowering Charybdis. Richard knew that anyone he did not claim would be fair game for whatever the demon desired. He fixed the demon with a steady eye. "They all are."

The demon turned the scarred half of his face toward Richard, and when he spoke, his voice was without any trace of warmth. "That is a lie, Priest. Be careful. I have some acquaintance with lies, and dominion over those who tell them."

Richard swallowed and felt a trickle of sweat run down his back despite the cold. He knew there was love in the world for even this prince of darkness, but he also knew that the demon wielded terrible power. Richard spoke evenly. "You are right, of course, your majesty. I have an implied covenant with the magickians. But this one," he pointed to Dane. "This one is not under my protection."

The demon looked at Larch and Charybdis, not liking the reduction of his menu but somehow knowing that Richard had spoken the truth.

73

THE DARK PRINCE bowed low and stretched a bony hand toward
Dane's face. Kat's mouth gaped open as she watched the demon. As
soon as the demon's fingers touched the man's face, his skin turned
from flushed red to an ashen blue. "Shhhh, it's okay," the demon said
with almost sincere tenderness. "No one will ever, ever hurt you
again. I promise. I am your savior, and I have come to deliver you.
Everything is going to be *all right*. Your suffering is finally at an end."
A ghostly ball of dark blue light shone in the prince's hand as he
raised it to his mouth. In a moment, the blue light was gone,
enveloped, even devoured by the crowned demon.

Nourished by the rich man's soul, Articiphus drew up to his full
height and faced Richard. "You are still in possession of the ring?"

"I am," Richard answered, holding out his hand. The demon
flinched and took a step backward. "I also know how to use it, and
what it does. And why you find it so...distasteful."

The demon swayed over him, which Richard took to be a kind of
nodding. When the dark prince spoke again, Richard felt the chill of
his breath. "You have released me from my servitude to these cretins,"
the demon waved in Larch's direction. "I am in your debt. At sunset

tomorrow, I will seek you out and pay that debt. You have some items to be delivered—have them ready."

Richard bowed, both out of respect and as an affirmative response. The demon turned and strode with slow, deliberate steps toward his dragon mount.

At the sight of the demon prince coming straight toward her, Jamie began screaming again. Dylan shushed her and tried to hug her to him to comfort her, but this time she was not bound. Watching the demon advance, she wrestled herself from Dylan's grasp and ran for the open double doors, trailing an ear-splitting shriek after her.

"I'll find her," Richard said, heading for the doors, "Terry, this place needs a banishing ritual, pronto. Dylan, first aid—I know Kat's got a couple of scrapes."

"Aye-aye," said Dylan, hauling himself to his feet with a groan.

Richard picked up speed in the dining room, shaking his head at the wreckage. At the threshold of the hallway, he stopped and listened, trying to determine which direction the girl had gone in. A fresh scream sounded to his right, and he lurched into motion. This was the direction of the elder Dane's room, he knew, and he had little doubt that the nightmarishly gaunt old man would frighten the little girl, even just lying in his hospital bed.

When he was halfway down the hall, the scream abruptly stopped as if someone had pulled the plug on a stereo. Richard added a burst of speed to his sprint.

As he rounded the corner into Dane's room, however, he stopped cold. "Ah shit," he said out loud. The old man wasn't in his bed but lay in a tangle of bones, like a pile of discarded clothes in the middle of the room. Beside the pile was Jamie, who smiled a positively vicious smile and looked at him with red, glowing eyes. When she spoke, the voice that emerged was dusty, ancient, and malevolent.

"Greetings, Priest. Did you lose something? Or, perhaps, someone?"

"Holy shit, Duunel, she's just a little girl!" Richard pleaded, "You can't possess her!"

"Oh, but I can. In fact, I am!" the demon said, walking in a circle, a bit hesitantly, trying out the new body. He closed the little girl's hands into fists and uncurled them again, a look of relish lighting up her once-angelic face. Richard could only imagine the satisfaction that came from the articulation of joints not stiff with arthritis and age.

"It's not fair to her," Richard tried again, "she hasn't had a chance to live her life—you can't take it away from her."

"What do I care for her life, Priest? I am a demon! What do I care for fairness? I am a demon! I fight for what is right for me and mine, and if there are losses along the way, then so be it! Do not think I will weep for her. But perhaps I will weep with her..." and he flashed her little lashes, crocodile tears welling up in her eyes.

Richard knew he was being mocked, but he did not allow himself the luxury of rage. The effects of the vision were still lingering in him. He understood Duunel's points even if he didn't agree with him. His first impulse was to raise the ring and lash out at the demon with the very thing it feared most, but even as he considered it he knew he could not do it. He had seen what the ring did, and he knew that for someone—or something—like Duunel, there was no difference between the ring and a weapon of mass destruction. The vision was violence for the unprepared.

He hesitated again. He could *bluff*. He would not use the ring, but Duunel could not know that. He strode forward and raised his hand, the ring shining with ruby luminescence. Duunel took a step back, and a wave of terror fled over the little girl's face, but then the evil smile reasserted itself. "No..." the girl's eyes flashed, like a reflection of the ring. "If you were really going to use that to compel me, you would have already done it. Besides, a vision like that"—he shook the blonde curly head in mock-pity—"well, it could snap a little girl's mind, couldn't it?"

Richard's own face betrayed him. Duunel was right, of course. It had almost snapped *his*. He grasped at the only remaining straw he could think of. "Perhaps we can make a deal," Richard said. "Come out of this little girl, and you can inhabit me."

Richard could hardly believe the words issuing from his own mouth, but he knew they were the right ones once he heard them. He knew from the vision that all things would be well, that there was, ultimately, nothing to fear, however much pain and suffering there might be in the meantime.

"Why would I want to do that?" asked the demon, the little girl's face registering something like pity.

"Because she's a little girl. She has no freedom, no privacy, her movement is restricted, and because once her family starts to notice her odd behavior, your new body is going to be subjected to electroshock therapy, psychiatric drugs, and possibly restraints. It'll be old man Dane all over again, only this time without the groovy morphine or demon-pal nurses. Is that what you really want?" Richard saw the little girl waver, could almost see the demon in her brain thinking. He pressed on. "You come into me, and I'll make room for you. We'll be...roommates. You won't take me over, and I won't shut you out. It'll be temporary, until we can agree on another host that will be more suitable for you." Richard had absolutely no idea what sort of host he would feel okay about Duunel inhabiting but he didn't have time to consider that just now.

He watched the little girl shift back and forth from one leg to another, thinking. Every moment the demon inhabited her, the more tenuous the little girl's grasp on reality would be, the less likely she would be able to be fully restored. Richard felt the press of time and struggled within himself for how to hurry it along.

"Look, Duunel, I don't like the idea any more than you do, but it's better than sacrificing a child. We just saved her—don't take her away again. If you inhabit me, we'll be able to move about freely. We'll eat and drink and smoke pot. We'll have sex—"

"Not with men, you perv."

"Okay, not with men, not while you're in here."

The little girl's face still registered uncertainty. But finally she nodded and pointed at the ring. "Take it off."

He did, drawing the ring off his finger and, slipping his hand through the slit in his cassock, placed it in the pocket of his jeans.

"Open wide," said the demon. Richard did.

TUESDAY

74

THE *BOOM-BOOMING* of the drum drove Dylan downward, through the crust of the Earth, through the portal between waking reality and the Otherworld. As he climbed steadily onward, he resisted the vertigo that the whirlwind events of the last couple of days threatened to inflict. Instead, he struggled to keep his focus on the rock in front of his face and the narrow, winding path leading downward, downward.

But discipline had never been his strong suit. His mind rushed back to the moment when he and the others had burst into the elder Dane's hospital room to see Jamie holding Richard's hand, with the old man's discarded body in a heap at their feet. Dylan had dropped to one knee, pressed Jamie to his breast, and squeezed her tight, a hug she returned in earnest. But what haunted him most, after the whole blasted ordeal, was the sad and tired eyes of his friend, Richard. There had been something unnerving in his weak smile, something that Dylan had not been able to put his finger on. They had all left then, Richard to drop the Serpentines off at their lodge and Dylan to return Jamie to her home.

Crossing successfully to the Otherworld, Dylan headed through the mist toward 924 Gilman, toward his power animal, Jaguar, and that elusive oblate, Mikael.

He wouldn't have given the look in Richard's eyes a second thought were it not for one thing: Richard had not come home afterward. Dylan had called twice, before he went to bed and after he got up. Both times Richard had answered, both times he insisted he was all right, and both times he had been evasive as a greased sow. Dylan scowled through the haze, feeling very uneasy. Something was *not* right with Richard, he knew it in his bones. But Richard wasn't saying.

Eventually, Dylan saw the amber streetlight above the punk club cut through the fog, and he followed its hazy beam. He skirted the edge of the building to where he had left Jaguar and Mikael last time.

There, as he had been expecting, was Jaguar, sitting patiently, his long, black tail whipping to and fro in an unconscious rhythm. Dylan stopped, confounded. Mikael was nowhere in sight. Dylan cursed inwardly, and suddenly all of the stress, all the frustration, all of the rage of the past several days caught up with him, and he could no longer contain it. "Where the *fuck* is Mikael?" he exploded.

Jaguar did not reply but only blinked calmly and after a few moments rose and began padding away.

"What the hell?" Dylan called after him. "Am Ah supposed to falla you?"

Jaguar looked back at him then turned again and glided into the mist, his mottled black fur reflecting gold in the amber light.

"Fuck!" shouted Dylan, and he began to jog after the great cat. In moments, he had caught up, and, placing his hand on his power animal's flank, they walked side by side for some time.

He realized how mad he was at Richard. He was the sub-prior, after all. If something was going on, by God he should know about it. Especially if it were something that could affect the order, or Richard's ability to lead it. Dylan felt excluded, and it was not a feeling he enjoyed.

A few minutes later, the fog began to part again, and Dylan's shoulders slumped when he realized where Jaguar had led him. "Not again," he said aloud. "Ah'm sick to shit o' this place," he complained to the cat, but Jaguar ignored him and led him up the steps of the Dane mansion.

Inside, they crossed the foyer and went down the long hall to where they had descended into the catacombs. Jaguar led him there now, padding soundlessly down the narrow stairs into dark.

There were no lights, yet Dylan found he could see pretty well—just one of many weird aspects of the Otherworld. But as soon as they reached the bottom of the steps, his blood ran cold within him. The dim cave of the catacombs was crowded, so crowded that he could barely move. And every one of the souls packed into that underground tomb was the shade of child.

Dylan fought back sobs as he realized who they were, what they were doing here. *They are the souls of the children Dane has killed*, he thought. *They must be.*

As he walked down the hallway, the children followed him with their hollow eyes, pleading, yet each one defeated by despair.

Then, near the end of the passage, he saw a tall, lanky figure, familiar beneath his appalling shock of black hair.

"Mikael, dude, Ah am so fuckin' glad to see you." He raced forward to embrace his friend.

Mikael was holding the shade of one of the children, but he gave Dylan a squeeze with his free arm.

"Dude, don't tell me..." Dylan began.

Mikael nodded grimly. "He told them he was liberating them."

"From what? Life?"

Mikael shook his head. "I don't know what old man Dane did to him when he was a little boy, but it left him convinced that childhood is one dangerous, rotten place to be. He told them he was their savior, their deliverer."

"Fuckin' whack job's more like it," Dylan answered. "So, these kids...they're all dead?"

"Shhhh..." said Mikael. "They're scared, and they're traumatized."

"Ah..." said Dylan, comprehension dawning on him. "They're *stuck*."

"Exactly." Mikael nodded, stroking the hair of the little girl he was holding.

Dylan clapped his hands and looked around. "Hey, y'all, listen up," he called to them. "Mah name is Father Dylan, and me and Mikael over there are your friends. We love you, and we are not going to leave you alone again. So be brave, and take heart. We're all going to walk out of this place now, and we're going to take you to a good place, where there's lots of light and people who you know and love. Your grandmas and grandpas, uncles and aunts, and some of you, even your moms and dads. Who wants to go?"

He had expected a cheer, but their spirits were too beaten. Instead, he saw them nod their heads, their wide, brimming eyes hardly daring to hope.

Dylan led the way, and they began to ascend the stone steps together. Dylan walked hand in hand with a child on either side, guiding them through the opulent yet accursed house and down the wide marble steps. He nodded at Jaguar padding triumphantly to his right. "Hey, Jaggy," he asked. "You know the way to Heaven?"

He was almost floored to hear the cat respond in an even, booming voice, "All roads lead there eventually."

Just then, from behind him, Dylan heard Mikael's voice singing out, confident and clear, "I looked over Jordan, and what did I see?"

Dylan laughed aloud to hear it, and as he did so, he felt the tension drain from the knot in his chest. He answered back, in a voice not quite as sweet, but every bit as joyous, "Comin' for to carry me home..."

As he sang, Dylan looked over his shoulder at the long stream of children behind him, a slow and silent parade of souls. *Mebbe*, he thought, *by the end of this journey, we'll have them singing.*

75

DYLAN OPENED his eyes and oriented himself in the room—Mikael's room, with light streaming in through the wall of windows, and the expectant faces of Susan, Kat, Terry, and Brian hovering above him. Susan laid down her drum and said in a voice containing both fear and hope, "Well?"

In answer, Dylan rolled over and got on all fours. Crablike, he shifted sideways until his face was directly over Mikael's unconscious head. Rearing up on his knees, Dylan pried Mikael's mouth open. Then he bowed down, looking for all the world like he was about to kiss him. Instead, he blew in Mikael's mouth. Then he blew again on his chest. Then, he smacked Mikael hard on the arm. "Giddup!" he called, too loudly for the little room.

Mikael's eyes flicked open, staring directly at Dylan.

"God, you're ugly," he said.

The entire room exhaled a sigh of relief, and then pandemonium set in as everyone spoke at once.

Mikael just lay there with a goofy smile on his face. Kat could stand it no more, and she fell upon him, covering his mouth with hers.

Suddenly everyone went silent, stunned by the kiss. They were even more stunned as the kiss continued. And continued.

"Kat," Brian broke the silence, "the man has to breathe, or he'll lapse into another coma."

She giggled, and it broke the spell. She rose up on her arms and stared into his angular face. "You're some guy, when you can make me fall in love with you while you're asleep."

His eyebrows shot up. "Kitten, I was already smitten before I left."

Then Susan and Terry and Brian were upon him, hugging him and crying tears of relief.

"Where's Dicky?" he asked, finally rising to a sitting position.

The room went silent, and no one looked too sure about how to answer. Finally, Dylan ventured, "We don't know. Ah talked to him on the phone, and he says he's okay. Ah'm gonna go see him after the baptism. He's negotiating the translation of the angel. Ah can't imagine that would take so long, but that's what he says he's doin'."

Susan looked skeptical, Brian looked worried, and Terry scowled, barely concealing his anger.

"Ah know, somethin's not right, but until we know what it is, we can't fix it," Dylan finished.

"I just hope it's something within our power to fix," Terry said, crossing his arms. "Anyway, I've finished sacristying downstairs. Everything's ready. When're the Swansons going to get here?"

The doorbell rang downstairs. "Uh, that'd be now," Dylan said, and jumped off the bed.

Downstairs, Dylan greeted the Swansons and shook the hands of an unfamiliar couple that they introduced as Jack and Emily Estudillo—Jamie 's godparents. Dylan then paid an extra special hello to Jamie. She kissed his large, flat nose, and he made a face. Standing up, he whispered to her father, "She seems okay."

"We had some nightmares last night," he confided. "But yeah, she seems okay today."

"Ah wouldn't be surprised if them nightmares lasted a while," he wanted to add, *even into adulthood*, but he decided against it midsentence.

"We're so grateful to you," Connie Swanson said. "We thought we'd never see her again. What in the world would Satanists want with our little girl?"

He opened his mouth to argue that the Serpentines were not Satanists but decided against that, too. It just wasn't necessary. He smiled a tired but professional smile. "Ah tell you what, let's baptize this child so she'll have even more protection against them kind of folk."

He bid them all sit in the chapel and hurried off to vest. Susan came downstairs and greeted them, offering to take their coats.

In a few moments, all were gathered around a crystal bowl of water on the altar. Even Mikael, though weak, leaned on Kat and beamed at the scene before him. Dylan held Jamie in his arms, the little girl wrapping her arms around his neck.

"Jesus said, 'Suffer the little children to come unto me," Dylan began the liturgy, "meanin' that it wasn't just the adults who could have a relationship with Divinity, not just the smart folks, not just the rich folks, not just the mature folks, neither. And thank God for that, or none of us would be here. Nah, he said, 'Let the children come,' because even the simplest soul, those with little or nothing to contribute, those without much experience or wealth or smarts is as welcome as anyone else in the Kingdom of Heaven." He turned to face Jamie and rubbed noses with her. "And that means you, little one." He pointed at the big, messy icon of Jesus plastered across the whole of the wall. "See that? That's a picture of Jesus. And see? It's made up of lots of little pictures. Jesus is the eyes and ears and hands and feet of God on this here Earth, and he is made up of all of us. And as soon as we sprinkle this here water on ya, you'll be a part of him, too. Ah know that's a complicated and deep kind of thought, but is that okay with you?" She nodded. The Estudillos looked at the icon with something approaching horror, and then at Dylan like he was out of his mind.

"Are you...Catholics?" Jack Estudillo asked.

Dylan ignored him and motioned for the Estudillos to come

stand by him. He transferred Jamie to Jack's arms, and she went willingly enough, treating it all as if it were a game.

Dylan faced the parents. "Do you promise to see to it that Jamie is raised a good person?"

Her parents nodded. Dylan leaned in and whispered, "Ya gotta answer out loud. All of yas."

"Yes," both couples said, a little nervously.

"Do ya promise to cherish her as a gift from the heart of God?"

"Yes."

"Do ya promise to pray fer her and set a good example fer her?"

"Yes," her parents and godparents nodded earnestly.

"Do ya promise to take her to church now and then and tell her how much God loves her?"

"Yes."

"Do ya promise to take her to Baskin and Robbins at least once a week for ice cream?"

Jamie's father froze with his mouth open, about ready to agree, when Jack Estudillo repeated, "Are these priests Catholic?"

"Do you renounce Satan and Satanists and everything evil and icky?" Dylan continued.

"Yeees," the parents and godparents repeated, not at all sure about this.

"Do you renounce all those things that might distract you from the love that fills your lives—the love of God, and the love of one another?"

"Yes," they agreed.

"Do you trust in Jesus Christ to save and protect you?"

Jamie spoke up, "I trust *you*, Father Dylan!"

"Well, that's fine," Dylan said, "Ah'm just a little part of Jesus. How 'bout it, parents?"

"Yes," they all said together.

"Waal, I reckon that's good enough," Dylan turned to his housemates and addressed them, "Will you who witness these vows do all in your power to support these people in their lives of faith?"

"We do," answered Terry, Susan, Mikael, and Brian as one. "We do," Kat said, a heartbeat later.

Dylan motioned for Jamie to hop down and come close to the altar with him. She slid from Jack's grasp and walked up to the high table, barely able to see over the top of it.

"Lookee here," Dylan said, showing her the crystal pitcher of water. "What do you think is in there?"

"Water?" Jamie asked, chewing on the back of her hand.

"*Holy* water," Dylan said. "Special magick water that protects people."

"Oh for crying out loud," Jack Estudillo whispered. Emily slapped him on the gut.

"Let's say a special prayer over the water, okay?" He picked Jamie up in his left arm and held her against him. With his right he lifted the pitcher.

"God, you are truly awesome. In the beginning your spirit moved over the face of the deep—that's the waters, little one. In the time of Noah —remember the ark?—water washed clean the face of the earth, so that there were no more icky people. Then, when Moses came along, God parted the Red Sea, and all the people of Israel walked to safety on dry land. Then, lots later, Mary nourished Jesus in the water of her womb—"

"Okay, this is too much," Jack complained.

Dylan ignored him and pressed on. "Then John the Baptist poured water over Jesus's head in the Jordan River. A Samaritan woman offered him water at a well. Then Jesus washed the disciples' feet. What does all this tell us, little one?"

Jamie shrugged.

"It tells us that God really, really likes water! And he uses it for all kinds of symbolic things—"

"I'm sorry, Connie," Jack shook his head. "This man cannot be a Catholic priest."

Dylan raised the pitcher up and poured a long stream of water into the bowl. Jamie's eyes lit up as the arc of water hit the bowl and splashed all over the chapel. She jumped up and down and giggled.

Then Dylan set the pitcher down and jumped up and down with her. "Isn't this fun?" he asked her. Still jumping, she nodded with big, dramatic jerks of her head.

"Okay we're gonna talk to God, now," he put his finger to his lips and said, "Shhh…"

Then he straightened up and held his hands over the water. "Hey, God, why don't you come on down into this here water? Fill it with your grace and blessing so that Jamie here will always feel loved and protected and comforted. Make her, by this action, part of your Son, Jesus Christ, so that she might continue his healing work in the world. Amen."

He leaned over and whispered to her. "Are you ready?" She nodded. "Okay, here we go. Pick her up, Uncle Jack."

Jack scowled at Dylan but lifted Jamie so that her chin was nearly resting on the bowl.

"Jamie, Ah baptize you in the name of the Holy One, Creator," he dribbled a little bit of water on her forehead. She giggled. "Liberator," he dribbled a bit more, "and Comforter." He faced her and rubbed noses again. "How was that?" She nodded enthusiastically, still dribbling water.

"And now, friends, with this oil—"

Kat lifted Mikael's hand off her shoulder and stepped forward. Dylan cocked his head at her. "What's up, Kat?"

"Me, too."

"What do ya mean?"

"I mean, baptize me, too."

Mikael and Susan exchanged quizzical but amused glances. Terry hugged Brian closer to him, and they both beamed at her. Kat cleared her throat, "Look, whatever you guys have, I want it. That guy there," she pointed at the icon, "is *nothing* like any Jesus I ever heard about before, but dammit, he talks to me, and it's time for me to answer. So, hell yes, I renounce Satan and Magickians and Republicans, and if Christians are what you guys call yourselves, then goddammit, I want to be one, too."

Dylan turned to Jamie. "Excuse her French, little one. What do you think? Can she be part of your party?"

The little girl looked at the black-haired young woman uncertainly. "I *guess* so," she said eventually.

"Should we let her be part of Jesus?" he asked her. Jamie nodded her head again in big, rapid movements. Dylan set her down and motioned for Kat to come closer. Kat leaned over the bowl, her long black hair flowing into the water. Dylan dipped his hands in three times, and each time poured water over the top of her head. "Kat, Ah baptize you in the name of the Holy One: Creator, Liberator, and Comforter."

"Amen!" shouted Terry. He then handed a golden oil stock to Dylan.

Dylan dabbed his thumb in the oil and made the sign of the cross on Kat's wet forehead. "And Ah seal you as Christ's own forever." He then knelt and did the same to Jamie.

Rising, he wiped his hands on an old, stained corporal. "Peace be with you!" he called out.

"And also with you!" his housemates responded as one.

"As we close this celebration, let us greet one another with a sign of peace." He then gave Jamie a big hug then turned and embraced Kat as well.

It was hugs all around then. Kat was leaking tears, but her smile was broad, and Dylan felt so happy he almost forgot about Richard. Almost.

76

THE SKY WAS THREATENING MORE rain as Dylan and Terry headed out down Cedar Street toward the Gallic Hotel. They walked largely in silence, not knowing what to expect when they saw Richard. Dylan shifted the mirror from one arm to the other, careful so as not to remove its covering.

Richard was waiting for them in the hotel's café. He was reading a Charles Williams novel, a steaming cappuccino on the table in front of him.

Dylan waved at him, and he rose to greet them. He gave each of them a long hug. Dylan felt the sadness and the love pouring out of his friend during that embrace, and he returned it wholeheartedly.

They sat, and Richard pointed his finger at Terry. "I don't need any judgment from you."

Terry opened his mouth to protest, but nothing came out. He looked hurt. Richard looked down. "Look, I'm sorry, that didn't come out right. I'm always my own worst critic. But you, Terry, are a close second."

Terry looked at Dylan for help. Dylan shifted and avoided Terry's eyes. "Ya can be a little rough, dude."

"I care!" Terry protested. "So, sue me for caring! At least I'm not as bad as Brian."

"No, but there's a difference between you and Brian," Richard said, the beginning of a smile curling his lip. "Brian will badger me into wearing a coat. You'll make feel guilty for not putting it on in the first place."

Terry narrowed his eyes and looked at Richard funny. Dylan noticed. "What's up, Ter?"

Terry's eyes grew wide. "Richard, do I need to get up and walk away from you for my own safety?"

Dylan was confused. "Dude, what are you talking about?"

Richard held up his hand. "I was wondering how long it was going to take you to catch on, Terry."

Dylan was watching Terry closely, and he knew what he was doing—reading Richard's energy. Suddenly, Terry stood up and started backing away, eyes wide. He pointed at Richard. "You're not alone in there, Richard."

"No, I'm not. Now sit down before you scare the other patrons. Nobody 'in here' is going to hurt you."

"Would someone tell me what's going on, please?" Dylan asked. "'Cause Ah'm jus' way too tired fer twenty questions."

Terry sat down warily. He looked at Dylan. "Richard has a demon inside him," he said.

Dylan exhaled deeply and slowly. "Waal, that makes sense. That's why you can't come home. The house is warded. So, what sort of varmint is it?"

Richard's eyes flashed red, and when he spoke it was another voice that issued forth. "The sort of 'varmint' that feasts upon the souls of errant priests. So, watch yourself."

Dylan scrunched up his face. "It's Duunel, isn't it?"

In a moment, the red glow had passed, and Richard's voice reasserted itself as he nodded. "We've got...joint custody of the body. It's a little crowded in here, but it's not as bad as I thought it would be. It's inconvenient, and I would never in a million years have thought of some of the shit he comes up with—twisted and brilliant, but trust me, more you do not want to know—but it's okay." He looked profoundly sad, and Dylan's heart went out to him. "I'm just so tired, and I really, really wish I could come home."

Dylan put his hand on his friend's arm and squeezed. "Yer not the only one on the outs," he said consolingly. "Remember Bishop Tom? He's probably flying home right about now, feelin' pretty low, Ah'll wager."

Richard jerked suddenly as if remembering something. Dylan watched as he fished in his pocket. With a dramatic slam he placed Solomon's Ring before them.

"What do you want me to do with that?" Dylan asked him, picking it up with not a little trepidation.

"Send it to Bishop Tom." Richard smiled broadly, chuckling audibly. "He needs an episcopal ring, after all. If this one doesn't afford him respect, nothing will. Besides, if he activates it accidentally, it'll do him good. He could probably stand to be reminded what a good guy he is about now."

Dylan nodded, pleased with the plan. He put the ring in his pocket. Then he looked pensively at Richard. "Y'know dude, thar's somethin' Ah've been wonderin' about."

"What's that?"

"What old man Dane ever did that so twisted his son's soul. Do you think you could ask...you know, Duunel?"

Richard smiled sadly. "I already did. You know how most Satanic Ritual abuse is just urban myth?"

"Yeah, false memories and such," Dylan responded.

"Well, in this instance, it was real. It seems old man Dane was consorting with demons for years. Alan Dane watched him kidnap and ritually sacrifice children for at least a decade."

"So not all of them kids Mikael and I led away were the younger Dane's victims?" Dylan said, understanding dawning in his eyes.

"Right."

"Thet makes sense, 'cause there were an awful lot of 'em, and some of them looked like they was straight out o' the Brady Bunch."

Terry was nodding. "The younger Dane must have suffered terrible PTSD. No wonder he wanted to rescue them—to help them make their exit painlessly before his dad could do it ritually."

"Yes," Richard agreed. "And in his mind, since his own father was capable of such atrocities, weren't all parents? Didn't all children need to be rescued? He really did see himself as a savior, twisted as that seems to us."

"An' what about that whole overthrowing Heaven thing? Obviously, that campaign didn't get off the ground," Dylan said hopefully.

"I think Dane's patronage sort of derailed the lodge's plans, which I guess is a good thing unless you consider what would have happened if he had succeeded." Richard stared at what remained of his cappuccino. "But don't sell them short. The lodge is down but not out. I'll wager this isn't the last we'll hear of them, or their nutso coup. In fact, when I've had a chance to rest up a little, I've been thinking of giving Larch a call and suggesting a game of chess over sushi. Nobody minds being grilled quite so much when sushi is involved."

"Thet's always been mah experience," Dylan agreed.

They sat in silence together for a few minutes, mulling the whole affair over. Then, tentatively, Dylan reached over and put his hand on Richard's arm. "So, dude, do you still hate yerself?"

Richard smiled a large, sincere smile. "I don't hate Duunel, I don't even hate Dane. I don't hate Mussolini or Stalin or Hitler. I don't hate spiders or cockroaches or meter maids. How could I possibly hate myself?"

Dylan leaned forward and mussed at Richard's hair. "That's the kind of shit Ah like to hear from you, you sorry fuck." Richard caught his hand and drew him into an awkward, across-the-table embrace.

Terry's eyes were wet when Richard looked at him again. "Dicky, we brought something for you. We brought the mirror."

Richard checked to see that the mirror was intact and set it aside.

"When are you due to meet Articiphus?" Dylan asked.

"Sundown. Soon."

"You'll also want to give him this," Terry said, pulling a manila envelope out of his habit.

"What's that?" Richard asked.

Terry smiled. "There are several things in there. Among them is a note for our friend the angel, written by moi in Enochian." Terry's smile broadened. "Let's just say they're *instructions*."

77

"Greetings, fags!" Astrid said when Brian opened the door. The last light of day shot through an opening in the storm clouds, bathing the afternoon in an odd orange-pinkish glow.

"Ah'm not a fag," protested Dylan, who was stripping the altar in preparation of the evening's scrying.

"Get in here, you old tranny," Brian said, giving her a hug.

"You and your ass-buddy coming to my housewarming on Sunday?" she asked.

"Wouldn't miss it," he said, taking her coat. "I'll be bringing *petits fours*."

"God! Can you get any more gay than that? A sack of cookies would do the job."

She gave Dylan a kiss and began to unpack her scrying materials from the old bowling bag.

"Where's Dicky?" she asked.

Dylan wasn't sure how much he should say. He just stared at her for a moment. She cocked an eyebrow at him. Finally, he said, "He's delivering the package. The one we're scrying on."

She nodded. Dylan knew she was kind and sensitive, regardless of her gruff persona. He knew that she knew that there was more to it.

"Uh-huh," she said. "So, I hope you guys aren't planning to make anything else disappear."

"*We* didn't make the avocados disappear," protested Terry, coming into the room from the kitchen. "*Or* the dogs. We've been trying to *stop* it." He put his arm around Brian and gave him a wet kiss full on the lips. "We *did* stop it."

Just then, a pounding erupted from the ceiling. The thud came again and again, accompanied by piercing female shrieking. A small cloud of plaster dust wafted through the air of the chapel. "Either you've got an exorcism going on upstairs"—Astrid said, wiping the altar clean of plaster dust and carefully placing the scrying stone —"or some lucky wench is *getting some*."

"Mikael and Kat are...making up for lost time," Dylan explained.

"Did I hear the door?" Susan came out of the kitchen, rubbing lotion into her hands. "Oh, hello, Astrid. I'm so glad you could come on such short notice."

"After what I saw last time? I wouldn't miss it." She pulled the light black blanket out of the bowling bag and draped it over her shoulders.

The others were seated in choir and waited as Astrid closed her eyes, relaxed her muscles, and meditated. After a few moments, she pulled the blanket over her head and began her gaze.

Dylan leaned into Susan and took her hand. She squeezed reassuringly. He looked up and saw Terry and Brian almost mirroring them in the opposite choir, hand in hand, looking anxious.

Brian broke the silence. "I think we're hoping for too much, here."

"Could be," Dylan agreed, "but mah plan is to have faith until it's horrendously and irreparably shattered."

"Okay, gang, I'm getting something," said Astrid, her hips wagging behind her.

"Whatcha see?" asked Terry. "And I don't want to hear anything about Brian's anus."

Brian's eyebrows shot up, and he wiggled in his seat, smiling. The late afternoon light poured in through the chapel windows, signaling a break in the rain.

Astrid wagged some more. "Okay, I don't really understand it, but here's what I see. There's an angel. I think he's the same one we were following last time. He's unconscious, in the gutter. Okay, guys, Swedenborg never mentioned a homeless population in Heaven, but that's exactly what this guy looks like."

Kat and Mikael appeared in the doorway to the living room, their hair arrayed at shocking angles. "Well, someone's radiating," Susan said. It was true, Dylan saw. Kat was flushed, and even Mikael looked like he had actual red, human blood in his veins for a change.

"Hi, Astrid," Mikael called, a little too loud.

"I'm under a blanket, not down a mine shaft," Astrid reminded him. "And I think I'm also looking at the angel Kat's brother is in. Hi, Kat."

The beatific satisfaction on Kat's face melted into concern. She sat in the choir next to Terry and held on to Mikael's hand as he stood beside her.

"He's passed out cold," Astrid said. "He's alone, too. No, wait, someone is coming toward him. Another angel, carrying a package. It's heavy as hell, too. The guy can barely move it."

"What does the package look like?" asked Terry.

"It's big, like a covered painting," Astrid said. "The new guy is kneeling by coma guy—"

"Hey, a little respect," Kat said indignantly.

"Sorry. Angel B is kneeling by Angel A. I'm trying to make out the markings on his clothes. Terry, does *elosyin* mean anything to you?"

"Mah money's on 'mailman,'" Dylan guessed.

"No, it means 'physic.' He's a doctor."

"Who knew they had doctors in Heaven?" Dylan asked no one in particular.

"Of course they have doctors in Heaven," Astrid snapped from under her blanket. "What would the earthly doctors do when they got there if there was no work for them? And what would happen when angels got sick?"

"Ah guess I didn't count on angels gettin' sick is all," Dylan admitted.

"Okay, turning our attention from *third-grade Heaven* to the real thing," Astrid continued, "Angel B has uncovered the package. It's...a mirror."

"That's it, all right," Terry looked at Kat and nodded. She held his eye and nodded back.

"It's glowing. I mean it's really shining. A bright purple light is coming from it—no, the light is moving, floating free of the mirror! It's blinding, people for blocks around are shielding their eyes. I can't see what's happening. Oh, now it's diminishing. I *think* the light was absorbed by Angel A. He's stirring, at least."

"He's dead now, isn't he?" Kat asked.

"No, he's waking up. Aren't you paying attention?" Astrid said, but Dylan couldn't tell if she was really irritated or mocking.

"No, not the angel. I mean my brother. Isn't he being...shoved out of the angel's body? Isn't he simply...dissipating, now?"

"I don't know, Darling," Astrid's voice was softer, now. "I just know Angel A is awake."

Kat blinked back tears and clutched harder at Mikael's hand.

"He seems to be okay. A little disoriented. He's shaking his head, holding his head, shaking his head again. He's trying to stand. Angel B is giving him a hand up..."

"Way to go, Angel B," said Brian.

"Angel A is standing. He's leaning against a building. Now he's standing free. He's looking at the sky. He's trying out his hands. They work."

"He did have trouble with the hands," Terry remembered. "Must be nice to have his own back."

"Okay, Doctor Guy is checking him out. He's feeling at his head. He seems to be meditating..."

Terry turned to Brian and fixed his fingers to either side of his head. "My mind...to your mind..." he said, with mock-pained dramatic pauses between every syllable.

"There's more important things in the world than Kirk-Spock slash fic, faggots," Astrid commented.

"Not much," Terry protested.

"There *is* food," Brian suggested.

"And sex," admitted Terry, "but even that's better when I can be Kirk."

"Oh sure, that would fly," Astrid interjected, "if Kirk were a nelly midget."

"Who says Kirk can't be a little nelly?" Terry pouted.

"Can we focus, please?" asked Susan, rolling her eyes and crossing her arms.

"Okay, Doctor Angel is giving Homeless Angel an envelope."

Terry sucked in a deep breath and rocked back and forth. "Good, good!"

Astrid's tail wagged to the left. "He's opening it. He's reading something..."

"A letter," Kat said. "Terry wrote it."

"There's something else in the envelope, too," Astrid went on. "Magazine clippings? Could that be right? What, you didn't want to send him into the next world without reading material?"

"They're pictures," Kat said. "Of things that don't exist anymore."

"Homeless Angel Guy is turning toward the city center..."

"Can we give him a new name?" asked Susan. "'Homeless Angel' sounds disrespectful."

"It sounds like a pulp novel," Dylan suggested.

"Or a Lifetime movie," Terry added.

"He's nodding at the doctor, turning the corner. He's heading straight for the *Azaziazel*—"

"That's the Hall of Forms, again," Terry said, daring to be hopeful.

"He's climbing the steps—much more easily this time, I must say."

"I kind of miss the guy," Terry said, cocking his head wistfully.

"Okay, this is a tricky transition for me, same as last time..." Astrid paused, momentarily still beneath the black blanket. "And we're in! Takes a minute to adjust to the light. Wow. Okay, I know I've seen this before, but...wow."

"Ah never lose my sense of wonder in seeing the Grand Canyon again," Dylan sympathized.

"Or Notre Dame Cathedral," added Terry.

"There's Eva Kadmona in the center, and everything you can *think* of is spinning around her in an orbit, some of them look like their ellipses are as long as a football field."

"I don't like the fact that everything revolves around this woman —" Susan frowned.

"Yeah, but what else is new?" Dylan quipped. Susan punched him in the arm.

"Ow, Darlin', that really hurt," Dylan rubbed at his arm.

"Well, actually, looking more closely at it now, there appear to be nested fields of relationships among the objects," Astrid corrected herself.

"How positively Whiteheadian," Brian pursed his lips, considering it.

"Yeah, but these archetypes are not evolving, that I can see," Astrid answered.

Brian chewed on that, placing a hand on Terry's knee.

"Eva is a gravity point, with lots of things in orbit around her, but she's also in orbit herself—it's just slower, more subtle."

"What is she orbiting?"

"I don't know—she's moving too slowly."

"She's the archetypal woman, all right," Dylan added, wincing from another anticipated blow from his wife. She ignored him. Despite her grief, Kat smiled at this, although it was obvious to Dylan that she was trying not to.

"Pretty much everything we use or eat, though, is orbiting her," Astrid said. "I gotta say, sadly, she is not my type."

"You mean she's pretty? That's gotta be disconcerting," Brian snorted.

"I'd say, 'Go fuck yourself,' but you'd just enjoy it," replied the blanket. "Okay, our angel friend is holding up one of the pictures... and he dropped it to the ground. He's picking it up...and dropping it on the ground."

"Maybe he's hoping it'll just start orbiting?" Terry suggested.

"Mebbe it's like a kite, yah gotta kinda get it started," Dylan offered.

"I think our boy is on the same wavelength, Dyl," Astrid said, shifting her hips in his direction. "He's running around Eva, holding the paper out like a paper airplane or something. Oh! Shit! He tripped—stepped into the orbit of a porcupine..."

"That's gotta hurt," Mikael winced.

"Ah...but the paper didn't fly with him. It caught its orbit, it's flying by itself. It's rounding out, taking on dimension and...mass..." She was breathing heavily now. "Friends, we have avocado!"

"Yea!" Everyone cheered. Dylan hugged Susan, and she wiped at a tear.

"He's looking around. He's looking for something. He can't find it. Wait, maybe he's onto it, now. He's holding up another magazine page. Now he's running with it. He's jumping over the armadillo...he's letting go...it's in orbit! It's filling out...it's...a *weird-looking bird*?"

Kat looked sheepish. "It's a dodo. I always thought it was sad that they were extinct. I'm sorry?" she cringed.

Mikael laughed out loud and hugged her to him. Brian looked concerned and asked, "Isn't there some kind of prime directive against this kind of thing?"

"He's got one more sheet. He's running...running...still running. This one is bigger, apparently, more momentum is needed or something. Anyway...there it goes...bigger...bigger..."

But before she could declare what it was there was a scrabble of anxious nails on the kitchen linoleum, and then Tobias bounded into the room, all hair and tail and jowls. He was wagging so hard it looked like he might break himself in two. He sprang right to Dylan, leaped up, and began slobbering kisses all over the friar's face.

Dylan hugged at Tobias, catching a fistful of mane and burying his face in it, weeping openly and unashamedly with relief and joy.

Everyone crowded around the dog, reaching out to touch him as if to make sure he were real.

"He's...different." Susan commented. "Redder."

Dylan collected himself enough to realize she was right. The golden lab was decidedly more auburn than he remembered.

Terry turned to Kat, "What kind of dog was in the picture?"

"Red? A big red dog. I don't remember what kind," she said, grimacing slightly.

"Who cares?" Dylan laughed. "Red dog is better'n no dog any day!" As he ruffled the dog's fur, Tobias turned over and begged for a belly rub.

"Well Ah'll be damned!" Dylan exclaimed. Written backward across the dog's stomach, like a faint purplish tattoo, was the word *Viagra* accompanied by the faint face of a smiling young couple.

Kat put her hand to her mouth, "Oh my God! There was a Viagra ad on the other side of the dog picture I cut out!"

"You mean that every dog on the planet is now a walking, eating, and pooping advertisement for the Pfizer Pharmaceutical Company?" laughed Susan out loud.

"You cannot buy that kind of publicity!" Dylan announced with a hearty guffaw. "Can we invoice them for that?"

"The angel is looking around," Astrid announced. "Now he's heading for the door...the angel has left the building!" Astrid pulled her head out from under the blanket and raked at her wiry blonde hair with her fingers. She beamed at the sight of Tobias, leaping up and licking almost everyone there. Then, abruptly, the dog turned and wagged into the kitchen. Slurping noises were immediately audible.

Brian stretched. "Toby has the right idea. This calls for champagne." He followed the lab into the kitchen.

"Ah only wish Dicky were here to see this," Dylan added, a wave of sadness washing over his features. Susan squeezed his hand, commiserating but saying nothing.

"Uh, guys..." Brian called from the kitchen. "Come see this."

As they filed into the kitchen, Terry started laughing. There, in the very place where the bowl of guacamole had been sitting days before, was a mass of green pulp, dripping off the table onto the floor.

78

JUST AS THE last of the sun sank below the horizon, the first spat of rain hit Richard's cassock. He pulled it more tightly around him and stood at the curb, looking at the warm, cheery lights of the friary. He dared come no closer—the warding, which Terry no doubt had already set in place again, would not allow it. He was, after all, a vehicle for a demon, and he had yet to see one that could defy Terry's wards.

He fought back a surge of sadness. He knew his friends would be celebrating their victory, and he longed to share it with them. His love for them rose up with a lump in his throat, and he uttered a small, pained cry as he swallowed it down.

Against his momentary despair, he summoned up the memory of his vision—and marveled at the pain and uncertainty that comes from the limits of human perception. If only everyone could see how connected everything was, how safe, how ultimately okay it was all going to be, there would be a lot less suffering in the world.

He felt Duunel shrink and hide at the memory of the vision. It was comforting to know that, even if he was inhabited by a demon at the moment, he was not defenseless against it. All he had to do was conjure up a memory, a visual, even just the *feeling* generated by the ring to send Duunel scurrying for cover.

Things could be worse, he told himself. But it didn't really help. He was not, after all, in the only place in the whole world that he wanted to be. He opened his mouth to say, "God hates me," but he stopped himself because he knew now how completely untrue that was. And with that thought, Fr. Richard Kinney turned his back on the welcoming lights of his home, an exile from the Kingdom.

CLAIM YOUR FREE BOOK

To find out more about the Berkeley Blackfriar's universe, download your free copy of *The Berkeley Blackfriar's Companion*. Includes photos of main characters, a complete glossary, a walking tour of the Blackfriar's Berkeley, recipes from Brian's kitchen, a short history of Old Catholicism, a Q & A session with author J.R. Mabry, links to music and videos associated with the books and more!

Click on BookHip.com/DXDCAS to get your free copy!

REVIEWS

If you enjoy the Blackfriars books, please help other people find them by leaving a review. Please consider leaving an honest review on amazon or kobo or wherever you buy books. Thank you!

Keep reading!
Turn the page to start the next book now...

THE POWER
Berkeley Blackfriars • Book II

PRELUDE 1

Amid the shrieking of the dying and the stench of the dead, the Ong Khan Toghrul crested the hill and reined back his mount. His eyes burned from the smoke. He squinted, trying to assess the scene. Behind him were five hundred men, all of them Mongol warriors, faithful Nestorian Christians ready to lay down their lives in the cause of the Savior.

His nostrils twitched at the stink, and his horse shied with impatience. "My Khan," said his lieutenant from behind him. "What are your orders?" But he was not ready to answer. His eyes flicked to the city walls, which were still holding against the Crusader army. *Although this is hardly an army*, he thought, taking stock of the wasted might of Europe before him. Most had been slaughtered. Here and there, living soldiers were clustered—no, *huddled*—apparently without leaders.

His lieutenant moved parallel to him, and touched his elbow with a mail-gloved hand. "Jahn?" he said. "Jahn, the men need direction. This is a killing ground..."

Toghrul nodded his assent. "Yes, but it will not be ours." He turned to face his lieutenant. "Tsogt, send messengers to these soldiers of Europe—those that are left. They can die or fight under our banner. It is their choice." Tsogt nodded briskly and began barking orders.

Toghrul watched as horsemen sped off toward small pockets of soldiers spread out across the battleground. With a grand gesture, he signaled an advance. He watched the Christians of Europe gawk with wonder at the great Christian army of Mongolia speeding over the hill to save them.

Within the hour, the Christians of Europe had either been assimilated into his ranks or dispatched by the sword. Fortunately, only a few had objected, and they were those who pretended to leadership. Jahn Toghrul spat. *Leaders in name, perhaps*, he thought bitterly.

Only one of their so-called leaders had joined them. The khan summoned him, and when the man appeared before him, he sank to his knees instantly, though it was obvious he was a noble. *Here is a man who knows the intrinsic hierarchy of warriors*, Jahn thought, and dismounted to speak to the man without shouting. "I am the Ong Khan Toghrul, king of the Kerait Mongols, called Jahn at my baptism. You are?"

"Sir Philip of Longacre, of England, sire." The man's tunic was torn, his hair matted with filth. He kept his eyes on the dirt.

Wise man, Jahn thought. "I have heard that you who follow the Bishop of Rome consider us heretics," Jahn said, a testy edge to his voice. "Is this so, Sir Philip?"

"I...I know nothing of this, my lord." The man looked quickly from side to side, but he did not look up. Jahn fingered the Talisman of Amitiel, which hung on a cord from his neck. It grew cold. "You lie."

The man looked down at his knees, and his face turned beet red. He nodded furiously. "That is what they say, my lord." He held his breath, but then blurted out, "But it is not...my own opinion, sire."

Jahn's eyebrows raised. A bemused smile crossed his lips. "Really, Sir Philip, and are you in the habit of questioning the teaching of your bishops?"

Sir Philip's face was so red that it seemed ready to burst. "Um...no..."

There was no way out of this, Jahn knew. He did not suffer fools, but he was not entirely without mercy. "Tell me what has happened here."

The man nodded, visibly grateful for the change in subject. "Two weeks ago, we laid siege to the city. Twenty thousand of us."

Jahn scowled. "Twenty thousand?"

"Yes, my lord. The Egyptians fought well."

"I see that they have." There were scarcely four hundred men left. Together with his own horsemen, they would hardly make a thousand. "How did they accomplish this?"

"They...they are charmed bowmen," Philip said, spluttering for an explanation. "They have demons shooting at us. And then, there are the raiders."

"Tell me about the raiders."

"They attack us at night. They attack when we are besieging the city—when our backs are to the hills. They are led by a sultan, Al-Kamil, they call him. He is like a ghost."

The khan grunted and stepped away, surveying the sandy hills. "Sir Philip," he said, "you will not be false with me again. Tell me, will your men follow you?"

———

The siege was hard, and doubly so since half of his men were wasted guarding the army's rear flank from a Saracen army that might or might not appear. They did not, and by midday, the tower door folded in on itself with a booming crack that the khan heard from half a mile away. The European Christians swarmed into the tower. The slaughter was quick.

Tsogt rode to him, fierce and breathless. Blood stained much of his mail, the Khan noticed, but was relieved to discover that it was Saracen blood, not his lieutenant's. "We have the tower, my khan." Jahn nodded curtly. "Many of the Saracens laid down their arms," Tsogt continued. "I thought...you might want to talk with them."

Jahn smiled grimly. "You know me well, Lieutenant. Lead the way." Within minutes, the khan was striding through the tower door, which was splintered beyond repair. Before him, Saracen soldiers knelt as he passed, averting their dark eyes. His own men stood behind them, swords at the ready, drunk on the victory of the day.

But the khan knew better. *A tower is not a keep*, he thought to himself. *We still have much to do*. When he came to the end of the corridor, he stopped and turned regally. He looked down on the Saracen before him. "Tsogt," he asked, "how many are they that live?"

"Exactly a hundred men, my khan." Tsogt answered quickly and with confidence.

Jahn drew his sword and with one swift motion, severed the Saracen's head from his body. "There!" he shouted at the men on their knees. "Now there are ninety-nine, one for each of the ninety-nine names of your heathen god." The Saracens quaked, but they dared not raise their eyes to the Mongol king. Some of them mumbled prayers in Arabic.

Jahn stepped over the body, its blood spilling over the stones of the floor, creating a slick crimson pool. He faced the next Saracen, who was visibly shaking. Jahn clutched at the Talisman of Amitiel and spoke, a note of kindness entering his voice. "You, Egyptian, what are you called?"

"Mohammad, Sire." A spreading stain on his breeches betrayed that the man had just wet himself.

Jahn sniffed. "I dare not say the name of your heathen prophet, for it is offensive to the Lord of Heaven. Tell me, Egyptian, where is Al-Kamil?"

The man's eyes grew wide, but he said nothing. The khan placed the flat of his broadsword at the man's neck and slowly turned it so that its razor-sharp edge came to bear. "You will answer," Jahn said quietly.

"I...I do not know."

The talisman grew cold in Jahn's hand. "That is a lie," he said over his shoulder to Tsogt. "Egyptian dog, called by the name of the blasphemer prophet, you are lying, and the cost for lying to the Lord Khan is death. But I am a merciful king, and I will give you one more chance to live before you see Hell. Where is Al-Kamil?"

In answer, the man squeezed his eyes tight and shook his head. With a flourish, Jahn cut his throat, the blood of his neck creating an arc in the air as the sword flashed past. "How many are left, Tsogt?"

"Ninety-eight, my khan."

Jahn looked out the window and measured the sun. "Good thing the day is still young." He stepped to the next man, huddled on the floor, and placed the flat of the blade against the quaking man's temple. Jahn looked up at his lieutenant, and smiled. "Hell will feast well today."

PRELUDE 2

HOLY APOCRYPHA FRIARY, BERKELEY, CA

A half hour before anyone would stir in the old farmhouse that served as the friary of the Old Catholic Order of Saint Raphael, there was a rustle of wings in the yard. The cherub touched one foot to the earth, then the other, and paused to gain his balance. When he straightened himself, he stood nearly nine feet. His hair was white like bleached wool, and his eyes shone with fire.

Beneath his arm was a package wrapped in cloth that glowed in the dim light of dawn. The angel knelt and unwrapped it, unfolding the cloth with care and laying it aside. He had uncovered a mirror framed with rough wood. He propped it against the house near the back door and turned to go.

"Hey!" a tiny voice shouted. "Where the fuck do you think you're going? Where am I? Are you just going to leave me here?"

The angel turned back, lowered his face to the mirror, and placed a raised index finger to his lips. "Shhhhhh," the angel whispered. Even so, his voice rolled like thunder.

Looking around to be sure that no one had been disturbed, the angel waited. He heard no shouts, detected no movement—only the twitter of birds and the distant honking of early morning traffic. Satisfied, the angel turned to go. He made to launch himself, but just short of flight, he clutched at his chest, stumbled, and fell to the grass. A low moan shook the earth.

A short time later, a muffled barking pierced the air, followed by the slam of a screen door. A large yellow Lab bounded out onto the lawn, barked once, froze, and sniffed at the air. He dropped his nose to the ground and began to follow the scent.

In a moment, he was hovering over the angel, drooling onto the divine countenance. The angel opened one eye and saw an enormous black membrane, slick with mucus, whiffling and snuffling with curious abandon. The angel reached up to touch the nose, choosing it as his point of entry.

PRELUDE 3

LODGE OF THE HAWK AND SERPENT, SAN FRANCISCO, CA

Stanis Larch lit the censer and then stood back in a posture of prayer as the smoke, fragrant with frankincense and myrrh, filled the temple. Once the air was thick with haze, he approached his Enochian table and sat on a high stool. The table was covered with symbols and signs carved precisely according to the instructions of John Dee, the court astrologer of Queen Elizabeth I.

Reverently, Larch removed a red velvet cloth from its place in the center of the table, revealing a shiny black stone about seven inches across and two inches thick. Larch breathed deeply and uttered an angelic invocation in the Enochian language. Closing his eyelids halfway, his focus became soft, and he rested his gaze upon the stone.

He concentrated on his breathing—even and deep coming in, long and slow going out—freeing his mind of concepts, and likewise freeing his eyes to see whatever the spirits chose to reveal.

At first, he only saw wisps of nondescript images flashing here and there in the stone. A gauzy flash of white, the momentary appearance of a horse's head neighing, the spinning of a distant crown. A pickpocket looked over his shoulder, caught in the act. Larch watched him cringe in shame, and then run away out of the range of the stone's vision.

The picture blurred again but resolved into a vision of white lace. A young woman stepped out of shadow into full view and faced him directly. She was so beautiful that Larch caught his breath—he had to concentrate to get his meditative rhythm back. Like the surface of a pond, the disturbance in his meditation made the vision blur and fade. But as he unfocused his eyes and settled back down into a contemplative state, the young woman appeared to become more solid.

He became aroused just looking at her. She appeared to be about twenty, and her lithe form was barely hidden by the wispy gauze that covered her. Long, light-colored hair hung nearly to her waist, and her nose turned up in a fetching, sprightly way. He could see the points of her apple-size breasts clearly, and they moved from side to side as she swayed back and forth. It made him crazy. There appeared to be a slit in the gauze that hung to her ankles, revealing a leg that seemed just a little too long, yet ended just a little too soon. Larch ducked to see if a change in perspective would afford him a glimpse just an inch higher beyond where that slit ended, to where legs joined together maddeningly just out of sight, but to no avail.

"What vision do I behold?" he spoke out loud.

"What vision are you looking for?" the young woman answered playfully.

"I seek Wisdom," Larch said.

"Oh, you'll have to go a very long way up the food chain to find *her*." The young woman shook her head. Golden bangs fell over her eyes in a way that Larch found absolutely irresistible. If this were a human woman flirting with him as openly as this ghostly vision seemed to be doing, Larch knew he would already be out of his clothes.

"Who are you, then?" Larch asked. "By what name may I call you, and what are your powers?"

"Call me Pim," the woman said, twirling her hair fetchingly and raising one leg as if ready to begin a dance. She didn't dance, though. She seemed merely to be playing with him. "And as for powers, I don't have many. But what I do have, I use pretty well." She *was* flirting with him; Larch was sure of it.

"I am a man with many questions," Larch said carefully.

"I'm not what you'd call a very *smart* spirit," Pim answered, a little apologetically. "So, I don't really know if I can help you."

"I want knowledge," Larch said.

"Oh, poop on *knowledge*," Pim said, with a little wiggle. The urgency in Larch's groin leaped as he saw her breasts bounce. Did she notice? Of course she noticed. It was all on purpose. "But I *can* give you something much, much better."

"And what is that?" Larch asked.

"I can give you *power*," she said, sucking on her index finger.

PRELUDE 4

SAINT JAMES'S EPISCOPAL CHURCH, THE BERKELEY HILLS

Reverend Felicia Dunne closed the door to the sacristy and turned the key in the lock. She spun around, placed her hands to her cheeks, and squealed. Her girlfriend, Jan, mirrored her perfectly, and they shrieked at each other in glee for several seconds before proceeding to hop up and down.

"Oh my God, Baby," Jan said, placing her arms around her partner's shoulders, "You did so good today."

"I did, didn't I?" Felicia nodded, almost in tears. "Oh my God, I think I did!"

"They are going to *love* you!" Jan said, adding in a singsong voice. "But not as much as I do." She drew her partner in for a kiss, which was long, luscious, and slow.

Felicia held her partner's head lovingly as they kissed, Jan's dreadlocks feeling rough on the reverend's fingers, her perfume intoxicating to her, inflammatory. When their kiss broke, Jan said, "As sexy as the...what do you call this, Honey?"

"A chasuble," said Felicia.

"Right. Sexy as that thing is, I can't wait to get it off you."

"I don't see anyone," Felicia giggled.

"You know the Altar Guild is going to be pounding on that door any minute," Jan warned.

"I think we have time for another kiss." Felicia put her nose on Jan's and stared deep into her brown eyes. "Do you think the sermon was too harsh?"

"Honey, you got to tell these white people like it is," Jan playfully switched her accent, sounding an awful lot like Felicia's father. "'Cause if you don't, they ain't gonna respect you for a moment. You know that's true."

Felicia felt her partner's thumb trace her cheekbone, and she smiled. "I know that's true. It felt right when I wrote it. It felt right when I preached it, too."

"It *was* right, Baby," Jan said, switching back to her own voice. "These folks are going to stand behind you." She raised herself up on tiptoe, pressing her lips against Felicia's again. The priest squeezed Jan's ample body against her own, and breathed in her scent, her head swimming with desire.

Just then a flash filled the room. Felicia drew back and looked around, alarm spreading across the features of her face. She heard the sound of a chair scooting back, and the figure of a man stood up, blocking the light of the tiny stained glass window that supplied the sacristy with natural light.

"My wife told me that these things were easy to use." The man's voice was deep and sonorous, possessed of an educated Louisiana drawl. He held up his hand, and Felicia saw the outline of a smartphone. "I don't like modern things, generally, but she insisted. I've never used the camera before, but I couldn't let such evidence just... well, evidence is ephemeral, isn't it?" The man stepped closer and smiled. After a few uncomprehending moments, Felicia recognized him.

"Oh, it's you, Bishop." She relaxed, but not much. Bishop Preston was new to the Episcopal Diocese of California, serving as an interim suffragan for Bishop McClary. It was he who had installed her today as the rector of Saint James's. "I didn't realize you were here."

"Obviously." His voice was grave. He placed the smartphone in his pocket. He looked at Jan with disdain and made a dismissive *scoot* motion with his hand. Felicia exchanged a worried look with her partner. "You should go," she whispered. Jan shot Bishop Preston a poisoned look but stepped quickly to the door, turned the key, and let herself out.

"It was a beautiful service today," Bishop Preston said gravely. "I'm just sorry there was so much wasted effort."

"What do you mean?" Felicia felt her panic level spike.

"Well, I understand that the good people of Saint James's spent years looking for just the right rector. And now they are going to have to start all over." He had begun pacing, his hands behind his back. "Pity, really. Very sad. God's people deserve better." He cocked his head at her, and she heard his unspoken words loud and clear: *they deserve better than you.*

Felicia realized that she was sweating now. "I...I don't understand."

"Oh, but I think you do. You've been hired under false pretenses. You lied to these people."

"I did *not* lie to them!" She allowed a flash of fury to erupt in her voice.

"Oh, but my dear little pickaninny pervert, you did." He stopped pacing for a moment and smiled. It was an ugly smile. "You see, Sweet Pea, a sin of omission is just as wrong as a sin of commission. I know you didn't tell these people you were heterosexual—you wouldn't *lie*, after all. But you didn't tell them you *weren't* a pervert, either, did you?"

Felicia said nothing. She realized that her hands were balled up into fists. She willed them to open and felt the coolness of the sacristy's air on her palms. "Bishop Preston, I know you are new to this diocese," she began, her voice betraying her fear. She plunged ahead, "And so maybe you don't understand the kind of place it is."

"Do you think I'm an idiot, Sweet Pea?" the bishop snarled. "Do you really think I did not know the kind of sin-sick cesspool I was stepping into when I came to this place? Do you think our church raises fools to the episcopacy as a matter of course?" He waited a beat but did not let her respond. "My wife and I came here because our daughter is sick. You knew that, right? She's still sick, so we're still here. I volunteered to help because, well, I'm retired and I like to be useful." He smiled the kind of smile that an alligator might display just before eating a wounded rodent. "This is not the kind of place I would *choose* to live. It's a diocese populated by hippies, activists, and perverts of the most unrepentant variety—such as yourself. Hell, you may be all three."

Felicia kept her mouth shut. He had her on two out of three as she'd always been more preppy than hippie.

"But from what I've seen, there's a big difference between this diocese and this parish." He gestured toward the grand, wood-framed, gothic-arched architecture of the sacristy, and, she imagined, beyond it, to the rest of the building. "The homos might run this diocese, Sweet Pea, but they do *not* run this congregation. This is an affluent congregation, a *Republican* congregation. They are not fond of perverts."

He gestured to the smartphone in his pocket and began to walk toward her. She felt his menace increase with every step. "I wonder what your vestry will make of your sacristy shenanigans? And on your very first day as rector? What other indecencies await them? Their imaginations will simply *reel*." He stopped with his face mere inches from her own. "They deserve better. I will see a letter of resignation on my desk by tomorrow. Am. I. Clear?"

Felicia saw her future crumbling. Her heart nearly beat through her chest. The chasuble felt like a sheet of lead hanging from her shoulders. She felt faint, and stumbled to a chair by the door.

"Here, let me help you," the bishop said, taking her hand in an icy grip until she had settled into the chair.

"A letter" she repeated, staring straight ahead at nothing. "A letter!" she jerked upright. A flash of insight stabbed at her brain, and a bolt of hope struck at her heart. "Wait here, please," she said and